'Dystopian novels of faith, power and resistance crop up regularly. So the form can feel stale. Yet this assured, involving debut finds a new vehicle – although one that knows its own tradition – to explore this ground . . . Wood sketches the back-story with crafty discretion, while a richly imagined setting allows the fable to flourish with the minimum of preaching'
Independent

'Wood conjures a time-warped world in which xenophobia, resignation and defiance fight for expression, and where unpleasant truths about human nature are conveyed in convincingly archaic slang. At its best, the result recalls the less fantastical parts of Philip Pullman's *Northern Lights* trilogy'
Financial Times

'This tale of faith and power from a young British writer is bound to get tables talking . . . An exploration of gang terror with whispers of *A Clockwork Orange* and a nod to *Lord of the Flies*, the novel also has shades of 2006's film *This is England*. But it's the surprising tenderness and cliché-free sentimentality that sets this story apart. Vibrant and evocative language give a tangible bitterness to this sharp story about lives saved, and doomed, by religious faith' *Stylist*, **Book of the Week**

'Wood's use of language is deft and ambitious . . . Wood is only twenty-seven yet her writing already has distinction'
Literary Review

The Godless Boys

NAOMI WOOD is the author of *The Godless Boys*,
which is currently being adapted for the screen,
and *Mrs. Hemingway*, which has been published in
more than ten countries around the world. Naomi
studied at Cambridge and has a Masters degree and
Doctorate from the University of East Anglia. Her
research for *Mrs. Hemingway* took her from the
British Library to the Library of Congress, and to
Ernest Hemingway's homes and old haunts in
Chicago, Paris, Antibes, Key West and Cuba.
She now lives in London.

Also by Naomi Wood

Mrs. Hemingway

Naomi Wood

The Godless Boys

PICADOR

First published 2011 in paperback by Picador

This edition published 2015 by Picador
an imprint of Pan Macmillan, a division of Macmillan Publishers Limited
Pan Macmillan, 20 New Wharf Road, London N1 9RR
Basingstoke and Oxford
Associated companies throughout the world
www.panmacmillan.com

ISBN 978-1-4472-9313-2

A CIP catalogue record for this book is available from the British Library.

Printed and bound by CPI Group (UK) Ltd, Croydon, CR0 4YY

Visit **www.picador.com** to read more about all our books
and to buy them. You will also find features, author interviews and
news of any author events, and you can sign up for e-newsletters
so that you're always first to hear about our new releases.

For Mary Wylie: 1914–2007

And for my parents

England

It was the summer they burned the churches again.

Sunrise broke over Berwick: the shadows clipped close to the walls; the sky broken only by Saint Gregory's spire. Laura checked the rear-view mirror. There was no one around.

It had been a quiet journey here. Someone higher up in the Movement had told them where to meet and what time; no more. They had travelled for an hour or so, no one saying much, the glass bottles, full of petrol, clinking against each other in the boot. The two men had both taken the back seat, one in army green, the other in black.

As the car had pulled in to the church lane, there'd been a moment, sitting there altogether, as if someone were considering saying something, perhaps *good luck*, or *goodbye*, but nothing was said. Instead the two men took the cases from the boot, and, as casually as worshippers, they walked toward the church, a case held tight in either hand. And Laura had stayed at the wheel, waiting.

She watched the first smoke start to drift upward from Saint Gregory's, drawn away on the wind, then building into a column, the smoke getting darker, richer. So here it was: the Secular Movement, alive again. Not since 1950, since the Church had taken power, had England seen such violence. And in the intervening years? God had come down on England like a cage, and all those involved in the violence of 1950 had been expelled to the Island. But the Secular Movement had retrenched and grown stronger, and, though they had been quiet until now, in the summer of 1976, the churches burned again.

Glass broke, somewhere close. Still there was no one on the Berwick streets. There followed a louder explosion and she thought – surely someone would wake and come to look, but no one emerged.

Last week, Laura had helped cut the petrol with tar so that it would better stick to what it caught. As she took Sarah to school she wondered if the other mothers might smell it on her. Soon, it would cover the pews, and then the curtains and the paintings, and anything else that was in its path. The two men would be launching the last of the glass-bottle bombs, now, lighting the soaked wicks and throwing them hard into the church windows. Laura thought she could smell fuel, probably from the boot – its metal stink flattening the air.

Blue light suddenly filled the car, strobing the mirror. Laura scrabbled for the handle but the door didn't release. She couldn't find the lock. Where was the lock? This was not her own car. The plastic snapped when she pulled at it. When she was outside the sounds of the siren filled her ears like water, and then she began to run.

Her teeth smashed against each other as she ran past terrace houses. Sleepy faces emerged from net curtains. From some way off a car screeched. She should have stayed in the car. She should have driven away. Somewhere in her mouth she tasted tin and blood. She should have driven away home. *They will persecute me for their names and I cannot give them up!* She thought of her husband and Sarah, her daughter's hair the colour of rust. What was she doing here, saving these strangers?

The big grey sky made the two men seem smaller than they were in the church yard. One had a flaming bottle but he dropped it when he saw her. The other scaled the far hedge and dropped out of sight before she had even said the words. 'Police! Police!' The heat was starting to come off the church now. Then the other man began to run.

'Police, police!' That's all she had managed and she knew that she too should run but she didn't: she had stopped running altogether. Why this impulse to save these two and not herself? She had no care for them; felt no sense of decency, and yet here she was. Steps ran toward her; there was nowhere to go, she wouldn't be able to make it to the hedge in time. A hand clamped her neck, another jerked her arm up, and then she was level to the ground.

In the cell, in Newcastle, she would remember the taste of gravel on her tongue, and the blood, from before, when she'd bitten down on her lip.

Laura saw the boots of the other policeman run on. A window of some stained and colourful Biblical scene smashed to the ground. 'Godless bitch,' the policeman spat in her ear.

Laura lay unmoving. Sirens circled as the fire grew stronger.

The Island

Ten Years Later

The Island

1. The Island

England, across the way, though it could not be seen tonight. The Sound was long and still. The boy crouched by the hedge, moonlight white on his skull. Underneath him was Lynemouth Town, slipping down the hill slope toward the sea. A few lights were on here and there but mostly it was dark. You could think, up here, that the Island might be alone in this, this sea; a great glob of earth, with nothing else for miles but water.

Looking at the Sound like that, looking so deceptively calm, always made Nathaniel think of his da, and how the sea had gobbled him up in its brackish waters. His da's boat would be out there, its keel dragging along the seabed, his body wet and strewn.

His da was one of the first men of the Secular Movement to be expelled to the Island, in 1951, a fact which made Nathaniel very proud. Jack Malraux had been a plumber in Hartlepool before being found responsible for one of the church-burnings in the summer of 1950 and deported here.

On the Island, Jack's trade was fishing and he'd done well from it. Nathaniel remembered the excitement of greeting his dad in Warkworth Bay when he came home for the weekend, and the rolling sound of the chains fixing the boat to the pier. When he left again, on the Monday morning, Nathaniel would accompany him down to the jetty, in the plum-blue mornings, in the winter months when the Island was all diamonded frost and sheeted ice, his hand in his father's hand, as they walked down toward the water's edge. Nathaniel would watch the boat leave, his da waving from the deck, knowing himself to be a softly shrinking dot in the distance, as his father sailed away to fish.

It was an English boat Jack had sailed out on. An English boat Jack had gone down with. No rocks or storms; most likely the caulk had given and the boat had sunk. Nathaniel imagined the English laughing when they had given the Islanders that boat, they must have known it could not be seaworthy for long.

A very English murder, this: unseen, bloodless, far away in time.

The moon was a dab of light now, not much more, what with the clouds tonight. Nathaniel wondered if there might be a twin of him, in England, a bald boy too, looking out across this sea, thinking about him. He wondered if his English twin also imagined descending on his scalp a cudgel to watch the blood ream. He'd like that; he'd always imagined English blood thick, like a pool of liquorice he'd seen melting one day last summer. The boy ranked his da's death as one of the Island's finest humiliations at the hands of the English. Worse than the Newcastle riots, worse than the Secular Deportations of '51 or '77; his da's death in that English boat rankled most.

*

Nathaniel set off up Marley Hill. He was a bald boy with a long throat, dressed in tight trousers and a military jacket, with gold braid on the epaulettes. The sleeves were a touch short and the studs of his wrists were frozen in the night. The trousers too were short of his ankles so that they showed the slope of his boots, which had been his da's, and which he'd given a rollicky-polish this evening to prepare for the scrap tonight. The boy wore handkerchiefs in the boots to stop his feet slipping. Red braces swaddled him neatly like a baby.

That afternoon, in his ma's bathroom, he'd smeared something on his lips called Pomade Divine. He knew it was meant for hair but he smeared it richly on his lips. On the front of the tin was a man with slick hair and a leer; Pomade Divine tasted of apples.

The hill was steep and the grass nearly bald with the Island's shearing winds. It was freezing, but he wouldn't shiver: because what was November on the Island but a cold to knock the breath from you? And leafless trees, and freezing nights, and the wind from off the Sound enough to make your balls into clams?

In the dark peat, further from the path, mushrooms grew, a whole moony lot of them. Something about their soft bright bonnets made him feel sick, or maybe it was not that, but the gills underneath, that made him pure want to heave. Nathaniel looked out for the Island's flowers his da had told him of: bog cotton, sandwort and rock-cress, but it was too dark to see anything but the mushroom domes. Just before the hilltop he ambled over to one of the swelling white patches and mashed the mushrooms into the grass.

Warkworth Bay was visible now and you could see where the skerries were from the waves' white froth. The pier, which would welcome the English boat tonight, had disappeared in the dark.

Nathaniel placed his boots down hard, since a misplaced foot could send a boy tumbling off the cliffs to the Sound. Where up at the summit Warkworth Town had been a shimmer of white, the houses now reared above him, their walls thick and coated in sea spray, the slated roofs dark. Handkerchiefs slipped gently in his boots. He wondered when he would fill them.

Shop awnings were going mad in the sea's fetch, and the Islanders were scurrying about beneath them, thronging the grocer's, and the fishmonger's, their coats billowing out from them, big as sails. Nothing much had changed in Maiden's Square since the emergency powers had brought the first men and women of the Movement here in 1951. In an elegant hand, the signs that hung from the shop fronts read: *Stansky & Sons* (above the fishmonger's), *Buttons* (above Mrs Bingley's clothes shop), *Caro's Launderette*, *Forrester's Funerary Services*, and a grocer's, doctor's, and hardware shop, for 'tools, cutlery and hardware', and 'oils, paints and varnishes'. And in rippled black glass, the walls unpainted, unlike the rest, the museum stood at the northeastern corner of the square. Walled in photographs, it told the Island's short history, and held the books and pamphlets the Church sent over to educate their godless kin. Mostly, they ended up graffiti'd – often by Nathaniel and his boys.

The boat, which was called the *Saviour* and came

weekly from England with supplies – potatoes, genera-
tors, rope, fish-tackle, medicine, newspapers and religious
propaganda, amongst other things – did not deliver cigarettes. In fact, there had been no cigarettes on the Island
in the past thirty-six years. The Islanders had always seen
it as yet another form of punishment from England, though
the men could have lived a lot longer with their untarred
lungs, had it not been for the Sound filling them up so fre-
quently, and fatally, with its lusty waters.

Nathaniel, however, had cigarettes. Tonight, he lit one,
not caring who saw him. The shoppers gave him a funny
look. He grinned: a smile which broke his face in two like
a split egg. He stretched out on the bench, waiting, and
watching. Mr Forrester, in the funeral home, was working
at his desk. Two girls from school were walking arm in arm
from the launderette; one had a dress draped over her arm.
Nathaniel winked at her and told her he'd take her somewhere nice in that; she flushed and looked away. Fish-skins
glistened in the monger's. Arthur Stansky went about his
work, pausing here and there to drag scale and innards
down his pinny. Arthur was a bloody mess but he seemed
not to mind.

And there Jake came, lumbering along, a little late,
something about his get-up – which was the same as
Nathaniel's – a little askew, the jacket too tight about the
middle, the boots a little dull. Aye, his boots could do with
a polish. He didn't look like a Malade; not like him; not as
sharp by halves. Jake was an enormous boy, a head taller
than Nathaniel, with his arms hanging down to those
hands the width of a spade apiece. His soft bulk always
surprised Nathaniel, as if a separate, leaner Jake existed in

Nathaniel's imagination. Aye, there was something whale-like about the boy, something gentle but irritating about the boy's great tonnage.

'I told you not to let your hair grow so long,' said Nathaniel, when the boy was close enough. Bristles spun from the boy's crown.

'Aye,' Jake said, scratching his head.

'Well?'

'Mam's asked me to grow it a bit. She says I look like a victim of summat, when I'm all shaven, like.'

'On yer bike, Jakob. Your mam's got nowt to do with it.'

'I can't help what she says.'

'Did you say you were a Malade? That this is what our gang is for, now? That all us boys are like this?'

'No.' And then: 'Aye.'

'And what does "No. Aye," mean now?' Jake shrugged and eyed Nathaniel's cigarette hungrily. 'How is your mam?'

'Well,' said Jake, 'and Mammy Malraux?'

'Fine,' and then, to goad him, 'When is your mam to invite me to fish supper?'

'You know you're not allowed back to mine,' Jake said, and Nathaniel knew this but still liked to crab him about it. Just to get Jake upset was pleasure enough for him.

They watched people come in and out of the shops, carting their plaid trolleys or shopping bags, their faces flat in the lamplight. Nathaniel and Jake were waiting for the rest of the gang, the Malades, waiting for their skulls to come bobbing down Marley Hill toward Maiden's Square.

Tonight, Nicholas Tucker was to be initiated into the gang.

They didn't speak for a bit, and Nathaniel was reminded of Jake's habit of wetting his lips, over and over again, furtively, with his tongue. Nath was about to reprimand him, but something about his eyes, their baleful stare, hooded by the wide flat lids, stopped him. Jake's hands, on the spread thighs, looked babyish. Who knew where the bones were in those things?

'Can I have a cig, Nath?'

'No. I don't have many left.'

'Are you getting no more from the Boatie tonight?'

'No. Not tonight. Got nothing to exchange them for.'

'Your ma's pills?'

'There's not enough left. I have to leave some for her, aye.'

'Have you been taking them?'

'Stop crabbing me, Jake! You're an old woman at times. My ma forgot to order more. So no pills, no cigarettes. We'll get more next week.' Nathaniel squashed the cigarette onto the bench. He had smoked it too quickly and a yellowy sort of nausea passed from his gut to his throat. An explorative belch made him feel better. Arthur held a fish by its tail in the monger's waxed light. Without taking his eyes off it – *It might be skate! And how long was it since he'd eaten fish!* – Nathaniel said: 'When are the boys coming?'

'At six. As we arranged.'

And though he knew the answer already he asked, 'And who is it? Who's to be the Freshcut?'

'Nicholas Tucker.'

'Lumme.' Nathaniel's hand over his scalp produced a lovely rasp; he wondered if only he was party to the sound. 'What a good idea. Did he suggest it himself?'

'Aye. Said he wanted to be in the gang. So I said I'd ask you.' Nathaniel nodded his assent, then slipped off the bench, and tilted his head for Jake to follow him.

Buttons was a big long shop with all the original fittings and fancy ironwork. A bell rang as they came into the shop, which was warm, much warmer than outside. Mrs Bingley emerged, took one look at them and her face turned stern. An elderly lady with white hair and thick calves, she wore a paisley dress with brown tights the colour of the peat on Marley Hill. Mrs Bingley folded her big soft arms across her big soft chest. 'What do you want, now? I'm not wanting any trouble. It's too late in the day for that.'

'Hallo, Mrs Bingley. Nice to see you, too. We're not causing trouble. Promise.'

Mrs Bingley touched her hair, pushing up the curls; they had a lavender tinge. 'How's your mam?'

'Well, well.'

'You shouldn't be causing her any more ache than she's already got, you know.'

'Aye, I promise you, Mrs Bingley. I want to buy Ma a present, that's all.'

'Like what?' Old-fashioned dresses hung from the walls as well as corduroy trousers and tweed skirts. There was a sharp smell, as if the clothes had brought with them the scent of the boat's bilge. 'This is all I have.'

'Mrs Bingley. Now, now, now. Is there nothing new here?'

'Oh no, dear. We haven't had any clothes from England since six months now. I have a mind of having a word with the Boatman.'

'And why don't you?'

'On your way, he'd scare me half to death. Not on your life am I talking to an Englishman. No. It wouldn't be proper.' She looked both prim and thrilled by the thought of converse with an Englishman. 'Imagine his churchy hands on me!' For a moment, her gaze was far away. 'On with your business, now. What did you have in mind?'

Nathaniel shrugged. 'Something for my ma.' Mammy Malraux needed something new, something to lift her spirits. He didn't know what to do; he worried after her. If only he could be as good to his ma as he intended to be . . . but the wall of smoke that hung in the living room, the intolerable warmth, the long blab of the television set . . . That living room sent him mad for the scrap, so that as he sat for hours in front of the gas-fire, all he could think of was the boys, the Malades, his gang! He knew he disappointed her, but he couldn't seem to help it. 'I don't know. I'd like to buy her something. So that she might think about stepping out here and there. She doesn't leave the house, aye.'

Mrs Bingley suggested one or two dresses much the same as her own, but they were all drab. Nathaniel held up the dresses to himself in the changing-room mirror. 'Nothing slimmer? Or slimming?'

'This is all I have,' she said, gesturing around her.

A clapping sound came from the outside, of boots against the flagstones. It must be six. The boys passed the length of the glass, their scalps passing in whitish blur, settling near the stage, talking excitedly.

'Let's off, now, Nathaniel,' said Jake. The boy stared through the cold glass, his gigantic hand now banging the pane and waving to the boys outside.

'Oi! You leave well alone of that window, you hear!' Mrs

Bingley's eyes shuttled from the gang outside to the boys in her shop. Her whole face had gone a shade of crimson. '*I told you*, Nathaniel, I said I don't want any trouble. You sharking about outside my shop does not help business, d'you hear me, son?'

'Bye, Mrs Bingley!' Jake said as he pulled open the door and ran out. Cold air burst in. Nathaniel put the dress back to its rail. He did his best syrupy voice for her, as if he were talking to his own mam, and took her plump old hand in his. 'Don't you worry, Mrs Bingley. We'll be right as rain. Don't you worry about us. We're Island boys, we shan't be any trouble!' And he gave her hand a squeeze, before dashing into the square.

The Malades were a beautiful bunch, in the way that scraping the scalp of all the fuzz brought out their bonny eyes, their full boys' lips. What slick little outfits they had managed! They were all dressed like Nathaniel and did not wear much, for November. Their mams pure despaired of them, urging an extra scarf on them, or a more sensible jacket, which they always – in fear of Nathaniel – refused, because who might know what kind of mood he was in, whether the humiliation might be a whole-scale attack, or something worse; total exclusion from the gang. They were all so pale; no one darker than a candlestick. But there was something very pretty about them, too, quite a nursery of daft infants.

The boys gossiped about the Islanders, who might be showing signs of churchliness and who might be their next target. They talked about their mams and what they were up to. For those fortunate enough, they talked about their da's on the fishing boats, and what they had done with them on the rare weekend that they were back on Island soil.

One boy stood apart. He looked nervous, and was moving a finger up and down his collar. He was a good-looking boy, soft-featured, younger than the rest, his eyes darting from Nathaniel to Jake, not knowing which one to settle on. He stood in front of Forrester's funeral parlour. 'All right, boy,' Nathaniel said to him across the way, 'you're right at the dead centre over there, aye. Why don't you come and have a chat with us?'

'Aye,' he said, but he didn't move. In the latening evening, the night had become cooler still.

'I hear you want to be in our gang.'

The boy took cautious steps toward them. 'Aye,' he said.

'Have you been to the museum, of late?'

'I went last year.'

Nathaniel's laugh was high and easy. 'Not good enough. You have to go often – many times – once a month, maybe, or every week, so you can ken your past. You've got to see the church-burnings, you've got to see how the Movement were kicked out of England in '51, and then again in '77. You've got to see how easy it is for faith to hijack your head! Oh, aye, you've heard what your mammy has said, and your da, as he dandled you on his knee before the fire. But unless you go to the museum, and often at that, you won't understand the English mentality. You won't under-stand how God has grown up around the English like cobwebs, while they weren't paying attention, and how it could, any minute, here, if our boys aren't alertful of the signs. You've got to go so you can understand who you are.

A child not just of Mammy and Pappy, aye, but of the Movement. So it's baneful shocking, you see, to hear it was a *year* ago you went.' The boy's lips trembled. There was nowhere to hide his shame and it rose as a pink wave from his throat to his brow. 'Och, now, Nicholas, not to worry. Next time, aye?' And Nathaniel chucked him on the back of his pate, lightly, and smiled at him, so that Nicholas lost the watchful look and he smiled back, hesitantly. 'I like your hair, Nicholas, did you do that yourself?'

'Aye,' he said.

'Did your mam blub when she saw you?'

'She gave me a right bollocking, yeah.'

The boys were a ring around him now, their baldheads half in shadow, half in light. Some of them laughed, remembering how their mams had been when they too had shaved their scalps. 'Well, you're all done now. And your scalp shines like a lovely penny. Now we're just going to ask you a few questions, get you to commit to some things. We've all taken the oaths. Don't worry. No fish heads or guts or any of that daft shite you might have heard of. No, boy. Just some firm moral matters of principle, which you might find in any tough boys' gang. We're a good lot, us, but we don't like casuals. Understand?' Nicholas nodded his head. Nathaniel leaned in and said very tenderly, like a father might, 'Then you'll be a Malade, like me, like Jake, like all of the boys, and you can help us with the cause.'

Nathaniel looked around the group. 'There is a ring of spies on this Island, working for England. Trying to get us back into God's acre. Soon the Island will be as faithful as London! Aye, aye: the walls of the church are not built in the freezing air but in the ramparts of the heart! Here, an aunt may be praying at night. There, a brother may be caught reading the English rag – or worse, fingering pages of scripture. One moment they'll merely be faithful, the next moment they will be at Warkworth beach welcoming English warships. So,' he turned to Nicholas. 'This is what I'm going to ask you. Have you ever been a Got?'

'No,' the boy said.

'Are you sure, now?'

'Aye.'

'No one in your family, either? A Got? A believer?'

'No.'

'Tell me, boy, have you ever believed? Have you ever felt the blood of God in your veins? Or heard his words in your mind?'

'No.'

'Are you sure of that, boy? We'll understand if you have. It can be nice. The soft babble of God in your ears.' Sweat had pricked high on Nicholas's forehead. Where his skin had been white it was now greenish about the chops, froggy and damp. 'He's a great comforter to those lost at sea.'

'No.'

'Not a prayer, sweetheart? Not a moan for a mollycoddle when Pappy popped his boots? The sea is cruel to us, you couldn't say we're not in baneful need.'

Nicholas's voice was barely a whisper. 'No. Nothing. I promise.'

The boys were tense and ready. Their boots kept edging them closer. He felt a great ministry within him, a great stillness, holding back until they were really at the dampish verge. Though Nathaniel's sight was fixed on Nicholas, the other boys hung, weightless, in the corner of his vision. 'And if your ma had gone all syrupy with faith? And decided to spy for England? Or your da? Would you tell us? Would you let your boys in kin know of the failings of your family?'

'Aye, aye.'

'What about your sister? Lovely Charlotte? If she were spying for England, trying to get the Island back to the Ministry, would you tell us, so that we could treat her how she deserved?'

'Aye, aye, I'd tell you.'

'One last thing; then you'll be just like us: a Malade, through and through.' Nathaniel reared his fist and caught his knuckles on the boy's lips. Blood issued from his mouth, as red as jam.

The boys' laughter was a distant sound as if they were a great way from him, beyond the Sound, even. Nathaniel slipped his index finger into the wet hollow of the boy's mouth. 'Now a Malade,' he said again, 'through, and through.'

For a moment, Nicholas was aghast. Something hallucinatory about the blood coming from – where was it? His tongue? Or had it been his nose that had burst? It was a brown taste in his mouth. Seconds passed, and he cupped his face in his hands: he had expected this, this predicted violence. And it had not been so bad. And so he smiled, the blood like a tonic on his tongue.

Nathaniel cooed, 'Aye, Nicholas,' and ruffled the baby spikes of his hair, declaring the boy one of the gang.

Oiled on all of this sudden affection, Nicholas smiled with the blood still coming from his lips and gums. He spoke quickly, lightly, laughing, 'See I knew you'd do that. Knew it. Knew I was in for some questions, and then a bit of the scrap. But I was ready. Ha! Yes. Now I'm a Malade, a marauding Malade, just like you!' Nicholas mopped his chin with a hankie.

Jake called: 'Down to the Sound now!'

'Off with you,' Nathaniel said, because the whim took him, 'I'm not going down to the Sound tonight.'

'But the dunking, like with Sammy, and me '

'No. That's not part of the game any more. We don't go down to the bay any more.'

'I'm only saying that when I was a Freshcut, there was a dunking in the Sound after the Square and now—'

'Not any more. *Listen*, Jake. Listen to what I say.'

Nathaniel lit a cigarette and passed it between the boys so that the earthy smell of tobacco filled the square. The boys smoked, concentrating hard. They looked with some degree of fascination at the smoke now clouding the air, and the ashy, not unpleasant tastes in their mouths. Jake refused the smoke, his mouth pouting and cross.

'All I envy them for. Those cigs.' After the boys had had their smokes, Nathaniel had the last of it then flicked it out across the square. It went burning in a pleasing arc. 'If the Gots had their way, faith'd spread through the Island like the flu. If someone sneezed you'd catch God in your nose. No, no, no, there's more to life than sacrificing everything for Old Man upstairs.' His face cracked into a philosophical smile. 'But they make a fine cigarette. I must say that. And it hurries them up to Kingdom Come, so at least the cigmaker is possessed of all his senses.'

A wave of tiredness passed over him, as it always did,

and Nathaniel felt that familiar restive feeling – not dis-satisfaction, quite, but something close to it. This always happened after the scrap, as if the violence were not big enough to dispossess him of some sad and unknown memory. 'Who's on for Wednesday night, then?'

'Eliza Michalka?' said Sammy.

'Nah,' said Nathaniel, 'I'd rather stare at that pudding all day than throw rocks at it. Another time. Once I've crabbed her, perhaps.'

'As if you could crab her without paying for it.'

'That I could, Jakob Lawrence, I'd be down to the Grand and have her pudding before I could even ask for the spoon.'

Jake looked away, as if embarrassed.

'Mrs Richards, then,' said Sammy.

'The maths teacher! Lumme,' said Nathaniel. 'Why? The evidence?'

'I hear she talks to the girls after school. Teaching them Bible and scripture. It's thought she's in contact with the English. She's a spy, all right. Through and through.'

'Grand,' said Nathaniel. 'We'll check her out. We're all on dispatch tonight and tomorrow night. See who comes in and out of that house from seven o'clock onwards. We don't want to crab her while the big man is there. All right, boys?'

And the boys ran from the square, following Nathaniel, this gang who would come and clap faith from any beating heart. The night was now a dark black lump, but they knew the Island instinctively, like worms in soil, and they were happy, the whole sleek lot of them. Six Malades now, aye.

Oh, life was a laugh, a lark, a love, on this Island of his!

2. Miss Eliza Michalka

Tonight was no especial occasion: Eliza had stood any number of hours in that doorway, come seven o'clock, under the sweep of the museum's shadow. Arthur Stansky had not yet seen her; not tonight, nor the other nights she had come to watch him, with all the rapture of a child at a television set.

Eliza had arrived at Maiden's Square just as Caro was closing the launderette. She had made some show about getting a dress that she knew would not yet be ready, all the while keeping her eye fixed on Arthur in the fish shop opposite. The launderette smelled of carbolic and made her nose itch. Caro had shrugged her shoulders and told her it was not yet ready, and that she was closing, mumbling something about having it up to here with this Island and these boys at their tricks. Eliza did not know what to say, offered some platitude or other, and stepped from the launderette to the museum's doorstep, jamming herself down into its shadow. Arthur would not see her here.

The monger's let out a square of yellow light. Under the window frame, deep maroon tiles; above it, an awning, with gold lettering. Eliza thought the fish shop the nicest place on the whole Island; the most perfect place. Beatrice Spenser was now Arthur's last customer: she was not really dressed for the cold, and looked rather wan. Beatrice was a deportee from the second wave – one from the 1977 boat – and she had never really mixed in with the other Islanders, save finding someone to father a child with her. Who he was, was a mystery to everybody. Eliza knew – just as everyone else did – that Beatrice Spenser would tomorrow slip into the museum and steal the English newspaper that was brought on the weekly boat. Beatrice missed home, Eliza thought, more than the others.

Arthur, however, was always kind to Beatrice. Eliza wondered what pleasantries they might exchange: the intemperance of the weather, perhaps, or details of the latest catch, or what the English boat might bring the Islanders tonight. Eliza had had only the most minimal of conversations with Arthur these past couple of months. What would she give, to hear him talk of cod or the cold?

Arthur pulled a long slender fish from the ice. Tenderly, as if it were a newborn, he held it from its tail, the fish flashed in the light, Mrs Spenser nodded her head, and he slit it down its belly with a long grey knife. He pulled out bladder and intestine and who knew what else from the hole. Mud-coloured and stringy, he washed the mess from his fingers. He grated the fish and sheared off its scales, which flew into the air like sparks. Oh, to be that knife; to be that fish! Wrapped in paper now, the fish was bundled under Mrs Spenser's arm, and she said her goodbyes.

Moments passed when no one was in the shop. The monger moved to the doorway, looking to the square from the gridded glass: tall, good Arthur. He seemed to be searching for something. Eliza shrank into the museum's shadows, wondering, if their eyes met, if he would see her. She doubted that.

The memory came back to her, painfully, as it always did, of the night they had spent together at the Grand this summer. It had been very warm: her room had seemed to creak with the heat, the air wriggling as it became stickier. She remembered, outside, the press of grey clouds above a strangely still Sound. A storm was approaching. She remembered Arthur's ropey, sweaty hair, his waistband too tight, as if he too were expanding in the softening heat, as if he were only kept narrow by the Island's winters. She remembered his parting words: 'Forgive me, Eliza.' Then months had passed, the cold had come, and nearly nothing had been said between them.

And now, very late November, and nightly she came to Maiden's Square, to stand and watch him, in the shadows, constant as a ghost.

In bloodied apron, Arthur proceeded to clean the shop. He moved a cloth against the glass and marble, pushing the scale and bone and blood into the claw of his other waiting hand, as if he were returning his countertop to a state of grace. Eliza wished dearly that she could lay herself naked down on the tablet, near the skate, and the sole, and the salmon, and find herself a thing of Arthur's worshipped hygiene.

He let go the handful into the bin.

Into a bag he gathered the old fish, put on a coat, unlocked the door. He switched off the light so that the square was dark. Arthur was invisible, now, just like her. The lock clicked again. Now he would set off toward Warkworth Bay – but he stopped at the door as if he had detected something. Cries of gulls scratched the air. Why had he not begun the walk? Had he seen her? Was he coming closer? Would he shout at her, or dismiss her as a lunatic? Eliza stayed very still and did not breathe, wondering what on earth she would say to him if she were discovered here.

He fiddled with some keys, and then set off. His shoes rang against the flagstones until he reached the peaty ground, and then the sound and sight of him was lost. She was disappointed; she had half-hoped for discovery. The herring gulls moaned. Eliza stepped out of the dark, straight into the soft bosomy front of Mrs Bingley.

'Oh,' she said, with Mrs Bingley looking equally frightened. Buttons had been dark; Eliza had had no idea anyone was still in the square.

Mrs Bingley held her hand at her breast and breathed heavily. 'Eliza Michalka, for pity's sake, stop haunting this doorway! Do you not think I have enough trouble with these boys? If it isn't them, it's a full-grown woman sharking about my shop and causing me trouble.'

'I—'

'I don't want to hear it. Not a moment's peace! This Island will be the death of me yet. Keep away from my doorway, miss, I've had enough hassle for one evening.'

'I'm sorry, Mrs Bingley, I didn't mean to scare you.'

Mrs Bingley flicked her eyes from Eliza's head to her boots. Her mouth clenched a little. 'What are you doing here, anyway?'

'I,' she paused, 'I came to see if you had a delivery from the Boatman.'

'The English boat is here tonight. We collect the goods

tomorrow. You know that. Why doesn't anyone know that? This Island's all gone soft.'

'Aye. Aye. Silly of me. I'm sorry. I'll come tomorrow, then.'

'Shan't you be on your way, then?'

'I'm waiting for a friend . . .' Arthur would be coming back soon. She willed Mrs Bingley to leave the square. 'Janey.'

'Bet you are. Don't get cold, then. You'll turn to ice at this rate.'

'Aye. Goodnight, Mrs Bingley. Safe on.'

'Aye.' Mrs Bingley muttered into her scarf and set off. Eliza saw Arthur returning and she slipped back under the museum's gable. His empty bag now blew open in the wind as he stopped to chat to Mrs Bingley. Then he returned to his apartment above the monger's.

The rooms above Stansky & Sons gave out a watery glow. She saw a shadow move against the north wall before she saw him. No doubt he would create for himself a handsome meal of fish and potatoes, though perhaps he tired of it during his labours. Perhaps he hankered for meat, though there was none to be had on the Island. The Islanders had never had meat: it couldn't come on the benefaction boat, and they couldn't rear livestock on the hill here. Beef, pork, lamb; Eliza wondered what they tasted of. Perhaps, like an expensive piece of furniture.

Arthur sat. At one point she thought he put his head in his hands and wept. But when he stood, he took a newspaper from the table and he moved to what she knew was the living room, and Eliza left.

*

She walked away from the square very quietly, heading for Warkworth Bay. She knew she should not torment herself with the sight of all that good fish only just on the turn, but she thought of it as a kind of offering, one that Arthur made to the world, and why should she exclude herself from the bounty just because she loved him, and he no longer loved her back?

Down at the bay, the birds circled the bluff, diving and picking from the fish flesh; all beak and wing and claw. How like ghosts they were, so white in the dark, but infinitely more solid, quick, and sure of their purpose. What a hash she'd made of tonight. Eliza had sworn she would talk to Arthur, but she hadn't even got close to the shop front.

On her brow that evening, Eliza had penned the word *Courage*, close to her hairline, underneath her fringe, to encourage her to talk to him. She had made a habit of this since starting at the Grand (that June, and so unwillingly!), pulling up her fringe and penning little messages of hope – or self-pity – on her brow. One word, or two, like *Courage*, or maybe *Resilience*, or maybe *Take Heart!*, and she'd go around the Island with her blonde lock of hair covering the words, murmuring the message in her head, hoping for inspiration.

But tonight! What a coward she was. *Courage!* Pathetic. She had no courage. She felt like that fish Arthur had shorn of all its scales: dull, and missing its brilliance.

The sound of a boat came up from the harbour. The tide, too, was quickening. It must be the boat from England. Eliza left the gulls and took the steps down the cliff face, toward the beach.

When she reached the sand, the boat was already docked, with its pale orange top, life rings on its railings, and the black belly of it bringing up the sea spray. Eliza crouched behind the rocks, so that for the second time that night she would be hidden.

The engine stopped. A big bow wave travelled to the beach, then the sea was almost flat and waveless again. Nothing could be seen through the cabin's windows. The name of the boat was written in large yellow letters on its side: the *Saviour*. The Boatman, bald and fat, shut the door of the cabin and unlatched the cargo door. Eliza had heard of him – many of the Islanders were frightened of him – but had never seen him; not in the flesh. He walked down a series of steps and came back up with a box of supplies.

Here, then, was the English benefaction. Ever since the emergency powers, and when the weather permitted it, England had weekly delivered the Islanders their goods. It was done at no cost whatsoever, so that those lost in the night-time of the Lord could eat, and think from what hand they ate; use light, and think from where this light had come; fish, and know who it was that provided them with twine and hooks. Most of the time it was accepted with a sneer, since there was no way of showing the English their rebuke, and since there was no possibility of rejecting the charity.

The Islanders received the *Saviour* with a heavy heart, though without it they would have died, or gone mad. They did not like to think of themselves as beholden. Not to the English. There'd be another boat next week, but then it would not come again until the new year. Aye, the Islanders were left to cope alone for the winter, when the winter fogs would come, thick as mud, and make passing the Sound an impossible task.

Tomorrow morning, the men would come down to the jetty and distribute the things as they saw fit; to the fishermen, the plumber, Caro, the doctor, the grocer and Mrs Bingley, if there was anything in there for her. You wouldn't steal; people didn't steal English things, which were English at least until they turned up in the shops and had to be paid for. Theft would be what the English expected and so the Islanders did not do it. The Boatman shifted the first box to the end of the pier. It looked a heavy thing and he stopped for a cigarette at the end. He looked rather peaceful, sitting there, despite the threat of foreign turf; he could almost be waiting for someone.

Eliza made to leave, when something on the boat caught her eye: there, on the deck, a girl stood. Just as the birds had solidified the air, here stood a presence of breath and blood and bone, rendered from the dark. The girl stood still, quite white, looking into the Island. She turned around to the massive Sound, that breadth of water before the North Sea began in earnest back to England, and then she turned again to the Boatman. He had nearly finished the cigarette.

Eliza felt her heart club as the girl climbed over the rigging and onto the pier. A stowaway? An *English* stowaway? On the *Saviour*? She started to edge down the pier, and Eliza's eyes darted from the girl to the Boatman, urging the cigarette to slow itself of its burning. The girl walked quickly down the pier, her eyes trained on the cigarette's orange light. No sound issued from her step. Just as the Boatman took his last smoke, and flicked the end to the beach, the girl reached the shore and dropped to the beach, crawling between the pier's legs, where she was lost again in darkness.

Over the next twenty minutes the Boatman brought the rest of the boxed provisions to the Island. He was still oblivious of the girl. Eliza concentrated on the dark tent under the pier. She could see nothing of her, which could only be a good thing, for now.

The Boatman stayed a few minutes longer, after his labours, idling by the boat. He had a small box in his hands. He lit another cigarette. When he finished that one he gave up and without further fuss stepped back into the boat and shut the cabin door. Moments later, the engine gunned and the waves began foaming again at the beach. The engine smoked as the boat turned. Eliza watched the mast until it disappeared into the sky and sea.

As soon as the *Saviour* had gone, the stowaway lunged toward the cliff. As she came toward the rocks, Eliza saw her water-blue eyes and freckles, dense as a bruise against her skin. The girl's hair, the colour of rust, flew in the wind. Eliza let the girl climb the steps and go over the top, before she too gained the rutted boards, intending to catch up with her at Maiden's Square, and, if her courage served her well (she pressed her fingers to her forehead – *Courage! Courage!*), she would talk to the girl and tell her she could spend the night with her at the Grand. They might be friends – the English girl, after all, would be sore pressed to find another on the Island. She wondered what on earth the girl was doing here.

Eliza arrived breathlessly at the top. The girl was gone. She was not even on the path toward the square. The fish, too, all gone, and the gulls with them. Eliza's stride broke into a run. Halfway to the square she stopped suddenly, looking back toward the Sound, terrified that minutes into being on the Island the girl might have jumped. Then it would be Eliza's fault for not acting quickly enough. Another score in the post for her inaction! No, no, she thought, hurrying along to Maiden's Square, a good English girl, one with faith and God and all manner of things she could not imagine were the privilege of that country's children, would not give up so easily.

Up here, the houses shone with the salt from the Sound, brought to the innermost part of the Island in rough storms. Arthur had probably finished his dinner, now, and might be doing his dishes; good man. Eliza just saw the girl between the museum and the hill: what a quick-ferreted thing she was to move at such a pace, and for someone who could not know the Island. Now, now, she might catch up with her, and ask her about London, and Walkmans, and churches, and motorways, and England! Eliza hurried along, no longer caring if Arthur saw her, when she caught the sound of other footsteps, apart from this time, they were following her.

The boys surrounded her quickly, like a leaking organ suddenly circled in blood. All her breath left her in an instant. Eliza turned around to see if there was anyone else left in the square but knew there would be no one, and then she craned her head to see if she could still see the girl. The rucksack, and the orange hair, slipped agonizingly from view. She might take any path from there; any road or pass, any which way. *Damn them*, Eliza thought, *damn them*.

She took a step away from the scalped boys but they were already a ring around her. 'Hello, dear.' This was Nathaniel; she did not know the names of the others.

'Evening, Nathaniel.'

'A fine night, Miss Eliza. We don't often find you in the square at this time.'

'No.' She looked around her. 'I was running an errand. For Musa.'

'At this time? That's awful late.'

'I might say the same to you. What are you doing here? The lot of you. You should be at home with your mams.'

'As you should be with yours.'

'My mam's dead; you know that.' He showed nothing. 'What are you doing? You've been told to stop it now. This sharking about.'

'Aye. And we haven't put a person to their displeasure. Not tonight. Isn't that right, Jake?' A tall boy nodded, touching his finger to the jacket's braiding. There was another boy with a bruise that looked just fresh. The ring of them seemed closer though she knew they had not moved. Eliza told herself these boys were nuisances, merely. Nathaniel lit a cigarette; where did he get them from? 'And your ma, what does she think about this? Her only son, skulking about the Island smoking English *cigarettes*. Shame on you.'

'She doesn't care.' Nathaniel touched his hand on her hip. 'Do you care, do you care for me, Eliza?' His lips were close to hers. He was sixteen – somewhere around that age – but he had the height over her.

'Get off me.'

'Oh. Firm with me now, are you?'

'Aye. I'll be firm with you yet.'

'Why? Do you not like us? Are you a woman of faith? A Got, lady?' This was Jake, now, stepping forward. Something about him made Eliza's courage shrink.

'A Got? On your way.' She tried to square herself up to them; she only just now counted how many there were. 'I was born on this Island, just like you.'

'Have you been up at church?' Nathaniel now. 'The old ruined one at Lynemouth?'

'Even if I have, it's none of your business.'

'Every bit of our business,' said Jake. 'If you're an English spy.'

Nathaniel walked the length of the stage, wagging his finger into the air, as if he were a mathematician vexed by a problem of logic. 'What I can't square is how you might carry on, dear Miss Michalka, in your line of work, with your heart pumping your devotions and with your other hand pumping—'

'Stop your mouth.'

He swivelled around, fingering his lip. 'Stop it for me.' There was a moment's silence before the gang cracked up. Loudly now, Nathaniel shouted: 'Stop my mouth, Eliza, our lady of the Grand!' He jumped from the stage and joined the ranks around her. He leaned in as if he was about to kiss her.

A window flew open above the monger's. Arthur tilted from the pane, his face obscure in shadow, his hand on the catch. 'Oi! What're you doing down there? Off with you, now, boys, before I sort out the lot of you.'

Nathaniel smiled, daftly, as if to say he was only joshing, and with a lady they both knew to be very pretty.

'Here, now, Mr Stansky. We didn't mean no harm. We were talking to Miss Michalka.'

'Aye. And I'm sure she's had a lovely time talking with you and has had fair enough. Be off with you now, boys. Scram. On you go.'

There was something about Arthur that Nathaniel could evidently not resist. Certainly there were fair few people whom Nathaniel would bow to. 'All right, Mr Stansky, sir. Good night, Miss Michalka. Safe on.'

Nathaniel started whistling some desultory tune, and set off, with the boys following, down the side of Mrs Bingley's, and followed the road the girl had taken. Before he was lost from sight, Nathaniel turned and gave her a crooked grin, before the gang disappeared in the night.

A gull squawked and then the square was empty of noise. Eliza turned back to the window to thank him, but when she opened her mouth Arthur closed the catch and fiddled with the lock. It was as if in closing the glass he had just shut the very entrance to her heart. He had saved her, and then damned her, in the time it had taken to open and close that window. The light went. And the square was once again flooded in darkness.

3. Lynemouth Town

Lynemouth Town was the oldest quarter of the Island. Narrow, curling streets; terraces many times extended; sloping slate roofs: the houses had been built into whatever cranny the steep side of Marley Hill might afford. From aboard a fishing boat the town was said to resemble a crumbling amphitheatre sliding down the hill. There was still the old system of numbering the houses, with the odd number on the landward side, the even number on the seaward. It looked more of a series of fortifications than a town: slats for windows, or windows showing from just under the gables; high walls, shut doors. There was not much colour here, everything carried in the general umber of the terrace roofs; it had none of the bright awnings of Maiden's Square or Arthur's iced fishes. Some way off, further east and higher up, a burned-out church topped the town, where, roofless, moss had crept over the stones for thirty-six years without much remark.

Eliza's brothel, the Grand, was a large terraced house down the side of a back alley, behind the more insalubrious of taverns that kept late hours. The Grand was not in a good state. Columns were blackening with dirt. Slabs of flagstone were missing from the steps leading up to the door. Behind the house there was a scant garden not much used. The windows sat in deep recesses and drainpipes croaked in the Island's high winds.

It was a sorry sight, the Grand, sorrier still that in 1951 it had lived up to its name, the cat-house itself where Jack and Margaret Malraux had once met in the bar, and talked, and laughed, and hatched plans for a grander life away from the churchly eye of England. It was where, so soon after deportation, the new Islanders came to eat and drink and fall in love, and there was a general exultation that somehow, despite their expulsion, they had won the war against the Church. In the fifties, the Grand had always been busy, as a bar and dancing hall, and then in the sixties, when things had turned quiet, it had turned into a brothel, although not very successfully.

Now, the Grand was often empty. It had the smell of the sickroom, as if the new freedom of the Island had somehow set in the rot.

There were several rooms and three girls, including Eliza, employed there permanently. Musa, the proprietor, did not have the money to spend on a renovation of the place. Damp grew, sponging the skirting boards and ceilings. Cobwebs hung woolly from its ceilings. A woody smell came from the rooms – mulchy and sour – which the girls had become used to, but the men could smell distinctly on their entrance. Musa had brought in Eliza this summer to inject something new into the failing state of affairs, which had worked, briefly, until she too had just become old hat.

This morning, at the mirror in her room, Eliza contemplated once again her brow. What words might mark the day? The eyeliner knocked against her teeth. Since coming to the Grand, Eliza had daily kept this small ritual. It was a way to cope, she guessed, with the everyday invasion of privacy that the job brought with it. A man might knock at her door at any time, and though they tended not to, it still prevented her from completely relaxing. And there were so few customers these days that the girls could never refuse them.

Eliza was Mr Carter's favourite, with his high forehead and rather lipless grin, but even then he might only come every fortnight or so. Still, when she had been more popular this summer, she had found this trick a good one to give her some space. Her first word written there had been *Escape*, so that she might imagine the possibility of not working here or living on the Island. Her second word, the next day, was, of course, *Arthur*.

Sometimes, on trips to the grocer's, when she would be faced with the open hostility of one of the Island women in the queue (they looked down on all the girls from the Grand), she reassured herself that on her brow, under her fringe, she had written *sour-faced bitch*, so that when she smiled politely at their cold stares she knew precisely who had won. Often, she wrote his initials, *A.S.*, or his initials and hers, *A.S.E.M.*, in tiny letters along her hairline. Sometimes she chose abstract words, such as *meekness*, which she didn't have, or *plenty*, which she also didn't have, or this word *escape*, even when she had no route to do that. At her pluckiest, she wrote the word *England*: the land to which she dreamed of going. Aye, regardless of what she did, if Arthur did not want her, she wanted out of this place. Whenever Eliza saw another woman with a fringe she wondered whether they might write these words at their hairlines; was tempted too to flick up the flank and scan the brow for words. One day, on walking into a tavern in Lynemouth Town, she almost pushed back the bangs of the barmaid to see if there was a sentence or two. What might it be? *Ale*, perhaps; but on looking at the lined face and slack mouth, perhaps *ailing*.

Perhaps it should say, *Fuck off, Nathaniel Malraux!*, as a statement of defiance to the boys last night. She had been upset by their crabbing of her, down in the square, but she knew they were only bored and getting up to mischief. They would not disturb her so easily.

Alternatively, it was Mrs Page's funeral this afternoon – perhaps it should be in reference to that. Eliza had been the gravedigger since she had left school, and had buried every Islander who had died these past six years. Perhaps she could pen the word *grave*, to mark the solemnity of the day as well as its thrust. Or *Victoria Page*, in memory of the dead woman.

She didn't mind being the Island's undertaker, though the salary was not enough to live on. When her ma had died, in June of this year, Linda had been heavily in debt, and Eliza had practically to give away the baker's she had owned. Once the creditors had been paid, there was very little left (£35, in fact), and, with Arthur grown cold, Eliza had been forced to take the only job that was going: at the Grand.

Across her forehead she decided to pen:

find the girl

Yes. That was the thing; that was the thing. She would do

a good job for Mrs Page this afternoon, but to find the girl was the hidden imperative of the day. Eliza moved the fringe back down and checked that the words were hidden.

With the words now penned, Eliza stepped out early on Tuesday morning. *Find the girl.* Aye. It was even colder than yesterday. Clouds moved fast about her, rushes of grey. She decided to forgo looking in Lynemouth Town, since it was unlikely the girl would have skirted all the way around Marley Hill to here without freezing to death. Instead, Eliza took the steep cobbled road out of the Grand, walking east. The town was not even close to waking up, its fronts shuttered and doors shut. She walked past Linda's old baker's, which had been renamed since Eliza had sold it. She could barely look at the loaves lined up on the shelf.

A few people here and there were getting ready for the day, but this place was poorer than Warkworth Town and few had constant work aside from the gutters at their stations, curing fish. The smell those shops gave off was of salt and seawash, and you could find a fish-curer easily from the yellow colour of his hands. Eliza weaved through the narrow streets. Lynemouth Town was a place for the night, not the broad eye of daylight.

She made it to the old ruined church before catching her breath. She was sure the English girl would look for somewhere remote and secluded, near here, perhaps, or the Eastern Bay, to keep hidden from view. Lynemouth Town spread out below like a fur. The girl would surely avoid the town.

The burned-out church was made of slate without

mortar or cement. It must have stood here for centuries, serving the Island's Christian community before the Movement's arrival in '51, and the godly folk had opted for resettlement in England. A moss had made the old stones nearly completely green. Rocks and other slabs stood at the base of the walls, as if the church were steadily tumbling toward the Sound. Down at the shore the sea sucked at rock. The sky hung low over the roofless walls.

There was little left to indicate it had once been a place of worship: an iron cross at the top, merely, which hadn't burned. Pews were overturned and no books were left. The arches were charred and black. At the entrance Eliza noticed that someone had cut the letters INRI into the bluish moss, and she wondered what it meant. It was probably the work of these boys; some anti-English graffiti.

Eliza wanted to stay a while, she liked the way the wind was stopped at the church's walls, and felt, somehow, as if her agitations were calmed here. But Mrs Page's funeral was at one o'clock and she would have to be at Forrester's by noon. With some of the £5 fee for burying Mrs Page, Eliza might buy herself something new from Buttons. A new scarf perhaps, or some socks. It was freezing cold and it was only to get worse as the December fogs came.

She walked on. There were children about in many of the houses, and Eliza reckoned on it being half-term. The houses were larger up here with bigger gardens, and they looked out rather defiantly over the sea. Few Christian souls had wanted to stay on after 1951 and the houses they had left were taken over by the deportees, and the excess were run to ruin by the Island kids. Eliza stayed five minutes outside one of the empty houses she had found but, after seeing no activity, she walked on toward the Eastern Bay.

She wondered – would a girl of English origin – brought up by the Church and fostered in its teachings – look different to the Island girls here? Would God somehow strengthen the whites of her eyes so that they were brighter than her own? Make her hair more flaxen, her nails less soft, her skin more luminous? Eliza had not seen the girl up close: only the red length of hair and the freckled skin. Eliza thought it wonderful: to be brought up believing in some kind and gently steering presence; to have a much stronger stake in some infinitely wiser thing than yourself. Nothing could be wasted, not in God's eyes; no. Eliza imagined that the girl would be boundlessly positive, since isn't that what the Church made you believe in, in the irresistible rightness of every act? Eliza had never believed in God – how could she, she had never been taught – but she had always thought that – given a different life in England – she would have been a natural at it. But it was too late for that now.

As Eliza walked, nearing the Eastern Bay, she wondered, again, what the girl was doing here. It was hardly a place for a holiday. Perhaps she had come to proselytize. Perhaps the girl had come to rescue her. Maybe she had come to find someone. Eliza made a silent vow to help her, and hide her, if she could.

The Eastern Bay was rough and the sand was scraggy and dark. Its currents made it too dangerous to fish and boats had often run aground here as they aimed for Warkworth pier. Breakers smashed against rocks. Its beach was often clogged with the drift of seaweed, and only birds alighted at the sand. Eliza fancied going down there but it was no time to be a daredevil, not with the girl to find, and Mrs Page to bury.

Eliza continued onward to Sea View Road, checking the houses. John Verger was in his living room, reading. Another man was watching television. One or two women poked their heads out of the curtains, wondering what she was doing sneaking around. They probably thought she was sharking about for another body for Mr Forrester. Eliza smiled nervously and almost retreated before she put her fingers to the words. *Find the girl.* Time was getting on. As she gained Marley Hill and then began footing her way down to Maiden's Square, Caro Kilman, mistress of the launderette, came running after her. She was wearing a big red coat that tied neatly at the waist; she was always well dressed, was Caro. Her auburn hair, set perfectly in a curl, was shown off by the purely grey sky. She said: 'Good day to you, Miss Eliza.'

'And to you.'

'And will you be assisting at Mrs Page's this afternoon?'

'That I will. And yourself? Will you be attending?'

'Aye. Aye.' Mrs Kilman gave her a cool look. 'You're a brave soul to be helping Mr Forrester like this.'

'It's not so bad.'

'Aye, well.'

'He pays me for it. It's not as if I'd be doing it for free, now.'

'No, well,' Caro said, 'I guess we all must pay for our fish. But you know, I haven't seen you much in the monger's these days.'

'Just haven't had the appetite for it.'

'Not since your ma's death?'

'No, not since Ma died, aye.'

'Well, it will return soon enough. Mark me. A fit young woman like you can't be on the tatties all the time now, no.' Caro had that knack of seeming both cold and caring: Eliza had never felt at ease with her. 'You'll be needing some fish inside you. Or you'll risk anaemia, you know.'

Eliza reassured Mrs Kilman she'd go to Arthur's and buy herself some cod with her wages. Mrs Kilman smiled at her but in a sceptical fashion. She gave her an odd look so that Eliza checked her fringe was in the right place and that the words could not be seen.

'Mrs Bingley said she bumped into you after you were at the launderette, last night.'

'Aye?'

'Well. I thought maybe you might be going to Stansky's, after mine, but you didn't. I just wondered what else you were doing, down at the square, when you couldn't get your dress.' Eliza shrugged. She was not in the mood for interrogation, especially not from Caro. 'You and Arthur used to be good friends. More than good friends. We don't see you two together any more. Did something . . . happen?'

'Nothing happened. We broke it off.'

'Oh. It's just . . . it was very abrupt, wasn't it, after your ma's . . . demise? We all thought you two would be together. But then you went to the Grand, and, of course, you can't expect a man like Arthur Stansky to be making his home with someone from the Grand, oh no, dear.'

'Well. That's the choice of Mr Stansky, of course.'

'It's just, well, something must have happened? No need to keep such a big secret, Eliza: you can tell me. I was very good friends with your ma, of course, she always did confide in me.'

With that laughable fact, Eliza said her goodbyes, absolutely wishing to be as far away from her as the Island would permit. She watched Caro descend the hill to the square. There was no one more gossipy than Caro Kilman; and no one she desired to speak with less about that night with Arthur. No one knew what had happened, apart from her, and Arthur, and Musa of course. And that's the way it would stay.

It was now nearly noon. Mrs Page's funeral was at one. Eliza gave up the search for the English girl and headed back to the Grand. She would have to change into something more fitting for the funeral: Mrs Page was to be buried by her today.

4. An English Girl

The girl stood unmoving in the light of the window. Dirt trimmed the bottom of the mattress where she had slept last night. The taps dripped. Half a broken mirror reflected back the room and her red hair, which looked as sumptuous as a gift of God. The house was derelict, but it would be Sarah's home, for her week on the Island.

Last night, after the ten hours she had spent in the hold of the boat, after creeping under the pier and then stealing across the Island, her legs had felt mercifully free, as if unpinned from restraints. The adrenaline too had made Sarah fast, her eye alert to any movement or shadows. She had had the sense of a pursuant, up until the square, at which point, though for no particular reason, Sarah had seemed to lose them. In the dark, she had been able to see very little of the Island, save the chalk-white houses, and occasionally, people in kitchens and lounges. The houses had a look of battleships.

Sarah had walked for an hour in the cold and salty air, footing her way carefully, but going fast if anyone seemed to be approaching. It seemed to take her an age to move through the dark, as if she walked through water, through a flood plain. Coming down the hill, the sea and sky were a block of dark before her, and she couldn't tell where the road might end and a cliff begin. She walked, wary to stop, but knowing she had to rest soon, lest she should freeze to death before she could even begin the search for Laura.

Sarah stopped at a row of darkish houses, with overgrown gardens and no sign of anyone about. All of the houses looked shabby and uncared for, some of the windows smashed and the hedgerow overgrown. She walked until the end of the road, circled back to check no one was behind her, then chose the house closest to the bay.

It was white and small and all of its windows were still intact. Sarah crept into the front garden. Once there had been a gravel path running up to the door but it was now covered with weeds. A track ran along the side of the house and she pushed aside brambles, her hair snagging on thorns. For a moment, Sarah thought someone was there, ahead of her in the back garden, but then a bird took flight and flapped against the branches. She waited moments, holding the knife, now, ahead of her, then she pushed the pine door and went into the house.

There was a kitchen in the first room, which smelled of old bread, empty rooms downstairs, with an upturned sofa and greying curtains. A staircase led to a landing where there were bedrooms and a long-abandoned bathroom with spots of rising damp. There was no one here.

Sarah waited for minutes, up in the bedroom overlooking the road, waiting for someone to appear, but no one did. And then, at midnight, after the exhaustion of the boat trip, during which, out of fear, she had been unable to even doze, she had curled up on the grubby mattress and fallen asleep surprisingly easily, sleeping until morning in the bright green sleeping bag she had brought with her from England.

Now Sarah stood at the window, in the weak stir of light. Over the roofs the sky was slung over them like a greying bed-sheet. She was cold, and had kept all of her clothes on from last night. In her hands, she held the newspaper article, the one that had brought her here. Her mother's mugshot looked out onto the world rather stunned, as if Laura were surprised to see it again.

For most of her life, Sarah had been told her mother had run off with another man. Her father had sat her down at the kitchen table, one warm July evening in 1976, and told her Laura had left them both, to start a new family with someone else. Sarah had learned the word *affair*, Laura had been having an *affair*. He said everyone was very upset with Laura for what she had done, it was a very bad thing to have an affair. Even the police were very upset with Laura, and that's why they had come to visit.

But in this past week, everything had changed. Now she knew the truth. Sarah looked out to the Island's vast sky, the flat long sea. This Island might be her mother's home. This Island might have been her mother's home for the past ten years. Laura Wicks was not an adulterer, but a criminal.

At the window, Sarah opened the article she had found last week, that had been folded these past ten years and kept in the cellar. Along the creases the ink had gone, but there was still more than enough to read. Her mother's eyes stared out from the mugshot, grey and light, her hair in the blonde bob that Sarah remembered. The article was from the *Newcastle Chronicle*, dated July 5th, 1976.

> Laura Wicks, of Trimdon, County Durham, has been arrested on suspicion of aiding the bombing of Saint Gregory's Church in Berwick yesterday. The Minister of Saint Gregory's, Rev Ed Williams, who was at the church early, died this morning from his burns.
>
> Wicks, a mother of one, was found on the scene; the two men she was with, and who launched the missiles, had already escaped by the time the police arrived. All three are thought to be members of the Secular Movement.
>
> It is thought Wicks had no part in starting the fire, but was the driver of the getaway car and alerted the two men to flee.
>
> The Secular Movement today issued a statement of responsibility for the church bombing, demanding the repatriation of criminals from the Island back to England and for the reinstatement of Secular rights.
>
> The Church issued a response saying it would not negotiate with terrorists.
>
> This has been the worst summer of secular atrocities since the emergency powers were issued in 1951, and is the thirteenth church fire in the North-East alone.
>
> After the Unrest in 1950, approximately 500 members of the Secular Movement were deported to the Island. This is the first orchestrated action from the Secular Movement in twenty-six years, and another mass expulsion is likely to follow.

The Secular Movement, which comprises members who use civil and violent protest against Church rule, are demanding the reinstatement of rights for non-religious people in England and the release of all non-religious prisoners on more minor charges. The Movement has called this the Sunday Agreement, but the Church has not yet entered into any negotiations on this matter.

A source from the Party has commented that the Sunday Agreement is looking less and less likely because of the violence this summer.

Ms Wicks, 26, has so far remained silent on the identities of the two male suspects, despite extensive questioning. Wicks will be held under emergency powers until sentencing.

Sarah wondered if her mother's act that July day ten years ago was an act of courage or an act of disgrace; whether it would be forgiven, or merely forgotten. The bruise on Sarah's wrist where, last Sunday, she had fallen on the cellar steps was starting to yellow. Her slipper had disappeared between two of the slats; going down to find it, under the step-boards, into the dark, it was then that she'd found the box of secrets, and found the article that had led her here, to the Island.

Sarah left the window and unpacked her warmest clothes, the socks, the comb, the toothbrush, the empty bottle she had used to pee in on the boat. She unpacked the knife but thought better of it and put it back in the bag. Half the bread was spoiled: last night, waiting for the boat to leave, and under the pier, her bag had lain unnoticed in a pool of water. But there was still margarine and cheese and a tin of corned beef, which she would save for the weekend when the food situation might become more desperate.

Sarah decanted the sopping half-loaf to the bin and saved what she could. She was already hungry but wouldn't let herself eat yet. It would be a week of hunger, she guessed, while she searched the Island for her mother.

She caught sight of herself in the mirror as she went about gathering her things. Silvering at the edges, and with spots of rust, it rendered parts of her invisible, and she was struck by the idea that perhaps she had changed, that coming to the Island had already marked her. She had spent a night here, mostly asleep: she could hardly have changed over ten hours. But she saw something in her eyes, hard, blank, as if she had entrenched her real self much further back, much further away from this new world. She wondered how the Island might have changed Laura, and whether she would even recognize her. She wondered, too, what the people were like here: unshepherded, free, but sad perhaps – they were free only in this patch of earth. Sarah had come from an England where God had swelled the schools and the boardroom and the banks, where the Church operated in sober distinction to the ways of the past. Sarah did not know anything but the croon of Church comfort and the presence of God in her like a second eye. And now she was here, after finding the article on her mother, after journeying to Newcastle and waiting at the docks for hours for the *Saviour*, and after she had stowed herself into the hold of the boat, in this most atheist of Islands.

The thought was terrifying and thrilling both.

Sarah packed a bag with a hastily made cheese sandwich, the torch, another jumper, the knife. At the taps, she washed out the bottle three or four times and then filled it with water; it still had an oily taste.

The path on the carpet was worn as if a multitude, not a family, had at one time taken these steps. The whole house smelled off. In the kitchen, where Sarah had come in last night, there was still crockery stacked at the sink and glassware in the dresser. Yellow scratches marked the length of a long wooden table. A chair was pushed back from the table as if its sitter had only just, violently, departed.

There was a strong smell outside, possibly a pond at the bottom of the garden. Someone with great care had planted a border of stones around the flower beds. A child's toy train had been kicked under the uncleared leaves. She wondered about the child's hand that had once motored the train through the home behind her. The child would be much older than her now. The Christian family that once lived here now probably lived in England, cosy, and church-going, having moved on from the resettlement village in Newcastle to pleasanter neighbourhoods, the memory of the Island merely a shrinking picture. Sarah remembered pictures of resettled families from her history books: their look of palpable relief, after they had cleared the Sound, and come home to England.

At the front of the house, Sarah flattened herself to the side wall. A man was walking past, elderly and bald, wearing tweed. He was talking to a young girl, asking her what she was to do this week, with school off. He kept on saying, 'Aye, aye,' very softly. Sarah looked at the soil around her feet, almost purple in the furrows, convinced that the man, if he found her, would grab and question her, convinced that her strong English scent would be carried on the winds, like a blood-stench, toward him.

When she could hear them no more, Sarah edged beyond the house. Its details she committed to memory: the long white walls, the drainpipe across its front, the loose branches of the hedge and the scruffy gateposts. On the lintel, in a friendly gesture, the words *Swanscott House* were carved.

Sarah tried to keep her eyes only on the path but she kept sneaking looks at the Islanders in their houses. They were doing normal things: laundry, reading the newspaper, cooking, cleaning. Sarah had expected more liveliness, somehow, as if the Islanders' behaviour might always be motivated by their irreligious fury. They had been expelled, after all; and they were all criminals – or the sons and daughters of criminals. As was she, she now supposed: the daughter of Laura Wicks.

At the hilltop, the sea was the colour of silt or ash or something close to it. There were two towns, down below, one light and airy; the other, packed and over-built, some-how making her think of the corned beef she'd brought in the tin. Only the grander one had a jetty, and this was where, she guessed, she had come last night. Behind her was the line of empty houses with Swanscott House, close to the strip of beach, where the breakers splashed against the rocky stacks, and where a slick of grey light winked.

A woman, in red, smiled at her, which made her feel nervous, and Sarah turned and walked much too quickly toward the bigger town, knowing, as she was doing this, that she was only going toward more and more Islanders. Sarah felt as if her blood had a scent, and that its hot spill would carry, somehow, on the wind. As if they might smell the meat she'd had for dinner on Sunday. She knew from her history books the Islanders had no meat: the English thought it would weaken their fortitude – as if the walls of the heart might be thinned by the absence of pork chops, and God might more easily sneak in and lodge Himself there. It was a tactic she had read about in her history books, and Sarah had thought the Church mean for it, as if you could teach God through the lessons of deprivation. It hadn't worked, anyway, the Islanders were no closer to God's bosom than they had been in '51.

Sarah pulled the coat closer to her, much closer, as if it might somehow contain her English reek.

All the grass was scrubby and flat, going down the hill, and mushrooms grew patchily, round and browning at the edges. She wondered, with her half-loaf gone, whether she could pick these and eat them. As she walked the sun came out and the clouds started to move off, and there were patches of blue, though the day became no warmer. With the brightening of the Island she felt better, and resolved to have a look around the town by the bay.

The square looked to Sarah much as a square in England might, without the church, she supposed, at one of its sides. Instead, the fishmonger's was the biggest place here, with the biggest awning, and people hovering about it as if it were the church. Flagstones were washed clean by the sea air; as were the roofs, which were low and slate and shone in winter light. Narrow windows barely broke the masonry. A few gulls wheeled on the winds; their wings massive, their eyes, when she caught them, somehow jealous, as if they envied her the turf.

Sarah pulled her hood closer. A few people came in and out of the shops. Every face she scanned for a likeness to Laura, but she didn't know where to put herself without attracting attention. Not close to the monger's: there were too many people near it. Neither did she have much inclination to be near the funeral parlour. There was a notice on the glass front. A funeral, today, near a place called Lynemouth Bay, at one o'clock, for a woman called Mrs Page. Perhaps she would go there, stand at a distance from the burial pit, to see if Laura might be in the congregation. Perhaps Mrs Page had been her friend.

A woman in a shop called Buttons looked her up and down and then looked away, chatting to another lady of the same age. A boy, with a bruise the size of an apple on his chin, narrowed his eyes and took some steps toward her before his mother called him back. He could only have been about twelve but he looked quite menacing, with his bald head and military garb, as if that mark of violence meant he had the capacity for it. Sarah felt for her knife, and followed the scrape of the sign into the museum.

There was no one inside. Sarah hid for minutes, just in case this boy was to come and cause trouble. When he didn't, she came out of the vestibule and slipped into the room.

The first picture on the wall was a map of the Island, pointing to Warkworth Bay, Lynemouth Bay, and the towns above them. She thought she could make out where Swanscott House would be, above the eastern quarter, which, she was pleased to see, looked rather uninhabited, with fewer houses than the rest of the Island. It had aged pictures of women picking at a quarry, men in old-fashioned clothes, an old 'kirk' above Lynemouth Town, and then the Islanders' resettlement, in England, in 1950.

The narrative continued under the black-and-white photographs, all taken during the Unrest. There was a picture of English identification documents from 1947: light-coloured if issued by the Church; darker if they were from a civil authority. There was a photograph of the elected Minister who had asked the police to do stop-searches; and those with darker papers were given a harder time. The Minister said that Englishmen had gone on too long in the night-time of the Lord. He said every Christian would do well to bring his dark-paper neighbour to Sunday service. He said it was right that better Christians got better jobs. He said it was right that those practising the values of the Lord were rewarded in heaven *and* on earth. The Minister said that Christian folk should pity the Godless. Then he said if they wouldn't respond to charity then the Council had the right to use more aggressive tactics.

A photograph showed a sign above a surgery which said 'No Godless Here'. There was a photograph of a boy with a black eye and one of a policeman with his truncheon poised. After-school clubs were no longer for the dark-papered children. There were two long queues outside a segregated school. Doctors could only treat people of their kind; this was in respect of people's wishes. A map showed boundaries re-drawn along the lines of Church congregations so that the Christian Party won again up north and, said the caption, 'most of the English were pleased with this.'

In the next photograph there was glass everywhere. Secular shops were looted and no one came forward to press charges. There was smashed glass on the roads most days. The Church Youth liked to take cricket bats to knees; the secular gangs liked to use golf clubs so that the altar boys' ears would ring and then they wouldn't hear the babble of God any more. There were photographs of kids bruised and happy as if they craved another beating, their eyes wide and thrilled. English policemen held guns toward a merry gang as they held their dark papers toward the lens. Photographs followed of people throwing rocks through church windows, then nail bombs, then glass-bottle petrol bombs. This was the work of the new Secular Movement, in 1949. A Sunday school was bombed and many children were killed.

In 1950, the Christian Party took government and that was the summer the churches truly burned. There was a sense of siege to the Northern cities. The first thing the Party did was to make the Secular Movement illegal. Anyone left with a darker paper got it swapped, if their family meant more to them than politics, or God, and besides, if you didn't pay a tithe to a church you didn't get a vote, so there was not much good to be done with darker papers.

Riots broke out and the photographs showed an old woman dying with her dark papers still grasped. There were hands nursing bloodied noses; policemen with batons poised midair; noiseless screams; shields braced; heavy boots stamping. Hundreds of protesters died. There were placards saying GODLESS OUT and THE GODLESS ARE WOLVES. There were cars burned out on the roads. The Movement occupied the Newcastle Town Hall and the police made a blockade. When the police took the Hall it was filthy with shit and old food and rats.

A state of emergency was called in London. A policy of containment was discussed, and emergency powers were drawn up. There was a photograph of the Prime Minister signing a paper: the title of it read 'Act for the Displacement of the Secular Movement from Problem Areas'. All members of the Movement were to go.

At the Museum's back wall, photographs showed men and women walking with heavy bags. Some of the women were very smart, in well-cut skirts and coats with fine fur collars, they wore upturned hats, and dark red lipstick. There was a strange look to them, with their flat mouths and pinprick eyes: they seemed faintly bored, as if their indifference were a form of protest.

That January, in 1951, five hundred members of the Movement were deported to the Island. Their families followed later. Some of the photographs were over-exposed but the points of their eyes were shadows. Dark identification papers could be seen falling to the waves.

In the next room, the narrative continued after 1951: England's long happy fifties, sporadic resistance in the sixties, and then suddenly the great wave again of violence in that big year, 1976. Sarah analysed the photographs intently, looking for Laura. There were more church-bombings, riots, the murder of two members of the Christian Party. There were photographs of the Newcastle riots and a summer hot with church fires. A photograph of a man hanging from a tree, neck chafed from the rope, his head lolling. A fat woman lay dead in a pit, her big breasts exposed. A second wave of deportations followed in 1977. This was when Laura would have come. Sarah searched, looking for a photograph of Saint Gregory's, for a burning church at the end of an avenue in Berwick. There were any number of churches with their pulpits burning but none in particular that looked like Saint Gregory's. Sarah searched too for the two men Laura was with that day: but she had no names and no faces to identify them with, and searched instead for the words Saint Gregory's, or Berwick, or Laura Wicks.

There had been no more deportees after 1977. In the last section, it said that the Sunday Agreement, finally signed in 1983, had secured the relaxation of compulsory religious attendance, the carrying of ID cards and the release of minor Secular prisoners given their good cooperation on all crimes still outstanding. The final sentence observed, rather melancholically, that nothing had been achieved insofar as returning the Islanders back to England.

At school, Sarah and her friends had all been told the Movement had gone willingly. It had been a ceasefire, and the members had opted for resettlement, to stop the Unrest. But here there were guns and blindfolds and a man hanging: the Godless on one side, the Church on the other. This had not been the story told to them. Sarah had been fed one story when the truth was very much other. Well, she supposed, Laura's 'affair' was only her father's contribution to the national lie.

Sarah waited there, in the museum, until one o'clock, amongst the walking men, and scared women, and merry policemen with waving guns, waiting for the funeral of this Mrs Page, which her mother might – or might not – be attending.

5. The Grave Courtesan

Heat swelled from the living room's gas-fire. His mam sat in the big old chair, her face as clear as the clock-face above her, wearing her housecoat and slippers. When Nathaniel saw her, nested between the fire and the side table, some block of misery sank him. 'All right, Ma,' he said to her quietly, from the doorway, so as not to give her a fright, 'am off now.'

She batted away the smoke. 'Where you off?'

'Down to the square. And then to Lynemouth Bay.'

'What for?'

'Mrs Page's funeral. You asked me to go. Remember?'

'Is it Tuesday already?'

Nathaniel nodded.

'Aye. Aye. Good lad. Your da would have wanted you to go.' She looked at him and narrowed her eyes. 'You're not going with the boys, are you?'

'No, no.'

'Tell me you're my good lad?'

He told her he was her good lad and then she looked away from him, out of the window to the garden. Nathaniel came to the chair and stroked a lock of her hair. It was so brittle he could snap it. 'All right now, Mammy M?'

'Aye.'

'What's got into you?'

'Nowt.' Her gaze was fixed somewhere in the middle air between the window and her chair. She looked worried.

'Now there's a lie.'

'John Verger was here yesterday, asking for you. About some book you'd borrowed.'

'Oh, aye.'

'D'you know the one?'

'Aye. It's a daft thing he lent me. I'll return it soon enough.'

But Nathaniel couldn't remember where he'd put it. He had tried, in truth, to ignore its existence as much as he could. A book of scripture and paintings, Nathaniel had shuddered as Mr Verger had shown him 'the hidden glories of English faith', and shuddered too, at the tremble of delight in the old man's voice. Verger had delivered a little lecture, telling him about how he had found himself unexpectedly in the church after falling off one of the pews, and describing some miracle act of calling, culminating in this act of theft from the museum. Nathaniel had felt very moody with him, as the old man argued for the consolation the volume might bring 'to someone still grieving'. At this point, Nathaniel had purely wanted to punch him, or gromick up his supper on his lap. But Verger had been his da's best friend, and Nathaniel hadn't had the heart to reject the book. It was a frightful thing, with Christ babied and bloodied on every page, and Nathaniel had no more than taken a few looks before putting it aside in some drawer or cupboard and lost it for ever.

'Well. He'd like to see you,' his ma said, 'and he is a kind man. Your da always talked very highly of him.'

Nathaniel could never seem to persuade his mam of how tiresome Verger was. 'Aye . . . but he's always wanting to talk, always a little sermon about this or that; I can't stand it.'

'You be good to that man, Nathaniel Malraux. He was your da's best friend,' she pointed the cigarette at him, 'just you remember that.'

'Aye, Mammy, aye. I didn't mean anything by it. Let's stop this now. What'll you do today?'

'There's a soap on the box I want to watch.'

'Shan't you go out?'

'Not today, Nath, not today.' He held her wrist; it was tiny. He felt again he could snap it, and felt sorry bad that he kept on thinking of snapping her, his own ma. The poised cigarette was now almost all ash. Nathaniel moved her hand to the ashtray and tapped the cigarette gently. 'Smoke 'em slowly, Ma, I didn't get any more this week.'

'Oh. Did you not?'

'The Boatman wants those pills you get. And you forgot to order them. So no more cigs for a while.'

'I'll get some more. For next week. Commerce with an Englishman, I can hardly believe it sometimes. My own son. Cheeky monkey, eh?'

'Aye, well, let's not complain while we enjoy them, aye?'

Margaret looked up at him and patted his hand gently with hers. 'When'll you be home?'

'Tonight. I'll be here all tonight with you, doll. And we'll have supper together and watch the telly-box. How's that sounding?' Should he chance it now? 'Maybe I could go to Arthur's and buy us fish supper?' His mam didn't answer but looked out again into the garden, her eyes full of vague alarm. 'No. Well. Not if you don't want to. I'll be here any-way, this evening. All right, doll?' His mam patted his hand and told him he was her good lad. She put out the cigar-ette in the ashtray and her eyes slid back to the telly set.

Nathaniel stepped out into the cold air and sucked it up by the lungful, glad to be shot of the warmth. A few trees here and there, but everything had the look of being dwarfed by the sky. He felt happy to be setting out. An edgeless cloud topped the hill this morning and, making his way to the top, now surveying the harbour and houses and the men working down at the herring stations, Nathaniel felt more than ever the happy king of this dark isle.

Within the half-hour he was down at Maiden's Square to meet Jake as they had planned. Nathaniel had hoped to interview Mr Forrester about Mrs Page and her anaemic demise, but when the boys walked into the parlour, Mr Forrester was fast asleep, his narrow back facing them, snoring gently. The two boys crept past and Forrester did not wake.

Behind the shop there was the mortuary and garage. The mortuary was a tiled room of white enamel; cool and very clean, with a chemical smell, flat and strong like chlo-ride. A window was built into the back, though it was seldom that a person looked either out or into the colour-less room. The garage, next to it, kept the Island's only car, a black old rattlebox whose creaking chassis could be heard over the whole measure of the Island. Petrol was delivered by the English boat once a month and the car was used sparingly, in emergencies, and for those whose emergen-cies had emerged with less than happy outcomes. It had a long bonnet and at the tip a logo that meant nothing to those born here. The garage, to Nathaniel, smelled of his da's garage where Jake and he had first shorn their scalps: a mixture of turpentine, grease, paint, oil.

The car looked as if it were waiting for them. Nathaniel got into the front seat and made Jake get in the back, and he pretended he was a taxi driver, just as he'd seen on the telly, and Jake told him where to go and they chatted as they saw the English people on television did. They put on funny voices to imitate them. Nathaniel made Jake bob up and down as if the English road they travelled was a rutted one. When the boy paid from a book of invisible notes Nathaniel said that he would give him a reduction on the price since Jake was a friend.

Jake thought it was the nicest time they had had together in a long time, probably since the summer, before things had turned strangely fraught between them.

A single door joined the mortuary and the garage. When Jake had paid, and after they had swapped places so that Jake was the taxi driver and Nathaniel the chatty customer, the boys shut the cab doors quietly and crept into the mortuary.

It was very still in there, and cold enough that Mrs Page gave off no smell. 'Can you believe it, aye?' said Nathaniel, staring wide-eyed at the closed casket. The two boys were as immobile as Mrs Page and stood together away from the coffin, their shadows no larger than them on the glossy walls. 'Mrs Page, Mrs Page. I remember her giving me a shilling if I ever came to visit.'

'Are you off to Lynemouth Bay for the funeral?' asked Jake.

'Aye. My ma asked me to, like.'

'Is it Eliza still doing the Tongue?'

'Aye,' said Nathaniel.

'Wouldn't mind dying so much if it meant going on her Tongue,' said Jake. 'Me on the tip of her Tongue, oh yes, I could see that all right, though I shouldn't hope for it, I suppose.'

The light coming in at the window was grey and the boys' skin was grey too. 'Go on, then, Jake, open the box.'

'On your way!'

'Why? Scared?'

'No. Just don't want to.'

The boys stood there looking at the coffin, both unmoving.

'Scaredy cat.'

'Am not.'

'Y'are so. It's not nailed or anything. Eliza will be doing it in an hour or so, anyway. You're more fearful than a woman, then, is that what you're saying? More fearful than the doxy herself?'

Sullenly, Jake went to the casket. His hands had a tremor to them but he wouldn't show the other boy. He told himself Mrs Page was dead and couldn't do anything to him now. The wood was surprisingly heavy but soundless in its springs. Jake could not make out much more than a body recumbent in the dark. He brought the lid up further, the underside of it rougher than the top. A sweet smell rose as the lid came to rest on the hinge.

Mrs Page was dressed in Buttons' finest: a plaid skirt, tan stockings and sensible shoes for the lower half; for the top, a plain shirt and woollen cardigan. Everything in her outfit, all the separates, seemed so stiff that if she were flipped over there might be nothing covering her undersides. Jake imagined her bottom squashed fatly against the coffin base. Her skin had a waxy look and her eyes were closed as if they had been sealed with glue. Her lips too had lost their colour. Mrs Page's hands, with knuckles gleaming, held each other over her middle.

'Oh my,' said Jake, and then he burst out laughing. 'She looks just like your ma.'

Nathaniel came round to the box, viewing Mrs Page over the tips of her brogues. 'She looks nothing like my ma,' he said, rather tonelessly, as a sadness pulled at him, because she did, she did, she had just the look of Mammy Malraux! He felt almost like he might blub. He'd come here with Jake to have a lark and be thrilled by the pathos of it, but now an awful spreading sorrow came over him, so that his lids scalded and his cheeks burned. He said something like, 'She looks more like *your* ma,' but she looked nothing like Mammy Lawrence and they both knew it.

Nathaniel closed the lid and then slapped Jake very hard on the back of the skull. 'You say nothing of that ilk again, Jakob Lawrence.' The boy rubbed his head and gave Nathaniel a narrow look, but did not push it.

With some urgency, and without closing the box, the boys left the room, suddenly spooked. Mr Forrester was still facing Marley Hill, but now reading a newspaper spread over his knees. At his crown, he had a bald spot the size of a penny piece. He turned on his swivel chair as if he'd always known they were in there, but laughed at them as they tried to make excuses. Mr Forrester asked what they were doing, and the boys spoke at the same time, until Mr

Forrester gave up, and, after some pressure from Nathaniel, he measured them up for a coffin apiece, until Jake mentioned something about stinky Gots, and how he'd liked to bury a bleeding Englishman in one of these coffins, and Mr Forrester got huffy. The two boys left to play Belly-Up and Shark before he had time to deliver a bigger sermon.

Eliza watched the boys come out of Forrester's, but chose not to comment. She was having a hard enough time snaking around the square so that Arthur would not see her. Last night had been such an embarrassment, with Arthur having to come to her rescue, and then not uttering a word to her. Aye, he had made it quite clear he wanted nothing more to do with her.

Arthur had been her mam's friend, really. Linda had always had a great deal of time for Arthur Stansky. But in the time between Eliza's ma having her first heart attack, and then the second, it was Eliza and Arthur who had become inseparable. It started when Arthur began calling round to the flat, above the baker's, offering some brill or bass wrapped in an oilcloth, his face shiny in the pool of lamplight. Eliza would watch him from her window, as if he were under a lens, a small thing, like an insect of particular curiosity.

She had felt things happening. They would sit at the table, after her ma had gone to her sickbed, talking, until very late, sometimes holding hands, sometimes there would be a kiss. He never smelled disagreeable, despite his profession, and his hands, so roughened by his job, always seemed marvellous to her. Aye, things were developing, gently, gently. They would go out for long walks up and around the Island, he'd sometimes take her out on one of the fishing boats, or guide her hand as he showed her how to gut herring. It was an exquisitely lovely time, wrapped up, as it was, with the grief for her ma, as well as the tender thrill of being with him. She liked the way the Islanders looked at her when they were together, that June: knowing that she had bagged the best man on the Island, and she was proud.

But then her ma died, and their little relationship – that hadn't even started yet, not in earnest – had suddenly collapsed. And the worst thing was, Eliza couldn't even work out whose fault it was.

Maiden's Square was busy at lunchtime. There was a queue of people outside Kilman's launderette and a shuffling line outside the fishmonger's and the grocer's. All around the square there was a reek of fishbait and seawater.

Mrs Bingley was standing with another woman and nodding toward the two boys settled now on the stage. 'I hear,' she said, 'they are sharking about the Island, looking for English spies. For anyone they suspect, you know, of having some English connection. A sorry state of affairs. Not in this day and age. You'd think we've had enough, after thirty-six years, without being persecuted by our own, aye.' The other lady was nodding vaguely and stole a look at them. Eliza took heart that if they were talking about the boys, that meant the English girl was not yet known to them. Mrs Bingley would surely have words about this were she to have seen her, this flame-haired foreigner. Eliza wove past them, avoided Nathaniel and Jake, and found herself at Forrester's.

Forrester's office was warm and musty. Everywhere there was disarray, with old books, notes and newspapers stacked above one another, though it looked necessary, as if the dead's dispatch depended on misrule. Forrester looked up and closed his paper. 'Eliza! How's business?'

'Grand, thank you, Mr Forrester. And yourself?'

He looked about the room, and lowered his voice. 'Between you and me, Mrs Page is a jolly good turn-up for the books. Business was looking rather glum; not enough dead.' He issued a finger urgently toward her. 'Not that I'd wish anyone to go, that's not what I'm saying. But I run a business, aye, love, and I need the money. A funerary home needs its dead as Arthur needs his fishes.' A raised eyebrow. 'And someone needs to feed his fish. Get my ken?' He closed the book of accounts on the desk. 'And I'd always rather see more of you, Miss Eliza. We don't see much of you any more at Maiden's Square.'

'No. I . . . I've been very busy.'

'Business must be very good.'

'Business is business. Other things have been distracting me.'

'Ah! Men, then; boys.'

'No,' she smiled; a sealed, sad, smile. 'Not that either.'

'Ah,' he sighed. He looked down at the chewed pipe. He applied a handkerchief, frowning. 'I always thought of you and Arthur, maybe . . . one day. You used to enjoy stepping out together when your ma was . . . in decline.'

'Not any more.'

'He had such a penchant for you, you know, and now he mopes around the monger's like a lost fish. I can't fathom it. I never see him anywhere but the square, and you're always in Lynemouth Town.' Forrester shrugged, then stuffed some loose shag into the pipe, poking it down with a blunt digit. 'He sleeps and eats and drinks in that pokey attic, you know, above the fishery. Being with all that trout, day in, day out, it can't be good for a man.'

'No. I can't imagine it is. Well, anyway, he's not interested. He barely says a word to me.'

Forrester's eyes flicked back up at her. 'No. Well. No, he doesn't *seem* to be, but perhaps he's only shy, perhaps—'

'Y'are sweet, Mr Forrester, but Arthur Stansky hasn't said a word to me in quite a while now.'

'Well, I hope you haven't quarrelled. He used to have such a soft spot for you.' Memories flooded her: a warm day spent on Marley Hill, when Arthur had carried the picnic in his shrimp net; swimming at the beach in Warkworth Bay when his lips had tasted of kipper. For a moment, the memory was so strong she thought her limbs were in water. 'He sometimes asks me if you're ever around the square.'

'He does?'

But she stopped herself asking more. It was impossible. Nonsense. Arthur only asked Mr Forrester so that he might know how best to avoid her. 'Look, Eliza, dear, tell me. Did something happen? You don't have to keep it to yourself, you know, if you want someone to talk to.'

Eliza cleared her throat and offered her hand. 'Can I get the keys, Mr Forrester?'

'Aye, aye. Oh, I'm sorry: Alison's always telling me not to meddle. Here,' he said, and he gave her the ring of keys, but did not let go. 'These lads. Over there.' He nodded over to Nathaniel and Jake, who were chasing each other about the square. 'Are they much trouble?'

'Not to me,' she said, wondering why she had so quickly lied.

'Well, they do say some funny things. About Gots and spies on the Island. A load of old nonsense, of course. Who out of any of us would want union with England? In this day and age!'

'I don't know.'

'Whipping up trouble for the sake of it. What nonsense. Well, well. Let's press on, eh?' He dropped the keys in her palm. And then he kissed her on the forehead, as a father might. 'Dear, Eliza. You're a good woman, a good woman. Your ma would have been proud.'

Away from the bluster of the square, the mortuary was always very quiet and very still. Whenever she was called here, Eliza would stop a little while in the back room, which seemed so luminous a spot as to render the rest of the Island shadowy and dark. Eliza put her hand down flat on the cool wood. A perilous job, this; burying the dead.

The Pages had chosen a dark, heavy wood, and she was pleased that they had spent a little more of their money. It always made her job easier. Mrs Page's features were damp and yellowy like a bread pudding. Her clothes were probably her best, washed and laundered by Caro Kilman. Mrs Page had not been a slender woman, and her body went right up to the clothy bulges of the box's padding.

Something in Eliza seemed to flag at all this. The memory of her ma's funeral that summer came back to her.

Mr Forrester had arranged all the sundries but it had been Eliza who had clothed her, pinned Linda's hair back into the soft waves she liked and brushed a rouge on her cheeks. Eliza had been burying the Island's dead since she had left school at sixteen, but it had been Mr Forrester who had pushed the Tongue's button that day; this was, finally, a job she was spared.

Since that June, it had been a bad year. The loss of her ma, the poor sale of the baker's, then Arthur's rejection, and the terrible job at the Grand . . . At every step, Eliza had expected a redress to her lot. The world had turned so ungenerous! In six months, she had lost nearly everything, and the Island now seemed a sorry little dump. Eliza thought of her future here: each day played out in long similitude to the last, amid the encroaching winter, when the snow would come to the Island, and would not shift, not for months, and she would stand outside Arthur's fish shop, waiting like a rag-picker, like a beggar, come to scavenge off him what she could.

Mrs Page looked on, calmed of all agitations.

With some envy, Eliza closed the lid.

It was warmer outside. The clouds had gone now, and the sky was blue and high. When enough people had gathered behind the car as was respectable, Eliza gunned the engine. It was a quarter to one. She drove slowly and the cortège followed. From their homes, people watched the car, as it went, rattlingly, to Lynemouth Town.

Eliza kept an eye on Mrs Page but let those gathering proceed as they wished. She took the opportunity to keep an eye out for the girl, expecting her to rear, unexpected and russet-coloured, amongst the Islanders. There was no one at Warkworth Bay, where she had seen the girl last night. Eliza doubted herself for a moment, wondering if she had dreamed of the girl between the beach and the square. Waves collapsed at the sandbar. She remembered the words on her forehead, that she had penned this morning – *find the girl* – and she knew she had not made the stowaway up.

Then the cliffs began swerving crazily inward, gouging gaps of enormous air, and Eliza concentrated on the road until Lynemouth Bay.

The air outside the car was a briny slap. Eliza checked the distance between the boot and cliff edge. Her heart lurched. How the waves scissored the light from up here! Her mother had told her that they bury their dead, over there; over there, she guessed, looking out, lay England. Eliza thought it crude and unromantic, to stop up a mouth with earth. She would much rather be buried at sea, to let her hair open and close like the skirt of a jellyfish. The Sound's beauty – though it was barbarous, aye, she knew that enough – calmed her. She forgot momentarily of her troubles, of Arthur, her dead ma, the English stowaway, and thought of the task ahead. Mrs Page was to be buried by Eliza today.

The Islanders had caught up with her at Lynemouth bluffs. In the congregation, she noticed Nathaniel was there, though the other boy, Jake, was not. Eliza positioned herself some way away from him. He raised an eyebrow to her but she had no desire to speak to him. The rare November sun brought a lovely light to the scene, and the grass on the cliff looked almost polished. It had its moments, this Island.

By half-past one the congregation had fully arrived. There was Caro from the launderette, Mrs Bingley from Buttons, John Verger's bald head poking out like a par-boiled potato. No Arthur to be seen. The reflection from Mr Forrester's round spectacles occasionally caught the Islanders in the eye and they squinted after him. He motioned for quiet.

'Now we are all here, I would like to thank you for coming, to celebrate the life of Mrs Victoria Page and to say goodbye. Mrs Page, as we all know, was a kind, caring woman. She was always trying to do right by people. It is a great loss to us, and to our little state, to have her leave us. Often, life might be said to be hard for us.' He looked down to his feet. 'Whether or not we believe' – and here he looked squarely at Nathaniel – 'we are all exiles now. We came from the Unrest – whether it was 1951, or '77 – and many of us did things, in those days, which we now might regret; which we may even regret every day. It was a very bad time, but in the light of everything else, we acted how best we could, in the name of progressive, not regressive, ideas.

'Now, in 1986, we find ourselves on this rock, and we do not seek any more unrest upon our heads. As part of the Movement, we fought for freedom, and that is what we have here. Freedom. It is not much, not enough to feed our children with or provide for our families,' he smiled, 'not enough to weave a banner with, but freedom is a good thing, and we would not have it, even now, in England.

'But enough of politics. We lead small lives. Over

quickly. Mrs Page's conduct was good and generous. In the midst of private hardship, we might remember her example, and remember Mr Page, who will need his neighbours now, more than ever, in these dark days. I cannot give you the reassurance of the priest at the casket, no promise of sweetness nor of light after we're gone, but I can say that goodness does not go unremarked. Not at all. To Mrs Victoria Page, then.' And the congregation dipped their heads, as if in prayer.

Mr Forrester gave a nod to Eliza. She broke from the rest of the group and went to the back of the car, opened the trunk, and unfolded the stretch of metal. It was topped by a belt of red cloth and nominally, amongst the Islanders, it was called the Tongue.

Mr Page came to the back of the hearse and drew a sprig of heather from the coffin's bouquet. He laid a hand down on the coffin, his palm down. The gesture did not last long. He rejoined the congregation with the flower still grasped.

Eliza gripped the pulley handle. With the grease cold in the cogs, it was always difficult to begin, but the coffin started moving out of the trunk, along the Tongue's conveyor belt. Eliza took the handle with two hands, drawing it round and round, watching the congregation, blackly rapt, as the pointed coffin emerged out of the boot. She kept on going, her forearms made strong from the brothel now strong for the Tongue. The casket edged along the belt, inching along, so it seemed as if the waves frothed about its end. Her forehead was licked with sweat.

With Mrs Page now a third down the Tongue, Eliza stopped to get a breath. Looking up, she saw – she was sure of it – the English girl, standing far away, right at the back of the crowd, unseen by anyone else. The girl was small and thin but her hair fell in brassy locks. In the sun, the red hair had a yellow glow to it. Under the freckles her skin was white as bone.

Eliza's heart sank; she could hardly stop the wheel now! Her grip slipped from the handle and the wheel did one revolution before she was able to reclaim it. Forrester looked at her alarmed. She managed a few more turns, going faster, really, than she should have done. When she was able to look up again, the girl had evidently noticed she had been caught, and had once again disappeared.

The coffin had, by now, travelled most of the Tongue and its top, pointed like a sword, weighed down at the end so that the car started to creak. Mr Page gave a moan. The car looked as if it should toss the box, like a horse wanting to buck its rider. Eliza gave the handle three quick cranks and the coffin was now halfway out into the air and the car groaned madly, and the weight of the box was beginning to tip, and then it teetered at the edge, and then was almost diagonal, until Eliza felt the car give, as the box and body of Mrs Page toppled into the Sound.

Moments passed and Eliza wondered if she really had just dispatched Mrs Page so brutally, and then there was a great splash, and the congregation sucked in a collective breath of air.

Gingerly, Eliza tiptoed over to the cliff edge to check the rocks. She had missed them. No leg or limb could be found kicking into the air. The coffin was nowhere to be seen, and the Sound was sliding around but more or less flat again.

Eliza had always taken great pride in her funerary duties, but Mrs Page had been dispatched in a shockingly brisk manner. Had the Islanders noticed her inattention, her unseemly haste? The English girl had captivated her. But no one seemed any wiser. Mr Page wept a little, others gathered around him; Nathaniel was smoking a cigarette – she wondered how he procured them? – and women huffed and puffed at the sight of him. Eliza folded up the Tongue back into the trunk, and shut the car doors.

Mr Forrester came over and gave Eliza the envelope with her fee. He put the pipe in the corner of his mouth. 'Were you all right there?'

'Aye,' she said, smoothing out her shirt.

He said: 'You just seemed distracted, that's all.'

'No. I'm sorry. A few things on my mind.'

'Well. Not to worry. No one noticed.' Forrester leaned in closer. 'Let's hope we might get a lick of someone else soon, Miss Eliza. My bets are on Mr Kilman. He has bad blood, the old anaemia, I hear.' He gave Eliza a peck on the cheek and a squeeze of her shoulder. 'And sorry about this morning. I didn't mean to harp on about Arthur. It's a private matter, and I understand that you're not wanting anything there.'

'Aye,' she said weakly, into the sun.

When the crowd had gone, Eliza drove the car back to the garage. She kept a lookout from the cab window, but the English girl did not appear to her again.

Wednesday

6. The Woman

Sarah woke that morning in the disused bedroom. Light slanted into the room but made it no warmer. In the chill, which leaked in draughts under doors and between panes, it felt as if her skin were bluing; as if the cold were a colour rubbing off on her. Dirt was building in the nail-beds. The strands of her hair clumped and gave off a brownish tang, but the water from the taps was too icy to think about. She was too warm in bed to move, and the room too cold.

Sarah felt for Laura's article, which was still in the pocket of her jeans. Folded and unfolded so many times in the course of this week, it was now soft and limp, like a worn piece of cotton. The now-familiar photo still shocked her. Sarah mouthed the word 'Laura', as if speaking the word might better her chances of finding her. All this time she had felt so angry with her, that Laura had felt so easily able to abandon the family, on a romantic whim, and never contact them. Now, things were so different.

Sarah had found the article a week ago last Sunday, while the meat from the butcher's was on the kitchen counter, and her father, folded into the sofa, was snoozing after church. The meat – it was pork – had been cold in her hands, as she laid out the medallions in the oven dish, when the boiler pipe had started clanging again. Sarah

79

didn't like to go down to the cellar – it was dark in there, and frightening – but it wouldn't stop until she had levelled a kick at the barrel.

There was dust everywhere down there, thick as a fur, and the bulb only gave a weak light. Vaguely she could hear her father's snores and the sound of the afternoon television; the races, perhaps, at York, or another Sunday service, gone long into the afternoon. At the foot of the stairs, growing through a crack in the floor, a mushroom was struggling into the dark, round and glossy as a blind eye. Sarah thought there was something eerie down here, and frightening, as if someone might lock her in, and choose to forget about her.

She took the steps two by two, but on the fourth or fifth – she wasn't sure – she lost her footing and fell sharply on her knee, her wrist scraping the stair-board. She put her mouth to the cut and the blood was warm. Her slipper was lost between the stair slats. Sarah climbed down and pressed herself between the banister and the wall, so that her hand went groping into the dark. She touched dust and cobwebs, but could reach nothing.

Eyeing a broom propped against the opposite wall, Sarah swept the handle over the stone floor. It brushed against her slipper, and then knocked against something else, boxlike and hollow.

Light and airy, in the arc of the broom it came quickly toward her. There was almost no weight to it. Sarah handled it carefully, like she would that mushroom should she have grasped its stalk. Dusty Sellotape sealed the box; and it was this that made her mind race. For so long, Sarah had asked her dad about Laura, asked about where her mother was and how she could get in contact. What was this box doing, sealed and secret under the stairs? Her father would never answer her straight, not directly, and neither would anyone else in Trimdon. Sarah carried the box carefully upstairs and then, wordlessly, as if nothing had happened, she proceeded to make dinner. Pork medallions. Apple sauce. They went to church and the butcher's every Sunday; the ritual was important to them, to the little family; her and her dad.

After dinner, while her dad was washing up, she cut away at the box's tape. Folded into squares, a newspaper cutting lay flat at the bottom of the box. Sarah's mind leapt to the contents. How many times had she found resemblances in women along the High Street, or trips to cities, her eyes keen to find Laura's blonde bob and freckled cheeks and nervous smile? Every Christmas she had hoped for a letter, or a soundless telephone call in the middle of the night.

Suddenly, there, on the newspaper sheet, there was her mother's face, looking up from the grey-and-white wash of print. It was a delicate portrait, though it wasn't intended as such: Laura's head tilting, the eyes shy, and the lips slightly open as if she had just spoken, or was about to speak. Unguarded and expectant, she looked as if she could be waiting for a blessing; her lips waiting for the host. This woman, though; this woman. Where had she been for ten years?

Sarah's eyes raced through the story, as she learned of Laura's crimes, which were not, as Sarah had understood them, crimes of the heart, but crimes of the Church. For ten years, the news of the mother had been kept from her. And here was the truth: her mother had been working for the Movement, and had driven these two nameless men to a chosen church in Berwick, on July 4th, 1976, and helped them set fire to it. A Minister had died because of them. Sarah imagined Laura in the cold car with bloodless knuckles holding the wheel, ready to drive at the first sound of sirens. But then she'd been caught, and the other two hadn't. *If found guilty,* the report said, *she will be deported to the Island.* But how was Sarah to know if this had happened? Was there a ledger, somewhere, a great English account of those who had and had not been expelled?

There were sounds of footsteps. She pocketed the article as her dad came in. He said goodnight and kissed her on her forehead. Her and her dad. It felt as if it had always been like this.

Out of the warmth of the sleeping bag, Sarah dressed rapidly in her old jeans and jumper. The article she folded neatly into her back pocket. She would need evidence, were she questioned, of who she was, and what she was doing here. At the mirror, she washed her face and rubbed it down with a towel. It, too, could do with a wash; it smelled of bread, somehow; of old dough.

But then, everything smelled of food. Her stomach was knotted, as if it were being squeezed in the claw of some big beast. There was a faintly sour taste, as if the duct between her stomach and mouth was filling with old food in protest at not being fed. Bread and bread and bread, that's what she had eaten since leaving Trimdon on Sunday, but it didn't seem to fill her up. The tin of corned beef glinted at the bottom of her rucksack: she had intended to keep it until at least the weekend, but now she was starting to weaken. Her hunger seemed constantly there, weightless and floating, like a net on water. She had to save the food; she could not predict how this week would go.

Sarah had been hungry since the funeral yesterday. Laura had not been in the congregation. She had had a good long look at the people there, before that woman, with the blunt fringe and yellow hair, operating that strange car, had clocked her head on. The woman had not looked at her menacingly, and Sarah wondered if she could seek her out, if this hunger continued, and beg of her something to eat. There'd been a boy, too, handsome, tall, whose polished skull had fairly winked at her in the winter sun. Perhaps he might be worth asking. There seemed a kindness to his eye.

Sarah had eaten plain bread last night for dinner, before falling asleep early in the grubby room. Hunger made her tired. She had dreamed of Laura, standing in the hallway, just a shadowy figure but Laura all the same, holding the door frame, tense, as if ready to flee. Her mother had been saying her name, over and over, and the tone was scalding, as if the shame of the crimes belonged to the daughter, and not the mother. And then, dreamlike, there had been the image of a man, pawing lamely at the windows of a burning church, and two faceless men running away. Sarah had woken early, cool with sweat.

This morning, in the room, Sarah spooned the beef into her mouth, though she knew she should not, knew these were her reserves until it got really bad. After two or three bites she closed the can again and put it into her bag, guiltily, as if she were ashamed, and left the house immediately, with the smell of the meat on her breath.

Sarah took another route, this time, walking up a coastal road past the bay, toward Lynemouth Town. She had been here yesterday but had fled the funeral so quickly that there had been no time to look, not properly. If only she might find a woman, bearing herself with all of Laura's qualities, in one of these cold stone terraces, she could ask her the question and then spend the week deep in conversation. There was so much she would give to talk to her, merely to say that she had missed her, greatly, and that she wished Laura could be at home with them. Aye, another hunger altogether had filled her these past ten years.

There was a large building with a sign saying the Grand, and then a string of houses, tighter and closer together than the ones she had seen in Warkworth. Cloudier than yesterday, the Island looked dun; as if, without the sunlight, it was left browned, and in need of a lick of paint. The houses, too, looked squashed and somehow grievous. Sarah tried to peer into windows but everything was mostly shuttered, and the winding terraces and tall flats meant it was impossible to spy.

Meat was oily on her breath from the beef she'd had that morning, tasting pink and wet, tunnelling down her nose and on her lips, as if she were a movable abattoir.

As Sarah walked toward the summit of the hill, her hunger seemed to set in motion a loop of images from the museum. The nude boys with their blindfolded eyes. The man hanging, shot in lancing light. The big woman in the ditch. Sarah had never seen pictures like this before.

The photographs from the Unrest shown at school had been of well-presented ladies and gentlemen lining up in an orderly fashion for the deportation boat. Lessons had taught her the Secular Deportation had been an agreeable compromise between the Church and the Movement. None of this violence had been aired. Sarah took the road downhill that would take her to the square, where she would have to find something to eat.

She had already begun to feel affection for Maiden's Square: its cool, autumnal colours, rich smell and familiar shops. Aye, this could almost be England, if you looked at it in slanted fashion.

She aimed for the grocer's, between the launderette and Buttons. There was a customer being served, the grocer, in green overalls, just like at home, weighing what looked to be old vegetables. The shelves were full enough with produce, though it was all cans and nothing much fresh. All the tins were brands she knew from England; they must have come over with her on the benefaction boat. The shopkeeper gave her a funny look and the other man behind him turned around too and she felt herself warming under their gaze. She smiled weakly, and as soon as the other man turned around, she grabbed three old carrots and left the shop.

So that she wouldn't be seen, Sarah walked fast down to the beach. Finding her home from Monday night, in the sheltered bit under the pier, she started on the carrots. She pulled the scarf tighter about her neck and let her hair down, so that it might provide her skin with more of a buffer to the wind. The Trimdon cold was nothing compared to here. These winds. That sea. The taste of the carrots, orange and metallic, was perfect, and their crunchiness felt as if they had cleaned her teeth.

Sarah had walked for a few hours more, looking into houses and avoiding the gazes of Islanders, when she came to the house. It was as if, in the grey and dying landscape, her eye had landed on an exceptional flower, though pale and hard to see.

A woman stood in the kitchen.

Dressed in blue and grey, with freckles over the bridge of her nose and her hair in a blonde bob, the woman stood reading a newspaper on the kitchen table. The skin about her eyes was drawn, and her hair was a little darker than it should have been.

The house was not remarkable, though the roof was rather small for a house this size. Nothing could be seen through the upper windows, though the curtains were unclosed. A chimney, lined with lichen, rose into the air and a trace of smoke was piped there. It didn't look warm, or inviting.

In distinction to the rest of the Islanders – none of the yellow fluorescence of the woman down at the funeral, or the tubby man of the monger's, or the polished sleekness of the boy at the cliff – here was a woman, slender and small, who had such a likeness to Laura that it stopped Sarah there for minutes. Pegged between the gateposts, she then noticed a boy at the kitchen table. His eyes and cheeks were rather sunken, his hair flat and crudely cut. The woman and boy – her son? Sarah's half-brother? – did not talk much, the occasional mouthed syllables here and there as the boy asked for more tea, or the toast. The woman poked a fish slice into a frying pan, turning only to the voice of the boy behind her. Brown and oily and curved, the fish looked like a kipper, and Sarah's memory of its smell filled her nose and her mouth grew wet, looking at the distant food.

Even with Sarah's own distrust, even while Sarah persuaded herself that she wouldn't just stumble upon her, she knew this woman, ahead of her, was familiar. And if it were Laura? What would she ask her? How should she announce herself? Sarah had schooled herself, manfully, she had thought, in coping with her mother's absence. But how would she cope, she wondered, with her reintroduction back into her life?

She had been there for a few minutes or so when the woman looked toward the garden, and Sarah panicked. She did not want to be caught here, not yet. She launched herself down the road, back to Swanscott House, resolving to come back tonight, in the dark, when it would be safer to watch this woman, who might be Laura.

7. Arthur and Eliza

Aye, things had been going well with Arthur, until her mother had died, and Eliza had found out the true scale of her family's bankruptcy.

On the discovery of the debt, Eliza had sold off the baker's, and the apartment above it with her ma's few bits of furniture. She had managed to pay off all the debtors, but there was nearly no money left, and Eliza, in the coming few days, would soon have nowhere to live. She had traipsed down to Warkworth pier when the fishing boats came in, and asked one of the fishermen for a job, but was very quickly laughed off. She went to the curing stations too, in Lynemouth Town, but was told, also unequivocally, there was nothing here for her. And then, one night, at a pub in Lynemouth Town, Mr Musa had offered her a job at the Grand. Privately, she had balked – she was hardly desperate enough for that.

With a few drinks in her, and wobbling down the Island paths, Eliza had gone straight over to Arthur's, convinced that he would, of course, let her stay. And so she had gone to him and asked if she could move in. Though she had not meant – move in – more like, a temporary stay, a few nights on his sofa. She was sure he would say yes . . . and yet, what he said, was no. She wondered if, drunkenly, she had not explained herself very well, because he had gone bright red, really very warm in the monger's cool light, and said, 'But this is all too soon! Move in together? You mean live together? But . . . ' his eyes had gone searchingly around the monger's, to the countertops, chopping boards and knives – 'Eliza. I'm sorry, no, we can't live together, not yet. I'm sorry.'

Eliza had been too embarrassed to tell Arthur about the state of her finances. Thirty-five pounds to her name! She would not ruin Linda's good name. Rejected by Arthur, she had gone straight back to the pub that night, and then, with more drinks in her, shots bought for her by Musa, she had gone, sobbingly, rashly, to the Grand.

When Arthur had found out she'd taken Musa's job he had refused to speak to her. The relationship was off. Both were smarting with the other's rejection and no communication was made for some weeks.

But if their relations were cool when Eliza had started at the Grand, they all but froze when Arthur came to her, one hot summer night, to engage her, not in conversation, but in business.

The Grand did bad business on the Island but it meant this morning she had the time to escape and look for the English girl. She went through Lynemouth Town, passing the old baker's on the way, and down to the bay where she had dispatched Mrs Page rather hurriedly yesterday. No one was there. Eliza walked on toward Warkworth Town, gathering a few of the wild flowers she found along the path. She searched the square and the museum and contemplated going up to the cop shop and declaring a missing person. But how could she declare a missing person who was not even registered as being here? Eliza circled round the Island back to the ruined church (perhaps the girl's religious sentiment might lead her back here?), and then went home to the Grand, the gorse now wilting in the warm palm of her hand.

Forlorn in her room, Eliza mooched, putting the flowers in water, wondering what she might pen under her hair today. The room had a petulant air to it too, as if it were also sulking about having nothing to do. Eliza held the fringe back toward her crown, regarding her brow. Perhaps she might take something sharper to it; a knife, perhaps, and tattoo herself there. Hours passed. She counted her money in the side drawer. With the fee from the Tongue as well, there was now £40 in total. What might she do with it? There was so little to do on this Island.

Eliza wondered what England was like and what it might be like to live on an island not so much an island as a long, seemingly boundless country with hills and rivers and meadows and cities. The postcards she had of the countryside fascinated her: the tall trees, and grazing cows, and big castles. Linda had sometimes told her of London. *Lon-don.* It sounded mad, purely hectic: the traffic, the dance clubs, the parks and bedsits. All that, though, had been before the emergency powers. It might be somewhat more sedate, now.

Eliza thought, much, of England: because she craved seeing anywhere that was not here. She thought everyone in England would be marvellous and warm and caring toward each other. She thought that they had it all figured out: surrendering this fruitless freedom for some infinitely gentler authority. Aye. That's what Eliza craved. She just wanted someone to tell her what to do. Not. It wasn't that; not really. She just wanted someone to talk to.

She hoped dearly that the English girl was alive and safe. If only she could find her she would offer her haven here, in the Grand; Musa might not notice. But along the tricksome Island paths, curling terraces and long bays, the empty houses and lump of Marley Hill, Eliza had no idea where the girl was, and, faintly, her hope of finding her was beginning to fade.

Musa showed up later at around two that afternoon.

'Where have you been all morning?'

'At Maiden's Square.'

'Well, thank your lucky stars, girl, you're off there again.'

'Why?'

'I'm hungry.'

'So?'

'You're to buy me my fish.'

'But that's Janey's job.'

'Janey's bloods are up. She can't go out. She's ill.'

'Pony. She's always complaining. Harking on this or that. She's so meaty herself she'll never get close to anaemia.'

'Eliza. Are you currently working? Are you otherwise engaged? Are you, might I venture, busy with the delicacies of a man's heart? I don't think so. Here. Now. Two shillings. A kipper. Make it two. No complaints, girl, you get it easy enough already.' His manner suggested more than fish was at stake. And he was right – she didn't have anything else to do – not in the manner of work – and there'd been no customers all day. 'Give my regards to Arthur,' he said, leaving the room.

By the time she reached Maiden's Square, Eliza was terribly nervous. The square was empty, aside from a gull fatly perched on a rooftop or two. Above the monger's she saw the window into Arthur's living quarters, but the curtains were closed. Eliza squeezed back her shoulders, cleared her throat. Without being entirely conscious of what she was doing, and with less than a flicker of consent, her legs took her into the shop.

Dark, wide-winged skate lay flat next to narrow trout. Monkfish gawped. There were purple octopus, rusty crabs, orange lobster, and a box of roe bubbling close to the glass. A salmon was spliced down its middle. A hundred filmed eyes stared at nothing. Everywhere, the smell of cold fish, ice and brine, and everywhere, the sight of moist skins and scales. Red plastic chains hung between Arthur's station and the back room.

Eliza hid behind the slow queue of women. Mostly older women, with thick ankles and set curled hair. With their bulging bellies and toothless frowns, the fish looked at her with wet disinterest. There was no one in the line she knew, and no one behind her, so at least the inevitable embarrassment might be kept between themselves.

Minutes stretched, and each customer in front seemed to have an endless list of requirements: herring with its head off or on, a plaice with a less brown skin, a sprat that didn't have quite such a feral look to it – the woman's voice was a whisper here – since this was where their uncle had died; in those exact waters, and they really shouldn't be eating it because – what if they were eating Uncle Roger? But the children couldn't live off turnips the whole time, now, could they?

Why not, thought Eliza, *I go without fish, day in, day out; I do not eat of Arthur's bounty.*

Two women spoke in quiet voices about the gang of boys and whether they should be afraid again; it was not new, this harassment. People always got het up about the threat from the English, about God being imposed again on their small Island. People – men, normally, and teenagers, mostly – always had it in their heads to create a little police force to check themselves of Gots. But it wasn't necessary. No one had gone back to the old faith.

Arthur prepared the fish for dead Roger's niece. The woman talked to him of the weather, and what he thought of Mr Verger's new sprightly ways, and did he think Beatrice Spenser should get out more, and might salmon help the constitution with all that protein? Arthur nodded amiably. And then, with the fish in her bag, the woman left, but only very grudgingly, because every Islander wanted to talk to Arthur for much, much longer. He was a kind man, and much liked.

Now it was her turn. Eliza looked at Arthur. The air stiffened. A hot wave came up her face. She managed a smile though she couldn't stop biting the side of her cheek. Arthur too had gone completely red. Had his forehead had that lick of sweat minutes ago? His eyes, though, were fixed on hers. 'Yes?' he said.

'Hello, Arthur.'

'Miss Michalka.'

The surname made her wince. 'How are you?'

'Fine.' He hadn't yet blinked. A thousand fish eyes seemed to be staring at her. 'Thank you.' He turned his broad back on her and cleaned his knife in sharp little strokes. Why was it she imagined that blade puncturing her throat and her blood puddling in his palms, he weeping over her dying frame? Her ma had always said she had a melodramatic streak. 'And yourself?'

'Very well, thank you.' Arthur looked about to say something else – opening his mouth, but shutting it again with a horrible snapping sound – and instead went back to cleaning the blade.

Eliza did not know what else to say. 'Well, two kippers then, please.' All joy was knocked out of her. Arthur placed the brown fish in paper and he wrapped it without looking at her.

'Grand,' she said. His eyes rounded. 'I mean—'

'That's fine.'

'I meant, fine, thank you.'

'No need to thank me.' He gestured to the space around him. 'It's my job.' Eliza slipped the coins over the counter top and wished she could place them in the shallow of his palm. Likewise, the bag of fish he slid directly over the plane of glass.

'Arthur, I've never felt angry because of—'

'No. Of course. Goodbye, now.'

She had been dispatched. Eliza whispered what she could manage – a weak *goodbye* – more into her collar than to him – and left the shop, to hear the bell trill her departure.

Eliza managed to get to Warkworth Bay before bursting

into tears. Oh, a fine victory; a veritable triumph! She kicked at the beach as if this might help. What a misery he had made her! She grabbed a handful of sand and threw it, ridiculously, into the air, and it came to rest immeasurably against the rest of the frozen beach. She wanted to open her lungs and scream, but somebody might overhear and think her mad. The grey breakers came ashore. It was stupid, the sea, with its stupid rhythm, its stupid sand and briny water, all for miles around and all for nothing!

Only two nights ago she had been on this beach, with such excitement, watching that brave English girl steal off Monday's boat. If only she had some of that courage herself. Wherever the girl was on the Island, Eliza hoped she was all right. She had so many questions to ask her. How had she come here? How had she stowed herself away on the boat? What was England like? What did the stretch of a meadow amount to? What did voices sound like climbing the walls of a church? And what was it like not to find the sea, staring at you from every which way, with all the dispassion of a dead man's eye? Yes, that was it, the sea: a great big eye, fogged and grey, and this Island nothing more than a piece of grit in all its salted juices.

Arthur's eyes, as well, too, too blank. When she'd walked in, she thought it might have gone well. She had even been rather pleased when Musa had asked her to go. A détente, perhaps. Not for the first time did she wish that she might be one of those fish nestling the ice-chips and awaiting the knife. How much she regretted that August night when Arthur had paid his visit to the Grand.

Furious that Arthur had rejected her, Eliza went at her

job with as much dignity as she could manage, and thence-forth they both avoided each other assiduously. Arthur was angry with her for accepting the job; Eliza was raging that he hadn't bothered to help when she had most needed it.

And then he had come one night, in hot early August, all breathy and half out of his wits, and bedded her, paying her beforehand. Never had she received a sum of money with so little heart. When he put the £5 note on the bed-side table he said, slurringly, 'I heard from all the other men what great fun you are, Eliza,' with something of a leer. He was a big man and must have drunk a boat-load to be that far gone. But when she lay down for him, tears dripped from his cheeks onto hers. And he asked her why, why, why was she here, as if it weren't completely obvious, that on her mother's death, she had been completely, and utterly, broke.

Eliza lay there all night, stony-eyed, while Arthur slept off the booze. Something in her hardened, and when he woke, he looked at her as if he were surprised to see her. 'Nice of you to come, Arthur Stansky.'

'Eliza. I— What happened?'

'You know what happened.'

'I— What have I done! Oh, what have I done!'

'Get out.'

'I'm sorry, Eliza. I'm so sorry.'

But Eliza was having none of it. 'It's all your fault I am here! When Ma died I thought we might be together! Did you not love me? And now I am here, in this,' she could hardly say it, 'brothel, because I have no money, and because you refused to help me!' Her voice softened and she held the bed-sheets in her fists. 'What happened? When

I came to you after Ma's death I asked for your help and you—'

'Eliza! I thought you were asking to move in with me!'

'I meant for a few days! A week! On the sofa! I had nowhere to go! I had no money, no home, no roof over my head—' Arthur did not say anything but looked sightlessly into the blue room. The light in there, from off the Sound, was like a wash of writing ink. 'Shame on you, Arthur Stansky, for the way you've acted. You're a disgrace. Coming in here, to bed me for that beggar's sum.' She pointed to the door. 'Out of my sight. I never want to see you again. I never want to talk to you again!'

Arthur held her wrists and said sorry, over and over. Then he said those words, 'Forgive me, Eliza,' but she threw his £5 out of the door and asked him to leave. She watched his broad shape weave down Lynemouth's alleys and wept in bed for the rest of the morning.

For months, in respect of her wishes, Arthur avoided her. At one point, in September, Eliza told him all was forgiven but he smiled at her politely, in rather a forced manner, and told her he couldn't be with her. He was cold and distant: every time she tried to engage him in conversation, he refused. Now, in November, he barely said a word to her. Nor she to him. She wanted to tell him his apology was enough, that her love had let her forgive him, but could not. She could only think that everything that had happened had ruined his feelings for her. She should probably move on, but felt she could not.

Eliza shook the sand off her shoes and stockings. Rock pools teamed with kelp and crab. The remains of three carrot tops lay powdered in sand; she kicked at them and buried them with her shoe.

At the cliff's headland, she stopped and looked out at the Sound. Musa's kipper she considered throwing back to the sea. Without quite knowing what she was doing she took a step forward. She saw above her the still clouds, and then down by her shoes, the grass so short and bald. She thought of her ma, and Arthur, and Nathaniel, and the English girl. *How the mind wanders*, she thought, *when it senses rest*. It was only a great shame that in dying one had to forfeit every minor keepsake; not the ghost of a memory, not the slender remembrance of a lover's face; not a breeze passing the hair on your neck. There would be nothing left of him for her. Nothing. And the relief of the pain stopping wouldn't even be felt; or at least, not for very long.

Eliza turned from the cliff, because it still meant an awful lot to her; this awful bold world. At least she had been loved, though she was loved no longer. Eliza turned back to the road. Musa was waiting. She at least might do something right, today, and rather than jump down into the comfort of the waves, she would deliver Musa his fish.

8. The Scrap

Jake did not want to hear this story again.

A few plants in the outhouse stood on the shelf, dry and dying. In there, when the tumble dryer was on, a warm mist filled the room and Jake imagined it would be like being in a jungle. Beyond the outhouse, the night was coming down, a block of mauve on blue.

It was too warm in the living room to think.

The gas-fire pumped heat. Its grille was as bright a blue as the sea at summer noon. When you turned the plastic knob sometimes it failed to ignite and the gas would leak and then when it did, the fire went up with a *woomph!* Jake wondered if Mammy Malraux's hair ever caught on the flames. It would light easily, her hair, coarse and dry as tinder-sticks.

Mrs Malraux's armchair was big and flowery and pitted with fag burns. The flowers now were vague as if her rump had smudged them. Even when she was not in the chair, it bore the shape of her hindquarters. Four worn points in the damson carpet took her weight. A bottle of buttercup syrup was on the side table, with pens, old lighters, and completed crossword puzzles. Little porcelain ornaments stood on the mantelpiece, and a golden brass bell, missing its clapper.

'Och, Nathaniel, you've heard it clear enough. I shan't tell that story again.' Mrs Malraux put the cigarette so far into her lips that when it came out the tip was wet. The big armchair made her as squabby as an infant. Her big calves glittered in the stockings; her bosom rested on the waist-band. Pointing to Nath's boots, and gesturing with the cigarette, she said, 'They were your da's, you know.'

'Aye.'

'Have you filled them out yet?'

'Ma!' the boy said, looking quickly at Jake, who didn't respond.

'Only asking.'

'Go on, Ma, tell us now of the boat.'

'No. Not now. You've heard it clear enough.'

There was silence for a while and then, with no more prompting, Mrs Malraux began. 'Aye. Well. It was about '47. I was fourteen, two years younger than you, now. There was all this bother around, about whether they were religious or civil papers you carried. When my da heard of the Unrest he got very upset. Ma too. Suddenly the police started asking you to show your papers, and it would say, you know, whether you were a member of a church or whether you were non-affiliated. Some people we knew started going to church just to avoid the hassle – and it was hassle, just name-calling, before it got rougher. I asked my ma if we could go to church and she said no. I wanted to go because my friends went, aye, and so people would stop picking on me.'

'But you didn't go?'

'No.'

'Aye. Good, good.'

'Anyways. The police started giving people a hard time, too, especially the boys, who were easy to pick on.'

'How?'

'Stealing things. Beating them up. My cousin came over to ours once with a huge black eye and we didn't need to ask, we already knew. I remember soon after Da left, someone threw a rock through my window. Ma was terrified. Da was working for the Movement by then, all of us knew it but we didn't say anything and we knew we weren't allowed to say anything. Things were hard at school. We started to be taught separately. We couldn't go to games after school with the other kids. I missed my friends, more than anything else. But they were told by their own parents not to talk to me.

'Gangs started up, there were beatings on either side, with cricket bats and golf clubs; anything they could lay their hands on. It was happening in America, too. Then it got worse, because the Movement started to fight back. Suddenly a church was attacked. Nothing like that had happened before. People had thought most of it was going on between teenagers, you know, and some bad police. Then another one, another church, the next week, and then another, the week after, was burned down almost to rubble and people were blaming it on the Movement.

'That was when Mammy moved us out of Newcastle but we were too late. People knew of my family 'cause of Da's sudden disappearance. You could tell a Movement family by their daddy's absence on the weekends. Da was involved in the Newcastle sit-in, in the town hall. That was where he was caught.

'They started talking about expulsions, deportations of

the worst offenders. About a loophole involving the Church and its powers. Emergency powers.' Margaret sniffed a little, here. 'We were served with the papers for the boat, and we were told Da would join us there. All the families were told that, I think. My mam believed them, I suppose. But there were lots who never made it. My da never made it. Someone from the Movement told us he'd died in a holding cell in Sunderland. My ma didn't leave the cabin for the ten-hour trip. Not once.'

Margaret stared at some dead point in the air. 'We smuggled a hand-gun in my drawers all the way across the waters and I was going to put it to the heads of one of the English police when I found out my da had died in one of their prisons. But when I saw my mam's face, I couldn't do it. I couldn't do it.' Margaret's eyes were glassy now, but then she smiled, a sad sort of smile. 'So we ended up here. And Mammy made everything very nice for us, as nice as she could. And then I met your da.'

'And?'

'Another story, aye. On with you, now. There's telly I want to watch.'

Nathaniel could never tire of this story. He loved to hear it. Jake was playing idly with a bowl of potpourri, his fingers digging down into the scented dust. His soft bulk loomed in the evening. 'Did you hear that?' Nathaniel asked. 'The story of my ma?'

'Aye.' Jake wiped the brownish powder on his jeans. It let out a hot flowery stink. The sky had turned violet now as the sun dropped amongst cloud.

'Up to, then, surly Turk.'

'What's that?'

'Need to get changed, aye, be ready for tonight.'

'Where are you off?' Margaret asked, with some alarm.

'To see the boys.'

'Better not be up to no good.'

'No, Mam. Are you to watch the telly-box, now?'

'Aye.'

'And what are you to eat?'

'There's a pie in the freezer.'

'You need some fish, Mam.'

'Don't harp on that now.'

'Your bloods. You've got to think about your bloods. You'll get anaemia.'

'On with you. I'm going nowhere fast. Now give me a kiss and tell me you're my good lad.'

He went over to his mam and planted a kiss softly on her bony brow. 'I'm your good lad, Ma.'

She leaned back into the armchair; contented. 'But you'll be here tomorrow, aye, when I wake up?'

'Aye, Mam,' he patted her hand, 'I'll be sitting at my chair when you walk in here.'

'Then I shall set the porridge for you tonight.'

Nathaniel's bedroom was colder than the living room but less pressing. A single bed with a plastic headboard was in the corner, and covered in a bedspread of purple flowers. A large brown wardrobe was wearing away to a lighter colour at the top, the wood flaking like a callus. It had all of Nathaniel's costumes in it, and it was a cherished thing indeed.

Nathaniel was nearly naked in not much more than pants, and the light gave his skin a mollusc gleam. There was some elegance of manner to Nathaniel that Jake envied, the long-tipped fingers, perhaps, or his lean stature; the way there seemed so little in the way of excess. Jake felt a little plump around him, as if merely Nathaniel's presence wadded him again in baby fat. Nathaniel looked very good with his hair like that, the bristle just showing, as if a match could be lit on the scratch. Jake had re-shaved his scalp last night, after Nathaniel had asked, and his mam had given him what-for, complaining again that he looked 'a victim of summat'.

Nathaniel was talking to him about the girls from school. He said he fancied Bridget, thought she was a looker. Jake said, 'What about Charlotte?'

'Nicholas's sister? A pudding!'

'Aye,' said Jake, 'I think she's lovely.'

'Tell you who *is* lovely,' said Nathaniel.

'Who?'

'Eliza.'

'The doxy from the Grand?'

'Aye,' said Nathaniel. 'But she's the prettiest girl on the Island. One day, Jake, I shall be the first of our boys to have her, and I shan't pay, mark my words I shan't. Och, she is a brass looker!' He pulled on his trousers and a shirt, which was so starched Jake could hear it unfolding like a box. Nathaniel looked to the mirror. 'I would love to fuck Eliza. Eliza Michalka! Doesn't bother me that others have had her. I think she's rum. I think she wants some of this, too.'

'Aye? What makes you think that?'

'Just the way she looks at me, like. Appraising me of my boyish wares.' He pulled on the red braces. 'Pass me a hanky, Jake. Make it two.' He turned back to the mirror, inspecting either side of his face. 'D'you know,' he said, watching the handsome chops go at the words, 'you can tell if a girl's shaved or bushy or whatever by the sound of their piss? If it's just one long stream it means she's still got a bush on her but if it's a spray you know she's shaven as your scalp, Jakob Lawrence. As shaven as your scalp *today*, that is.'

The other boy was standing with the chest lid open, staring down. Nathaniel had expected Jake to laugh but the boy said nothing and did not turn. The upturned lid reminded Nathaniel of the coffin they had opened yesterday, and a thrill rolled down him as if some damp corpse like Mrs Page might be in the chest. Imagine that, Mrs Page softly slumbering the night away as Nathaniel dreamed in bed. He remembered the dead woman's skin, with its film like the mushrooms up on Marley Hill. Had the water started its seep into the coffin yet? Surely now the old woman would be completely submerged; just like his da, he guessed, wet as a fish.

Jake did not move. In his hand two red handkerchiefs bunched. He gave a laugh, and there was something crowing in it. 'What's this?'

'What?'

'This.' Jake turned. A book was held between two fingers. Jake looked directly at Nathaniel, his eyes knowing, as if he had thoroughly crabbed him. He flicked through the pages. 'A book of paintings? Of godly paintings? Look, with verses running down the sides of them.' He turned back to the first page. 'And with the Museum's stamp on it? Now, now, now, Nathaniel, I didn't know you were one for such wares.'

'Look, it's not mine.'

'Aye. Whose is it, then?'

Nathaniel didn't say anything.

'Because it's in your room, in this chest. Which would all suggest, you know, that it's yours.'

'It's John Verger's,' Nathaniel blurted, without thinking.

'Mr Verger's?'

'Aye, look,' said Nathaniel, striding over, 'Verger gave this to me a while back. When he'd just lost his job, and he was all sad and messed up. He was trying to help as I was upset about my da. He was my da's friend. No need, now, to be picking on Mr Verger.'

'But, Nathaniel. He's a Got. Look at this stuff. There's God on every page.'

'It's just a book, Jake, it's nothing.'

'And how did he get it?'

'He took it from the museum. In a fit of boredom or misery or whatever. It's just a book, as I said, put it back now.'

'Just a book! Their whole system is *just a book*. Just a book is what sent us across the waters.'

'John Verger gave me it when he was in a bad place in his head. Listen to me: he's over that now.'

But Jake was no longer listening. 'I bet he's praying every night, asking for a big squelchy kiss from God on his for'ead!' Jake's eyes danced. '*He* should be tonight! Not Mrs Richards! He's even more of a threat than her!'

Nathaniel tugged the book away from him. 'Now listen to me, John Verger is not to be touched. He—'

'Why?'

'He was my da's friend! My da's best friend. Are you not listening? It means he's got immunity.'

'Immunity?'

'He's no spy – he burned churches to be here! He loves this Island!'

'How do you know?'

'Just because! You wouldn't understand, ken. He was my da's best friend. Your da's at home. You get to see him every night. Mine's dead.' His voice went quiet, choked on a hearty love for his dead da and the fact he would never ever see him again. *Never*; the thought crabbed. Quietly, now, he said: 'John Verger was the man who introduced my mam and my dad. Without him, there'd be no me! He's not to be touched. D'you hear me? He's done with this book. He's no believer, he's no spy, and he certainly doesn't work for the English. Look, we can burn it if you like, or throw it in the bin, I don't care; but we don't touch him. Ken?'

Nathaniel dropped the book into the chest and closed the lid. It slammed with more of a noise than he had hoped. He took the handkerchiefs and was surprised to find them so warmed from the boy's hands. All night his feet would be resting on the damp sweet cloth. Nathaniel shoved them into his boots. 'No more of it now. We don't touch Verger, you hear?'

'Aye,' Jake said, but he didn't move: he was looking out, flatly, toward the sea. His eyes seemed to be full of a new kind of knowledge.

With their pockets full of rocks, the gang ran up the steps of Warkworth cliffs and along January Road, with Nathaniel leading the charge. They went up the steep side of Marley Hill to Mrs Richards' house. It was an old house with small windows and a long enough box hedge to hide behind. Since Monday night the Malades had been doing sorties here, watching for when Mrs Richards came in and out, and when she went to bed. Nine o'clock was figured the best time, since that was when Mr Richards often went down to Lynemouth Town for a drink or two at the tavern, and Mrs Richards was alone. At this time, Sammy Carter reported, Mrs Richards liked to read the Bible and copy maps of the Island, intended for the English when they eventually arrived on the warships.

A light was on in the kitchen. The house was broad and low, beetled to the ground; the upstairs, low-ceilinged, warrenish. A light was on in a bedroom. 'Now,' said Nathaniel, 'listen. Sammy, you're to stand guard at the top—'

'What? I always miss out on the good stuff!'

'Don't whine, boy. You've got to help.' Nathaniel's eyes flicked toward Jake, remembering the flat look of the boy at the window that evening. 'Jake did it last time. On your way.'

Sammy sloped away to the top part of the road. The other boys waited, giggling by the hedge, glad it had been Sammy who'd been sent for lookout.

On Nathaniel's signal, they started launching rocks, their wrists flicking toward the walls. Rocks ricocheted from the plaster and the drainpipes. One hit the lintel and splintered the wood. All the boys laughed soundlessly. Nathaniel borrowed a rock from Sammy and threw it hard, imagining that there was a real-life Got in there, or imagining the policeman's face, the one who'd escorted his mam here, the one she'd wanted to shoot. Nathaniel knew that before the boys were men the Island might be reclaimed again into the English Ministry. Perhaps they *should* crab Verger, Nathaniel thought, as he threw another, perhaps he was an English agent, working for the church. His da's friend or no, he couldn't protect Verger forever.

Nathaniel watched them, his Malade boys, the whites of their eyes flashing wet and silky, their arms going like mad trying for the window, until a rock found the upstairs glass and there was a sound of smashing, sounding blameless, and fairy-tale, in the winter night. They all ducked down behind the hedge, their shoulders rolling with the pleasure of it. Jake couldn't control himself and a long loud laugh escaped him.

A woman's voice, afraid, cried out: 'What was that?'

The shadow disappeared; a face appeared at the window. It must be Mrs Richards. Nathaniel imagined her in maths class and here she was, cold at the broken window and scared. 'Who's there?' The laughter was louder now from the four boys crowded behind the hedge. 'Tell me who's there!'

'We want to know,' said Nathaniel, still squat, his back facing the hedge, 'if you're a Got, Mrs Richards?'

'What are you talking about? A Got?'

'Don't get narky with us, we're not getting nasty with you. We just want to know.'

'What are you talking about?'

'Whether you have a babble with God on occasion? A little prayer? A little word with him up top?'

Their teeth and grins were wet in the darktime.

'A babble?'

'Aye,' said Nathaniel, 'a babble, babble, babble.' The boys repeated him saying 'babble, babble, babble' over and over again. 'Do you think to heaven when Master's at it, Mrs Richards? Was it your first time with Master on the marriage bed, seen as you're Got, or were you a naughty girl before he got his paws on you? You're a Got, c'mon, stop denying it! We know this about you!'

'On your way now, boys,' she leaned out of the window, craning to see them, 'before I come down there and crab you myself!'

'Tell us, Mrs Richards. We want to know. What do the English ask you to do? How do they ask you to spy on us? In what manner will you tip the Island back to 1950? Is it maps you're drawing for them, late at night? Or is it propaganda you're writing, is that it?' Nathaniel was coming along, warming to his speechifying, when Jake stood, quietly, unexpectedly, and launched a rock straight toward her face. It struck Mrs Richards on the cheek and she wheeled away, aghast. 'Jake!' Nathaniel said, but the boy was laughing and the other boys were laughing with him. In the shadow, you could see Mrs Richards clamp her hand to her face and then a violent sob.

Nathaniel told them all to scarper. The gang made off, but, since the cut of the jeans had once again stopped the juice at their knees, they ran like idiots, yelping for their needled feet in the moonlight. Sweat pricked on their bulbed skulls and down the sides of their faces. In the corner of his vision, Nathaniel saw Mrs Richards' pink nightgown flapping about, as she came out of her house and onto the road. She grew ever smaller behind them, and all around him the boys' eyes, wet and keen, followed him steadily down to the darkness of the Eastern Bay.

When he was sure they had lost her, they shared a smoke to get some calm into their blood, and each boy went his separate way; rum, and a little bit scared, too, lest they should be found out for this unexpected violence. Had they really crabbed a teacher for an English spy? It was best now that all boys should be at home and watching telly, so their mams could all happily lie for them if the police came calling. They'd meet all together again on Friday night. Jake went larking off with Sammy, and Nathaniel watched them, waiting for them to leave the Eastern cliff before he too set off for home.

The sea below him kept up its steady croon as he walked along the bluffs. The night was low and still. It had been wrong to throw the rock at Mrs Richards, and he hadn't given Jake permission for it, but it was a bit of a rol-licky thrill, too. Now he felt cool and calm, as if his whole body had risen up a purer thing from some claggy bog.

He pushed away the thought of Verger's book, and shared a cigarette with himself, jets of smoke joined the Island night. Though he enjoyed the scrap, he often faced the end of the night with a sad feeling that it was all, somehow, not worth it. Even, although it was harder still to admit this, that there might be no English spies on this Island, and that worse than coming to invade, the English might have pure forgotten about them. Out of sight; out of mind. He had started this gang with such a clear idea of revenge for his da's death in the English boat; and yet he seemed no closer to satisfaction. Still, the boys would meet one last time this holiday then that would be it for the week. Then they would be back at school, and they could enjoy a more leisurely pace of harassment.

The night was dark and quiet. He wondered about turning back, to Lynemouth Town, contemplated scaling one of the walls up to Eliza's bedroom, but this lonely finale, that greeted every night like this, was dragging him down, and all he wanted to do was go home. To his mam, aye, his old mam.

It was on walking up Fairview Road that he saw the figure crouching down behind the hedge. At first sight, he thought it was a boy, come to launch rocks against the windows of a Got, but then he saw a flash of long red hair. He stepped on the cigarette and hid behind the cold bricks of the long terrace. The girl crouched by a hedge. A small amount of light was let out from the kitchen, but then, minutes later, the light was snapped off, and it was dark again. He saw the shape of the girl move away from the hedge. Who was the girl watching, at this hour?

Nathaniel kept at a safe distance. She had replaced her hood so that the brass colour of her hair was obscured. When Nathaniel passed the house, he peered into the kitchen but could see nothing – nor could he remember who lived here. The eastern bit of the Island, uninhabited, more squalid than the rest, was not a place for a boy like him.

He followed her onward. The girl walked purposefully, but there was something in her manner that suggested she was frightened. Panicked. She seemed to be making wrong turns, ending up in dead alleys, roads he would not follow her down because he knew they went nowhere.

The wind was flat now, and the trees stood, stirless, in the night. Nathaniel was sure he had never seen her before. He would have remembered a girl such as this. She was beautiful, aye, he could see that, even from the distance.

She walked on; quick, despite herself. She stopped above the eastern beach where the boys had gathered not an hour ago. The sea was a great black bowl before her. She turned back and walked until she came to a house. It was one of the derelict ones, one of the old Islanders' which hadn't been lived in for years. What was she doing, staying here?

Nathaniel waited behind the hedge as she went in and climbed the stairs. In the front bedroom, she came into view. She had a mane of hair; brass and ginger: as if she were a girl coined from something else; a metal, not flesh. She appeared sometimes at the window: the rare shadow, the skin seldom seen behind the glass. Her skin was so freckled it was as if she could have been born in a bowl of dust.

After a while, she came to settle at the sill. A tree obscured her and all that was visible was her fingers. She was reading a piece of paper, it might have been a newspaper. She breathed into her hands, and then rubbed them together. They looked pinky-white but he supposed if he were there standing above her they would be all mottled brown. At one point, she spread her fingers across her whole face and she began to cry, lightly at first and then a whole shake-and-heave, her shoulders joining in with the dance. Her mouth must have been a real twist of it. Even from the garden, down below here, Nathaniel could see how pink she became under the freckles on her neck. It looked winsome, all that pink. After that, he couldn't see her for minutes, and then the light snapped off, and the dark hung about him, loose as a silk.

9. Sarah's Story

Home, now, if it could be called that. Sarah sat by the glass, looking down into the inky depths of the garden, her breath fogging the pane. There was no streetlamp on the road; neither sky nor house nor sea could be seen. In her hands, she held Laura's article.

For some hours this evening Sarah had stayed behind the box hedge. The woman read a book by the fire, the pans above her shiny and brass, her eyes skipping over the words and glancing, occasionally, into the garden, with a look somewhere near dread. Sarah ate two slices of bread by the gravel and thought about the corned beef in the can then stopped herself. Only Wednesday. She had five more days of this. The boy – the woman's son – was nowhere to be seen.

The woman ate dinner alone and then washed the dishes.

She settled again by the fire, with the book on her lap, when some birds suddenly took off from the tree, and startled her. The woman looked out toward the garden as if she suspected someone of being out there, and left the room abruptly, leaving the kitchen in darkness. Sarah, taking this as her cue, left immediately.

*

From the sill, now, in her own room, Sarah contemplated a prayer. For years in England, she had given up on this. At church, she bowed her head as everyone else did, but she didn't believe prayers would do any good. Assuming the posture, she thought about patience and peacefulness and God's good grace, but then her mother was still absent, the fact was immutable, and what words Sarah did launch into countless mornings and soundless nights had always seemed so unanswered.

In church, while everyone else was praying, Sarah studied a portrait of Christ that hung above the altar. Hardly any of the cross could be seen under the lit skin. His fingers, crisped in pain, curled inward to his palms. The loincloth billowed as if a wind disturbed it. A slick of darkness clove the narrow thighs, the knees were pressed together; as were the calves. Blood loosened from a colossal nail. The toes, like the fingers, were curled, holding on to the wood. The eyes looked tired, not boastful. The mouth was open, a plug of black.

Sarah had always held Him as an example of patience. Waiting for her mother, she might try to be as patient as Him. She could try. But it had been a long time. And she had almost given up.

And then it had come, this stroke of luck, this losing of a shoe, and then the way to find Laura had become clear.

After the trip in the cellar, the discovery under the step-boards, Sarah didn't go to school. Every day, instead, she made a clandestine journey to Newcastle Library, to the room with the archives. Sarah didn't tell her dad what she was doing and went to the library in her school uniform.

In the first few days, Sarah checked the newspapers: the

Evening Post, the *Chronicle*, the *Morning Daily*. In that July week of 1976, there were numerous articles about Laura and Saint Gregory's. Sarah found the article in the *Chronicle* but with stories all around it, and advertisements, for toothpaste, amongst other things. It was always the same picture they used: of Laura looking up, curious, somewhat bashful, as if there were a hand hovering over her holding holy water. There were photographs, too, of the Minister, the one who had died in the church, one of his eyes swollen closed, and his skin, blackened between crisp hospital sheets.

Sarah read the other stories from that summer in 1976: more church-burnings, a riot in Doncaster, more protests for the Sunday Agreement. Sarah thought she detected some public sympathy toward the Movement, but then a Sunday School was bombed, again, as if the vileness of 1950 was obliged to repeat itself, and the calls for expulsion seemed to get louder. Rubble was pictured in a scorched-looking street, and a line of policemen stood with shields braced. There were scores of arrests. Burned-out cars looked like bees, dead in summer.

Around Christmas, all stories of Laura disappeared. There was nothing else. The two men Laura was with had not been named anywhere in the press, they were called 'the unidentified suspects of the Saint Gregory fire'. But by December, all mention of them, too, disappeared, so that the trio of Saint Gregory's seemed to have vanished from all reports.

In the first days of March, in 1977, there were court reports from the Movement's trials. There were several groups asking for leniency, others demanding expulsion.

The Church in London insisted on another expulsion, arguing there was no difference between the severity of the crimes in 1950 and 1976. Sarah read through the trials, expecting at any moment to get to Laura's, but again, there was no mention of Saint Gregory's. It seemed as if Laura had dropped as easily out of the public narrative as she had her own family's life. Days in, Sarah found a list of those expelled in 1977. There were a hundred or so names written on the sheet, but the name Laura Wicks was not there.

Later in the week, Sarah changed course. This time, she checked English prison records. She checked all the way from July 1976 to the present: all the female internees under 'W'. Still nothing. No Wicks. Sarah then found all those imprisoned for minor secular crimes and then all of those discharged under the Sunday Agreement, which had made its difficult way into law by 1983. Laura was not on either list.

On Friday, just as Sarah was beginning to give up, as she scrolled the microfiche and yellowing records, she happened upon another picture. It was of the deportation boat, the last one, in the spring of 1977. The title read: 'The Last Boat: England Prays for Peace'.

And there she was, unmistakably, on the boat, her blonde hair thrown by the wind, her eyes, this time, retreating, defensive, cast down. Choppy waters surrounded the hull. Laura's face was the only one really picked up by the photographer. She was hunched into the wind. Two men stood behind her, and Sarah wondered if they might be the two men, the 'two unidentified suspects' of Saint Gregory's.

Sarah copied the photograph twice: one for herself, and one for her dad. Perhaps there had been some official oversight, and her mother's name had been left off a list, or some necessary secrecy which meant her case had not come to court, but she had been deported anyway. A mistake had been made – evidently: because Sarah was sure it was her mother, staring out, bleakly, into the gun-metal top of the Sound.

That Sunday, they went to church, her and her dad. Sarah had not yet mentioned anything about her discoveries, and she didn't know if she would. She didn't want to be dissuaded from what she was going to do. Sarah looked at the portrait of Christ as the rest prayed; His expression seemed encouraging.

After church, they went to the butcher's, as they always did. It was called Wroxham's. In its window, there was a luxurious display of cuts. The smell of the meat outside the red-brick house was a suggestive stink: the display was grand, even a little obscene. Pork medallions ringed in fat, brassy lamb shanks and red steaks were all laid out on a red-and-white chequered cloth, garlanded with parsley. Geese hung on low-slung hooks from their bluing throats; beaks downturned as if coy. In a lozenged line, sausages hung, diced fat near skin. The slick dark liver seemed to hint of some unnameable pleasure. This was God's meat.

Church-people queued up in hungry silence, eyeing slabs of turkey breast, mauve kidney, countless chipolatas. The knife by Wroxham's block was already bloodied. A sign at the shop front said *Pickled Tongues in Freezer*. Eggs nestled in straw.

Sarah said something about the smell, told her dad to order the lamb at the window's front, and went down the butcher's side alley. Out in the yard, there was a smell of warm blood and bone. Sarah lit a cigarette. In the pantry, pigs hung from big hooks. Unhoused of their innards, their bristled ears flapped over their skulls. Sarah sucked harder on the cigarette to block out the smell. The pigs looked like children on their first day at school, their heads hung in snouty commiseration. The front trotters, still muddy from the last-touched field, dangled from airy stomachs. All that space in what was once stomach and heart and bladder; the ribs curved now around empty air. What vessels these once were, wobbling little lives of fat and food, mud and udder, until they had come to the butcher's knife and all life had leaked from the wound.

She remembered from her history books how there was no meat on the Island. Did her mother miss this? The butchers? The slabs of all the red and white meat? She wondered what she was like, Laura: living alone, on this Island, in that sea, with no meat in her for the decade.

Sarah crushed the cigarette out under her boot. She would go to the Island, before her courage fled her. She would go and try and find her. With a sidelong look at the hogs, she went back into Wroxham's.

That night, Sarah made the dinner. They ate the lamb in companionable silence, and her dad went to bed early. He suspected nothing.

Sarah packed a bag: warm clothes, some stocks from the kitchen (corned beef, water, margarine, bread), and, at the last minute, she slipped a knife into the bag. She left out the extra photograph of her mother on the boat, and drew a long arrow to Laura, writing underneath it – 'I've gone to find her. I'll be back as soon as I can.'

That night, by way of three buses, she made her way to Newcastle, down to the docks, with her backpack heavy against her shoulders. Behind a red crate of fish tackle she waited, then watched the Boatman go to and from the depot with these boxes and sacks, netted bags of food, heaving and sweating in the cold November air, unloading them into the hold of the boat which was the *Saviour*. Then he left the boat unattended, for a piss or a pint she didn't know, and Sarah knew it was time.

She left the shadows. She walked down the steps to the boat, put her hand to the cargo clasp. She looked at her own freckled hand and withdrew it very quickly, as if scalded. She was scared. She would be back in a week. The next boat was Monday, but there wasn't another one for the winter. She had to go; now; she had to make sure. Footsteps sounded from the back of the depot. Sarah pulled open the hatch and bundled inside to the dank and rooty smell of potatoes. Minutes later the front cabin was unlocked and Boatman stepped in, the boat lowering under his weight.

The engine gunned.

She was on the boat. In ten hours, she would be on the Island.

10. Introductions

Nathaniel woke early. On his bed, a box of sunlight from where he had left the curtains unclosed. Through the window, branches shook in heatless light. Without its leaves, there was something bare and pure about the tree, like one of his boys. Nathaniel liked things scraped of fuzz if they could be. His own scalp could do with a razing; the bristle rasped against the pillow.

The duvet was lumpy in places and flat in others; he was warm only if he did not move. Nathaniel would lie in bed like this, on schooldays, until the last moment possible when he would have to rush and wolf down his porridge, so as not to be late for the bell. He did moderately well at his lessons, but something about their big silences made him lustful, on leaving the school gates, for something rotten. And it was a pleasure, of an evening, to tramp about in big boots with his funny boys, though when he came home he always felt sorry bad that his mam sat up and waited for him alone.

Now this girl was on his mind. Following her last night, her strangeness coming off her like a stink, he had no clue as to who she might be. Her face had been ghostly, shrouded by the hedge and then the hood. Nathaniel would've thought she was one of the boys, crouched and

ready to smoke out a spy, had she not been so fully possessed of all that hair. When she had walked away, she
hadn't been confident; he could tell that the Island paths
were unfamiliar to her. And when he had come to her
house, and seen of her what the window would give – the
flash of hair and the skin so white it could have been bone
– Nathaniel settled on the fact that he had never seen her
before; never once in his Island life.

It was *possible* she was some Island girl, born a baby at
the Grand, perhaps, and kept in a drawer, and only just let
out to roam the Island in the inky parts of the night; or that
she was some fisherman's daughter, come off the herring
boat; or maybe even that she was some sort of mermaid
washed ashore, which would explain the phosphorescence
of her skin. He imagined her emerging from the sea, half-
naked and faintly fishy, with her hair pelt-like and dark,
the little breasts dropping beads of the Sound's cold water.
He might stay in bed for much longer, just thinking of the
girl like that.

She could, of course, be a new deportee. But they hadn't
had anyone since '77. Not a soul. And besides, there would
have been some announcement, and people would be talking about the extra boat, you wouldn't be able to escape
the gossip about a family moving in. And besides, new
Islanders didn't just end up in old squats by the Eastern
Bay.

Mermaidy and lushly wet, her skin glossed in salt, he
thought of her limbs slipping between his underneath the
purple flower-print.

But her provenance, that's what he should think on.
No new deportees, no fisherman's daughter, no girl of the

Grand, so what was she? And who was she? Why was she not at school with the rest of them? And why was she staying in that abandoned house?

He thought on anything unusual he'd seen lately. Jake had been narky these past few days but there was not much unusual there. Verger had given him the odd book but that had been months ago. Apart from that, he'd heard nothing new.

But he remembered how agitated Eliza had been at the square on Monday, how distracted, even before the boys had crabbed her. What time had that been? It couldn't have been more than ten minutes after the boat had gone. And then he began thinking, really putting his noggin to it: what if the girl had been on Monday's boat? What if she were a stowaway, unknown to the English and Islanders both? And if she *were* a stowaway, it was possible too she was an English spy, come on a mission to report on the Island! Perhaps the English were truly coming back to reclaim the Island, just as he'd told Jake when they'd set up the gang. If she *were* a spy, if she *had* come on a mission to report in the Church's interest, Nathaniel would need to think about what to do. There might be so much God in her veins he would have to beat it from her. He imagined her now, not as the lustrous mermaid, but as a bloodied girl on the sands of Warkworth Bay, with all that orange hair fanned about her like a crown. Aye, if she were a spy, Nathaniel and his boys might find out the truth with their fists. And what a rollicky lot of scrap that would be.

When he rose, he dressed quickly; it was so cold. Lean all the way to his chops, in the northern light his skin was almost blue. He put on one of his da's old shirts and found new handkerchiefs to stuff down the boots. In the chest he saw the silly book of John Verger. It had been a mistake to keep it. He should burn it, or bury it, before any of the other boys found it. Or just take it back to the museum and no one would be any wiser. He didn't like the fact that Jake now had leverage on him. But he ignored it for now, pressing as it was to find this girl before anyone else did.

He ate breakfast. The toaster's grid lit up red and he warmed his bony fingers on the heat; when he drank his tea he warmed his nose in the cup's steam. He wondered whether he should call round to Jake's and tell him he had found this girl, but his heart sank at the prospect. Wherever he took him, the boy drained a thing of its sweetness. Aye, that was Jake, with his big humpy ears, observing the world with bland insolence. No, Jake would not get the spoils of the girl; not yet. Whoever she was, she was Nathaniel's, for the while.

The toast snapped; the jam was raspberry and sweet. He shoved the crusts in the bin. Not for him, curly hair.

The boy made his way over to Swanscott House. He was fair excited to see her, and so he stepped lightly across the Island, though he knew he could not be caught, not when it was barely eight o'clock. All the boys would be softly kipping at their mam's; getting in their rest before school started again.

As he turned at the top of the hill, the full light showed the Sound at its best, almost so that he thought he might detect England, faint as a smudge, across the way. *Are you from there?* he almost asked the waiting air. *Are you a spy?*

Four roads went down the hill in four directions and he took the one leading to the Eastern Bay. From some way up he saw a slick of oil or light near the rocks at the beach and wondered if some treasure or some such thing had come aground there. He would take a look later. Perhaps the little toy boat she had arrived on. He came off Marley Hill to the abandoned road of houses, and, finally, to her house.

In the window of the upper room he saw that the girl too was awake. Her shadow slid across the wall, crisp in the cold sunshine. There was something a little slower about her today, her features flatter. Nathaniel crouched by the hedge, the jeans nipping. Strange, a little, that in his fists he did not hold any rocks. The shadow of smoke curled on the far wall. Was she smoking cigarettes? If she had cigarettes, did that confirm her Englishness?

At the back of the garden, a pond let off a muzzy smell. With still green algae on it, he thought of his da's boat covered in the same slime then pushed the thought away. He tried, instead, to think who had lived here before, in this house, but he thought perhaps it had always been empty, at least, since he'd known it. The whole street, in fact, was empty, and going to ruin. The back door was in a bad way and open on the latch. There was a yeasty smell inside the kitchen and dirty crockery stood by the sink's side. Cabinets and drawers were still open. Little thought had gone into abandoning it, rushing as the family probably had been, in the Christmas of 1950, to escape the incoming tribe. He checked the other rooms were empty, catching himself in a mirror, surprised at his scalp's dark cap of hair. Aye, it could do with a razing.

His da had not looked fast enough for a house, if this was the kind of home which had been on offer in '51: it was big and grand, if dirty, but that could be helped. There was no chance, however, of moving his ma out of their house: she would never leave it. Not even for a trip to Maiden's Square, never mind packing up for better quarters.

He stopped at the window and smelled it, dimly, on the air. It *was* cigarette smoke. How had the girl procured them? Neither he nor the boys would have sold on cigarettes. It was clearly against the rules. Or perhaps Jake had found her here already, and was sharing cigs with her and chatting. Perhaps they were already at the old gromicks, his big hands pawing at the freckled breasts, and the thought stopped Nathaniel cold.

He turned from the glass and suddenly, like a phantom, she was there, looking at him, from the landing. Her face was still. Her skin was very white, as it had been last night, but in the breadth of a second she had blushed so deeply that the freckles were now surrounded by the colour of blood. He'd like to put his hand there to feel the warm rush of it. Her eyes flashed.

The girl was wearing a rucksack, jeans, heavy boots, heavy anorak; no Island girl might be wearing garb as bad as this.

'Who're you?' she said.

Nathaniel did not answer; surprised as he was that it had been her to ask the first question. He continued to the landing and she went back, a little, toward the room he'd seen her in last night. Behind her, clothes sat in uneven piles and the room was a mess. Now, he blocked the stairs and any exit down. The girl said again, but this time in a whisper, 'Who are you?'

'How is it now,' Nathaniel said, moderating his tone to one of kindness, 'you don't know my name?' And he edged closer to her, coming up to the last step. He was right, he thought, she *was* foreign to here; he had a feeling about it. Something about her voice, her accent, and the cigarettes as well. Pink ringed the girl's eyes; maybe she had cried the night through; maybe she'd been at the old shake-and-heave since he'd left her. It was freezing in here, enough to make the tears come to any man's eye, never mind a doxy such as she. The girl was tiny, really, one quick move and he could have her by the wrist or the hair. And he got that feeling, like how it was after school, when he wanted nothing more than to move, to do something, in order to shake off some vague and unknown sadness.

She said: 'I don't know. I don't know you. What are you doing in this house?'

'I saw you here last night, lamb, I saw you outside that house. Then I followed you here.'

'You followed me here? I didn't see you.'

'Aye. Aye.' He took a step closer. Still kindly, kindly: 'And these cigarettes. Who did you get them from, now? I didn't give you any, and none of my boys would have sold them on.'

'I wasn't smoking any.'

The girl looked adrift, out of her depth, as if her head was bobbing along the Sound's grey water.

'I smelled it.'

'From a shop. I bought them in a shop.'

'Did you now?'

'Yes. Yes I did.'

Despite the cold he saw her brow was damp. Her nerves excited him. 'And you know, now, you can't buy them in a shop, like; you know that, surely.'

Her blue eyes flicked to the side of the room. 'Someone gave them to me.'

'Who?'

'A man,' she said, 'down at the square.'

'Who?'

'I don't know.'

'Who, doll? I didn't catch that.'

'I said *I don't know*.' Nathaniel took another step toward her. He'd crabbed her now. She was all flushed about the skin as if she really was terrified, her eyes flitting about the landing, looking for another exit. She had less and less space now in which to move, and she looked to the back window, as if to gauge its distance from the ground.

'Who are you? If you're not from here, where are you from?' The girl said nothing. 'Look, I've never seen you in the square, nor at school, nor at Lynemouth Town. Are you a baby from the Grand only just discovered? Or have you just come in from the sea, washed up in a boat wreck, a mermaid perhaps?'

The smell of smoke hung in the room like a premonition of her confession. Cigarettes! No Malade would have given her a cigarette, not without crabbing her first. Now she would have to admit it, that she was on Monday's boat, that she was some Evangelical spy on an English mission! What would he do with her? Bundle her up and lock her in the room? Alert the boys to the great English danger within these walls? What a scrappy week it would be, if she were a spy!

The girl stepped back so that she was against the wall, and then suddenly, as if with a sleight of hand, she held something out toward him. Nathaniel couldn't identify it at first, so quick had been the gesture, but she moved it toward him and he saw what it was. Light caught the tip of the blade; its length was grey. It was neither a big knife nor a long one, but it was there, held between them like a torch. There was quiet in the room for a bit as they regarded each other and they wondered who might win this. She held it very still; her hands did not shake; her eyes did not move from him. The blush, which had fairly soaked her face moments ago, had disappeared. No one had ever pulled a knife on him before; no one. He wouldn't be so afraid were he not certain the girl was scared enough to use it. His blood did its surge, as if fairly *he* were the one being crabbed for a spy. He should have played this softly; he'd gone at her too hard.

The girl made a jabbing motion with the blade. 'You come no closer. I've heard of you, all right. I know who you are.'

He held up his hands. 'I'm sure you have. Nathaniel Malraux, miss.'

'Aye. Nathaniel. Yes: I know you.'

'Put the knife down, miss. I promise I won't hurt you. I was as surprised as you were, that was all.'

'You don't intimidate me,' she said, with no sign that she would lower the blade. 'I don't want to be intimidated, you hear?'

'Aye, aye. I hear.'

Slowly, she lowered the knife, but did not put it away, instead, she held it loosely by her side. She said again: 'I just don't want to be intimidated.' Then she did something quite unexpected; with the knife still there, she patted her bag and brought out a pack of smokes, expertly flipped the top with one hand, and offered him one. The tips were lined up perfectly, and smelled good: earthy. Nathaniel took one, as did she, and she lit both of the cigarettes, then put the knife back into the side pocket. Two curling lines of smoke rose.

The girl slid down the wall and sat at the skirting. He joined her there: smoking, watching her smoke. The cigarette tasted unbelievably fresh, without the taste that it normally had of an old brown piece of furniture. There was something leathery and strong to the smell of it, like his da's old tin of Pomade Divine. The girl did it well, the smoking, like she was mistress of it. Lots of practice, he supposed, back in England, where you might buy a pack for merely a cherry. And then she smiled at him, so that he knew she wouldn't bring out the knife again.

'A fine cigarette,' he ventured.

She didn't say anything. Something moved in the garden, and he followed it; when he looked back she was still watching him.

'So you don't have cigarettes here? That's what I'm to learn from this?'

'Aye. You're right about that.'

'Oh,' she said, 'I see. So you want to know where I got these from.'

'Aye.'

The girl looked at the lit end and sighed through her

nose. 'Well. I'm guessing you might know this already.' She took a deep breath. 'I'm from England. I came on the boat. On Monday night.'

'How?'

'I hid myself in the cargo hold. When the Boatman wasn't looking.'

'I knew it! A stowaway, aye, that makes sense! I knew I'd never seen you before, not at school, nor down at the Square.'

'And you saw me last night?'

'Aye. Spying on someone – outside their house.'

'A woman. A woman's house. Do you know whose house that is?'

'No idea. The light was off by the time you left, remember? Why? Want me to make enquiries? I could go have a looksy – I'd know her by name, if I saw her.'

'No. No, don't do that.'

The girl looked down toward her lap, almost guiltily, and he remembered himself as a Malade, and what he was here to do. He made his voice gruffer. 'Why were you spying on her?'

'I wasn't spying.'

'What were you doing outside her house?'

'Watching. Looking. She's someone I might know.'

'Oh, yes. I see. Have they contracted you, is that it, to watch my isle? To spy on us and get us back to God's acre?'

Her eyes were quizzical, confused. 'A spy?'

'Aye. Come to watch the Island, and report back to the Church.'

'No,' she said, 'no. I'm not here to do that.'

'Oh, really? And how am I meant to trust you on that?'

'I give you my word.'

'An Englishman's word is worth nothing.'

'I'm not an English man.' The girl pulled a piece of paper from her bag and handed it over to him. 'Here,' she said, 'read this.'

Nathaniel read the article quickly; it was like any you might find in the museum. Churches burned; the Movement arrested; the promise of expulsion was made. 'And bravo, bravo to them; but what is this to me?'

Her voice was small. 'My name is Sarah. I'm Laura Wicks' daughter.' As she smoked she narrowed an eye against the sunlight. 'Mum was accused of Saint Gregory's ten years ago. And then she disappeared,' Sarah clicked her fingers, 'like that, without a trace. So I've come here, to try and find her.'

'Oh, aye, and why now? Ten years on?'

'I found the article by accident. In my home. In England.' She laughed, but quite mirthlessly. 'For ten years, my dad's kept up this lie, that she was with another man, with another family. But that's not true. I found article after article on her in newspapers from that year. And I'm convinced she was sent here, in 1977, when the last of the Movement were taken here.'

'Your ma, aye? 1977. A lot of people came that year. A lot of people.'

'Have you heard of her?' she asked.

'I can't say I have. But it doesn't mean she's not here.' Nathaniel pointed to the article. 'Mind if I keep hold of it?'

'This isn't a story. I swear. I'm here only to find my ma.'

'Aye, aye. No need to protest. I just want to have a look at it, think on it a bit more.' Nathaniel tucked it into his jacket pocket. 'And this woman, whose house you were outside last night, you think that was her? Laura Wicks?'

'I've looked over the whole Island. She's the closest, so far. But I don't know if it's her. She's the one that's nearest, yes.'

Nathaniel stood, and walked over to the banister. His grin stretched from one ear to the other. 'Are you hungry?'

'Yes,' she said, 'starving.'

So this is the way he'd master her. 'I'll come back tonight with something to eat.' He flicked the cigarette to the back of the landing and it smoked thinly under the windowpane. 'In the meantime, I have some advice for you, which I suggest you ken. If you see any dandies dressed like me,' he gestured toward his clothes, 'it'd be best to avoid them. For your sake, merely. If my boys find out you're English they'll go for your throat.'

'But my ma, she's part of the Movement, she worked to help—'

'Hush now, Sarah. Listen. I shan't tell a soul if you manage not to get yourself discovered. I've read the article,' and he patted his jacket here, 'and, according to you, you've come to look for your long-lost mother who was part of the Movement. Which is interesting, very interesting. But what scant evidence you have for this makes me uncomfortable. Aye. And you don't want to know what Islanders do with unwanted Englishmen. Or women, for that matter. So keep a low profile. Don't talk to anyone. I'll come back tonight. I'll bring you some food. I give you my word.'

She squashed the last of her cigarette onto the carpet. 'And what's the worth of an Islander's word?'

'A bucket of fish; I don't know. You're just going to have to trust me.' He gestured again to his costume. 'As I said, if you see anyone dressed like me, don't talk to them. You'll only find yourself in trouble. And that knife won't help you; not with my lot.'

'I'm not lying,' she said. 'I've got no other business here. No business of spying, I swear.'

He'd been a fool to be scared of her. She was, most likely, soft as anything, with all her English comforts. But she was a peach if ever he'd seen one! A peachy pleasure! He took the stairs two by two. Not a spy then, but a daughter of the Movement. That made things better.

Or perhaps, just more complicated.

11. Bream

Later that morning, Nathaniel sat in the living room, which was so warm he felt as if he were being cooked. Porridge bloated him. Beside him, the oats were still glued to the bowl. He resisted looking at the newspaper article, now folded in his jeans pocket, but he thought of the girl often, that challenge to her eyes, the neat long line of smoke from her cigarette, that knife between them. Her skin and freckles; milk and mud! Poor old thing, how frightened she was! He felt something fold within him: a softening. Aye, he'd expected to feel a jolly fury, a merry rage, on discovering she was an Englisher, but instead, sitting here now, watching the telly-box with his ma, he felt a long, light curiosity. Cowled in her Englishness, that much was true – and yet she was a daughter of the Movement. So it was a noble lineage, like Nathaniel to his Jack Malraux was Sarah to her Laura Wicks.

What a week this could be, with no school, and with little Sarah Wicks in tow!

He'd done a few hours of telly-watching already, with the heat sending him into a soft loop, thinking of the girl. The gas-fire creaked, its bars blue. His mother's pink jumper – with a diamond of small holes at the breast, revealing here and there a greying brassiere – had stains down the front. What had happened to his mam? She would move her leg to and fro, saying she had to dance to keep the blood in it, it tended to deaden. And she laughed, empty sort of, and it was then that Nathaniel wanted nothing more than to leave the house.

'All right, Ma.'

'Monkey.'

'Take a step out with me, Ma.'

'No, Monkey. Not now. Another day. Baneful tired today.'

Boredom made him hanker for something rotten. Sarah was in his mind and blood. When could he go back to her? This evening? This afternoon? He didn't like to leave his mam for so long alone, when he wasn't at school. Mammy changed the channel and an English copper in a navy suit ran after a young man. 'Time is it?' she asked.

'Noon.'

'Aye. Shall have my lunch soon, then. You hungry?'

'No, Mam, just had my porridge.'

'Oh, aye, so you did.' Margaret took a swig of the syrup. 'Aye,' she said again, smacking her lips then leaning back into the chair. 'Are you all right, Nathaniel?' she asked him, giving him an eyeful. 'You're ever so restless.'

'Aye.'

'Why don't you visit Mr Verger? He'd like to see you. He called around again for you yesterday. Asking about that book you'd borrowed.'

'I told you, Mam, I can't find it.'

'The book?'

'Aye.'

'Always was a very good friend to your da. Jack always

137

said how much he liked him. Well, you best tell him you've lost it, since he seemed to be sore for it.'

'He's always crabbing me, asking me to visit him, asking me to—'

'He was very good to your dad. I don't think you should be complaining that he enjoys your company. Jack wouldn't've liked that.' On the telly, a boy ran from two coppers, barely escaping them. Two cars collided and one of the bonnets was smashed up. Nathaniel wished he were there to see it: the roll and lurch of the metal. Oh, to be that boy! Exhausted and roughed up! And free to do what he pleased! 'And tonight, Nath, what'll you be doing?'

'Off out. Don't know.'

'With the boys?'

'No,' he said, 'that's tomorrow night.'

Sighing, she turned back to the set. The policeman programme finished and another started. It was a game show. A woman spun a big wheel. His mam turned back to him with a youthful look suddenly in her eyes. 'Nathaniel, my son, why don't you buy me a bream? A whole sea bream. I'll give you the shillings. Give you the money for it. Would you like that? You'll have to be in, mind, for tonight. It won't be ready b'fore seven.'

Nathaniel looked at her. 'Seriously?'

'More than the day.' She added, her head cocked: 'As long as you stop in for the night.' His mam fished out her handbag and pulled out three shillings and some pennies. 'A whole sea bream, now, mind,' and as she placed it in his palm she looked up with a timid smile, 'and mind it's from the Norwegian waters, good boy now.' Her hand had a tremor to it. 'If Mr Stansky offers you a fish from the Sound, you say no, love.'

Nathaniel kissed her on the cheek and was out into the hall pulling on his jacket before he had time to think, before he had time to say goodbye, going at a jaunty pace along Blackett Place, feeling the air cut his lungs. He started up Marley Hill. The first fish in months! Were the Islanders full of fish or were the fish full of them? This Island produced some tricksome questions!

No more veggies and po-tat-ies, he sang to himself.

The cold always did this for him; where in the living room he went lollygag in the heat, as soon as he set out he felt all of his boyish years. Perhaps he would take a detour and look in on Sarah and see if she was still there. He'd let her roam about a bit; he knew she wouldn't talk to anyone, and that the boys, warm in their mams' living rooms, wouldn't leave unless they were called out by him. And even if they did see her they were too thick to see her for what she truly was. Exotic and English and oh . . . quite lovely.

And tonight Nathaniel would bring her a bream sandwich and impress on her what a civilized lot they were. He felt happy. Maybe this is what England did to you; made you all oiled up, like a fish, as happy as a herring!

Still, he sobered himself – he was right to be suspicious of her. He'd have to investigate this story, just in case it was figs. Because what if she were a threat, what if this mother story were a pack of lies and what if she were here to fatten the Islanders with tales of God? He imagined his lean body turning into the soft babyness of Jake. No. Aye. He was right to be suspicious of her.

*

At Maiden's Square, Nathaniel smiled at some of the girls going into the grocer's, proud that today it was not vegetables he would buy, but fish, for there was to be *no more veggies and po-tat-ies*. He heard the fishmonger's bell and as he looked around, smiling as he was at the girls in the square, the two almost collided. Nathaniel's heart sank. Bream! The Island! The girl! The gang! Anything but John Verger!

'Nathaniel!'

'Mr Verger.'

A moment passed as they stood watching each other. Nathaniel couldn't help his dislike of the old man. He gave off a sweet smell like some old swelling fruit. Verger asked, 'How are you keeping?'

'Well.'

'And your mam?'

'Fine,' he said, 'you saw her yourself yesterday.'

'Good, good.' Verger's eyes were eager; his voice dropped to a whisper. 'And the book. Did you like it?'

'The book?'

'The book I lent you.' Verger took a little step toward him. 'Of the paintings.' His bag bulged with fish. The dicky bow, spotted and clipped, was fast to his throat.

'Oh aye, the paintings.' Nathaniel moved toward the shop. 'I seem to have lost it.'

The old man's eyes had lost their jig. 'Oh,' he said. His whole aspect seemed to sag.

Now the boy felt sorry for him, but it wasn't his place to be out socializing with an old man. Would his da be this old now? Or older? When Jack died he was still the broad fisherman. Not like this girlish old man, even if his da *was* marbling the seabed. 'I don't know, but I'll have a look, right?' Nathaniel pushed the handle, stopped, and turned back to him. 'Though you were a friend of my da's, which I understand, and I respect, all I'm saying is that you might be careful with a book such as that. Wouldn't want anyone to assume, you know, you were a Got.'

'No, no; preposterous,' said Verger, biting the side of his cheek.

'Aye. I know it. But the others mightn't. And I don't want you to get in trouble with the boys, ken? They've a wild eye for anyone who seems to be harking for the Church. My mam is very fond of you. All I'm saying is: use some discretion.' Then, louder, and with much stiff politesse, he said, 'Good day to you, Mr Verger,' and with the door open, he was hit presently by the salty waft of Arthur Stansky's fishes.

Arthur emerged through red plastic chains. He had been his da's boss – or buyer, really, of Jack's catch – and Nathaniel loved him as an uncle. The monger made him feel shy and excited, as if he were in the presence of some-one cut materially from the same cloth as Mr Malraux. Arthur had evidently forgiven the boy for Monday night, when he'd crabbed Eliza, or forgotten clean about it, or purely never cared in the first place. 'Nathaniel, boy! A pleasure! It's been awful long.'

'That it has,' Nathaniel said, somewhat uncertainly.

'What have you been eating? Stuff of the earth?'

'Aye. Potatoes. Endlessly.'

'How is your ma keeping, then?'

'As usual.'

'Ah. Not getting out much, then? She always was a greatly sensitive soul.'

'Aye. I can't remember the last time she left the house. She has a gromicky fear of the outside.'

'The sea especially, I imagine. It happens to all of us, aye, who've lost one to the Sound. It's difficult ever to go near it. Even to dip a toe in it.' Arthur laughed into his chin, a svelte, kindly laugh. 'Or to eat the fruit of it. Aye, well the Sound will feed and kill us both.'

'And are you well, sir?'

'Aye. Business is doing well. As well as one can hope.'

Arthur looked down into the counter. At five that morning he had gone to Warkworth pier to pick up the catch. Back at the monger's, he laid out the fish on the ice chips, pretending he was a painter setting up a still-life. The fish were cold in his hands, sea-soaked, and the smell of brine and seaweed filled the shop. He laid out split herrings, sea trout and brill, monkfish and flounder, and a catch of rockfish on the chips. Paying attention to the orange scale, the rainbow shine, the dark wet lids, he placed each fish in the counter with regard to hue and luminescence. A hunk of blood-red tuna he placed at the heart of the display. Arthur loved his fishes as he loved Miss Michalka: generously, instinctively.

Arthur had been hoping Eliza might come into the shop today, after the ham-fisted job he had made of everything yesterday. Now, he was prepared, and ready, and had made a beautiful display, and he'd practised being nonchalant and charming. But it was past one o'clock, and still she had not come. The lonely monger felt a rising desire to cry into the fish hearts and spleens because he was hopelessly in love with Eliza and she didn't care for him. Not any more.

How disastrously he had coped with her coming to him that night in June. With her ma's death, Arthur had felt suddenly, overwhelmingly responsible for her. He felt plunged into a crisis of commitment. They weren't even official. His immediate reaction to her request – to move in with him! – was a quick, bowled-over 'no'. He didn't have to live with her if he didn't want to. She had been too fast; far too fast. But he hadn't meant for her to join the Grand; not this; not at all. When he'd heard she'd done that he wondered if it was out of revenge. And then, righteous with envy, he'd gone to the Grand in August, because his friends had been talking about how enjoyable she was . . . what great fun . . . and in the morning she'd cried, telling him how broke she had been – and! Only begging from him a sofa! – he'd felt terrible; so ashamed.

And now she wouldn't speak to him, and he had promised himself he wouldn't get involved with her. He couldn't hurt her again; and he had resolved to stay away from her. And she would stay away from him, or made every effort to. It was agony.

Yesterday had been horrible; her face cold, her words polite; only her eyes soft and unable to be unkind. Oh, she was the Island's saint! When he had passed the kipper over to her he had thought that perhaps their hands might touch and he might feel the warm quick pulse of her skin. But she had placed the coins on the cold counter and then she had said it – the word 'grand' – and it had set them both off in disarray.

Aye, around her he was boorish and indelicate; overweight, and reeky of fish. She, however, was a great white dart of ice that would not melt. Oh, it was his entire fault: from the moment she had asked him for shelter, to the night at the Grand; the glare of the salmon only seemed to confirm this.

Still, he saved up his shillings and his pounds – for what, he didn't know, perhaps to buy a new shop that might enamour her to him, buy out Forrester's, or put a deposit on a house, where she might envision setting up a family with him. He would handle the fishmonger's and bring home what they had left of a day to feed the three or four little Stanskys who had by some good grace inherited their mother's looks, and ditched their father's nose. Or perhaps he might buy her something from Buttons – and present it to her on her birthday. When was her birthday, he would have to find out, but who could he ask? He couldn't ask her. Oh, would she ever forgive him? Could he ever forgive himself?

'Mr Stansky?'

The boy was looking at him.

'Sorry, son. Miles away. What'll it be, then? The eel makes a great spitchcock, Mrs Spenser was telling me. Or the ginpike, she has a lovely bite on her.'

'The ginpike?'

'Peachy fish. Something like trout.'

'No, Mr Stansky, sir, just the bream, please.'

When Arthur held the fish, tip to head from hand to elbow, the ice chips melted on his skin. 'That's an eight-ouncer. How's that for you?'

'Perfect.'

'For Mammy Malraux is it now?'

'Aye,' Nathaniel nodded and grinned. 'She hasn't cooked fish in months.'

'Ah. A special occasion?'

'No,' he shrugged, 'she seems to have it in her today, that's all. She seems to be feeling better, that is.'

'Well, she'll enjoy this one, that's for sure.'

'Mr Stansky?'

'Yes, son?'

'Is it from the Norwegian waters?'

'That she is.'

'Good. 'Twas what Mammy M requested.'

'Nowt wrong with that, son. Your da was a marvellous man. She must miss him. It was a great shame; and it happens too often, aye, that we lose one to the Sound.' Arthur wrapped the fish in paper, closing the fins into the package. 'Well, for you that is three and fourpence.' Nathaniel slid the coins over the counter. 'Enjoy it, then, son, it should be a good feast after your fast.'

The bell behind the boy rang and they both turned to Mrs Bingley, pulling a tartan trolley. 'Hello, Mrs Bingley,' said Nathaniel.

'Well,' she said, 'good morning, Nathaniel,' rather primly, but she hardly looked at him and started instead talking to Mr Stansky, rattling on about some theft from the grocer's. Well, if carrots were the only thing on Mrs Bingley's mind it meant the girl hadn't been found by anybody yet. And it meant Mrs Richards had not complained too widely of the crabbing she had received last night. A relief, on both counts.

Not a fish in months! And now it was this big fat fish

with its head and its fins and its tail! As the bag swung from his fingers and Nathaniel made his way from the square back home, he thought of Sarah's eyes on him and that ludicrous knife. She would never use it. She was too scared. But it had thrilled him, really, when she'd pulled it on him. Such an outrageous manoeuvre! He liked her better for it. He'd bring her some food tonight and win her over, so by the end of the week all she'd be looking for was cuddles and caresses.

12. Tea

In the late afternoon, Margaret prepared Arthur's fish. The slack-jawed bream fell easily from the paper and onto the oven tray. Margaret studied him and his deep frown. She didn't really want the fish to be in the kitchen. If it had come from the same place as Jack lay now . . . what if it had swum through his bones? My husband is a fish, she thought, or his bones are their beds.

Margaret Malraux did not know whether to weep into its gills or rip its head off.

She had developed this antipathy maybe a year or so after Jack's death. In the first year, her grief made it difficult to be squeamish, and when people came around (prim Mrs Bingley, or dear Mrs Page), with cod pie or clam casserole, she was not going to refuse. She knew, vaguely, that her boy needed to be fed and what he left she would eat without much pleasure. But as the bones of her bonny fisherman became, most likely, strewn along the seabed, Margaret developed a pure antipathy to the sea. She would not eat of its waters, not from the Sound, where the boat went down, nor, increasingly, from the Norwegian waters. No; she would not eat of the sea. She imagined Jack's molecules like plankton in its currents. Aye; now he was nothing more than mulch drifting in water, ready to be siphoned by mollusc or whale.

They had a fishless diet, Margaret and her son, because to eat fish was to entertain the possibility they might be eating him. And in the past few years she had stopped leaving the house so much, always afraid that the sight of the sea would send her racing back toward that grief.

But when John Verger came round yesterday night, he talked to her, in a worried fashion, of her son. He said that people were talking about some hooliganism in the square on Monday night. He said another boy had become involved in the gang – a Nicholas Carter, who wasn't older than twelve, and who now bore a bruise on his chin, supposedly from its connection with Nathaniel's fist. Verger said that the violence, and the intimidation, had to stop. Margaret told him how difficult she found it without Jack, mastering this boy of such wilfulness. Verger said he would be here to help, and he had held her hand in his, and that was when she had made her resolution to cook her boy a fish. It would be a way to keep him at home.

After all, that was what Nathaniel was always asking her, always saying that he could pick up something at Arthur's if she wanted. She would cook the fish for him, which would encourage him to stay at home, and keep him away from these boys. This would be the first step. Aye. Better meals had to be had. The Malrauxs would no longer eat potatoes.

Tentatively she slipped her finger into the wet body. Underneath his gills, the pouches of his cheeks, the tip of her finger touched the vertebrae, so sharp they almost pricked her finger. The backbone snapped between its head and tail, and Margaret moved its head to a plate. Its eyes, filmed and black, looked blankly at the ceiling. She regarded the flesh under the grey skin. How to make sense of her husband's death? Their love had been the only good thing about the Island. And now. Now there was so little to be consoled by. She couldn't understand it. Nothing could be extrapolated from the sea, from its tough opacity; its unerotic charge. The sea had devoured her husband! He had only wanted to suck up the air!

The Sound had taken away all comfort.

Margaret wiped the blade on her pinny. She pushed the knife in and spliced the fish open. Its translucent ribs left indents in the flesh. Margaret bent down to smell the seawater on its scales. *Were you near him*, she wanted to ask, *Were you near my Jack?* and then, *I can't do this, I'm frightened; I'm frightened of eating him!*

She stayed a while near its skin, breathing, slowly, slowly, until she regained composure and reminded herself that she was doing this for her boy. For he was the purpose, the meaning. She would feed her boy the fish to keep him from this gang.

Into the bream's belly she stuffed tinned anchovies and bottled capers. Margaret dropped the fish-head into the bin. The rest of the bream she put in the oven, and kicked the door shut.

If Jack were here he would know what to do. Was Nathaniel a terror? A hooligan? She just couldn't think it; he was such a bonny boy; he was not a boy who would harass, not a boy to terrorize. He was a lovely boy with eyes so blue. The pinafore she put back to where it always hung and she moved to the sink to scrape the scales from her hands. The flakes fell, sparkling in the water.

Margaret checked her hands were free from scurf and looked out into the back garden, with the clothesline, the bare trees and garage. Nathaniel was in there, fixing up Jack's workstation. There had been a time when she would pick the long red rhubarb stalks and make jam for husband and son. There had been a time when, home from a trawl, Jack and she would go out to watch the aeroplane fly over the breadth of the Island. It came on the last Sunday of the month and they liked to watch it and imagine the pilot's sense of freedom up there in the big air. They remembered, too, their once-cherished sense of freedom; which hadn't been freedom really, not in England in the late forties, but a sense of boundlessness, a sense that they could travel and go anywhere. But England had gone, disappeared in the wash, and with it, its roads and cities and ports, and though that sense of freedom too had disappeared, it had been replaced with their love for one another. It had been enough to sustain them; just. And now Margaret had her boy, and her boy only, and she would do anything to keep him from himself.

The plane would come this Sunday, she guessed, but she wouldn't go out to watch it.

The doorbell rang. It was unusual for Margaret to receive anybody at home, never mind two visitors in two days. She hoped it wasn't Verger again, at any rate; sometimes she couldn't bear his concern. Her hands she checked again were free from fish scale before opening the door.

Caro Kilman. There she stood, her auburn curls round

against the grey sky, wearing a plush red coat. As sturdy and polished as a first-class train carriage, next to Caro was a sleek creamy Labrador, with wet eyes and panting tongue. Directly, the snout was at Margaret's crotch. Caro pulled the dog back to her side with a smart snap of the leash. Margaret noticed the fine gloves. 'Hello, Margaret. Sorry about that. A nose on him.'

'It's fine. Hello, Caro.'

Margaret smoothed down her green plaid skirt and tried to give her hair a little volume at the crown. She always felt bad about herself next to Caro, who always looked very well put together, as she should do, being mistress of the Island's launderette. She had always wondered if Caro had held a little flame for Jack.

'Margaret.'

Margaret led her through the vestibule and into the hall, and Caro removed her coat, though it was not much warmer than outside. Underneath was a purple frock, cinched at the waist with a matching belt. The scooped neck showed a lovely oval of skin, quite pearlescent. Her perfume, something of roses, breasted the air, and made Margaret's nose itch.

The parlour was rarely used and cooler for it. Caro sat herself in the armchair, moving her hand over the dog's glossy coat. Margaret lit the fire. Underneath the parlour's window was the veneered box where Margaret kept Jack's letters. *Maggie*, they would start, invariably, and then some sentimental little thought – *I'm at sea without you*. She knew bits off by heart but tried hard not to read them. *Y'are a bag of cockles to warm any sailor's heart*. On long missions, when he would be out at sea for a month or so at a time, the ferry, that brought the catch back to the Island every Thursday, would bring her a letter too. But Margaret tried hard not to read them; they tended to make everything worse.

Caro put her ungloved hands toward the fire.

'Would you like some tea, then, Caro?'

'Please.'

When Margaret returned with the tray of tea and biscuits, Caro was staring anxiously at the ceramic cockatoo on the mantelpiece, as if afeared it would jump onto her lap. Margaret left the door open so that Caro could smell the baking fish and know that she kept a good house, and also so that the room wouldn't warm and Caro wouldn't be inclined to stay. Steam piped from the teapot's spout.

The dog had by now fallen asleep, snoring gently in front of the fire. Margaret placed the tray on the side table and then sat herself on the sofa. 'And Morris? How's his anaemia, if you don't mind me asking?'

Caro held her head up high as if stretching her neck. 'It does give him an ache.'

'Aye. I imagine.'

'Right pale, he is, with very little colour in his lips. And under his eyes, you know.' She pulled the skin down underneath her eye. 'All round here very pale pink; not red, like you or I. And his heart is shaky, too, what with the iron, you know, and not having enough of it. Me, I've never suffered from it. Have you?' Caro did not stop to hear the reply, instead flattening the dress over her knees, saying, 'I told Morris to eat more salmon. Arthur says this might help.'

'It's a chronic ache, then, the anaemia?'

'No, not as such; it doesn't affect him all the time.'

Margaret looked at the pot and wondered if she could hazard now to pour the tea, but it would be an embarrassment if it came out as bathwater. Margaret did not want to be embarrassed, not in front of Caro. Caro looked at an exact point on the carpet with a washed-out look in her eyes; when she looked up she was somewhat flushed. 'I'm scared for Morris. Seeing Mrs Page buried like that. She was quite young, you know, only sixty-five. It was a heart attack but she was very weak, very weak already from the lack of iron.'

'You can't die from anaemia, Caro—'

'You can if it gets really bad. Morris is sweaty, at night, like a radiator in bed with me. I've heard it causes heart palpitations. Palpitations!' Caro's eyes rounded alarmingly. 'That's a heart attack!'

For moments, neither woman spoke. Caro looked mournfully at the dog, Margaret looked mournfully at the picture of Jack and Jack looked at the sea, and, unbeknown to him, into the lonely soul of Margaret Malraux. 'Of course, it wasn't something my Jack was affected by. Anaemia. He was always a big healthy man. It must be hard for you, I can't imagine.'

'I expect,' Caro said, re-crossing her legs and smiling tightly, 'it is the same feeling as when you lost Jack in the accident. It is hard, sometimes, to get to the pity of another's suffering, but not impossible.'

Margaret stood and splashed the hot tea into the cups. She poured too much milk into Caro's cup and hoped it would make it cold, passing the cup and saucer over to her, while the dog snoozed by Caro's feet. 'Mrs Bingley is the same with Gordon. Washed out with worry, day in, day out, for his bloods. Aye, it is hard for us women. If we're not hard enough on this Island, oh aye, if there's softness left in us on any account, then the anaemia comes. Very cruel; life.'

Margaret drained her cup of tea, though it was quite hot, hoping Caro might do the same and leave with her fat dog. But she was evidently in no rush.

Caro coughed and then said: 'And Nathaniel?'

'Yes?'

'He was in the launderette last week. Acting very strange.'

'And?'

'And then I saw him outside in the square on Monday. With his friends. They were larking about in a queer manner.'

'Perhaps, as we didn't grow up on this Island, it might be hard for either of us to imagine what is normal, and what is queer.'

Caro placed her cup and saucer on the carpet and put her hands on her lap, neatly, like two hands carved of soap. The corners of her lips twitched briefly upward toward her eyes and then her expression became markedly more sober. 'Yes, well. Mrs Richards had a hard time of it last night.'

'And what is that to me?'

'It was reported to me that these boys were involved. Nathaniel, and his ilk.'

'Reported to you? Are you the new policewoman of the isle, then, Caro? Strange, I thought we already had a force fit for that purpose.'

Caro simpered. 'Mrs Bingley told me.'

'My boy does not parley with those hooligans. You can take that from me.'

Margaret looked out onto the street. Caro drank her tea.

'How is business? Nathaniel tells me he spends nearly all of his pocket money at your launderette. Keeping his fineries spruce.'

'Well, I'm not here to discuss Nathaniel's sartorial choices—'

'I didn't assume you were.'

'No.' Caro stood, as if being at the level of the cockatoo might confer her with some degree of authority. 'That I didn't. But what I do want to discuss with you, Mrs Malraux, is the issue of this gang. They're sharking about the Island for Gots or English spies or who knows what and I think it's a bad business. We hardly need thugs like that around, not any more, not after our troubles. Not in 1986, for goodness' sake. They're vandalizing things, harassing people—'

'Rubbish.'

'Poor Mrs Richards was hit last night by a thrown rock.'

'Are you implying my boy—?'

'Well, was he here?'

'Of course.' Margaret lied with ease: 'He was watching the telly with me.'

But Caro pressed on. 'Are you talking to him? Finding out the problem? He's a menace, Margaret, and people are scared.'

'How dare you tell me how to raise my child! He's a good lad. You just don't see it. You have no proof he was there; none whatsoever.'

The muscles in Caro's neck squeezed. 'Fine.' She stood and picked up her gloves, and with the tip of her brogues nudged the dog's belly. The Labrador woke and yawned. 'I only came to warn you, Margaret, out of a good sense in my heart. That Nathaniel should be—'

'Yes?'

'I only thought I might be a help. I care. And without Jack—'

'Thank you.'

The dog gave a bark and they both looked at him as if they wondered how he had got there.

Caro said quietly, 'Do you even know where he is now?' After the pronouncement of Jack's name, moments ago, Margaret assumed Caro was now talking about her husband. *Did she know where he was now?* What kind of question was that? Margaret imagined Jack's limbs dancing in the tide; the fish swimming between his bones. Her heart ached. Caro raised an eyebrow, persisting, leaning toward her as if Margaret were deaf, or at least incapable, saying: 'Nathaniel. Your son, Margaret. Do you know where he is?'

'Yes.' Margaret laughed. 'He's in his da's garage. Do you want to check up on him? Lend him a hand to saw through an English spy?'

Caro was now evidently fuming though her face remained expressionless. She turned neatly on her heel and walked swiftly to the hall. The dog followed lazily. Caro vigorously buttoned the coat with one gloved hand. It was dark in the hall and Margaret felt ashamed of the carpet. 'I only came as a friend, as I said.'

A waft of bream escaped from the kitchen.

On the front steps a broad wind hit the two women. The row of pebbledash houses gleamed, their slate roofs slick in evening rain. Margaret wrapped the cardigan closer; this was as far as she would come out. 'Enjoy the plane on Sunday, if you're to see it, Mrs Malraux.'

'My regards to Morris,' Margaret replied, but Caro had already set off, the dog trotting behind her. 'And his bloods,' Margaret added, but with very little voice.

From behind her, the oven bell rang out.

In its warm chamber she saw the fine skin blackening.

13. Fish Supper

There were cases of anaemia on the Island, but fewer than the Islanders thought. In the early fifties, when the deportees had arrived, a rumour had circulated that the lack of meat would drive them all mad, and it had become a long-term concern of the terrorist mothers to keep their children on a surfeit of iron.

Ever since then, preoccupied with nearly nothing else, not fighting the English nor petrol-bombing churches, the Islanders became obsessed with the imminent danger of anaemia, convinced that it was the fastest path to pack your child in a little box off Lynemouth Bay. The danger of the disease also furnished them with ample opportunity to visit the fishmonger's, which the late Stansky and now his son, Arthur, both handsomely presided over, in order to get their store of protein. But the only thing in their blood was a persistent and inter-generational hysteria, which brought down men and women who, in their previous lives, had brought down the sturdy brick walls of churches.

Further rumours circulated in the early sixties that the *Saviour* was taking back to England the very worst cases, for blood transfusions, in English hospitals. Rumours followed of patients fed up on pork chops and gammon. They said that to think of England was to teach a man despair;

to think of meat, suicide. But people talked in the square, outside Stansky's, working out if they could get back to England on the boat, for this was the decade when the boredom had crept in, when the age of the revolution was well and truly over, and the Islanders had to live within the bounds of their freedom.

The Island children didn't have the same hang-ups, they hungered for nothing, the taste of meat never once having passed their lips.

And though the craze for meat fizzled in the middle of that decade, the fear of anaemia never left them. When people died of heart failure, like Mrs Page, a rumour always spread that it was the anaemia that got them, even if they'd been the most loyal customers of Arthur Stansky. Mrs Page had had the spoon-shaped nails and yellow under-eyes and pale skin that had sent the rumour mill going, but she had died of a heart attack, last week, pure and simple.

Still, it was a bad mother who kept a household without fish.

Tonight's dinner, in the Malraux house, had been a grand feast, one Nathaniel hadn't been used to. For the months of eating tatties and turnips, Nathaniel would never have allowed himself to dream of this meal of bream.

Mammy Malraux was a wonderful cook, and it seemed to make her happy. He only wished she would do it more. The way she sat, smiling to her ears, when she saw him eat, he wished he could see that face more. It was a kind of joy that would stop a clock or crack the flagstones. She had looked awful sad of recent times. She always grew more melancholic in winter. But tonight she had even asked him to move the table into the parlour, so that they could sit at the chairs and not in front of the television. On the mantelpiece, Jack grinned down from the photograph.

Nathaniel ate as if he had not eaten in days. His mother watched him, her blue eyes (like his own, he knew) fixed on him. At one point she looked at him, panicked, and then looked at the bream. It was her first bite of the fish, but when she swallowed it looked painful, as if it had been a mouthful of bone. 'It's hard, aye, for me, this fish.' She prodded its side then dropped the fork noisily. Her pale yellow cardy bagged until her wrists. 'I can't eat. Because what if. Oh.' Her eyes flitted to the photograph of his da. Then she composed herself, and gave a weak smile. 'Don't much fancy it. Not tonight. But you go ahead. You eat. Have mine.' She slid her plate over to him and then rested her cheek on her fist. 'My good boy, isn't that right?' She ruffled the short spikes of his hair with her palm. 'My good bald boy, aye?'

And he swatted her away and said, 'Ma!' but that was the thing: she made his heart a rollicky softness when she spoke to him like this. He'd like his mam to put her arms about him; she squeezed his hand across the table. He felt a little bad, because he'd banked on her lack of appetite, and banked on her portion being available for Sarah. In fact, he'd even eaten his whole plate, so sure was he that his ma would eat nothing. 'That I am, Mammy M.'

'And you've got nothing to do with this gang?'

'No, Mam, I told you. Don't believe a word of what Mrs Kilman was saying. She's only out to get me since I stopped using the launderette.'

'Oh.' Margaret was surprised. 'Caro didn't say that. She said you were in last week.'

'Nope. Haven't seen her in a month. Thought I could do my vesties better myself, and she took exception to that. She's nursing the slight, that's all, and she probably misses the,' Nathaniel stopped, searching for the right word, 'revenues.'

'Ah,' Margaret said, softly laughing, in a sad sort of way. 'I see. I see. Caro didn't mention that. No, she didn't mention that.' She looked again at the photograph of Jack. The cockatoo grinned with birdish menace. 'Nathaniel, love, will you do something for me?'

'Aye, Mam, anything, anything you ask.' He would, he would, he'd drop off Lynemouth Bay if she asked him!

'Will you put that bird in the bin?' She tipped her head toward the china on the mantelpiece. 'I'm sick of it looking at me.'

'Aye, Mam, of course. I've never much liked it myself.'

In the kitchen, Nathaniel put his mam's portion in a roll, spreading it with a thick yellow layer of margarine. Nothing could beat a fish sandwich and he bet Sarah would be sore for it. He wondered when she'd last eaten something proper; and he wondered what this bream might win him.

He considered telling his ma the truth – that he was off to see a girl – but she wouldn't believe him and would assume he was out with the boys. Besides, it was only for the hour, just to give the girl a fright to her gilly-high shoes, before he'd back off and be sweet to her. He needed to know, definitively, that her story was no fib. So he could eventually tell the boys. And reassure himself, that he was bedding no Godly girl.

His mam was snug now, in front of the telly, and he'd

done the washing up like the good son he was to her. 'I'm off to the garage, now,' he said, and she nodded, gently, as he slipped out of the too-hot house.

Nathaniel walked east, over Marley Hill, and then skirted round past Mrs Richards', where he ducked down and walked close to the hedge lest she should crab him for last night. He smacked his lips of the left-over fish oils; rubbed them up a bit to make them soft as if it were Pomade Divine they had been treated with. He could still taste the dinner on his lips. A perfume of a most peculiar character: Essence de Bream. He took the scree carefully down the hill, lit a cigarette, caught something, some dead mushroom now slimed to the bottom of his boot, and scraped it off on the side of the pavement. The slow cadence of the Sound coming up from the shore was a winter music to his ears.

Aye, he had decided to act tough with Sarah tonight; give her a bit of a fright, and smoke out the lie if it was there. If she was spying, he'd discuss it with Jake: he would share the news reluctantly, but he needed another boy's ear to bend on this. It was too important to keep to himself. It was his duty, he supposed. What rotten luck if a cherry such as this one was a spy for English soil! A rotten lot, indeed.

When he reached the row of empty houses he paused to catch his breath; he'd come at quite a jog. The last house, at the end of the road, looked threatening to fall into the sea. All around it looked marshy and habitually overgrown, as if it had been built on waste-ground. It would be a wicked place, devilishly cold, in this month of November.

*

In the bedroom, the girl was all soft snorting rhythms, a small shape in the corner. Asleep, at nine o'clock! This Island must tire her English eyes.

The room was dark but he saw that the clothes had been tidied up since he'd glimpsed the room this morning. This, he approved of; he would have never treated his vesties like that, casting them about as if she took no care of her possessions. Before waking her, Nathaniel looked for maps or notes or photographs or anything that might give the girl away as a spy. There was nothing but clothes and the last of a loaf.

He had expected her to wake, but her breath was steady and her eyelids still closed. Her hair was all coppers and rusts. Her mouth was open, and he saw how her lips were lined white before the freckles started. The boy crouched down to her. He wanted to put his hand on her skin to see if it put out the lovely warmth that all girls seemed to have. She breathed softly, like an infant.

But he stood suddenly, as if her breath was rank, remembering himself. This girl was English. It was very likely she had come on some mission to spy on them. He thought of his da drowned in the flimsy English boat. Aye, the Island could never be second to a girl, even if she was a cherry such as this. He nudged her shoulder with the tip of his boot. Half-asleep, her eyes darted about the room in panic. 'What?'

'I brought you some food. Tea. Here.' Nathaniel switched on the light and saw that the rucksack, with the knife, was by the sink at the corner. 'Drink some tea.' Sarah sat up, blinking against the hard light. Her face had lost some colour. *Oh, Sarah*, he thought, *you're to be frighted tonight, and though it is for your own good, I'd just as well do this to my own mam.* Nathaniel poured the tea into the top of the cap and handed it over. 'Is that a uniform?' she asked him, her breathing louder, pointing with a finger. 'You were wearing it this morning, too.'

'Part of a group I'm in.' He ledged himself at the sill; the glass, at his back, was cold.

'Are you part of a police? I've heard there's a police here, and that they dress in strange clothes.'

'Part of the police, in a way. We police the Island, that's true.'

'For what?'

'For English spies. For people who want us to join back with England.'

'And there are people like that, here?'

'Oh, aye. Of course. People are bored of being alone. They want back into God's land. And the English want us back, too.'

'I don't think the English care.'

'What? Of course they do. We're a threat. And they've set up a network of spies on the Island in order to convert people. And with each prayer they send out, each hand they hold, each piece of scripture they read, they're building up the Church in their minds. Until the whole Island will tip back to the old way. And if the Islanders go back to faith they'll want union with England, and we'll all be lost!' Sarah leaned her head against the wall, looking at him. Something curiously blank about her blue eyes. Like his, perhaps. 'Oh, aye, you can never be too careful. See, what if they sent an Englishman who they *said* was part of the Movement, but really worked for the government? What if they were tricksier indeed, and they planted a girl who no one would suspect?'

The expression on Sarah's face didn't change.

Nathaniel stepped from the sill and took the fish sandwich from his satchel. He kept his eye on the bag by the sink. He came close to her, her head near the ball of his knee, the roll offered in his palm. She didn't take it, and her mouth was flat. He gestured a little with his wrist. She stared, sightlessly, somewhere in front of her. Perhaps he had crabbed her at the heart of the lie and she would now confess everything. But he knew she would not refuse the food and a moment later she reached up for the roll.

Nathaniel went back to the sill where the branches drubbed the glass. They didn't talk for a while as Sarah ate the buttered bread and bream, and she washed it down with tea. 'I went to the museum,' she said. 'I know what went on. I saw the pictures; I know what the Unrest did to your families.'

'Aye.'

'It was sad. Very sad. What happened. What the English did.'

'What you did.'

'No. Not me. Not my family.' She threw the foil to a corner of the room. 'My family have been just as broken by the Unrest. You read the article, so you know what my mum did for you.'

'Tell me it's not a lie, Sarah.'

Her blue eyes were as cold as the sea and just as sad. 'I told you. I told you the truth. I'm looking for her, for Laura Wicks. Nothing else. I promise.'

And it felt as if his heart were pure about to break its banks, so sure was he of her sincerity.

'Bet you were hungry?' he said, warmth now coming into his voice.

'Starving.' Sarah stood and stretched, and went over to the bag. He tensed, but she brought out the pack of cigarettes again and offered him one. With a match she lit his and her own. 'We tend to eat meat, back home, me and my dad.'

'Oh,' he said, 'my ma talks of that.'

'You don't have meat here, do you?' She leaned against the sink.

'Oh, no. Just the fishes. I'nt a finer thing than a fish, when you want that.'

'So you've never had pork? Or beef?'

'If it's not of the wet, I've probably not had a taste.'

'It must be strange. This Island. To live here.'

'No. I don't know anything else, it's not strange to me,' he said. 'Tell me of your ma, now. Tell me more of the story.'

Sarah tapped her ash into the sink. She observed herself in the glass, somewhat warily, then watched his reflection. 'When I was seven, my mum left. She was having an affair, Dad said. He said she'd run off with another man. For months I asked if she was coming home, if we could go and visit her, but my dad always said no. Looking back on it, I suppose, knowing what I do, it was an odd situation. People don't just disappear like that: there are arguments, and angry telephone calls. But Mum just disappeared.

'When I was a teenager, maybe thirteen or so, I began asking the neighbours about her, but there was a wall of silence. No one in the village remembered her, or they said they didn't know her, or they said they had lived somewhere else when Laura lived in Trimdon.'

'Your town?'

'Aye. My town. There's hardly any family on my mum's side and the ones there were wouldn't talk anyway. When I pushed Dad on it, he said he'd found love letters, and correspondence, but he said he wouldn't show them to me, said they were private, which I understood. I didn't really even want to see them. He said Mum and her lover were in hiding, because the Church wouldn't let them live openly, which would explain why we couldn't contact her. And so I accepted the story, I couldn't provide another explanation. And either way, Mum was gone, and I couldn't do anything about it.'

'And then?'

'And then I found out about the fire. Last week. I was down in the cellar. Our boiler, it makes this noise, the pipe's loose. I went down to fix it, but I lost my footing and fell and lost a slipper.' A weary smile. 'Who would've thought that losing a slipper might get you here?

'Anyway, the shoe fell between the boards and I couldn't reach it. It was too dark for me to see. So I took a broom and it pushed against a box. A shoebox. Just a normal shoebox, but it was sealed with tape.' Sarah lit the next cigarette with the one she was smoking and paused, pulling her fingers against the enamel of the sink. The wind outside was less fierce, now, against the glass. She coughed, and then continued: 'I didn't look inside. Instead, I made dinner. It was pork medallions, with apple sauce, but I bet you have no idea of what that is, do you?'

The boy shrugged.

'Later that night, I read the article, about my mum, and the church fire. I couldn't believe it. There was my mum's name: Laura Wicks, and her photograph, calling her a terrorist. A murderer. All this time I thought she was off making families with someone else. And there she is, on the front page, a political dissident.'

'Aye. Go on.'

'I didn't say anything to my dad. Not a word. Instead, I went to the archives up at Newcastle. I tried to find anything I could on her. Anything that would give me an extra clue. But I came to a dead end. I read deportation lists and prison lists but I couldn't find her name anywhere. I was about to give up. Then I found this.' Sarah bent over to her bag again and brought out another folded piece of newspaper. She handed it over to Nathaniel.

He held it out and looked at the photograph, brow furrowing. 'What's this?'

'That's her. The one in the middle, on the last boat here.'

'But there's no mention of her. Nowhere that names her.'

'Do you think I wouldn't be able to recognize her?' she snapped. 'That's her. I'm sure of it.'

'But it was ten years since you last saw her!'

Sarah snatched the paper from his hands. 'It's got to be her. Or else where can she be?' She was desperate-sounding, now, and knew it. 'They must have missed her off a list. Mistakes were made. Things happened so fast. She's got to be here. She isn't anywhere else.' Nathaniel came over to where Sarah stood at the sink. He moved some hair from her face and put it back to the gingery mass. Her eyes welled. 'I miss her,' she said, then, 'Sorry,' even quieter.

What empty houses they lived in, he and Sarah both! Here she was, one parent down, just like himself. He felt a stabbing bit of grief for his da, who had deserted him too, but not half as willingly. Then he got lost a bit thinking about his mam and how she had pushed the plate of fish over to him, patting his hand, unable to eat. He was about to bring Sarah closer when he saw her eyes slide to the bag and the knife.

He dropped his hand from her face.

'Aye, well, I haven't heard of Laura. But, as I said, people don't go out, people get scared, people stop in away from the sea.' He remembered his specific resolve to lay it on mean so that he could test her. What kind of Island boy would he be if he didn't have it in him? And what kind of Malade? He put his hands to her jaw and cupped her face. 'Or maybe your ma got so sick of the Island she threw herself to the Sound.' He laughed. 'You never know. Whether it's us who're full of the fishes or them that are full of us. Ha!'

Sarah looked up at him, her eyes flashing. Her cheeks too had that red rush to them, just the same as when he'd seen her this morning. 'And this mother story,' he said, 'I don't know. Could all be bollocks, aye, Sarah Wicks? Maybe she's in England making house with her fancy man. Have you considered that? That she may actually be fucking this man!'

'But the photo—'

'Who cares about the photo? There aren't even any

names underneath it! Who knows why you're here!' Suddenly he took a boot to whatever he could find, kicking over a plastic chair by the mattress, then stamping about a bit, mad with the thought that she might have made her grief up. 'Could all be a right load of bollocks, aye, Sarah Wicks!'

His breath was ragged now as he calmed himself. 'I shan't tell the boys of your being here, yet. But I wouldn't push it.'

Nathaniel had given her the bit of terror, as he had intended, but he didn't feel good for it, as he normally did after a bit of the scrap. Oh, but it was problematic, aye, the possibility of love with an English girl! As if embarrassed, he turned away from her and without looking round he said over his shoulder, 'Tomorrow. I'll come back for you at lunchtime. With some food. And as I said: don't talk to anybody.' And then he left without saying goodbye.

14. Maggie

All morning, Margaret had been upset about the bream. She'd barely eaten a mouthful; even watching Nath had been painful. How could she be his mother, cook for him, provide for him, ask him to stay at home, if it took so much energy and grief merely to make him supper?

For the past few days she'd barely got up out of her chair for anything more than a meal or the relief of her bowels, watching her boy swan in and out of the house. Knowing he was up to no good, perhaps, but not having the energy, either, to say or do anything. Aye, Caro Kilman was a gossip, and a pain in the neck, but perhaps there was some truth to her words.

It was just after breakfast. Margaret Malraux put a hand to the buttercup syrup then stopped herself. Instead, she walked into the cooler air of the hallway, where the phone was on the trestle mute. In the parlour, where she had sat with Caro yesterday, she twisted the blind so that the light of the day came. The room was not much brightened for it. Under the window were Jack's letters.

Margaret handled the box attentively. She did not do this often, but she was allowed, today, given how upset the fish had made her last night. She sat where Caro had sat, telling her limply of her child, and laid out the piece of paper on her knees. The paper, even flattened, sprang at the folds. She supposed, really, that she shouldn't read this. Not today. Letters were hard. His letters were hard. She supposed, if she were sensible, she should spare herself the pain of all these memories. But the bream had been so difficult to manage, and she wanted merely minutes of comfort.

March, 1977: The Sound

Maggie,

I was sitting here staring out to sea and I thought of you. The sea has been wild these past few days and it has given us no respite. This evening it has finally quietened, and I have the opportunity to write.

The catch has been tremendous, despite, or because of, the storms: the fish have fairly leapt into our nets, so sick are they of the sea below. Mackerel, haddock, even cod; the boat groans with the heavy loads. Whiting comes out of our ears! Peter has insisted we stay out for days further; hence the letter. I won't be home as promised, dearest Maggie, but a few days later; perhaps even a week. I wish it wasn't this way, but there's little I can do, what with the price of fish bringing in such a profit. Surely, they slip into the nets faster than you jumped into bed with me.

There, I was feeling melancholic, and even just writing to you has cheered me. Last night I thought about our first encounter. I don't know why. Sometimes these things transpire from nowhere. It seems to happen when I am at sea: the mind is left to wander, and here I am, with you, in 1951, at the Grand, remembering.

The Grand – that old cathouse, of all places! We were in the great dance hall (do you remember?), when everything was jubilant, and we celebrated every night, that we had, in some way, won the war – though, of course, we hadn't. But the triumph was there, and we were playing up to it: us, drunken, thrilled infidels.

You were drinking, what was it? It must have been gin; as always. You were sitting underneath the great leafy palm in the corner of the room. Your lips were red, I remember, and your dress green; fancy, with a big skirt on it. I remember thinking – this woman, this Margaret Malraux – for I had heard of you, heard about a ferocity that gave you the reputation of a lioness – I remember thinking that you were the loveliest mouse I had ever laid my eyes on.

You didn't hold my gaze for long, but carried on your conversation with your friend. Was it Frieda? I think it was. I said to Verger, should I talk to her? Should I offer to buy her a drink? He told me to take a flower from the vase and offer it to you. And so I did. My heart was in my mouth. I brought out a carnation, snapped off its end, and walked over. I tried to put it in your hair. I was drunk, drunk enough to try such a manoeuvre – I wouldn't have sober, that's for sure – and you turned around and swiftly slapped my hand away.

But then you danced with me. How can I thank you for dancing with me? I, who dance as if always aboard a boat, I should not have dared this, this of all things, to win your heart! It was a foolishness – but you forgave me, and these culpable left feet. Was it a waltz, or a polka? It could have been a jive, for all I knew. You said some words to me. Some words. Maggie, you said your name was, and I thought it the prettiest thing on the whole Island.

Maggie, dancing with you, feeling your head rest against me, you, you were the land of plenty. Even on this tiny island in the middle of the North Sea, which I felt had surely imprisoned me, I felt a sense of boundlessness. When I saw you, I knew I should happily live out my gaol term – a thousand-fold – with you here by my side.

Dearest Maggie. It is growing dark. I will have to stop soon.

It pains me still to leave you, early in the morning, in the darkness, when the sun hasn't even come up yet. I hope you know that. In the summer I close the window, before I leave, to shut out the sound of the sea, for I know you are jealous of it, and I do not wish you bad dreams. But it is good for me to be on the boat, to leave the Island sometimes – it's important to me, and of course you know that. The Island would strangle me if I didn't have a release from it. I find it, occasionally, stifling, and our Godless polemic – well, I have grown tired of it, and I do not care whether my neighbour believes in goats or sheep or flying fish.

At least, out here, on the wide open sea, I am free from all of that – out here, I contend only with the waves. The waves decide on everything I do: when I eat, when I sleep, even when I think about you. I am fastened to them, I suppose; they are my God, if there is one.

Do you see, the sea has made your Jack into quite the

philosopher. Indeed, it has seduced me into so many
things – letter-writing, drawing, philosophy – I promise
I shan't let it seduce me into its bed. For that, I am yours
alone.

The sky! A stab of light has emerged from what I
thought was surely night. I wish you could see it. But
moments have gone, and it has already disappeared.
When I write I feel as if you are here with me now, and
I do not want to leave the page. I will see you soon, give
a kiss to Nathaniel – I miss you, Maggie.

All my love, all my life,

Jack

Margaret placed the letter back on her knees, putting
the first page on top of the second. The fire roared beside
her. It was not right to make a habit of this; it was too hard,
but November was nearing its end, as it must. And the
bream was in her belly. And Jack was in the sea.

Tenderly, she restored the letter to the box. There
were more letters there, and they were all beautiful. She
shouldn't read these; not too often. They consoled her and
saddened her at the same time. Where was the last one he
had sent, she wondered, she had put it somewhere for safe
keeping and then lost it – if only she could find that last
letter, perhaps it might draw these matters of grief to a
close!

Footsteps ran down the stairs and she heard the doors
bang. There was a faint whistling, a high, chirpy tune.
Anxiety flooded her. Margaret snapped up the blinds
and wrenched the window from its jamb. It gave with

a cracking sound of paint. 'Where are you going?' she shouted to the retreating form heading up Blackett Place.

'Over to Mr Verger's!' and Nathaniel gave her a wave.

Margaret could tell, just from his voice, even yards away, that he was lying. How could fish be the only possibility, and yet be so impossible! Oh, what was she to do with her son!

15. Bloom

Nathaniel was there, at her adopted home, waiting for her, just as he had promised. He sat smoking on the sill, watching the front garden. All bristles and blue eyes, when he saw her he grinned. She felt herself warm under his gaze.

Sarah was glad to be home – she had spent the morning at the woman's house, this time creeping closer to the kitchen and crouching down near the garden wall. Yesterday, she had stayed away, telling herself it was prudent to search the rest of the Island for further possibilities of Laura. As Nathaniel had advised, she had talked to no one, and kept a low profile. And, as she had promised – this time to herself – Sarah traipsed the Island paths in search of another candidate. But everywhere she went, no woman was as persuasive as this one here, and, this morning, she had sat and watched, for hours, looking for all of her likenesses to Laura. But it was cold and lonely, and slightly perverse, she knew, spying on this woman, and it was a relief to be back at home, and talking to someone; no longer hiding.

'Where's your bag, Sarah Wicks?' She took it off and left it by the sink. 'I always have to be careful, you see, of that knife.' From his satchel he pulled out a foil square. 'Come with me,' he said, 'we can go somewhere we won't be seen by anybody else.'

There was not much sun, today, a spoonful or so in the sky. The two walked, mostly in silence, through the purple heather to the edge of the Eastern cliff. 'Down here,' he said, 'we'll be hidden. We won't be seen by anybody.'

The sea was rougher here because of the rocks. They made the waves choppy and big and when the sea came tumbling up toward the beach, and then sucked back, the pebbles made a grinding sound as if they were chains rattling against pavement. There were no houses around the Eastern Bay; only the thinnest stretch of beach could be seen from its cliff-top. 'Keep to the rocks, at the side,' he said. 'We're not supposed to go down here, but at least it'll be private, aye, and there'll be no one around.'

Sarah started footing her way down the rocks. 'C'mon, then,' she said, 'unless you *want* to be seen with an English girl!'

Nathaniel began his way down, but it was made harder by his tight jeans, which hampered his movement, so that she was much faster than him. It was irritating, how quick she was, descending like a topsoil come off in rain, when all he could do was place his boots carefully down the wet cliff face.

Level with the sea, a salty breeze met his face. If they kept away from the sandbar they would be fine. On a rock big enough for two, Sarah ate her sandwich and Nathaniel watched her, cautiously – he thought – so that she wouldn't notice. It was just a marge sandwich; there'd been no more fish left from yesterday night. He hoped she wasn't too disappointed.

Sarah was close enough so that he could feel her jacket against his own. It was surprising, how blue it got underneath her eyes; how orange the lashes were when she looked down to the sand. Dusted in freckles, they were hectic and went purely everywhere. He'd kill to see her angry again, like when she had coloured scarlet earlier on. When he saw her – no, when he thought about her – a warmth rolled in his blood. It was like the time he'd tried his ma's sedatives and felt his whole body go slack and calm but somehow strong; that was how she made him feel. Though she did not, exactly, send him to sleep; or hadn't, anyway, last night.

He sensed an affinity between them, that his empty bits were her empty bits too. But he was annoyed at her too. There was something aloof about Sarah, as if she thought her Englishness made her better than the Island's mob. Still the thought nagged at him, about how he should talk to his boys, of what he should do with her. He couldn't let them see her; not yet. They would assume her to be a spy; as he did; as he had. He imagined Jake placing a punch, and the blood gushing from her nose and lips. But to keep her a secret was somehow to admit her culpability. Still, he'd managed to postpone the meeting tonight, and that had bought him some time.

'Look,' she said, 'over there.' Tiered on the wind, gulls circled at the other end of the beach and wings flapped between the rocks. Sarah stood and started walking, as if she didn't have a fear of anything. Was she so undaunted by anything put in her way? Perhaps this was a very

English trait, as if God watched for every rock you might fall over and gave you a surging sense of confidence.

On her approach a gull launched into the air, its orange claws dangling as it flew. Nathaniel followed her toward the rocks, the wind turning with a foul smell, like a sewage, and it made him nearly bring up a reflux of Mammy's porridge.

Yards away, a fish's black eye stared up at them. The tail was silver-yellow, its body plump. Its gills were powdered in sand and its pink mouth gaped. Further on, there was another fish, its threaded fins striking the air. Sarah nudged it gently, so that you could see its heavy lids and snout flecked in sand.

She kicked it back to the sea, so that slowly, in the tide, it was carried off toward the Sound. The boy and girl watched the floating fish and it made them feel sad, indirectly, about their own lives.

By the rocks the smell was stronger still. All the birds had flown off now but were still close above them. A whole boat-load of fish were sunning themselves on the cold grain. Slipshod over one another, the fish were everywhere, a spill of organs and bones and scale. Some of the flesh had been eaten as far as the spine. A purplish air hung. Their greasy remains reminded him of the bream they'd had last night, and Nathaniel felt he would gromick at merely the thought of it. Razorous teeth grinned upward.

With each swill the Sound tried to carry them off but there were too many for that. 'A bloom,' he said.

'What? What's that?' Sarah looked up at him, then back, surveying the puddled graves. 'What's that, then?'

He pointed way out across the Sound. 'There's a band

of algae out there choking the fish. They can't get enough air, aye.' He walked downward to the water's edge. 'They drowned in the water and then were carried to the shore.'

'It's horrible.'

'Aye,' he said, 'but it happens. The Sound is a nasty business, at times.'

'Is it dangerous?'

'No. I mean. Not really. Just have to fish from the other side of the Island. Go into the Norwegian waters, like. Means less fish for the winter.' He saw in the sea the shadows of things: weeds, and rocks, before the sandbank veered. An uninterrupted stretch, the sea went right out to meet the sky, a line of the horizon jammed in between. Were he to close his eyes, he would know this Island from end to end. It was a grey sea today, bluish under its top. It looked so long, as if it were impossible that land could be found after it. 'My da's boat's out there.'

'He's a fisherman?'

'Was a fisherman. He's dead now.'

'I'm sorry,' she said.

'But this would be where his boat was. Across the Sound, aye, between here and England.'

'I'm sorry,' she said again. 'It must be hard.'

'Aye, well. Can't be changed.' The lump was so sore in his throat he thought he might be about to do the shake-and-heave. What an embarrassment, to be blubbing in front of an English girl! But still the big hot tear came and it came with a sense of weariness and gratitude. 'Sorry. I shouldn't be crying. I'm man enough now to take it. 'Twas a long time ago.'

'How long?'

'I was seven. Nine years ago.'

Neither said much, for the while.

'Thank you, for the food, for the sandwich, last night,' Sarah said. 'I thought you were angry. I didn't know if I would see you again.'

'You were lucky to get the bream, aye. My mam's not in the way of cooking much.'

'She's poorly?'

'No, not that.' It was all he could say and Sarah held his hand. When he brought it to his lips it smelled metallic, like tin. He wondered, again, just what he was meant to do with her. The light, obliquely from the sea, had turned her blue eyes grey. 'Ma doesn't get out much. Not after Da died.'

'Why?'

'She's scared, I guess, though I don't know what of. If I could only get her to move, to go out just a little bit. She sits in her chair all day, day in, day out, and I don't know what to do with her. If only I could get her to move! Just a few steps, perhaps, even out to the garden. But she won't leave, you know. She just won't do it. There's no point in even trying to persuade her.'

Another floating fish came on the next wave, eyeing the sky dreamily, as if lovelorn. Very gently, Sarah picked it up and put it next to the rocks. 'There's so many of them,' she said and they both watched the dead fish for a bit as if they expected something else to happen.

Suddenly, Sarah started to run up the yellow beach, her ginger hair flying in the huge wind off the sea. Her squawks made the gulls go crazy above them. Nathaniel gave chase, trying to catch up with her. They circled back and found themselves at the rocks. He cornered her so that he was very close, maybe a stride or so away. Sarah backed off then stood still and they held each other's gaze. She picked up a fish and thrust it out between them. The slime on it caught in the light. 'Be careful,' she said. You couldn't tell if her eyes were grave or playful.

'I'm more scared of that fish than I am of your knife.'

'I shouldn't be so sure, if I were you.'

The fish flopped, bending backward, and they both laughed, but she thrust it out again, jabbing. Nathaniel ran back a few paces down the length of the beach and then felt the hard pressure of it against his back. It landed with a wet slapping sound and then dropped to the sand. 'You're dead!' he shouted, and he raced back toward her, to the pool of fish, and grasped a fat one by his boot, and immediately threw it at her, catching her neck. Sarah fell dramatically as if she'd been shot and then turned over, belly-up, her laughs ringing out in the big sky.

He lay down next to her on the freezing sand. 'Sorry,' he said, still laughing.

'Aye,' she said, breathing heavily.

'Sarah?'

'Yes?'

'Are you to leave on Monday's boat?'

'Aye,' she said. 'That's the plan.'

'And your ma? You think you'll find her before then?'

'That woman. In the house. I think it could be her.'

Nathaniel cast his mind back to Wednesday night and the blackened kitchen. 'Do you want me to come with you? To see who she is. I'd know who she is, if only I saw her.'

'No,' said Sarah, 'I want to do this alone. I'll ask her in my own time. Tomorrow, perhaps. Aye. Tomorrow.'

'And if it is her, what will you say?'

Sarah laughed a little. 'You know, I don't know. I haven't thought of the questions, yet.'

They lay watching the birds watch them. The sand around them smelled of old seawater; the breakers were close, on the steep beach, not yards away. He imagined the bones of his da washing up on this shore, or glistening in the nets of Arthur's friends as they pulled in the trawl. 'Tell me about England, Sarah.'

'What do you want to know?'

'What it's like. My da used to tell me stories, about where he was from. But my ma won't speak of it; not much anyway.'

'Well, it's bigger than here, and busier.'

'And the Church? What do they do in your life?'

'You go to church on a Sunday. You say prayers at school. You have Bible lessons. You learn about Christ.'

'And you believe in it? All that stuff.'

'I did. And then I didn't. Not for a while. I don't know. When I thought about Mum leaving, it didn't seem to be right; it didn't seem to make any sense. And you? Despite yourself? Despite the Island.'

'No! Never.'

Sarah turned over on her side and rested her head on her palm. 'Never even thought it might be worth your while putting out a word or two?'

'No,' his voice straining here. 'Never. Do I believe in ghosts? Or spirits? Or magic? No. And I don't believe in God.'

Sarah smiled and closed her eyes.

'What's that on your wrist, there?'

She opened her eyes and explored the bruise with her fingertips. 'It's where I fell, on the cellar steps, last week. My lucky wound.'

'Why d'you think your da kept it? The article? I mean, if he'd lied to you all this time?'

'Maybe it was all going to come out at some point. Some grand revelation on my eighteenth birthday. I don't know. I don't know.'

Nathaniel stood, and then helped her up. 'Here, you can have it back,' he said, handing over the sheet from the *Chronicle*.

'Does that mean you believe me?'

'Aye,' he said, nearly managing a laugh, 'but don't push it.' He checked his watch. 'I have to go. Have to check up on my mam. Make sure she's OK. But I'll come back for you. Later this afternoon. Be at Swanscott House, aye, at about four or so, and I'll come back for you then.'

Birds circled overhead, waiting for them to leave. There was a boy, too, up at the cliff edge, watching Nathaniel and the girl at their larks. He wore the epaulettes and scarf and boots of the boy down at the beach, though he wasn't half so handsome, and he left before he was seen by them.

16. At the Malrauxs'

When the Secular Movement came to the Island, it was as if they vanished from the sight of an eye surveying them. All it took was the breadth of the sea to dispossess them of English standards. The new Islanders were disinherited of God and free to do as they pleased. They smoked and drank and made love as if everything they did was a fist up to that surveying eye (though they said they did not believe in it, aye, this eye). They hated God though they would not believe in him. They had parties in the bar at the Grand, drinking, drinking, there was so much drinking in those days, and couples would shack up in the rooms at the back, or walk down to the beach to the cold sand and look out across the waters to an imperceptible England. Those days were fabulous; if hinged, a little, on a feeling near despair.

The Sound was so long; other land, so far away.

In the sixties things turned quiet; and life returned to normal, back almost to the way it had been in England. It had become tiring, and boring, the novelty of being reckless, and people settled down to work. The Island became another little England, with its petty gossip, and harmless feuds, and small kindnesses, and it might have been England in all but name had the burned-out church not been left to nature's creep.

Lynemouth Town, was, by the late sixties, a place of ill repute: of dark pleasures, of taverns, and brawls, and brothels, and its bay was the place where the Islanders buried their dead. Most of the Islanders avoided Lynemouth, if they could, lest one might see a leg or limb knifing into the air from the rocks. In 1977, with the second wave of migrants come from an even more evangelical England, Lynemouth Town had done well again, peddling all of its naughty pleasures, but then history had repeated itself, and into the eighties the brothels and bars had emptied as people settled back to ordinary life.

But to Eliza's ma, Lynemouth Town had always been a place of toil and pleasure: where the prostitutes would stop, early in the mornings, and they would drink black coffee and eat the hot sweet rolls just fresh. Eliza thought them all remarkable women, with their thin red lips and arched brows, and she knew that Linda had loved their company too. They talked, with mouthfuls of the hot bread, about the previous night's happenings, while Linda vigorously kneaded some dough for loaf or bagel, and Eliza always felt slightly ashamed, though her ma had given her no instruction not to listen. Then again, her mother probably hadn't imagined Eliza going into the profession, leaving her daughter, as she thought she had done, in the capable hands of Arthur Stansky, fishmonger.

Eliza missed her ma. It didn't look as if time would help this. She had woken this morning and written the word *Linda*, high up near her hairline, and then smoothed the fringe down against her brow, holding back the desire to weep. There was so little to be done. What use mourning on this draughty Island with the sea like a rope around its neck? One lived and one died here. One hoped for respite, often it was absent, and when it did come, with the warmth of a summer's day or a gift of fish, one might believe this was evidence of some felicitous eye keeping care of you. But then the joy soon bottomed out, and life went on, just the same. No, there was not much respite on the Island; not here; not for them.

That afternoon, and all of yesterday, Eliza had been looking for the English girl but once again she had found dark houses, a busy square full of Islanders, and people on the roads, milling about the baker's or Caro's, or down at the pubs, but none by the English girl's description.

Up at the church she saw the breakers of the Sound. Eliza wondered what the iron cross might mean to some-one who was not her; what it might mean to the heart of this English girl. This was His station of sacrifice, Eliza knew that much. She sat for a while in its shelter, thinking that if the English girl were feeling homesick, she might come here for some consolation. The Islanders had been wrong to shove so much of faith away, and now they were stuck in the great loll of the sea like dead sailors on a ship. It was pride, nothing else, keeping them from asking the English for more help. They could ask them for more fish-ing equipment, tools to build more boats, more books for the school. They might order new clothes and furniture. If an extra boat was laid on, a ferry, perhaps, the Islanders could come and go as they pleased. How many lived here? Fifteen hundred or so? All of them – even to think about it made Eliza smile – could re-join the world!

But it was 1986, still too early, and the Islanders still too sore, to hope for this.

There was still a faint smell of carbon, in here, though the church would be about thirty-six years burnt by now. She wondered who had done it, this last act of defiance against England. Eliza put her hands on her knees and cocked her head, as if she were listening to a service. How grateful she would be to hear some words of guidance right now. She just needed someone to talk to. The Sound sparkled invitingly.

On Monday night, watching the girl sneak from the boat, Eliza had imagined talking to her about railways and Walkmans and churches and all manner of English things. But now, Eliza knew that if she found her, she would not ask questions of England, but tell the girl about her own life: of her time growing up here, of her ma's death, of her job at the Grand and as grave-mistress, and she would, finally, unburden herself of the secret of Arthur. But now the hope was lost, since the girl was lost, and what secrets she had were to be kept inside, or written in inconsequential letters on her brow.

By two o'clock she reckoned she would go home. Back to the Grand. Oh, but that hollow little room; those thin little curtains. *Linda.* Linda could at least say, on her deathbed, that she had had a rich life. Her mother had grown up in England and seen America before God had swelled across the globe. At least her ma had stood up for something. Now the Islanders were free to do what they wanted, and they did very little.

Eliza had come all the way round to the school-house; she must have been walking for hours, now, to get from the Eastern Bay to the north tip of the Island. The school-house was empty and a little eerie without the sounds of children. Too cold to carry on, Eliza walked up the hill and along Blackett Place and stopped, seeing Margaret Mal-raux's house.

The blinds in the parlour were closed flat. No slats of light came from within. Poor Margaret, with no Jack to help her with the boy, and Nathaniel such a terror. He was only bored; Eliza knew that, knew that the Island was as much a noose for him as it was for her; knew that he did not necessarily want to frighten, but only to break up the endless grey days. Eliza moved on, but stopped in her tracks.

She remembered, suddenly, the scent of his cigarette, the one he was smoking at Mrs Page's funeral. And the idea came to her with no effort, or forethought, but suddenly it was quite clear what she should do. If Nathaniel got those cigarettes, somehow from the Boatman, perhaps he could . . . Eliza rapped the door. Slow footsteps approached.

Margaret poked her head out from within. 'Oh, dear. I thought you were Mrs Kilman.' She opened the door wider and pulled the shawl closer to her neck. Margaret's blue eyes were sunk but sharp. 'How pleased I am it's you.'

'Hiya, Mrs Malraux.'

'It's been too long, eh?'

'Aye. Sorry about that.'

'Not at all. Not to worry. You look well.'

'As do you.'

'You lie.' Margaret cocked her head toward the living room. 'In with you, now, for a cup of tea, before I catch my death.'

It was just as Eliza had remembered: the brown-dia-monded carpet, the yellowy walls, the telephone on the trestle, the stairs curving to the first floor. In the living room, there were little ornaments all over the place, stacks of magazines and a radio. The cushions of Margaret's arm-chair dipped with the phantom weight. 'Eliza, dear, I hope you don't think I'm rude, can you bear to make the tea? My leg is sore and I can't stand on it.' Margaret dropped her-self into the chair with a sigh. Her breath came out rattled.

'Of course.'

In the kitchen there were tea stains on the counter-tops and rusty lids on tin cans and a smell of grease from the cooker. Crumbs gathered about a toaster, which was prob-ably as old as Eliza. Limescale flecked the kettle's insides and Eliza washed it out at the sink and put it to the boil. Everything – the floor, the spoons, the glassed cupboard fronts – had a slight tackiness to it, as if something sweet had spilled, and no one had bothered to mop it up. Eliza made the tea, giving the kitchen a bit of a clean as she went.

She brought Margaret her tea and took her own mug to the armchair opposite. She wondered if this was where Nathaniel sat. 'How are you, dear? Are you well? You look peaky,' Margaret said, steam curling around her nose.

'Fine. A little worn-out.'

'Aye. Work does that to you. How are you coping?'

'All right. It's hard sometimes.'

'Of course. Well, we all have to work. Until you get to my age, I suppose.'

'What did you do? When you were younger?'

'I worked at the herring station, but not for long. Jack

brought in more than enough, so I stopped that, as soon as I could.' Margaret looked down at her lap. 'My hands are still a little yellow from it, you know.' She tittered and then said again, 'And Jack brought in more than enough.'

'Of course,' said Eliza, 'of course.'

On the mantelpiece was a bell Eliza bet had been stolen from the church. Surely Nathaniel would be home soon. Margaret lit a cigarette and Eliza pretended not to notice. 'How's Nathaniel?' she said.

'Keeping out of trouble. Just. Do you know anything about this gang?'

It was then that Eliza fully understood what she was to do, otherwise she would have sat there and said yes, I know about this gang, she would have said that they had crabbed her on Monday night. She would have said: your son is a good-for-nothing, Mrs Malraux, and you should intervene before these larks turn into something terrible. But to say that would not help herself whatsoever, in what she had suddenly come here to do, and so, without hesitation, Eliza said, quite boldly: 'No. What gang?'

Margaret sighed. 'Mrs Kilman was in here yesterday telling me tales of this gang, that Nathaniel is the ringleader, and is leading them all into trouble. I said he's an Island lad, he's bored; he gets up to mischief. They shouldn't be so hard on him. They don't know what it's like. She doesn't even have any kids, so how would Caro know how they're meant to behave? And on this Island, of all places. They're bored, these boys, just a wee bit bored, and causing mischief.'

'Aye, of course. Of course. It's probably just games. It will pass, I'm sure. A phase, merely.' The tea was steaming in her hands and though Eliza had been cold all day, traipsing along countless roads in search for the lost girl, she was now intolerably hot. Perhaps this is what pushed Nathaniel to crabbing people, this great swell of heat. She removed her coat. 'And he's not mentioned anything? Of anyone?'

'No, should he have?'

'No, not at all, not at all,' said Eliza. 'But you know Nathaniel, always knows the most about Island gossip!'

'Aye, aye, I suppose,' said Margaret.

'Where is he now? Nathaniel. Is he around?'

'No,' Margaret said, her eyes drifting back to the telly. 'But he'll be back soon. He promised me that.'

Eliza ventured: 'I grew up here. It was hard. There's not so many children of your own age. Not many things to do. He'll turn out fine.' She was surprised at the finesse of the lie. 'He's just got extra energy and he doesn't know what to do with it.'

'Aye. That's exactly it.'

'Boys have so much energy,' Eliza continued blandly. 'If it's not girls then it's just some other trouble.' Margaret's eyes were now fixed on the set. It might be easier to do it like this, to catch her off-guard. 'These cigarettes, though, do you know where he gets them from?'

Margaret stared down at the one lit in her hand. There was something almost merry about the way she said it: 'Will you not tell anyone?'

'I shan't tell a soul.'

'He swaps them with the Boatman, for my pills. Oh, it is a naughty affair, but one that won't harm anyone, aye.'

'And what pills are they, now, Mrs Malraux?'

'Sedatives. They just make you sleepy, and so you can't

think about things. I get them at the doctors in Warkworth. But a cigarette's better, doesn't make you so tired after.'

Eliza laughed; so, it was as she had assumed. 'Very entrepreneurial of him. Very.'

'Aye. I know. A very entrepreneurial boy. He's a good lad.'

Margaret put out the cigarette and raised the volume of the television. She began to nod off. If Eliza did not do something this would be her, in forty years' time, dozing off, next to the fire, unable to hold or finish a conversation. Margaret would sit here like this, for thirty more years, this human engine covered in fat. Eliza did not want to grow old and alone on this Island. She could not allow it. If Nathaniel had this connection to the Boatman just as Margaret had said, then Eliza would try and use it as best she could. She allowed herself to begin hoping.

Margaret woke with a start, and smiled at her, flicking over a channel. Her jaw she cupped again in her palm. The television babbled. Eliza stood and went into the kitchen. Water spilled over her fingers as she rinsed the cup. Then a door slammed, out front, and then the inner door. The boy. Nathaniel. Eliza felt the cold air brought with him as he came into the warmth of the living room. Eliza's heart started to race. She would have to insist on his secrecy. But what if he told his gang? What if they came after her down one long and dark Island alley, for being a traitor?

'Nathaniel!' Margaret said.

'Hiya, Mam.'

'Did you see Mr Verger?'

'Aye.' Plainly a lie, Eliza thought, from the sound of his voice.

'And you gave him back his book?'

'Aye. That I did, Mammy M. He was right pleased with me.'

Eliza looked in on the room from the space between door and frame. The boy was pink about the chops and his blue eyes were dancing. He was in all that get-up again. He caught her spying; she blushed, and came back into the living room. The boy's eyes slid over her breasts and down her trousered legs. Nathaniel almost managed a blush himself. 'Why, hello, Miss Michalka, I didn't know you were here.' His mother's hands were in his. 'To what do we owe this pleasure?'

Eliza gathered her coat and fiddled with the collar. 'I was passing. You reminded me, on Monday night, that I hadn't seen your ma in a long time. I thought I would pop in.'

Without missing a beat the boy replied: 'Very kind of you.'

'Aye,' said Margaret. 'We had tea. Did I doze off now?'

'Aye. But I was beginning to as well. It's very warm in here.'

'Oh. I don't feel it. My feet are always cold.' Margaret wiggled her stockinged feet in the airless room. 'The toes are near purple in the winter. That's why I have the fire on. Because I don't feel it. The warmth.'

'Well, I think it's best I'm off now,' Eliza said.

'I'll see you out,' he said.

'Good afternoon, Mrs Malraux,' Eliza put out her hand and held Margaret's fingers, and they were indeed cold, just as she said. 'You keep well,' she said to her, although by now Eliza realized this might be the last time she would ever see her.

'Aye. Goodbye, duckie.'

Eliza squeezed her hand. Linda used to call her that.

Nathaniel's step was close to hers as they walked into the hall. 'You know you're welcome any time, any time, now.' He helped her on with her coat. 'Though best when my ma's asleep,' and he gave her a squeeze of both shoulders. He glanced up toward the second floor. 'Or I could visit you at the Grand? At your invitation, of course,' he laughed. 'I'm not a boy to pay for these wares.'

'Right.' Eliza smiled tightly. 'Can I have a word with you? Outside?'

Nathaniel opened the door and waved her on.

A cold skiff rose from the Sound but it was a welcome blast. Someone had gritted Margaret's pavement in the hope that she might ever move outside. There was no one on the road but still Eliza lowered her voice, and she came a little closer to him. 'Look, Nathaniel, your ma told me how you get these cigs.'

'And?'

'Well. What I'm saying is this.' Eliza cleared her throat and did not quite know where to start. It was imperative that he would agree and fundamental, therefore, that she said it in the right words. 'You exchange those pills for cigarettes, am I correct in thinking this?'

'Yes.' The boy surveyed the road. 'But it wouldn't be to your advantage to start spreading that, ken?'

'No. I realize that.'

'You didn't say nothing to my ma?'

'Nothing. Only what your ma told me. She knows you're using her pills, but that's it.'

'Aye. And she's a good woman who deserves a few good things. A few cigarettes will harm no man.'

'Aye. Aye. Right.' Eliza dipped her head toward him. Her heart felt fair near her throat but all she thought was: *I cannot end up like Margaret Malraux! Nor like my own mam!* 'But what I'm saying is this, Nathaniel. If you get these pills on the boat, then maybe you can get me on it too? Can you have a word with the Boatie? Get me on Monday's boat, sweet man.'

The boy's expression switched rapidly from astonishment to anger: he seemed affronted, as if she had insulted him. 'I am not in the business of getting people off the Island.' His voice was stiff. 'This Island is a place of beauty. Plenty! You have more than enough here.'

'I need to leave. I want to leave. I need to leave before I go mad here.'

'You'd be leaving us; me.'

'I know. I know.'

'Why? Why go?'

'Because I want to go somewhere that isn't here.'

The muscles in his jaw moved. 'Why?' he said at last. 'This freedom's a hard thing to ape. You won't get that in England. The land of God and Fury.'

Eliza thought of Margaret Malraux dozing near the fireplace. She thought of Mrs Page's coffin sliding into the waves. She thought of Arthur's face, and Mrs Bingley's, when they saw who was walking into the fishmonger's. 'Because I am unhappy here,' she said, looking squarely at the houses opposite. 'Because I don't have any friends, and I'm lonely. Because I'd like to see some place that isn't here, and talk to people not from here.'

'If you're lonely, doll, I'm here.' He hooked a thumb on the belt of her coat, pulling her closer. He smelled of soap and cigarettes; she saw his face, round and lovely: a thug and a beauty both.

Eliza disentangled herself. 'No,' she said, quietly, 'I need more.'

'And England? *England?* You want to go there? Why?'

Eliza shrugged. 'Because there's nowhere else to go, of course. I just want to get out of here.'

'Not this week. I've got a lot on my mind, doll.'

'But then the fogs will come. There's no other boat till spring. I can't wait that long. I'm scared of what I might do.' Eliza put her hand on his jacketed arm, stroked up and down a bit. 'I'm desperate, Nathaniel, you've got to help me.'

The boy sucked the air between his teeth. He warmed his fingers on his breath and then stuck them in his pockets. They did not speak for a while, then he said, 'It will cost you. I shan't do this for free.' He narrowed his eyes, calculating. He cleared his throat. 'If I get you passage on that boat, I want fifty pounds. At least.'

'Pony!'

The boy licked his lips. 'How much do you have?'

'Forty. And that's what's left of my ma's money.'

'Well,' he smiled, 'I'm sure you'll enjoy your winter to come.' The boy made a little bow and made to go inside.

'Forty-five! That's all I can offer. The Grand is quiet. I don't even know how I can make that. Only a few punters come any more. But I can try.'

'Then try you must. If it's there, the full fifty, you've got a place on Monday's boat. I can guarantee it. If not, get used to it; you won't be leaving. At least, not till next spring.' At this, he smacked a large wet kiss full on her lips. 'Won't charge me for that, will you?' And then he turned his back on her and shut the door, right in her face.

17. Jakob Lawrence

The summer of '86 had been warm. Jake and Nathaniel had spent each day building sandcastles and swimming in the sea. For the whole warm week they didn't stop larking about on the beaches, as if the summer had untied them from the imperative of being men, and the creamy wash of the Sound was lovely on their skin. They knew they were acting too young for their age but they enjoyed it even more because no one was there to observe and criticize. They weren't the Malades, then, and Nath wasn't the chief; and they didn't have the costumes, nor the cigarettes, nor the scalped pates. And in the sky the Northern sun was like a burst yolk. It was a very happy week and Nathaniel treated Jake with so much care.

One day, it was the best day really, Jake and Nathaniel were fishing with stick and bent pin and raw limpets at the bay. The rock pools that summer were busy with buttercrab and stickles and the most enormous amount of seaweed. When the boys failed to catch anything they started making castles, swiftly kicking them over, sending the sand exploding into the scorching air. They bronzed all afternoon. Heat was everywhere. By the end of the day they were pink.

As night fell late, they left the beach, with their towels slung over a shoulder, wearing knitted jumpers against the cool, heading over to the Malraux house. Warming up by the fire and licking their lips of salt, Mrs Malraux fed them margarine sandwiches and cups of tea with a topskin of milk. She fussed about so much Jake thought she was lovely and was allowed to call her *Mammy M*. And then she brought out some ginger nuts she'd been saving just for wee Jake and Nathaniel on a day such as this.

In summer, darkness came at midnight.

They were like brothers, that night, Jake and Nathaniel, and Mrs Malraux fussed over them as if they were both her sons. And Jake talked to old Mammy M, and told her how he was doing at school, and she said what a grand pair of boys they both were. It wasn't half as good as Jake's house, what with there being no rollmops, but being around Mammy Malraux herself more than made up for this.

But after that summer, Nathaniel changed. He started acting queer, visiting the museum a lot. At the start of school, in September, he brought Jake up to the nook on the west side of Marley Hill, pointing with his finger at the space he thought his da's boat kept under the waves. They came back again and again after school, to this place, Nathaniel talking of his da's death as if the English had murdered him with that boat.

Nathaniel harked on and on about how his ma was forced here, and made Mammy M tell the boys over and over how her family had been served with their deportation papers – as if she was any different from anyone else! Nathaniel started to talk about English spies, a network of them, operating on the Island at a buzzing frequency you couldn't quite hear. It scared Jake, the pictures he'd drawn, of English boats coming over and planes passing and dropping bombs. Nathaniel called it a crusade. He said it would happen if they didn't act soon. And so they had formed the gang one night after school, the Malades, for the protection of the Island.

The garage was very dark, that September night, when they first did it. Half-filled jars lined the shelves with nails and stops and hooks and hundreds of other things Jake didn't know the names of. There were smells of turpentine and solvents. This was a place indeed for a man like Jack Malraux.

Jake did Nath's scalp first. They spread out newspaper under their boots, and watched the shorn float down, big tufts of it, until Nath's scalp was completely bald. 'We'll get rid of them now, Jake. Any Englisher or spy on this Island. My da's memory deserves it, aye.' Nath then started off around the curve of his ear, and Jake laughed because it tickled with those trailing fingers and the buzz of the razor. He wriggled like a fish but Nathaniel didn't mind. He supposed Nath was the first Malade, officially.

When they came out of the garage Mammy M gave them what for and they stood there guffawing as she gave them slaps over their scalps for being so daft. But really she had no true idea of what being a Malade was about. Neither, it seemed, at times, did her son.

Nathaniel was nowhere to be seen tonight. Old Baldie Boots had cancelled the meeting, showing up at Jake's house this morning, saying he was poorly. He was probably at home, agog with Verger's book. It should be Verger for tonight, and Nathaniel knew it. It was just like Nathaniel to deem who was and who wasn't a spy, given some crazy rubric only he knew how to read. It wasn't fair. That was probably why he'd bottled it tonight, scared that Jake would choose Verger as the next target, and Nathaniel wouldn't have the balls to disagree with him in front of the lads. Well, he would see about that.

Jake squatted among the rocks, in the shadow of Warkworth pier, where the wind couldn't get such a lick on him. He watched Sammy ahead of him, skipping pebbles, and he watched Sammy's jacket, making sure the sea didn't get to it. Jake thought himself a kind boy, one who would do this type of thing for his friends. Sammy walked up toward the rocks and sat down beside Jake, closer than he would have thought necessary, since there was so much length to the beach.

'I have something to tell you, Jake.'

'Oh, aye?'

'Something important,' he said. 'D'you have a cig?'

'You know only Nath has those.' The boy sighed and looked uncomfortable, biting his lip and worrying at his shoelace. 'Out with it, then.'

'I saw something.'

'What?'

'I saw Nathaniel with someone, this morning. A girl.'

'From school?' Jake's heart began to race. 'Was it Charlotte?'

'No. That's the thing. She wasn't from school.'

'Eliza, then?'

'No. No. Not Eliza.' Jake's relief was palpable. 'You don't understand,' Sammy said, digging at a furrow of sand, 'I've never seen her before. Never in my life.'

'Oh, aye, and how can that be?'

'Dunno,' Sammy said. 'But I swear to you she's a stranger to me. But not to Nathaniel.'

'Go on, then.'

'They were walking along the bay, the rough one down at the eastern end. Calm as anything. I thought I could smell a bloom, and I wanted to have a looky. That's when I saw her – the girl, and Nathaniel, walking along the beach. I can't fathom where she's from. A grozzly girl like this, and I mean a real grozzly: she's a cherry! And there she was, larking about the bay with Nathaniel, and she was laughing all the time, and he was looking dead syrupy for her.'

'Who is she?'

'No idea, as I've said.'

'And then what happened?'

'So I followed them. At a distance, like, so they wouldn't crab me. And I followed her, and her lovely carroty hair, all the way to one of those houses, the empty ones near the eastern cliff.'

'Aye, aye. The row of them?'

'Aye. Called Swanscott House.'

'So where d'you think she's from?'

'She's not from here, that's for sure. I've never seen her at school. Nor down at the square nor down at Lynemouth. And no new boat has come with another family, has it?'

'No.' Jake scratched his scalp. He smelled onions on himself from dinner. 'I don't know. Perhaps a new family's come, maybe, in time for school starting again next week?'

'Nah! We would have heard of it.'

'P'raps she was on Monday's boat, come over from Newcastle!' Sammy's eyes were wild. 'An English spy! A missionary come over the waters to turn us Malades back!'

Jake laughed. 'Do you think so? And how would she have got on Monday's boat, then, clever clogs?'

'I don't know. Maybe she bribed the boatman, or sneaked herself into the hold. Whatever. All I know is she's not from here.' Sammy leaned closer toward him. 'And she's a cherry, or did I tell you that already?'

'Yes, Sammy, a "grozzly", as you said. What happened after that, after they got to the house?'

'I hid behind the hedge for a while. Maybe an hour or so, just watching them, like.' He coughed. 'Nothing much happened; they were just chatting, at the old chin-wag, like old friends, though he's never mentioned her before. So, you see, I don't know what his game is. She's a secret, if he hasn't mentioned her, and that makes me think, what if she is? What if she is truly English? Or what if she were a stowaway, even, forbidden cargo on Monday's boat? I wonder what we might do to smoke Christ out of her! I didn't know whether I should say anything, like, seeing as Nathaniel's the chief.'

'Nathaniel's not the chief. That's never been established.'

Sammy stood up suddenly. His bald head bobbed in the dark and his eyes looked the same inky colour as the sea. 'Let's see her now! Bet she'd like a bit of Malade, wouldn't she? Bet she's bored of English boys! Bet she's come to the Island for a sort-out! Couldn't find any slug' – at this he grasped his crotch – 'and wanted some of ours. I'd give the carrot some of what she wants, sure I would.'

He began to sing, crooning to the Sound, wheeling round and round.

> *Oh lovely, my peacheroo,*
> *Open up, see what I can do;*
> *Miss Carrot, open up the leafies,*
> *And let my Slug through.*

'Oh,' Sammy shouted to the brilliant dark, 'she is all ginger-fizzed loveliness!'

'Aye, aye,' said Jake, laughing.

'Shall we go and have a looky? Then we can tell the boys about it tonight. It's a Friday night – it *should* be a night for the scrap, just as Nathaniel promised. Just because he's getting syrupy with the girl doesn't mean we have to stay mooning about at the beach. Who knows? Maybe we can even have a bite of the crab ourselves.'

'Where's Nicholas?'

'Tucker? Don't know.'

'Is there anyone else we can take with us? In case we need, you know . . . ' Jake searched for the word. 'Reinforcement.'

'They've all stopped in with their mams.'

'Lazy biters. Well. The spoils will just be for us two, then.'

Swanscott House was white in the November dark, like a bone in soil. It rose thinly from the brambles and high grass; a fence hung broken from the hinge. Aside from the waves breaking at the eastern beach the road was quiet. Jake hadn't said anything since they'd left Warkworth Beach. He wondered what it meant if Nathaniel kept a secret like this.

Surely she should be interrogated, and yet here she was, supposedly coddled by the leader of their gang.

Sammy and Jake stood behind the hedge, watching and waiting.

After some minutes, Nathaniel appeared overhead. It was a shock, to see him in this room, though they'd known he might be there. He stood at the window with his hands on the leading looking out. Jake and Sammy giggled, knowing they were both thinking what it would be like to crab him as a spy. Jake wondered if he might find a rock here, and throw it at the window; wondered whether he could clip the cheek of Old Baldie Boots, as he had done Mrs Richards. He could have him for consorting with an Englisher. He only wanted to give the boy a bit of a fright.

Through the leaves, Jake saw the girl appear, rust-coloured about the hair, and freckled, as Sammy had said. He'd never seen her before, at school, nor down at Maiden's Square, and she was too young to be working the taverns or brothels of Lynemouth Town. Aye, he would have clocked a girl such as this. Sammy whispered: 'That's her.'

'I've never seen her before in my life.'

'Nor me.'

Jake's voice was full of longing. His breath clouded as he spoke. 'Oh, she is a cherry!'

'Is she not just?'

Nathaniel and the girl went away from the window; who knew to what long bed they might have descended? To what deep and lovely nest? There was something different about the boy, something darker about the skull. His scalp could do with a razing, that was for sure. The light snapped off though they had not left the room. The boy, in there, with the secret girl, with the light off? It only seemed to confirm that something wrong was going on, that she was a secret to be kept to the shadows. 'And you definitely think she was on Monday's boat?' Jake said. 'Did anyone see her coming off it?'

'No. No one *saw* her come off it – but it doesn't mean she didn't.'

'Aye, I suppose.'

'What's the alternative explanation?' Sammy was whispering and talking fast. 'Why, I know all the doxies on the Island. Stowaway or not, she came off Monday's boat, I'm sure of it. Lest she were washed up to sea in a shipwreck, I don't know. But I've never seen her before on this whole solly Island. I swear it.'

Sammy suggested that they confront him but Jake shook his head, and waved him on down the road. He said that they would ask him about the girl tomorrow at the postponed meeting. 'To crab him better,' he said, 'and in front of the gang.' It was a sorry business, not to be involved in your gang's affairs, and Jake and Sammy left the house with a hump of displeasure.

But Jake's face broke into a smile as he contemplated what they might do next. 'Now we know where he is, he won't know where we are.' Sammy asked what this meant, but Jake didn't answer. Instead they ran over Marley Hill and trotted down westward, where the Norwegian sea was like a big black bowl before them, and where the schoolhouse was silent, waiting for the boys' return on Monday, before they swung into Blackett Place.

*

Mrs Malraux's house looked as empty as Swanscott House. Jake told Sammy to stay outside, and that if he saw Nathaniel coming he was to come in immediately and start talking to Mrs Malraux in a very loud voice, and then Jake would walk into the living room as if he'd just come from the toilet. Mrs Malraux wouldn't know what had happened.

The door gave without a noise. The vestibule smelled of old lino. Jake pushed aside the next door, with the swirls of glass that magnified some bits of the stairs and shrank other bits, then shut it back to. A sound of light snoring came from the living room. Slow and steady under the thick bosom. Jake poked his head round the pane; there Mammy was, and, he'd guessed rightly, completely asleep. He checked the clock above the gas-fire. Nine thirty.

Jake came back to the hall, unsure of what he was doing here. Old Baldie Boots would kill him if he found him here. The peg on the wall waited for Nathaniel's jacket. He'd never been here when that peg held nothing.

Jake took the stairs. Nathaniel's room was quiet and cold. He crept quickly to the chest and opened the lid, rifling through the clothes until he hit the hard boards of the book. Jake had felt sick when he'd first seen these paintings of Christ. To be so *coddled*, he thought, with blurry distaste, to be so *watched*, was as abhorrent to him as his rare imaginings of what went on in England, with its damp and girlish God, and its feeble, pandering folk. Aye, the book only confirmed to Jake how much he loved the Island, with its electric air and dark seas and lightless winters, how little he wanted to do with the old faith.

Immunity? For Verger? Bollocks to that, aye.

Jake shoved the book in his bag and closed the lid of the chest.

Mammy's snores continued from the living room. Jake went cautiously downward. How long had he been here? Five minutes? Fifteen? In the living room, Mammy slept and the clock's long hand had hardly moved. He readied himself to leave, but he'd had so little time to luxuriate in Nathaniel's house alone.

The slat of darkness from underneath Mammy M's room was inviting. He'd never been in there. If Baldie Boots found him, he'd have his guts. He'd kill him. He'd tell everyone he was an English spy, and the boys would be at his throat before he might have a chance to defend himself. But it was there, the room: dark, cosy, inviting.

A sweet smell met him, on entering her bedroom, similar to his own mam's room. Moonlight, cut by the windowpanes, fell on the bedspread. The wadding of the duvet was lumpy, you could tell it was old. Could tell it might have seen a rollicking, all those years ago when Pappy Malraux was about. 'Jack Malraux,' the boy said, and then again: 'Jack,' to the moonlit bedroom, exultant in his sense of ownership in the dead man's room. There was a photograph of Nath's da on the dressing table with some old bottles of perfume and other pictures of Nath acting cutesy, twirling round with his da's ears when he was a baba. Mr Malraux looked a nice man, with that smile, and the fisherman's hands gripping tightly the ankles of his wee boy. And here he was, in Mr Malraux's space. The thought thrilled him in his body: to be like Nathaniel's da, master of the bedroom, and the sea, and his son.

Jake opened the vanity-table drawers. There were folded jumpers and blouses, all pastelly colours of wintry thickness, some looking bobbled and stained. No matter what they said or did, they couldn't get their mothers to dress better. Despite the suits their sons wore with such aplomb, the mothers seemed not to notice, and wore whatever drab thing came to hand, or whatever old English thing they might buy at Buttons.

More blouses yet in the second drawer, but this time he plunged his hands right in, hoping he might catch on to something secret. His hand touched a silky thing and something wiry. It was a beige brassiere; he wished it were black. He could put that in his pocket and use it for something, but he couldn't think what, so he let it go, shut the drawer and opened the third. Yellowing letters and old bills. Mammy M's original identity papers. On a darker paper, in a bold neat print, was the word NON-AFFILIATED; the word that had led them all here. It looked like it was written an age ago. Jake tossed it back to the pile.

He put his hand right down to the bottom, felt the cardboard edge and then there was something else, completely unexpected and cold in his grip. After all of the silks and slips, it felt hard and definite, very foreign to ladies' underthings. Jake turned it over in his hand, then put it to his nose to smell. Peppery, almost, and cold against his cheek. It was squat, littler than he would have thought. Mammy Malraux's handgun, smuggled here over thirty-six years ago; the one she had wanted to use against the English policeman. He might shoot her just to never hear that story again.

The front door banged. Jake stood frozen, with the gun

in his hand and the drawer wide open. Nathaniel's voice in the hallway shouted, 'Mammy!'

Sounds of disrobing. Jake pictured the peg where Nathaniel would hang the jacket. The shout again, *Mammy!*, a little more panicked this time, and then Mrs Malraux saying, *Aye, through here.* A light snapped on in the hall, and then there was talking.

Jake put the gun in the bag, with Verger's book. Crab-like, he edged out of the room, his back sliding along the walls, the diamonded carpet now a mess near his boots. The door was half-open and he saw through to the kitchen: Nathaniel, his back turned, the tensed cotton of his shirt and the 'Y' of the red braces. Jake's heart felt fair near his throat and sweat seemed to spill from him. He moved along the wall not taking his eyes off the boy. He found the gold handle of the inner door.

The outer door closed with no more than a clicking sound. Outside, Sammy was crouched behind the wall, looking sick with nerves. Motioning to him urgently, Sammy ran down Blackett Place, and Jake followed as quietly as he could, not saying a word, knowing how close they had come to the boy's full fury, until they were at Marley Hill. They stopped for breath. Sammy explained something about freezing in fright and being unable to speak the lie he had meant to say, but Jake didn't care. He was too relieved to care.

They went down Marley Hill quickly, their hearts keeping time with their boots. At Warkworth Bay, their lungs felt as if they were bleeding, they had run so fast. And at the cold sand, the air was like iced wedges and the sea was a long black lump with the pebbles grinding the night.

Realizing how close they had both come, Sammy and Jake laughed and laughed as the broad white birds wheeled in the sky.

And then, into the big open night, Jake fired the gun and the bullet went whizzing and his wrist flexed at the power of it and they did not hear the bullet come back down but they laughed and laughed and wiped clean from their minds the sight of Nathaniel and the English girl. They were high on everything they had seen, but more than that, the boys were high on having escaped.

18. A Bath

'Say that again, Mammy?' he said, shouting over to her from the kitchen. Nathaniel wolfed down the marge sandwich in not much more than three bites.

'I said I heard something, in the house.'

'And what was that, Mammy?'

'Something, I don't know.'

Nathaniel wandered into the living room. 'No, no, now, I told you, it was me. In the garage. I'm fixing up Da's garage, remember? Remember I came back this afternoon? After Eliza was here?'

'Aye, aye.'

'And then I went to the garage to do some work. I said I'd be there the whole evening, like, remember?'

'Aye. I forgot. I am daft. Sorry, love.' Margaret smiled, wearily, and switched off the television; it closed with a popping sound. 'It's best when you stay at home. You're a good lad, Nathaniel. Your da always liked being in that workshop. He said he liked the smell of it. It always smelled greasy to me.'

Nathaniel chewed at the next sandwich. Its yellow taste was bland, but he'd been nearly all day with Sarah, and was just about famished for anything. He didn't like to lie to his mam but he could hardly tell her the truth, pent up, as he had been all day, with an English girl.

'And did you get much done?'

'In way of what?'

'Whatever you were doing.'

'Much, much,' he said; and, in a way, he had.

Margaret looked around the living room, her eyes not stopping on anything in particular, then she started to nod along to some thought or other. 'And how about another fish, aye, for next week? Maybe after school Monday? A good feast after your first day back?'

'That would be grand, Mammy M, just grand. I think it's just ace you're back to cooking again. And then, soon enough, you'll be eating all the fish of the sea again. You'll see.'

'A bream? Or a sea bass?'

'Serious?'

'As the day.'

'Aye,' he said. 'A sea bass.'

'Good, well.' Margaret heaved herself up from the seat. 'I'm off to bed. You don't stay up too late. School's starting again on Monday. You don't want to be too tired. You're a good lad stopping in with me on a Friday night. I do appreciate it, son.' She kissed him goodnight.

Nathaniel sat by the fire as he heard his mam in the bathroom: the sound of the flush then the cranking of the taps. He wondered if she would wash her face. He was glad, finally, to be in the warmth. Sarah's house was such a block of ice. *Sarah's house*; those words were now familiar to him. That evening, after the strange little chat with Eliza, he'd brought Sarah over a marge and jam sandwich – it was all he could muster from the fridge – to talk to her, of Laura, and her home, and of England. Hours in, he'd noticed the lilac flush of her skin, and, holding her hand in his, he'd felt how cold she was. He'd smelled, too, a brackish waft from her; she had probably not washed since she had come from England. And so he'd brought her back home. Or had nearly brought her home; all that was stopping him was Mammy Malraux getting into bed.

Nathaniel went into Mammy's room, where the moonlight fell in oblongs on the quilt. He checked Mammy was not smoking in bed. He closed the drawers of the vanity table and then the curtains, so that the room turned dark. He sat with her until, minutes in, he heard the snores comb the air. A dreadful thought came to him, of Mrs Page, still in the casket, and Nathaniel left the room.

In the hall, he could smell everything intensely, as if he were a stranger here: the yellowy smell of nicotine was everywhere; on the wallpaper, on the carpeted stairs, in the mouthpiece of the telephone, in the fibres under his boots. What would Sarah think of his house? How could they go on living here? How could his mam never leave this house!

Nathaniel left with barely a sound, and jogged to the end of the road. 'Sorry,' he said, 'I was so long. Mam took a while to go to bed.'

'Can I not meet her?'

'No,' he laughed. 'Of course not.' He laughed, but this time gently. 'I told you that! I have a reputation to keep intact! Me! With an English girl? I don't think so. My ma might put a gun to your head if she knew you were English. Though I wouldn't let her. C'mon, now, come inside.'

They went a few paces and then she stopped. 'Nathaniel.' Sarah pressed his forearm. 'I didn't know whether I should say this. But I thought I saw someone. Running away. From your house, just after you walked in. I heard someone talking to someone else and then I heard footsteps running, but it was too dark to see. I couldn't see a thing.'

'I'm sure it was nothing,' he said.

'Sometimes I'm scared here,' she said. 'Sometimes I don't know what to think. I've seen your boys around. One with a bruise, he looked at me. Do they know I'm here?'

'No.'

'Should I be afraid? I don't know. I don't know how this Island works.'

'Sarah, Sarah. They don't know you're here. Only I know you're here. And if you see one, dressed like me, you don't look at them. Don't talk to them. Promise me you won't talk to them.'

'I won't, I've told you I won't. But I'm scared, sometimes.'

'No need, now; no need. You're with me now. And I'm the king of this isle, as I've said.'

Sarah did not look displeased with his home. At a theatrical creep, she followed him into the living room, where he set the gas-fire to full. She looked around the room, and then from the window into the garden. When she sat in his mam's chair she closed her eyes for a while. Odd: to see Sarah there, and not the constant form of Mammy. He let her rest as he made her up a sandwich. When he glanced over to her, she had closed her eyes, and was beginning to look better for the warmth.

'It's so nice,' she said, when he woke her with the jam roll. There had not been much left, even though he'd only had marge in both of his sandwiches. He'd ask his ma for some money for groceries tomorrow.

'Aye, too hot, normally. Most of the time I can't stand being here. Gets rid of my vigour. Holidays are the worst for that, when you're stuck inside, being gassed by the fire. Sometimes I think I'm going mad, sitting in here. Although you're sitting in my ma's chair.'

'She stays in here, all the time?'

'Aye,' he said. 'I can't get her out of the house. Not for nothing. Not for shopping, not for fish, nor for the plane.'

'The plane?'

He sat opposite her. 'Aye. It comes on the last Sunday of every month. Flying over from England. I think it might be some surveillance project, some way of spying on us. Others think it's off to Norway. Still, it's what people do; look at it, as it goes across the sky. It's a spectator's sport, to watch it fly across.'

'Oh,' she said, with her fingers pressing into the white loaf, and the red jam squeezing out just. She barely suppressed a laugh and giggled into the sandwich.

'An Island delight, aye, looking at the aeroplane,' and Nathaniel laughed at himself, at the silliness of it. 'We have such larks, here, you know. I'll be able to show it you in a couple of days. It's coming this Sunday.'

When he returned from the bathroom, Sarah was washing the plate, looking sort of dreamy as she watched the hot water and soap slip over her hands. The bath was running. 'I've put in extra bubbles,' he said.

Steam curled in the bathroom and the mirrors were already clouded. Nathaniel had laid out a towel and a flannel near the short green bath. He closed the curtains, though no one would be in the garden looking in. The bath was now nearly full.

'Here's your towel. And some shampoo. And a bar of soap. Sorry it's so cracked, like. I'm sure you're used to much better provisions in England.'

'Thank you.' Sarah looked around the room and he couldn't detect any signs of displeasure. Perhaps this wasn't so bad, compared to English standards. Her eyes darted one way, coy. 'Well?'

'What?'

'Are you going to leave?'

His face broke in two with his grin. 'Now what would my mam think if I was having a bath and not in the bathroom?'

'Your mam's asleep!'

'But if she were to check!'

'She's not going to check. She's asleep.'

'I'm sorry, Sarah. You either have a bath with me in the room, or no bath at all.'

'You're blackmailing me!'

'Aye. But I shan't look. Promise.'

Sarah sighed and he saw the red flush behind her freckles once again. Oh, what a cherry she was! How beautiful when angry! He wondered how far down the freckles went. He wondered if all English girls were like this, and, if they were, whether the Malades should really be crabbing them all for spies, or looking at them with somewhat more gentler intentions. 'Turn around, then,' she said.

The steam was thick and sweet and warm. Nathaniel looked at the wallpaper, starting to peel off, leaving a yellow underside. He traced the amber-coloured glue with a finger, wondering how on earth he could persuade Sarah to stay. Monday. Monday. Monday was far too soon.

Then he found the bit of mirror he was looking for so that he could watch her undetected. He caught her just as she dropped into the bathtub, managing to see a scrap of breast. Nearly – but not quite – a nipple. There was a suck of water and then the water went still. 'Can I turn around now?'

'Of course not! But you can sit there. On that stool. Facing the wall.'

Extra bubbles! Extra bubbles! What an idiot he was. What a chaste layer of foam covered her! In the mirror, all he could see was her head, with her ginger hair now tied in a topknot. A strand had escaped and curled on her neck like the fish-hooks you could see at Arthur's. She'd smell a whole lot sweeter now, though there had been something faintly thrilling about her before, and he had often, these past couple of days, day-dreamed of her taste as something like the seabed.

Sarah began to soap her arms and then scrubbed at her fingers with the nailbrush. She went at them hard and he worried about her skin going raw. As she leaned toward her toes, he saw her breast just coming out of the water, but he could hardly look, for fear he might jump into the bath with her. Her skin was pink with the heat; her eyes squeezed against the fog.

Then suddenly, like a seal plunging for food, she sank under the water. When she emerged her hair was glossy and black like a pelt. The water, which had heaved about her, now lapped gently the enamel sides. In her palm she poured the shampoo and then lathered it against her crown. Could he ask to soap the bubbles in her hair? To follow the line of her neck to the twin weights of her breasts? What a rollicky softness was rolling in his blood, what a terrible ache she provoked in him!

Sarah plunged into the hot again. She came up, all rinsed, and puppish again. Breathing the steam close to the waterline, she stayed like that for moments longer, then rose and said, 'Tell me about these boys.'

'The Malades?'

'Your gang.'

'What do you want to know about them?'

'Why are you frightened of them?'

'Frightened of them! Are you mad?'

'OK. Frightened of them for my sake.'

'You're the one that should be frightened. A gang like mine don't take nicely to English girls.'

Sarah stared straight ahead, her toe on one of the taps.

'Well. There's Jake. He's my second man. And then there's Sammy and Nicholas, he's a Freshcut.'

'A Freshcut?'

'Aye. He's the one you saw with the bruise. We made him a new member on Monday night.'

'And how did you do that?'

'Nicholas made some promises to us. He promised to always rid the Island of Gots. He promised to always report anyone he thought might be going back to English faith.'

'And how do you do that? Find someone who's gone back to faith?'

'Well, say if they're found with Church things, like a Bible, or scripture from the museum. Or say they coo at you, saying, "God bless," or you see them praying or rolling their eyes to heaven. Something like that. Then we'll go and investigate. Then we'll go and look for photographs or maps they've taken of the Island to send back to England.'

'And have you found people doing this? Drawing maps, taking photos?'

'We haven't found the maps, per se, or the photographs either, but that doesn't mean there aren't people here working for the English.'

'But if you haven't found any evidence, doesn't that mean they're innocent? I mean, they were deported because they were working for the Movement, I can't understand why they'd suddenly want to go back to the Church.'

'Because you don't know what loneliness can do to a man's heart. Your old English gentleman thinks he can do just fine without God and he goes round bombing the church in 1950 or '76. But the real test is not in England, but when they get here. They had to have a whole heap of courage when they drove up the church path to throw the petrol at the pews; but nothing like what you need to live here. This Island will make you meek and mild, if only for the promise that you may once in your life see somewhere that isn't here. Within days a Newcastle gent might give up his soul to God. And that's a fact. The Church knew something of loneliness, aye, how quickly it might draw us back to the homeland. That's why they sent us here. My boys, we're here to stop that.'

'And me? How do I fit into this?'

'You?' Nathaniel stared at the peeling wallpaper. 'You.' He couldn't see her at all but he could imagine her in his mind. 'I have to find some way of telling them that you're neither Got nor spy. That you came on Monday's boat as a stowaway and are looking for your ma. Jake will be the difficult one in this. He sees things in black and white. He can't understand the subtlety of being English and yet being no Got. That's why I don't want you to talk to him. He's thick as two planks sometimes but it doesn't mean he's not curious. And he has a nasty streak in him that I can't seem to temper. So you keep away, you hear?'

'Yes, sir! Don't worry. I can handle him myself.'

'No, you can't. And you don't even know that.'

He held the towel out in front of him to its full length.

'Close your eyes,' she said.

He heard the suck of the water again and then, as her back was turned, he saw the scissoring of her legs and a red foot the colour of blood. 'OK,' she said, 'I'm done.'

In his bedroom, Sarah wore a pair of his jeans and one of his shirts. From the look of her, you could tell she would be clean-smelling. If she wore his braces, she could almost be a Malade. He laughed to himself, imagining her with a bald shiny pate and bovver boots.

'I'm not taking any clothes off.'

'OK,' he said, 'neither will I.'

'Promise?'

He didn't say anything, and she gave him a dig in the

ribs. She sat, leaning against the bed. She brought out the photograph of the boat from her bag. 'I couldn't believe this when I saw it. My mum, just like that, staring up from this photo.'

'And you're sure?'

'It's her. She's here. I just know it.' Sarah looked up at him. 'This woman in the photograph. I'm going to ask tomorrow if she's Laura.'

'Do you want me to come with you? I might be able to help.'

'No,' she said. 'I want to do this alone.'

When they turned in for the night, they lay together like two chaste babies, and the heat radiated off her as if she were still in the tub.

'Sarah,' he said, quietly, 'I don't think you should go on Monday.'

'I have to,' she said. 'I can't stay. I came to find her. Then I've got to go back.'

'But Monday's too soon.'

'I know. But my dad's at home. Alone.'

They held each other tight as if, around the bed, there was the depthless Sound they could both so easily fall into.

19. Questions and Answers

The Island, then, was still fending off winter's fog. A heatless summer's day had arrived, the sky massive and blue, though the air was Novemberish and cold. White morning light pulled at the walls of the Malraux house.

Sarah's skin had lost the warm colours of last night. She was still asleep when Nathaniel brought her up a jam-sandwich breakfast, looking newly minted, fresh as a brass coin. 'Here, Sarah,' he said, squeezing a shoulder, 'I'm sorry it's not much, like.'

'I slept so well,' she said, blinking, and then devouring the sandwich as if she hadn't eaten anything in months.

When she rose she dressed again in his clothes. As she moved about the room the shadow on the wall matched hers, shape to shape. Light folded along the lines of the shirt. Nathaniel even put her in a pair of red braces. He clipped the metal mouth to the middle of her jeans and then brought the 'Y' shape up over her back and then brought them over her shoulders, his fingers quickly running over her breasts. He brought the metal mouth to bite at the waistband of her jeans. He did it twice, which made her laugh. She coloured warmly but smiled and held his fingers with her own.

'Now all you need is some boots. I could lend you some of mine but they're still too big for me, never mind a doxy like you.'

Lolling on the bed, he watched her put together the last of the outfit. Lit by the winter sun, he saw the velvety hairs on her cheek. All night he'd cradled that body, as if she were some ship's treasure washed up on the shale. He felt somehow special, as if he had been the one marked out to shepherd this girl in the ways of the Island. His da would have liked her. That was for sure. He'd introduce her to Mammy M, later in the winter, and they could reminisce about England.

'There,' she said, when she was done dressing: 'I look a fine Malade.' Then she did a funny bow, her hand wagtailing in the sheer light, her mouth easy, laughing still.

But he couldn't think of the Malades now. He didn't want them to botch this for him. And he stood and kissed her, with her laughing eyes still going in the daylight, but it was as if the boys were already prowling, down there in the garden, with rocks in their hands, waiting for her; as if their shadows, behind walls and hedges, had spilled over the Island's strong daylight like an ink, because she had merely said their name.

When they crept downstairs his mam called out to him and he said, 'Morning, Mam!' and then, silently giggling, they left the house to the Sound's winds, and Sarah remembered how cold the Island was, despite the sun. She should probably not have mentioned the boys. Nathaniel seemed to tense whenever they talked about them. This gang; she wondered if they were really a force to be reckoned with, or some band of bored boys with nothing to do.

On the steps was a grit someone had laid down, in readiness for snow. Light glinted off the drainpipes. 'You seem happy,' he said to her, as they set off.

'Aye,' she said. 'It's just. I'm ready to know.'

'About your mam?'

'Aye. Yes.' She smiled at herself. 'Do you think your mum heard us? Last night? This morning?'

'No,' he said, 'no.'

They began the walk up Blackett Place. Ahead, the road curved toward the square or up to Marley Hill. Over the way, there would be the woman's house, looking out, she knew now, over the Norwegian waters. 'Does it ever get warm here?' she asked. 'I can't imagine it.'

'Sometimes. For a few weeks. We had a hot summer, this year.'

At the end of the lane, he said: 'You know, I read somewhere that this road was occupied by crofters, before the deportees came. That they went to church every Sunday, and that Blackett Place was where the vicar used to live. Funny, to think of the people living here before us. And these people, too, with such a Churchly bent.'

He held her hand in his for a while.

Sarah thought of Nathaniel as a blessing, as if, several leagues from church, she suddenly understood what that word meant.

He dropped her at the foot of Marley Hill. Sarah wanted him to stay, so that she could see his reaction on viewing this woman, but he insisted he had to leave to the square, for 'some business needs sorting'. He said he would come back to Swanscott House that afternoon, and asked her to return there to meet him, later this afternoon, 'for your safety', he said to her, 'No one knows you're there.' And he walked away, down the long slope of road that led back to Warkworth Town.

Sarah stood at the hedge, alone, for half an hour or so, before the woman entered the kitchen. This woman who could be Laura. Sarah folded out the photograph, and the article from the cellar. She looked from one to the other. Moments passed; minutes went; Sarah kept attempting to go to the house but as soon as she took a step in the right direction her confidence fled her. Laura Wicks, who had been an adulterer for so much of her life, now, in a couple of weeks, transformed into a distinguished criminal. Sarah had longed for this moment for so many years, and now she couldn't work out what she would ask her. She wanted to know and yet not knowing was so much easier. Finally, she tucked the papers into her pocket and managed the long gravel path to the door.

The doorbell trilled. Then the sounds of footsteps came: measured; flat. The woman said something to the boy but Sarah couldn't make out the words behind the door. A chain rattled along the latch and the door opened so that the hem of the dress skimmed the porch and the woman's head poked out; like a bird with its ringed fingers around the door-frame. 'Yes?'

The red door narrowed. The boy appeared at her side, reaching a hand through her legs, bunching the cloth of her dress in a fist. His hands were still wet with soap. Sarah's mind emptied; what were the appropriate words to say? *Are you my mother? Am I your daughter? And is this, then, my brother?* The boy stuck the loose thumb of his other hand in his mouth and gave Sarah a sullen stare, stroking his nose with his finger. Some surge of disbelief threatened to send her back to the gates. 'Hello,' Sarah said, although to which one, she didn't know.

The woman scanned the garden from corner to corner and then craned her neck to see the hedge. 'What do you want?'

'I'm . . . looking for someone. Her name is Laura Wicks. Mrs Laura Wicks. She was deported here. In '77.'

The woman pushed the boy away from her; he squealed in protest. She guided him into the hallway, shoulder-ways, and shut the door behind her, so that the red door was flat again. Her hand came to rest gracefully on the knocker. Lilies; she smelled of lilies. 'Who're you?'

'Sarah. Sarah Wicks.'

'And who is that?'

'I'm her daughter.'

The woman took a big breath and her small chest puffed out. She was small-ribbed and sinewy, with very little skin or fat or muscle or anything between the air and her veins. Blonde and freckled, just like Laura, but there was something sharper about her, as if she had turned pointier in the cold. The woman strode past Sarah, down the gravel, to the gateposts. Suddenly she began to kick the hedge as if she were trying to beat out rodents from within it. 'Who're you with? Are you here alone?'

'Yes . . . of course. I'm not with anyone.'

'Don't lie to me, girl. I know you're with this gang.

What's your game? I don't know what you're doing, snooping around, but I don't like it. You stay away from this house. What are you up to? Hmm? Searching for English spies? Or just the faithful? I'm neither. Don't give me this lie of looking for someone.' The woman stood taller and said, rather defiantly: 'I shan't end up as another Mrs Richards,' then, narrowing her eyes, 'although I didn't know they had a girl in the gang.'

The woman marched past her, almost shoving her to the side as she regained the step.

'I'm looking for my ma, that's all, for Laura Wicks. She was deported here in '77. I came here to find her, to tell her—'

But it was obvious now that the woman wasn't even listening. 'Look, girl, I don't know who you are or what you want, but I want you to leave. For three days you've been out there watching me! Skulking behind the hedge, looking for the right time to come back, at night, is that it, to crab me? I have a son inside. What can I tell you? That I don't believe? That I am a woman of the Movement? I am all of these things. Do you not know how scared people have become of even leaving their own homes at dark? What a broken Island! What a place you've made this to live! The Island's a prison! There aren't any spies here, do you hear me? None are at this address. So leave me alone! In broad daylight, for goodness' sake!'

Sarah was at a loss about what to say. She kept her voice toneless and calm. 'I don't know what you're saying. I'm not involved in any gang. In fact, I'm English, as I've just said. I just wanted to know your name. Because I've been searching this Island for the past week, for this woman, my mother, and you . . . you look like her. Her name is Laura Wicks.' The woman's eyes looked out toward the sea and then returned to Sarah. 'Just tell me. Please. Look at this photograph. It's of the last deportation boat. Do you recognize the woman in the photograph?' The woman's lips bunched and then sagged. For a moment, you might believe she had softened, because something in her eyes seemed fluid and compassionate, almost as if she were about to weep. 'Or at least tell me your name.'

'My name is Beatrice Spenser,' she said, thinly, and then re-composed her features. 'I don't know what you're talking about. I don't know about Laura Wicks. Please leave me and my son alone. I can't help you.'

'Mrs Spenser?'

'Aye.'

Sarah put a foot on the step and the woman stared down at it as if suddenly outraged. 'I'm looking for an Englishwoman, who might—'

'There is no Englishwoman here. I am an Island woman now! And if you don't leave me alone, I shall go to the police – I will not be as silent as the others!' With her boot, Mrs Spenser kicked Sarah's foot off the step, and pulled the door shut.

The red door was flat again to the house-front.

And the woman waited, one arm across her belly, in the shaded kitchen, waiting for Sarah to leave. Sarah put the photograph back into her bag, and set off, as Nathaniel had told her, back to Swanscott House. Beyond the loss that this woman said she was not, in fact, Laura, Sarah was astonished: she had never, at any point, expected fury.

20. John Verger

John Verger had come over on the boat, like most of the others, in 1951. His had been low-level work for the Movement: scouting out weak clerical locations, passing on information between Movement members, advising on some of the more tactical legislation in the courts. But the police still had his number and he was duly escorted out of England with his dark papers and case. On the boat, he'd met Jack Malraux, and they had become firm friends, Jack working at the docks and then out at sea; Verger picking the quarry, quite a happy toiler at the rock. He had always enjoyed the difficulty of the work. In England he'd fancied himself as an intellectual; a radical objector; on the Island, he was surprised at his delight for the pick. He'd lost too many friends to the waters to think this a bad job.

How things had changed in these years. Verger had grown quiet when Jack had died, years ago. Jack Malraux had been his best friend on this Island; perhaps, his only friend. After Jack died, Verger carried on at the job but without much delight, and then he had stopped altogether.

Retiring had been hard. Days would pass so slowly. A wave might take a decade to break; night-time, a century. He tried to busy himself because he knew he was becoming bored, which was dangerous; that a man should not be without his labours. He hadn't brought a sweetheart from England and he hadn't met anyone on the Island either, despite Jack's best efforts. He hadn't minded so much, then; he hadn't felt much of a drive, for that. He seemed to miss, now, the presence of this woman: this imaginary wife with whom he might grow old, as if she had once existed, and had gone, as if she had left a clearance of ground which he now trod alone. Jack, too, was too absent.

In his retirement, Verger started walking the Island. He would begin at the Eastern Bay, to watch the waves rear and break on the skerries; then go down to Lynemouth Town, to watch the men in the pubs, and women slip into brothels, and children play on the roads, wondering which Islander might be expecting the next eternal salted bath – Morris Kilman, most likely, from all reports – and then he would go up to Maiden's Square to watch Arthur Stansky cut and quarter his fish; a man treasured, and adored.

Verger could not find on the Island the delight he had once, daily, experienced here. Perhaps, somewhat, he savoured this steady withdrawal, and though he knew it was bad for him, he did little to stop it. He walked with a sense of commitment to his nervous crisis, but still wondered when it would break. A weary curiosity came with him, on his walks, for his new-found depression, though it always finished, at night, in a much more serious case of bleakness.

Aye, nothing seemed as it had been. He longed for his job. He could not seem to lift his spirits.

It had been getting warmer – the ground no longer wintry and hard but damp and boggy – when he had seen the old church above Lynemouth Town and decided to pay it a visit. Perhaps he had not been here since early '51. The church was in a sorry state: the moss and lichen spreading, the beams stubbed and charred. Nearly roofless, nature had crept in, and, between the stones, the hill was visible, though there was neither clump nor clod of tree to see.

In the cool church John touched the stones, greened by the creeping plant. The moss was coarser than he had expected. He put one foot on an upturned pew, one on the skirting, pulling himself up to view the clouds: most of the sky was visible from here. A cross still rose at the steeple, it was wedged into the rock so deeply that had any man tried to pull it out, surely they would have met with failure. The iron cross had gone unburned. Wetted, now, by days of rain, the beads hung motionless from the bar. In the distance, the horizon sealed sea and sky together. And he noticed the letters INRI, at the centre of the bars, and he placed his fingers within the letters' troughs. *Iesus Nazarenus, Rex Iudaeorum; Jesus of Nazareth, King of the Jews*. He remembered that from school. He retracted his hand, though, as if the cross still burned from when Jack Malraux and John Verger set a match to this place, in the spring of 1951.

Abruptly, John felt his foot travel into the air where he had thought he would find stone. His hand scrabbled at the moss. His nail-beds filled with earth. His boot sought the pew again but this time it tipped, knocking him backward, so that he gashed his knee, and his head rushed with a sudden surge of blood.

The smell of the burned church was intense as if the

knock to his head had provoked a sudden sensitivity to the memory.

John sat himself on the cold ground. His breath came quickly; it sounded like a crab scuttling on pebbles. His knee was cut deeply and the pain started to thud in the joint. John's vision clouded. He felt himself sweating, despite the chill, and his fingertips burned. A great load of guilt rose in him. From somewhere, far off, he heard a bell, like the sacring bell he remembered from his school's chapel, which held him, stilled him, so that he did not think of his knee. Where could the sound be coming from? He looked toward the sky and the unmoving clouds. John thought of the little bell in the fishmonger's, and the bells of the police, and that bell of the church at home, in England, ringing in the body of Christ.

And then, on this day in May, in 1986, he heard the bell again, invisible yet ringing, pealing and rippling, and the epiphany was marvellous.

Verger did not feel in possession of himself. He felt very thirsty. The bell rang madly as if children played at the clapper. And a great, furious warmth rose up his face. Then his vision broke, in that he was able to see again, quite perfectly, and he sat there for a long time, searching for what wonder of bells he had heard.

How quickly time passed as he sat there. Jolts of pain from his knee bothered him only occasionally. Cloistered in the moss, Verger felt all the depression of that year lift off; he was impervious to the cold that night. There was a breadth of stars: their lights pulsed; the sea shone; everything seemed to tremble. Christ's presence was all around him. Verger felt touched by grace, and delivered.

John felt himself God's new servant, one who had been taught kindness, to himself above all things, in His roofless office. And, oh, it was a magnificent grace. The old man, now, felt enormously free; the guilt had fled him.

That week, he went to the museum to read scripture and prayers from the English newspaper. When he had conjured up enough courage, he stole the book of paintings from one of the museum's displays. There was an ecstatic thrill to the theft. But Christ, the man, up on that cross, knew something of the Sound, knew something of what it was like to endure the hardship of this Island – who was in some way the Island embodied. Verger wondered how the Islanders could not see that God suffered as they suffered – that He did not judge, nor censor, but loved, only, from afar. Nathaniel's blue eyes too, held in them this shock of love, as if his eyes too were made of the same stuff as Christ's eyes.

When he had given Nathaniel the book, the boy had resisted, and he had sulked. Finally, he had relented, though the boy was resisting still, saying he had lost it, but Verger would carry on schooling him, until he saw God's Message. It took one who believed in Him to be so angry with Him, Verger could see that, and he wouldn't allow Jack's boy to throw away his life as he had.

It seemed, to Verger, that he now understood a world he had never truly known before. It seemed he now knew this Island absolutely; as if he had uncovered the Island for its true, vast acreage, with the columned light of its long afternoons, pale breadths of sandy beaches, and this humane, rich muck under his step; this place where he would school Nathaniel into faith, then, at long last, he would lie down, and though his body would slip into the wash, his soul would be at rest here, in the earth, on the Island, at the church he had burned by the bay.

21. Stansky & Son

Nathaniel waited for him at the back of the monger's. The red chains, between the shop and the outside, swung lightly, bringing with them the smell of the sea. From here you could see the long slope of Marley Hill and its bald sides. You could see, too, the garage at the back of Forrester's, over the partition wall, and you could just see into the enamel-tiled room where Mrs Page had, on Tuesday, lain in state. Nathaniel remembered how Jake had compared dead Mrs Page to his mam, and how much he had fair hated him for it. The boy had such gall in him; such poison, to be saying things like that about a fine woman as Mammy Malraux.

He fancied a cigarette, but he wouldn't smoke out here, lest he should show any disrespect to Mr Stansky.

Nathaniel caught the reflection of himself in the windowed door: all throat and hairy scalp. His blue eyes looked as black as coals. What had happened in the past week, what a change had come over him! He'd barely had time, between waking and leaving, to dress properly. The eyelets of his boots sagged as if in disappointment. He pulled the laces fast, but he'd forgotten the handkerchiefs and the boots were far too big. He would have to spruce himself up before the scrap tonight.

The scrap. The thought failed to thrill him, but the boys would be down at the square, chumming about, playing Belly-up and Shark, waiting for him to come and have done. He hadn't heard a peep from the gang since they'd crabbed Mrs Richards. Their silence left him with a sense of disquiet. Surely one of them had seen her? Seen the brass flash of hair along the Island paths? No, no, no; this silence was troubling enough. And if they had seen her, why were they not talking of her to him?

Suddenly Nathaniel felt too old for this; these games; these boys.

Arthur chatted away genially to a customer and Nathaniel wondered when he would leave so he could come back to the pantry and talk to him of this girl! Sarah Wicks, soft in the bath. Oh, she was a rollicky sight! Coming out frothed from the tub! He wouldn't be able to stand seeing the blood ream from her mouth, maybe a tooth knocked loose, or a punched eye socket, all in the name of finding out if she was an English spy. He had to keep the boys away from her; at any cost, any cost whatsoever!

The talking came to an end and the monger's bell rang. Through the chains' big red links, Nathaniel saw someone leave; it might have been John Verger, or maybe Mr Tucker. Mr Stansky washed down a long knife, and replaced it at the magnetic strip, so that it joined the other knives, dove-grey and flashing in the clouded light. Mr Stansky's apron was spattered in so much blood and guts it must have a reek to it. Sucking on that apron would give a man protein enough for life; enough, even, for Morris Kilman to spring from his sickbed.

Still grubbing his hands against the pinny, Mr Stansky

came out the back and took a good lungful. 'Hello, our Nath,' Mr Stansky said, giving the boy a grin. Once again, Nathaniel felt that curling joy, as if he stood next to the emblem of all fishermen. Nathaniel liked to think that some briny lineage ran from Jack to Arthur to Nathaniel, though they were in no way related. He wondered how – professionally, like – he might get his hands on Arthur's knives. 'Hello, Mr Stansky, sir.'

'A fine morning.'

'Aye, that it is. Have you been down to the fish-boats today?'

'Oh no, that's Thursday for you.' Arthur put his hands under the pinny. 'That's when the catch comes in, on a Thursday.'

Nathaniel nodded, and mouthed the word 'Thursday' soundlessly, as if committing it to memory. 'It's a nice life, eh, running the fish shop?'

Arthur shrugged and looked down at the boots he wore for the monger's. 'It's harder than it looks.'

'What do you mean? You could have fish pudding every night of the week if that was your wont!'

Arthur did not say anything but stared off distantly in the direction of Marley Hill. Arthur's black hair parted perfectly at the centre; the quills were gelled hard. After some moments, the older man spoke. 'What can I do for you, lad? Is it Mammy Malraux? Are you needing a hand?'

'No, no. Mammy's fine. She even cooked your bream on Thursday.'

This brought a smile to the monger's face. 'And did she enjoy it?'

Nathaniel looked sheepish. 'Nah. She didn't eat a

mouthful. It's still too hard for her, she says. No reflection on you, mind. Nor your fish.'

Arthur picked some stray bit of gut or slop from off the apron. 'Well. You don't know how hard for her it's been; how hard. You must be understanding. Your mam's in fine fettle, you know, there's no need for her to eat the fish if she doesn't want to.' Arthur chuckled lightly, giving him an extra bit of chin as he looked down at the gutters. 'This fear of anaemia. It keeps me in business. Keeps my fingers skinning and gutting all day, you know, but it's nothing to worry about. You can survive without fish. It's just fear that keeps everyone coming back.' He leaned in toward Nathaniel. 'Though I'd like you not to spread that, ken?'

'Aye,' said Nathaniel, laughing. 'Your secret's safe with me.'

'So,' said the monger, still laughing into his bib, 'what can I do for you?'

Some moments passed as Nathaniel tried to get at the right words and tone. On such a delicate matter, he had to get it right. He put together the words in his head, rearranged them and then put them in a different order. Then he gave up, and said, quite simply: 'There's a girl.' And he felt like even on his scalp he was blushing.

'Oh, aye.'

'And she is a cherry.'

'Go on.'

'But she is not the right one for me. Not the right kind; not at all.'

'Not the right kind?'

'Aye. Not the right kind at all! I'll never be able to walk out with her, or share her with the boys. And I don't know what to do about it. I can't tell the lads about her; I can't even tell my mam. But, oh, she has me agog!'

'Is she from school?'

'Aye . . . sort of. But it's as if I didn't pay attention to her before. Like before this week, she didn't even exist; like I've only just noticed her. And I can't remember what it was like *not* to know her. And I can't remember what it is I'm meant to be bothered about with the lads. Ah, it's ruined me.' Nathaniel caught himself in the glass and saw again his scalp, now all fuzzed and dark. 'I'm half the man I was!'

'Ruined you? What are you talking about?'

'Aye. Ruined me. I'm in love.'

'And? Love's better than a whole month of summer.'

'The boys, they won't like her.'

'Who cares about the boys?'

'They're my lads, Mr Stansky. My gang!'

'No, no, no, Nathaniel. You've got it purely the wrong way round. They're your lads now, and you may think they're important, which they are, by all means, but this girl's got to go first. What's her name?'

Nathaniel coughed, looking a little strangled about the neck. 'I can't tell you. Just in case it comes out.'

'Being embarrassed of her, of what she is, of what she does, will only make things doubly – triply – worse.' Mr Stansky picked at some dirt underneath a nail. It was then that Nathaniel saw how tired he looked, how slumped about the shoulders. 'Trust me on that one.'

'She's going to leave me.'

'Leave you? How? She doesn't live with you, does she?'

'No, no, I don't mean that. Leave me; stop loving me. She might as well be across the waters in England by

Monday, for all she will remember me next week.' The boy slumped against the wall, his lips pouting his sorrow. 'You need to tell me how to persuade her to stay!'

'Is she so lovely?'

'Aye, Mr Stansky. She's all ginger about the hair, and lips so red it's like she's been guzzling berries.' Arthur laughed. 'And I don't want her to go.'

'Now, now, now. Enough of this. She's not going anywhere. Don't you worry, boy. You tell her how you feel and she'll stick right by your side. I promise you. It's the only thing to do. Forget all your fear and do the right thing, lad. Tell her how you feel, while you've still got the chance. I certainly wish I had.'

'How's that?'

Arthur sighed. He readjusted the belt under his apron as if to make better room for his guilt. 'I was in love with a woman once, and I loved her, as you said you loved this girl. But I too was scared and fearful of what people might think. Being the fishmonger, on an Island such as this, it gives you a higher sense of yourself than your worth. It makes you too proud, too proud, when you should be far more humble. It's fish mouths we have our fingers down, most of the time, remember,' he gestured with his hand, 'this is not the reek of the brothel.' Nathaniel laughed and then stopped himself, seeing the watery look in Mr Stansky's eyes. The monger looked back at the shop, and the wind brought with it a hearty stench of the sea.

'I loved this woman. But when it came to making a decision, I bottled it. We were courting a little before her mam's death, but when her mam died, and when she asked if we could be together, I said no. I didn't realize the consequences then.' He laughed mirthlessly into his chin. 'I didn't realize how broke she was. And then, because of my decision, she decided to do something which I became embarrassed over. By then, I didn't want to tell my friends I was involved with her; I didn't want anybody to know I had anything to do with her. And then I lost her.' Arthur clicked his fingers. 'Like that. In an instant. I was drunk, and angry, and I went to her and . . . oh. I wish I could take back that night! I'm such a fool,' he said, though Arthur's words were barely audible now.

It must be Eliza, must it not? The whole Island had a suspicion that he mooned about the Square longing for her. What a sorry state, Nathaniel thought, to be in love with someone who had no care for you. And for a man like Arthur Stansky! The fishmonger himself! There was no dignity to it, no, for a man like Mr Stansky to fall in love with a doxy like Eliza, and for her not to love him back. Mr Stansky would be better off without her. He'd be better off with her gone, settled in England, severed from the Island like a chopped tail. And there was no doubt of her uninterest: Nathaniel had seen that, plain on her face, when she'd shown up at his house, threatening to blub, telling him how much she wanted out of here. You simply wouldn't leave the Island if you were in love with someone here; no, the logic didn't work.

Meanwhile tears were welling up in Arthur's big brown eyes. Nathaniel too noticed the grey creep of stubble. How they were all sprouting, these men, he and Arthur both, with too much hair! 'I am sorry, Mr Stansky, I didn't mean to make you sad. There, there. I'd forget about her now.' Suddenly Nathaniel felt the father, and Arthur, his awkward son. 'No doxy's worth your tears, now. You should move on to another. One more pliant to your needs. You don't want to be troubling with a doxy like Eliza.' And then he said it, braved the awful truth: 'She doesn't care about you, Mr Stansky. The whole Island knows it. And I don't say that to harm you, in any way, aye, just to help you, that is, move on.'

Arthur wiped the tear away with the big fist of his hand. 'Aye, aye, I know. It's just, I'm always hoping that maybe . . .' He sniffed. 'One day . . . Well. You're right. It's over now.'

'I'm sorry,' Nathaniel said.

'No, no, no. Hark at me, all mawkish. Forgive me.' Arthur breathed deeply, steadying himself. 'It's been a strange week. I heard there's a bloom come in, and I'm worried about winter stock. That's all. No. You're right. It's right to forget about her; sometimes it gets to me, that's all. It's the bloom that's worrying me. Aye. There's reports of it on the eastern beach but I'm worried it will belt the Island and there'll be nothing to eat all winter. We can't live from provisions only. And I'm among those who don't want the Island to starve to death.'

'Will it be OK?'

'Of course, of course. We'll have enough to eat. I promise you.' Arthur dabbed now at his eyes with the corner of his apron, and then turned to Nathaniel, his face full of passion. Light glinted from the planes of his nose. 'Now you go tell your girl to stay. Don't mind your boys – they'll settle soon enough. But don't let her wriggle from you. They're slippery like that. First chance of escape and she'll take it. With both hands. D'you hear me, son? You do anything to make her stay.'

'Anything?'

'Anything, aye . . . within reason, that is.'

Anything. Anything. Nathaniel could, he thought, do something, something that would ensure Sarah would stay until spring. It was a little mischievous, but she'd come round to the logic of it, once she saw how much sense it made, and what a rollicky winter they'd have together. Especially, it seemed, now so obvious, that with Eliza's money, he'd be such a lord of it all! And when Nathaniel looked at Mr Stansky, wet-eyed and in need of nursing, Nathaniel knew he couldn't live the winter without his girl. To tumble into a depression such as this was surely death for a man! 'Thanks, Mr Stansky.'

'Well,' the monger said, 'I have a shop to run. I have to be off.' They shook hands. 'Oh, and Nathaniel? I like your pate. It suits you, a bit longer. Will you watch the plane tomorrow, with your mam?'

'That I will, if I can get her out. And yourself, Mr Stansky?'

'Aye. I'll watch it from the beach.'

But Arthur did not continue serving customers. Instead, he shut the shop at lunchtime, which was a rare thing, and much commented upon by passers-by. Instead, he went up to his apartment, took off his apron, his boots, and all of his clothes, and went to bed: overwhelmed by this morning's conversation, and, overwhelmed, above all, by his own true stupidity, at ever having let Eliza go in the first place. He slept solidly for the whole afternoon, and woke up feeling no better.

22. Money

Winter now, but then it always was. The day had started off looking sheer and bright like the first day of spring, but the afternoon had lustily rushed into cloud and grey, and then the whole pretence of day had collapsed into little more than night at barely three o'clock.

Already Saturday. Eliza still didn't have enough money for the boat. And here she was, enveloped in shadow, watching the fish shop. How many times that night had she watched a fish brought to the waxy light, and filleted by the man's deft hand? And not just tonight. Long autumn nights had been spent here, with the branches drubbing the museum's windows. The time the trees were in leaf seemed so brief . . . But from autumn to winter to summer, there would be Arthur, a constant pain and pleasure both. He would always be there to torment her: his belly canting forward from the belt-hoops, chatting amiably to anyone who was not her, amongst his treasured fish.

Eliza had waited in at the Grand all day for a customer and nobody had come. Not even Mr Carter. She kept looking in her bedside drawer for the banknotes but no amount of counting would conjure any more. It still amounted to £10 less than she needed. How could she make £10 in two days? It seemed an impossibility, but so too did spending another winter on the Island.

That afternoon, at the mirror, Eliza had pulled back her fringe and contemplated writing something. How about, *I'm staying here and there's nowhere to go*? How about, *My heart's too heavy to carry on*? Eliza had dropped the pen, fed up with the game, and her brow had been left blank. She contemplated going out to look for the English girl, but that hope, too, seemed dead. Nathaniel had stopped by the Grand and, like a cheerful hangman, had told her that unless she had the £50 for the boat on Monday, he could assure her she was not going anywhere. On his way out from her room, he had said, 'Feels awful to be so alone, doesn't it just?' but he was gone before she could ask him what on earth he meant by that.

Eliza imagined the fishmonger's to be like a church: a place of ritual, and uninterruptible silences. Aye, it was a sacrosanct place, even if it was for the butchering of fish. This was the holy place of the Island: the fish with their sheen and iridescence, flake and scale, fogged and bright eyes; the armoured crustacean and the slippery eel; this was where people came to talk, and be fed, and be reassured, by the wise and clerical silences of Mr Arthur Stansky. And here she was, the constant spy of the Island, unloved by him.

Eliza watched the bend and heft of the man at work. She thought: if I don't make enough money, and Arthur does not want me, I shall take myself off the cliff at Lynemouth Bay so that I may no longer have to live here. She would swallow all the brackish waters as easily as a liquor. She imagined her coat billowing behind her and the electric shock of her bones meeting the hard flat sea. Aye. She might be glad of that enough. And she'd spare the Island the expense of a funeral.

But rather than drumming up business or thinking of a way to earn the ten missing pounds, here she was again, watching Arthur move about the fishmonger's as if administering some office of grace. But he looked sad, or weary, drawn about the eyes. He had dropped Mr Tucker's fish, which was very uncharacteristic of him, and seemed to chat with little pleasure to a rather harried-looking Beatrice Spenser. Eliza wondered why he was so out of sorts. How dearly she wanted to steady his arm, to guide him to the ripened trout or gelatinous roe, and let him scrape his hands on her rank and grubby pinny. Then she imagined his hand clamped between her fleshy thighs, but she put that thought out of her mind immediately. Every erotic thought of him was barbed.

It was not to be. It was over. England called for her now. If only she could somehow make the £10.

Arthur said goodbye to a customer and turned the lock in the door. He looked out into the square, his face shadowed. *Oh, Arthur, if only you might love me*, she thought, *then this Island might prove a little richer, because right now, oh, what a pit of poor earth it is proving to be!* Eliza sighed, gathered her coat about her, and left the museum.

Caro Kilman was finishing up at the launderette. Eliza popped in to pick up the dress she had come in for on Monday. It was cosy in here, and the room was full of an odour that was not far from the smell of the mortuary. Eliza liked the scent of the powders and the liquids, and the sight of the clothes on the hangers. Everywhere, there was that smell which made the nostrils burn – well, everyone save Caro, with her nose and eyes that couldn't smart at bleach. The Islanders were poor in most things but liked their fineries treated just so.

'How are you, Caro?'

'Aye, well, well.'

'And Morris?'

'Keeping up as well he can, poor wee man.'

'Is it the anaemia?'

Caro moved her chin to the heel of her palm. 'Aye, his blood! Such a problem with his blood.'

The launderette also did shoes and there were open boxes piled on top of one another. They reminded Eliza of the boys' boots. A notice of goods for sale was pinned to the wall; herring lines and fish tackle. 'I imagine it's very hard.'

Caro said nothing but pressed her lips into a thin line and touched her generous auburn curls. She turned and Eliza watched the lavender dress dip slowly in between the racks of clothing. Caro hummed a faint tune, occasionally saying, 'Now where is it? Where've you got to?' Her voice was bright from behind the back of the shop. 'Found it! It's a lovely dress, Eliza, such a blue.'

Caro handed it over and the film squeaked on the counter. Eliza asked, hazarding the favour: 'Can you add it to the tab?'

'Aye,' she said, 'but you'll have to be paying this back soon.'

'No doubt, no doubt.'

Caro's bosom seemed heaving fairly near her throat. 'Did you hear about Mrs Richards on Wednesday night?'

'No?'

'A sorry story, aye.'

'What happened?'

Caro cocked her head to the side. 'Nathaniel and his boys. Looking for spies. Again. They threw rocks at Mrs Richards' window and then she was struck by one on the cheek. Had to have stitches.'

Eliza was dumbfounded. 'You're joking. I had no idea. I was only at Mrs Malraux's yesterday. She didn't mention it.'

'Aye, well, she wouldn't, would she? That boy's all she's got. She'd hardly condemn her own son. And she is very fierce of him.'

'They threw a rock! At her face!'

'Aye. Mrs Bingley said there was blood everywhere. And that Mrs Richards had a real fright of it. Ten stitches, she had, at the doctor's.'

'My. I didn't know it was so bad.'

'And I can hardly think who's going to have a word with him to put a stop to his behaviour, what with Jack no longer with us.'

'The police?'

'What are they going to do with them? They're not much older than the boys.' Caro leaned her bulk against the till. 'Some people shouldn't be allowed to be parents, you know. Letting Nathaniel roam about the Island, just as he likes! Those boys frighten the life from me,' she said.

'Aye, but you've got Morris. I shouldn't worry.'

'Oh, Morris. Morris is in bed all the time. You know I feed him up with whatever I can afford at Stansky's but it's still so bad. His bloods never seem to get any better. He's fair yellow, he's missing that much iron. And his nails: so weak and soft! And so pale underneath the eyes! Oh, seeing the sight of him near kills me! You know he hasn't been out of bed for weeks.' Caro looked up at Eliza, her eyes round and wet. 'I'm so scared for him!'

'I didn't realize it was so bad, Mrs Kilman. What will you do?'

Caro looked at her, suddenly alarmed, and her whole demeanour froze. Mrs Kilman sat up straight and gripped the bagged dress. Her voice was suddenly edged: 'Don't you come sharking about here, doll. Morris is going nowhere, d'you hear me? He's in fine fettle. Now I know it's winter and times are tight but you don't come round here trying to pick up another fare for the Tongue. It shan't be Morris, d'you hear me?'

'I would never— I wouldn't have come—'

'I don't care. You can say this or that but I know when you're sniffing about for money. The shame! Get you gone, now. Do you wish death upon my house? So you can make a fiver! My Morris is in good shape; fine shape. The shame of you, Eliza Michalka. What would your mother have thought!'

'No. I never said that, I would never—'

'Aye, and I know someone sniffing for business when I see one.' Caro pushed the dress across the counter, and then folded her arms over her bosom. Her gaze flicked to the door. 'I shan't add it to the tab. You can have it for free. But I shan't launder another thing for you, not on your life, d'you hear? Sharking about the Island, looking for fares for the Tongue! The shame!'

Eliza took the bag wordlessly and slipped out of the shop.

Shame curled in her breast. It was true. If anyone was ready for the Tongue, it was Morris, and it would have meant an extra £5 if he could – somehow – die before Monday. Eliza hated herself for thinking of it. But it had been worth a shot. She sloped away home, feeling hopeless.

23. The Burning Book

Night-time now was as lustrous as glass.

Nathaniel walked from Sarah's house, hands shoved deep into his pockets, the wind drying out his eyes. He couldn't remember the last time he was so cold; his neck was frozen. He felt unkempt: his hair needed shaving, he needed a wash, he'd smoked so many of the girl's cigarettes he felt sick. The boys were waiting, for their Saturday night thrills, as he had promised them, a big Malade meeting before school started again, and yet the anticipation that had once rallied him was now gone. Something in him had gone slack. Even when he'd made the quick trip over to Eliza's, to give her a bit of a scare, he'd felt so undelighted by his own threats. When he left, he could barely look at her.

The boy walked, fixed to the path. Grey trees were the faintest marks against the night sky. He hadn't been home enough; he should go home and see his ma, make sure she was all right. There was no point in doing anything if his ma was not all right; the woman of his life, aye. He'd like to turn and go back to Blackett Place, to be near the warmth of the fire, but he couldn't cancel another meeting. He walked on.

All afternoon, Sarah had been at the shake-and-heave. Nathaniel probably could have told her that that woman wasn't Laura Wicks. That he'd never heard of a Laura Wicks on this Island. And, if he'd really put his mind to it, that the woman down at the Eastern Bay was none other than Beatrice Spenser. But what good would it have done? Tomorrow they would go to the museum and check the log-book for Laura's name; and then Sarah would know, finally, that her ma was not here, and settle down to their winter of pleasure.

Nathaniel was tired. The afternoon had tired him. He wanted always to be with her, but it was as if all that brassy hair, the sheer colour of it, fatigued his eye. And if he couldn't be with Sarah then he wanted to be with his ma, not sharking about the Island with these bald infants.

Jake was waiting for him at the Warkworth bluffs. Nathaniel wanted nothing more than to go directly to the boys; he had no desire for a private chat. He nodded at him and tried to walk on to the square but Jake quickly caught up with him, and Nathaniel was forced to slow down, then stop.

'Where were you?' Jake said.

Nathaniel stopped. 'What?'

'We were meant to meet this afternoon.'

Everything about the boy aggrieved him: the pearly big ears, the slabby cheeks, the tubby middle. The big bland eyes.

'We were?'

'To plan for tonight, remember, you said that yesterday.'

'Aye.'

'To plan our target.'

'I get it.'

'So where were you? I called round to yours, and your mam said you weren't there.'

Nathaniel looked out over the bay. The sand was flat and the tide was out. The sea smelled off; or perhaps there was a westerly wind coming off the bloom. 'I was out,' he said, without looking at Jake.

'I know that already.'

'I was with—'

'That English girl? The one at Swanscott House?'

So the boy had seen her. Jake knew about Sarah. Of course he did. You couldn't keep one secret on the Island to yourself, not with Jake sniffing around, bored, and ready to spoil your fun.

'C'mon, Nath. I've seen her with my own eyes. I know she's not from here. I would be able to recognize a doxy such as that! Go on. Tell me. Give her up.' The big night air filled the bay. Could he push the boy from here and pretend it was an accident? What might he give to never see Jake on these Island paths again! 'Tell me who she is, Nathaniel.'

'She's from Lynemouth Town. You've never seen her before?'

'That's not true. I know that's not true. Tell me the truth, Nath.'

'Why! Why should I?'

'Because I'm your second man, Nathaniel. I started this gang with you on the same night. We share everything, remember?'

Nathaniel felt himself relenting: he would give the boy the minimal amount of information, just so he could get past tonight. 'You promise not to tell the boys anything?' Jake nodded. 'The girl. She's off Monday's boat. She hid in the hold. She's a stowaway, but she has no business of spying. Her ma was deported here on the '77 ship, for burning a church in Berwick. Sarah's come to find her.'

'Sarah? Sarah who?'

'That's her name. That's the girl's name. Sarah Wicks.'

'And her ma's name?'

'Laura Wicks.'

'Laura Wicks? Never heard of her. There's not a Laura Wicks from here to Marley Hill. It's pony, Nath, it must be, it must be, she's obviously making up lies. There must be some other mission she's on!'

'No. I believe her. She has a newspaper article, and a photograph of her ma on the boat. She can prove it.'

'But that could be anyone! Anyone at all. It's a story, Nath, a story, just so she can crab you and learn about the Island! And an English girl, in our midsts, we should be crabbing her for a spy!'

It was an odd feeling, not having the energy for a fight. Nathaniel looked at him blankly, curious about what part of his personality had deserted him this past week, knowing that if Jake had been like this on Monday, surely he would have swung the boy out to the Sound. 'Leave it out now,' he said, quietly, nodding over to the square. He cupped the back of Jake's neck with his hand. To his touch, the boy felt much warmer than himself. 'Listen, now, Jake, the boys are waiting. We'll talk about her – about everything – later, OK? Tomorrow, or something. Just not now, Jake, I don't have the energy for it. We've got all winter to find out what she's about; just let me find my way with her, at the beginning.'

'I *want* to see her.'

'No. You'll do so when I say you can.'

'No, Nath, now.'

'Listen to me.' Nathaniel squeezed his eyes; he felt a headache coming on. 'You can see her when I say. Not before. You're not the leader of this gang. I am. And I say not now. So leave it out.'

Nathaniel walked toward Maiden's Square and left Jake standing by the cliff edge.

It had been a long, disappointing week for any boy who was not Nathaniel. There was no mention of the boys' stay in their mothers' warm living rooms. They had been promised nights of thrills and all they had got was Nicholas at the start of the week and Mrs Richards in the middle. Tonight had to make up for this.

Nobody mentioned Nath's cap of hair although the others were all distinctly bald, aside from Sammy, who'd done something odd with his pate. The hair was shaved on either side so that the fuzz was in a central line. 'What's with the hair, Samuel?' Nathaniel asked. 'You look like your scalp's grown a cunt.' A nervous titter went through the group. Sammy stood next to Jake and tried to come up with a response. 'A fur, Samuel Carter, is what you've got. And we don't accept ladies in our circle, you know that rule very well. So get rid of it, lad.'

Nathaniel saw them cower a little, and the tiredness began to go. Aye, he could knock two heads together and watch them smash like eggs. Oh, he murdered for something. Was it the girl? Or these boys? Or the scrap indeed? He just needed to stop thinking. Really he'd be happy to be down at the bay, alone, in the dark, skipping stones, smoking cigarettes. Or at home with his ma. Sarah had ruined things, and perfected things, at the same time.

'Who's on, then, for tonight? I've an eye on Caro Kilman. She was around at my ma's the other night, telling such stories of us.'

'Caro Kilman's at my mam's,' Jake said, 'having tea.'

Nathaniel saw the challenge in the other boy's eyes.

'Did you not think, boy, did you not think it politic to try and dissuade Mrs Kilman from suppering with your ma? Surely better to nurse old Morris back to health!'

'How was I to know she was the target for tonight? I've not heard any English words from her. And I haven't heard anything from you, these past few days.'

The other boys exchanged glances and there was the sound of boots shuffling; edging away, a little, from the two boys.

'Don't answer back, Jakob Lawrence. The point is, you shouldn't have let her in! You should have said your ma was ill! So we could have had someone for tonight!' Nathaniel tried to relax himself. 'So who's next? Who's got a bright idea?'

'John Verger?'

'What?' Nathaniel stared at Jake. His mouth was dry but he kept his voice level. 'I have told you about this. About him.'

'Nicholas saw him down at the old church.'

'Is this true?'

Nicholas nodded his head vigorously.

'When?'

'This morning,' Nicholas said shyly. The bruise on his chin had greened in the past week.

Jake continued: 'Mooning about, sitting by the church walls. He looked to be having a molly time of it. And I think he's the one doing the graffiti, the ones that say INRI, or something like that.'

'I told you,' Nathaniel said, 'he's my da's pal.'

'Aye, aye,' said Jake. 'But I can't think of anyone else, aside from maybe the girl—'

'What girl?'

'I haven't seen her before,' Jake said. 'Copper-coloured hair.' He clicked his fingers, as if he were hoping for recall. 'What's her name?'

'I told you not—'

'Up at Swans—'

'Stop it, Jake.' There was silence in the square for a while. Nathaniel's scarf, as if oblivious, danced about in the Island's wind, jigging and whirling, as if a part of him were determined to escape. And then there was a terrible moment, really very terrible, when the boys congregated saw the eyes of their leader go brighter and wetter and sharper too, and there was a fear that Jake had upset him so much, that Nathaniel was about to cry. No one wanted that; not even Jake.

When Jake resumed, it was amiably, as if he were chattering to his mam. 'Aye. So Verger. And I'm not saying he's a bad man, no, but Nicholas saw him down at the church this morning and there's no denying it's a sure sign of faith.'

Nathaniel didn't want this. He didn't want things to get too deep. What would his ma say, if they went after John Verger for a spy? What would his da have said? 'Who else saw him at the church?'

'I did,' said Samuel, tracking a hand over the fuzz.

'And me,' said Nicholas.

'Aye! I know about you already, Tucker.' Nathaniel was in no mood for this. It was as if his gang was suddenly turning brutish beyond even his own ken. 'Fine,' he said – because better John Verger than the English girl, and what were a few rocks anyway? Or a few smashed windows? And what were the boys but purveyors of a violent sort of goodness – though Verger shouldn't be the target; not at all.

Nathaniel smiled at them, and, most importantly, Jake. 'All right, boys. A good spot, Jake. Verger it is. As you wish.'

Verger's house, up on Heath Rise, not much further from where Nathaniel had looked out over the Sound on Monday night, had an ill-tended character. Trees obscured most of the bottom floor's rooms. Branches scraped the glass. It was a typical Island cottage, not much looked after. 'I wonder where he is,' one of the boys said, at a faint whisper, as if in the presence of something to be revered.

'Down at the Grand!' Jake cried.

'Fucking Eliza!'

'Down on his hindquarters having his fill of God.'

Nathaniel had been to this house many times as a boy, with his hand in his da's hand, but never here, to do this. But if he couldn't let on about the girl, then Verger it would be – and maybe it was the right thing to do. It was idiotic for Verger to have given him the book, and he supposed the old man should be punished for it. Then there were the pep talks, and the reminiscences of England, and the lectures on his da – oh no, this all had to stop.

Rocks were thrown. Most of the boys were a bad aim,

most ricocheted off the plaster. Nathaniel saw how their eyes grew wide with it: the good generous violence. They threw their stones hard. 'The oldest Got on the isle!' Nathaniel shouted, joining in with the rest of them, and he felt the old pure love for his boys return. The boys were beauties, like babies; even Sammy, with his line of fuzz, looked a winsome sight. So this was goodness! This was right! It had a reek to it, but so must everything worth fighting for.

A window smashed. Jake had thrown the winning stone. The boys cheered and clung about him, rubbing his head with their fists. 'All right, Jakey!' 'Yes, Jakey-boy!' they said.

Jake was laughing and jumping about and pointing at the hole in the window. Where had the boy assumed this new power? Jake bent over to his bag and reached down into the satchel. The rest of the boys too had gone very quiet. Rising in Nathaniel was the knowledge of what it would be. His heart sank at the prospect.

'John Verger's been found with this book. A book of paintings of Christ! A real Got living on our Island, a Got more than all the others.' Jake flipped the pages and the boys gathered round to see. 'Look!' he said, pointing. 'For shame! The glory of Christ splashed on every page!'

'That isn't your book, Jakob Lawrence.'

'No. Aye. Whose is it?'

'It isn't yours.'

Sammy looked at Nathaniel, eyes wide and distressed. 'Have you seen this, Nath? Have you seen these pictures? Wow!'

'Gives me the gromicks!' said another.

'Give me a bucket, I need to heave! The rot's in my blood!'

'Aye,' Jake said, watching the boys turning the pages. 'A man so sweetened by the coddle, I bet he doesn't sleep without muttering a prayer.' The boys were quiet, softly abuzz. They'd never seen such pictures. 'A man. With a book such as this.' He looked directly at Nathaniel. 'I hate to think what he believes—' He stopped, brought out a lighter and put it to a page. 'Or what length he'll go to, to get the English back here. If the English aren't already here.'

Oily green flames jumped high in the night.

A sadness fell upon Nath as he remembered the old man outside Arthur's, grinning at merely the sight of him. He should stop Jake, but he couldn't. Not now; not any more. He thought of Sarah. No; he could not.

The burning book went straight into the dark hole of the room. For moments, all was darkness, as the boys stood and watched, rapt by this sudden escalation of violence. An acrid smell sliced the air. A curtain, clasped to a bracket on the wall, caught, and with a huge noise, the room filled with bright orange light.

24. Grace

Eliza applied the needle to the blue flame. Her hand was shaking; the needle quivered. It was four o'clock in the morning. The match went out, the needle turned from red to black. Eliza hesitated, then pushed up her fringe and stuck the needle in. She steeled herself against the pain, then pushed it in further, and began to write. Starting with the letter *V*, she punctured the skin down to the dip and then began the shoot upward. The letters seamed in blood as she began the *e* and *r*. Eliza felt as if she might faint but dug the needle in harder. In minutes, the name, finally, was cut into her skin. *Verger*.

Eliza had been sleeping lightly, at about ten o'clock last night, still waiting for a customer to grace her door with a £5 note, when she had been woken by what sounded like an explosion. From the window she saw the orange flames up near the viewing station at Marley Hill. Pulling on her coat, she winched up the glass, jumped onto the flat roof and rattled down the iron staircase. When she reached the road she ran as quickly as she could to the burning house but then hung back, yards away. A black net of boys idled by the house, but she did not stop them. One of them threw another flaming missile. She stood by and then the boys scattered: some down to the beach, some up the hill.

The fire was mounting, and smoke escaping through a smashed window. Eliza went up to the house, as close as she could get, and shouted Verger's name through the door, but the heat was tremendous and the smoke thickening. She wondered if she should go inside and look for him. What if the old man was in there, inhaling all that smoke? Eliza left the house blazing as the Islanders showed up with water pails and buckets, and a hose from the main taps.

Verger emerged, minutes later, a shadowy figure at the end of the road. Eliza thought he looked tiny, but as she neared him he seemed to get no bigger. When he looked at the burning house, he sagged. He asked her if it was his house and she said that it was. Eliza held him by the elbow and brought him back to the Grand. He asked her who had done it and she merely shrugged. 'I don't know,' she lied.

Eliza passed an inked swab over the bloodied letters and felt the sting. She had chosen black ink, the better for it to show. She should have stopped the boys from doing what they did. How wrong to think the boys were merely bored, merely playing games! Was that not what she'd told Margaret? And now here they were, the brutal lot of them, assaulting people, and burning down houses! But to turn them in would have meant no escape!

Eliza put the swab back in the inkpot. There it was now, his name, her guilt, tattooed on her brow.

'Eliza! Here!' Musa called, from some way away. She mopped up the word with a ragged piece of tissue, bringing off blood and ink together, and flattened the wing of hair against her forehead. 'Coming,' she said, wiping away her tears with the bloodied rag.

Rain came on Sunday morning. Verger stood at the window, watching the sheets of it, imagining parts of his house that had never before seen water grow damp, then sodden. There was something of the dirge to the fat heavy drops breaking against the roof of the Grand; something funereal to the slow spray against the window. The world outside was nothing more than a blur. His shirt, which the previous evening had been ironed crisp, was crumpled; there was an air of surrender to it. His dicky bow wilted at the edges. His hands hung, and the veins rose swollen within them.

The night spent – at a brothel! – had been fitful. A woman had guided him here last night, steering him by the elbow, when she had found him sobbing outside the burning house. He had felt out of his mind. He had felt as if he couldn't see. She stopped when he stopped, told him to mind his footing when the path became rutted. His house was gone, burned and gone. She had pulled him along, half-dragging him, when he had stiffened on seeing the Grand.

In the reception he smelled unusual smells. The woman was arguing with the man he knew as Musa. Verger pulled some pounds from his wallet and this made him quiet. Musa led him down a corridor and opened the door with a gold spiked key. Musa said, 'Ha, ha, should I send in a girl to see you, sir?' but Verger shut the door without a reply.

This room, he supposed, was a spare; blue, functional, little about it was decorative. In here, he was out of the way. Yes, he thought, leaning his shoulder against the window, listening to the squeaks of the Grand's sign in the wind, there was little to be done. His house was gone; Nathaniel lost. Long strings of rain slid down the window. Further out, it dripped off the terrace eaves across the street. The day, at least, in glum camaraderie, is in mourning for me, Verger thought; for what I have lost. A small comfort. The water soaked what it could.

Verger was brought tea and some porridge for breakfast. He sat and ate by the window. It was eleven o'clock, he must've been by the window for hours. He felt as if he hadn't slept at all.

The rain was letting up now, coming gentler. Verger opened the window; the air felt rinsed and crisp. He felt himself a slow servant of God – defeated, already, and by a mere child, at that. His Message was a low throb; a distant pulse. He had carried the Message to the boy and this was his recompense! Must he get down on his knees and thank God for his loss? How ungenerous was His reward! Oh, he could push his fist into the boy's face, and watch the blood ream about his lips, and feel it, just for a second, a moment of justice; of reprieve; of pleasure, even, and power. The smooth scalp he could claw in his hands.

The world did not make sense: not like this.

There was a tapping at the door. Verger feared, if it were the woman again with the tea, he might take this violence to her soft body. The door opened. Eliza. She looked just as she had on the day of the funeral, with that smart length of fringe, and the strong able body. Swollen eyelids gave her a hooded look, as if she had been crying for some time. So, it was Eliza who had brought him here last night. 'I hope I haven't disturbed you.' Her hand was still at the door knob, as if she were about to shut it once again and flee. 'I came to see if you were all right. If there was anything I could do.'

'No, no. You have not disturbed me. Please. Do take a seat.' Verger gestured to the armchair. He sat neatly on the edge of the bed, conscious he was sitting on a well-used mattress. He gave her a rueful smile, and she smiled back; this Eliza, this woman of kindness. And yet a whore, he knew that; they both knew where they were. Eliza played her fingers through her hair.

'How are you feeling this morning?' she asked. 'It must have been a shock.'

'Oh. Well. You know. My house – it's gone.'

Eliza looked down at her lap where her hands lay flat. 'Yes. Yes, I know.'

'So, my house is burned. Gone completely. That, I must accept. Everything is rubble, I suppose.'

'Do you,' she began, then faltered. Her voice was thin: 'Do you have any idea who did this?'

'No,' he said softly, 'I don't.'

She took a deep breath. 'I know who—'

'Eliza. It's funny how we haven't really met before. I mean, I saw you at Mrs Page's, and you did a very good job, but we haven't actually spoken, before now, have we? What is your surname, Eliza?'

Her eyes widened in confusion. 'Michalka.'

'Michalka. A Jewish name?'

'Yes.'

'So you weren't one of the deported, then? If you were a religious family?'

'No.' She adjusted the tone of her voice; she had evidently not come expecting this conversation. 'Ma came here voluntarily. She had had a hard life, she thought the Island might be a refuge. And it was, in a way, for her.'

'Germany?'

'No,' she smiled, 'London.'

'Lucky thing.'

'I . . . ' Eliza started, and swallowed, and then looked at him levelly. 'I know who. No. I know who did this.'

'Speak up, my dear,' he said softly.

Her voice was barely more than a whisper. 'You are a good man, I understand.'

'A good man?'

'Aye.'

'If I am a good man, then you are a good woman. If I had stayed outside my house I would have frozen to death. You took me back here. You rescued me. And now I am here, in this room, warm, at least, and alive.'

Her eyes were brimming with tears. 'I could have . . . I could have stopped them . . . but . . . those boys, I need to get out of here.'

'Come now.'

'It was wrong. I should have—'

'Aye,' he said, but gently. 'Wrong of them, not you.'

'But if I had reported them, on Monday, there would be no . . . oh!' Verger moved to the chair, kneeling, and put his arm around her. Her shoulders shook as she began to cry. 'I am a bad woman! Selfish. And nothing but a whore! Do you not see where I had to bring you back to? Of all places to drag you to, in your state of tears! I wish I could be finished with it all! To be done with it all! And I didn't stop them. I'm sorry, Mr Verger, so sorry. It's just that I want to get out of here.' She looked at him with her wide brown eyes and it was as if the light of God was singing in them. Yes! Singing from the iris itself. 'I want to leave so very badly.'

'My child! My child! Hush now. You are a spotless creature. You do not deserve anyone's blame. You couldn't have done a thing about it.' The woman fairly shook in his arms as if she were quarrying out all the misery. This woman, who opened men like clams, getting to their filthy spots of pleasure – it was this woman who so badly needed the Light! This woman, who sent the men off to the fish, the squid, the sharks, without so much as a mention of God's name! This was the very soul that needed grace!

The rain started again and they both looked toward the window from the blue pale room. Eliza pushed a tissue to her nose, her tears spent now. 'I *must* get out of here.'

He said: 'It will come. You will not be here for much longer, I promise you.' He cupped her face with his hands and she gave him a weak smile. With her other hand she swept her fringe from her eyes. Written on her forehead was his name. Fresh blood scabbed the letters. 'My name,' he said. 'You have my name upon your skin.'

'It was a penance. For not helping you. For not stopping the boys.'

'Oh, unnecessary. You cannot earn grace by punishing yourself.'

'I'd like that to be true, but I don't think it is.' She dissolved into tears again. 'Sometimes I think someone is punishing me!'

'Why?'

'Because everything I ask for – companionship, love, family – is denied to me. And I can't understand it. I think of myself as a good woman. One who thinks of others. And yet I never seem to get what I want!' She stopped sobbing and looked flatly out of the window. 'He is so distant with me, sometimes I think he barely knows I exist.'

'God?' John ventured.

'Arthur.'

'Ah,' he said, 'so we are talking of a man here?'

She sniffed. 'Arthur Stansky. He came to me every night when my ma was ill. And when she died, I went to him, and he rejected me. It was too soon, perhaps, but I didn't have a choice! I was broke. And I loved him, I really did. Then he came here, to the Grand. It was a very bad thing to do. And we haven't spoken since. Not really. I forgave him for that night, long ago, but he won't talk to me.'

'Dear, dear. He's ashamed. It doesn't mean he doesn't like you.'

'But I said I had forgiven him!'

'Aye, but the heart is a difficult thing to understand. We act contrary to how we feel, and we feel contrary to how we act. He is just ashamed of himself. I promise.' He laid his hand down on the crown of her head, as he imagined a minister might, and felt all the good love for this world that he thought, this morning, he had lost forever. 'You are too fine a woman to punish yourself like this.'

'Thank you,' she said to him, and took his hand and put it in her own. It was soft, her palm, and it suddenly reminded John of where he was. He retracted it quickly, although he didn't mean to.

'Sorry,' he said, quite ashamed of himself.

Eliza shrugged. 'What will you do today?'

'Salvage what I can. Begin again. Eke something of goodness from this thing.'

'You seem almost happy about it.'

'What else can I do. And you?'

'I am planning my way out of here. But it's a secret.' She smiled weakly. 'Don't tell anyone.' She seemed about to say something further but then stopped herself.

'Well, I wish you luck. You are too fine, too good a woman to be stuck here.' Eliza smiled thinly and turned in the eave of the door. 'Sorry,' she said, 'you know, about the tears. I've reduced the rate at the reception desk as you weren't . . . seen to. Don't let Musa crab you for more.'

'I won't.'

'Oh, and Mr Verger? Please don't tell anyone that Arthur came here. To the Grand. It was wrong of him, but I wouldn't want the whole Island to know.' Verger nodded his head. 'Then it is goodbye.' She smiled and said, 'And thank you.'

John returned to the window. Outside, the rain had stopped and a hole had found its way in the white mesh of the clouds, and what was left of the winter trees were streaked with sunshine. Aye, the whole world had seemed to give up its sulk. He remembered last May's epiphany and the feeling of God's friendship swelled his breast. He could burst with it, there was such a pride to this feeling, that he was so small and yet deemed so instrumental to the world!

And what was the burned lot of his house but merely the companion to the charred loveliness of the church. John had more than he needed, and was thankful for it.

25. An Article of Faith

They walked up the hill in silence: Sarah and the boy. Nathaniel's skull was all stippled, it looked almost like a spillage, too much of himself grown from what had been purely skin. He had been so . . . what was the word? Peeled, when she had first seen him; his forehead almost vergeless. 'Come down with me to the museum,' he had said to her, at home in Swanscott House. Sarah had looked up to watch him dress, the braces stretched and then snapped, the shirt as stiff as paper. He was grinning, urging her out of the warmth of the sleeping bag.

Yesterday, she had returned from the fruitless visit to Mrs Spenser and spent the afternoon crying and feeling foolish. What an idiot she had been to think that of all these people here she could merely pluck her mother out from within them! She had been a fool not to sweep the Island further; not to look for other possibilities. Nathaniel managed to calm her down, but when he left that evening she was weeping again: childish grief gripped her, all the misery she had felt on Laura's absence suddenly returning, ten years later. A failure; the whole trip had been a failure. Laura was lost to her; she was lost in newsprint and photographs; neither on the Island nor in England.

Laura had disappeared; and Sarah couldn't explain it.

She had been asleep when Nathaniel had tiptoed in, late last night. When he came down to the sleeping bag, he smelled, improbably, of soot. She found grains of sand in his ears and in his hair. She wondered if he was drunk and asked him that. He said he had never touched a tipple in his life. He fell asleep within minutes, his breath slowing, a carbon waft about him, the smell of fire on his clothes.

As they rounded the first bit of Marley Hill, Sarah saw the sea. The sun was high, heatless and white. Odd, how it gave no warmth. The rain had stopped but a fog was closing in at the bay. They walked in silence: Sarah, plonking along, ungainly in her walk; she hoped Nathaniel wouldn't notice. The boy's eyes ferreted the hill – watching for this gang, these boys. He was scared, she could see that much, though he carried himself as someone who knew nothing of fear. At the hilltop she saw the little town with its big houses and the square and the bay with the black pier. Tomorrow, she would walk back down it, knowing nothing more about her mother than when she had arrived. Nathaniel followed her line of sight down to the jetty. 'And you're serious about going? Tomorrow?'

She looked up at him, surprised. What else could she do? 'I can't stay. My dad'll be waiting for me.'

'Not even for the winter? Just for a few months?'

'No. Not even for the winter.'

'It's baneful hard, Sarah, hearing you say that.'

'Aye,' she said, 'and it's hard to say it. But England's my home.' He swallowed and looked out across the sea. 'I'll miss you, Nathaniel. And I'll remember you. I promise.'

He avoided looking at her. 'Come on, then.'

They headed to Maiden's Square, taking the steep of Marley Hill. Low and doleful, the trees up here were so thin it was a wonder they stood up to the Island winds. Sarah couldn't think of this Island in summer, couldn't imagine that its earth had, months ago, known something of warmth. No fierce heat; no warmth in the waters; no lambent light of summer at rest on the sea-top. No – she would always imagine it like this: wintry and November-ish, a difficult place for comfort. Nathaniel traced the bones of her spine as she walked. He was the Island's warmth, and that was all.

At the flat, he led her to the square, to the places Sarah always wanted to remember: the launderette, the grocer's, the fishmonger's, that shop down there called Buttons. In her mind's eye too she sketched a portrait of him. There was something to this picture of Nathaniel, or the antici-pated memory of him when she would be back in England, that was fragile, as if, at the windy mount of Marley Hill, he had been nothing more than a statue of ash.

He'd not yet told her what they were here for. The museum's door was hidden by the stage and its sign banged the stone wall, plangently, insistently, as the wind swung it. Sarah asked what they were doing here but Nathaniel didn't reply and led her on, pushing the door, and bringing her into the low-beamed room. In the museum he cupped her jaw so that her mouth was close to his. 'No one's here,' he said. He kissed her and his tongue darted into her mouth, the hand straying, scooping a breast.

She broke away from him. He watched her, alarmed, suddenly.

In the photographs, in the next room, there were black eyes and nostrils and slit mouths. Their fatigue came off the mob like a stink. Had he brought her here to shame her again? To teach her a lesson in her country's fine narrative? She felt, now, that she could not be shocked: some hardness of the Island had become part of her and she could not be moved or shamed.

'I think there is a logbook, here; I think they kept a log, of who came here and when.' Nathaniel stooped down to a cabinet, reaching for a thick red book, pulling it from the shelf and mounting it on a lectern. The book cracked as he opened it: the pages were rough-hewn, the paper heavy. At the top of the column *January 1951* was written. On the first page there were dates of birth and home towns, mostly from the North: Manchester, York, Newcastle, Sunderland. Lots of young men; at the beginning. The next date was that year's summer: more women, this time, and children: she saw the name Margaret Firth (he pointed here, and said, 'That's my mam, aye,') and then flicking through the pages she saw the dates went further and further apart. Until they came to a stop, in 1977. He said to her, very tenderly, and quietly, as if she were a child: 'And it's 1977 you're looking for? Am I right?'

'Yes,' she said.

Nathaniel turned the page. Sarah looked to the other room and her country's history seemed completely absurd – to get rid of people like this, and photograph them, to boot, in their Godless march to exile. She felt proud of her mother, for Saint Gregory's, for burning down a house of cold and moral probity. One could not just let it all happen. There were other things to account for, aside from God.

There was a long list of deportees in the summer of 1977: mostly those who had been convicted of the church-burnings in '76. She remembered some of the names from the deportation lists she had read in the Newcastle Library. There were a hundred or so names here until they came to a stop. 'But no Laura,' she said. 'No Laura. I don't understand. These would have been her contemporaries in the Movement. Laura was arrested for one of these church-burnings. I don't understand. How is it she's not on a prison list, and not on a deportation list either?' Sarah began to admonish herself, again, just as she had done all day yesterday: 'I see a stupid photograph then leap on the first boat out of England. I'm an idiot. A real idiot.'

Nathaniel scanned each name in the column until he came to the last name. 'Sarah? Who was the woman you talked to yesterday? Mrs Spenser? Beatrice Spenser?'

'Aye.'

'Well, look at that,' he said, pointing to the last name in the column. 'Looks like she was on the last boat too. Perhaps she knows something about your ma. Perhaps she's worth another try.'

'She doesn't want to talk to me.'

'So?'

'She made that quite clear, Nathaniel. That she knows nothing about Mum, and even if she does, she doesn't want to tell me anything.'

'C'mon, Sarah. She's the one most likely to know something. Your photograph shows the last boat that came here, correct? Well, turns out Beatrice *was on that boat*. She might know who that woman is. She might know who your ma is. Come on, now, doll.' He brought his arm around her and let the boards of the book hit the pages softly.

Hundreds of captive eyes seemed to follow her as she left the museum with him. Nathaniel almost had to pull her along. So Mrs Spenser was on the last boat here. It didn't really mean anything. And she wasn't up for probing her any more. She just wanted to go home, and be done with the whole thing – consign it to memory, and misadventure. Laura was lost.

Mrs Spenser's house looked tired, as if one more blast of wind could powder it back down to sand and stones. The jolly red door was fooling no one. For the first time, Sarah noticed the slight list of the house, how it seemed to lean toward the cliff and the suggestion, in the marshy front garden, of neglect. Loosened, the house might fly from here, with very little force whatsoever.

'She won't speak to me,' she said to Nathaniel, tugging at one of his cuffs, and eyeing the steep hedge warily. 'She doesn't know anything. Let's go, let's go back to the house.'

'She could have chosen a better lodging,' Nathaniel said, ignoring her. He gave a short, nicking laugh. ' 'Tis worse than my abode.'

He walked the gravel path; she followed, lagging. Nathaniel rang the bell when he saw she was not going to do it. There were the sounds of slippers and mumbled warnings, probably to the boy, and then the door unlocking. When Mrs Spenser saw who it was, she came out of the house and shut the door flat behind her. 'Yes?' the woman snapped, eyeing Nathaniel, then turning back to

Sarah. 'I told you, young lady, I didn't want to speak to you again.'

'Please, Mrs Spenser, I need to talk to you.'

'I have nothing more to say.'

Sarah gathered her courage. 'I saw your name in the logbook in the museum. You were one of the last ones here in '77. Which meant you were on the last boat, which means you might know something about that woman in the photograph.'

'That means nothing,' she snapped, and though her voice was full of conviction, Mrs Spenser reached out to the door handle, as if to steady herself, and her eyes flitted nervously down the trunk of Nathaniel's jacket.

'It means you might have been on the boat with her. It means you might know what happened to her after she came here. Laura seems to have disappeared. Please, if you know anything, it would be a great help to me. A great help.'

Beatrice pulled her dressing-gown closer to her throat. Between the hem and her slippers, the thin ankles were mauve with cold. 'Fine,' she pointed a finger to Sarah. 'You can come in.' She flicked her hand toward Nathaniel. 'But you can leave him out of it.'

'Fine,' he said. 'I'll wait out here, freezing to death.'

'I won't be long,' Sarah said.

'No,' said the woman to Nathaniel, and boldly, here, she took a few steps toward him: 'I don't want you outside the house. I *know* about Mrs Richards. Is your memory so short you can't remember Wednesday night? Wait at the end of the road. Not here.'

*

Sarah walked through the cold hall, Mrs Spenser followed. The kitchen was just as it looked from the outside, with the brass skillet pans on the hooks, the small fireplace and big stove. Nothing could be cleaner, or more polished. It was strange, for Sarah, to be inside, looking out; like being in a different world, the room untouched by sunshine, on account of the high hedge. 'Your son,' Sarah said, 'he's asleep?'

'Aye.'

'You brought him with you? From England?'

'No. I had him here. He's five.'

Beatrice filled the kettle and put it on the gas. The black iron looked heavy in her grasp. The stack of newspapers was taller than it had looked from the outside, and yellower, too, as if they had been there for some time. Damp and finely layered as a pastry, Sarah wondered why she kept them. 'You've been watching me for days,' Beatrice said, by the oven, choosing not to turn. Steam started to pipe from the spout, and she put her hands toward the heat. 'How did it enter your mind that this was an acceptable thing to do?'

'I'm sorry. I didn't mean to scare you.'

Beatrice turned, her eyes lively with anger. Blue and accusing, they reminded Sarah of her mother's eyes when she was annoyed. An angry blush had come up around the freckles. 'Well, you did. Those boys! They crabbed Mrs Richards on Wednesday night, and I thought you were coming for me. When you were outside – oh! I was so frightened! You have no idea!'

So that was it: Beatrice had assumed, yesterday, that Sarah was part of Nathaniel's gang. Hence her rage, yesterday, at being called on – not rage, however, but fear: Mrs Spenser was scared of her. Sarah said gently: 'I have nothing to do with them. I met Nathaniel by accident. He's fed me, these past few days, and given me shelter, and without that, I don't know, I might have been very ill. Whatever he has done in the past is not my business. I apologize, if I scared you. But I can tell you, quite certainly, that I have nothing to do with this gang. Nothing.'

The kettle whistled. Cups hung neatly from a rack above the oven. Looking no more pleased than when she had opened the door, Beatrice poured powdered milk into a jug and added water. She stirred it inattentively for some moments, the hood of the spoon clinking against the jug's sides, doing circles and circles, the other hand holding the small of her back as if she suffered from an ache. 'So where are you from? In *England*, as you said.' Her tone was mocking.

'Near Newcastle.'

Beatrice set the steaming cup down. Tiny flecks of milk floated on the tea's top. She smirked. 'Near Newcastle? And?'

'It's called Trimdon, just outside it.'

She looked at her quickly. Her expression had changed completely. 'Trimdon?'

'Yes.'

'And that's where your mother was from as well?'

'Yes. Look. I don't want to take up any more of your time, Mrs Spenser. But I need to know if you've ever heard of Laura Wicks.' Sarah took out the article and spread it on the kitchen table. Laura looked out, vague, her features smudged by wear. 'Here. Saint Gregory's. This is what she was arrested for. That's her, there.' Sarah indicated the date. 'That's the day after she disappeared. July 5th, 1976.' Sarah delved down into her bag, and produced the photograph of the last boat. 'And here is the picture of the last boat, in '77. There she is. And you were on that boat too, somewhere. I saw your name in the logbook. I know that you were on this boat. But I can't seem to find Laura anywhere. Not here, on this Island; and not on any documents either.'

Beatrice sat opposite her at the long wooden table. The tabletop was worn smooth, as if it had come, like driftwood, from the sea. 'I will talk to you, if you promise that you have nothing to do with this gang. Promise me. Mrs Richards had such a hard time of it the other night, I couldn't bear it if anything happened to my son. Promise me.'

'I promise.'

Beatrice held the edge of the table so that her knuckles showed white. She shook her head as if she disagreed with some thought or feeling in passing. 'Sarah. In this photograph, that's me. I remember that coat. I still have it, somewhere. It was so long ago. Nearly ten years, now, aye. They always said we looked alike. Me and Laura. You've mistaken me for your mother.'

'That's you?'

'Aye.' She tapped at the face Sarah had assumed to be Laura's. 'That's me.'

'That's *you*?'

'Aye. But Laura – your mum – didn't come here with the rest of us.'

Sarah's voice was little more than a whisper. 'Why? Why not?'

Beatrice stood and piled more logs into the grate and then warmed her hands against the flame. Without turning her back, she said: 'Laura was a friend, though we didn't know each other for long before I was deported. She was a kind woman. Very kind. I liked her very much. But we were different. She was a lot stronger than me.'

There was a moment or so of silence and then a log cracked. 'I arrived a little later than she did, in August, after one of the Movement's burnings in Preston. Laura and I, amongst other women from the Movement, were held in a female prison, in Sunderland. That was '76. When the police started interrogating me, about people I knew, deals I'd be willing to make, Laura kept on saying, *Don't believe them, they're lying, don't give people up*.

'But there was months and months of this. We'd be taken to a bare room, one of the "interview rooms", and asked the same questions, over and over again. The police kept on saying that if I gave them a name, of anyone higher up, they would get me a lenient sentence, in an English prison. They said that I wouldn't have to go to the Island. One of them hit me. But there wasn't much violence. They knew I'd give in – they recognized something in me, I guess.'

Beatrice turned: her face was rather haggard – as if this confession was going to be painful. 'And eventually, I did give in. I blabbed and blabbed, about any names, of anybody in the Movement I could remember. And I remember how your mother wasn't angry with me when I did it. She held me, when I wept, and told me everything would be OK. I couldn't be as strong as her. I just couldn't.'

'How do you mean?'

'Laura was so steadfast. She wouldn't give up the names of the two men she was with at Saint Gregory's. But there were consequences to this. Laura would come into the cafeteria with black eyes and fat lips. I think things happened to her that I wouldn't like to say. But she remained silent, no matter what they did to her. I admired her, very much, but I didn't have the same strength.

'When it came to the trials, though, in '77, Laura was excluded. Hers was still an open case. And when it came to the expulsion that summer, Laura was not on the deportation list for the Island. Finally, we all saw Laura's strategy. In keeping the secret, she had kept the case open, and saved herself from deportation. Of course, I regretted confessing. The promise of a soft sentence was not kept. We were all duly packed off on the boat, just as they'd always planned. And here I am,' Beatrice turned and gestured to the photograph of the boat, 'wondering if it might not be better to jump into the waves.'

Beatrice's face had cleared, as if by talking she had removed some weight of history pressing on her. In fact, she looked teary, as if she might be about to cry. 'Oh, I am sorry, dear, it's always difficult talking about the past. We avoid it, here, you know. It might drive us mad if we talked about nothing but England all the time.'

'Mum's in an English prison?'

'Aye. You know, I've been watching out for her. In the newspapers that come across on the boat. I thought that, maybe, with the Sunday Agreement, in '83, she might have confessed. They were letting people go, by then, "minor" members of the Movement who were cooperating. Still she didn't give up any names. When they announced the list of prisoners who were to be released, hers wasn't on it. I couldn't believe it. I couldn't believe her tenacity, her determination.'

'So she could have come back to us? Three years ago? And she chose not to?'

Beatrice shrugged and smiled at her sadly. 'Aye. Well. Your mother always had a very deep sense of honour, I think. Perhaps it was misplaced. I don't know.'

'Where is she? What prison?'

'She was in Sunderland. But she's not there any more.' She took the cups from the table and poured the cold tea down the sink, despite Sarah having had none of hers. The taps went on with a flourish as Beatrice rinsed the sink. Then she sat, and she smiled at her, quite warmly. The pans above her gave the woman a beatific look – there was a sense, perhaps, of atonement: as if speaking about Laura had comforted her. 'Now, Sarah. I am going to show you something. It may be shocking to you. It was a shock to me, too. I picked up the newspaper on Tuesday morning from the museum, as I always do, and for the rest of the day I couldn't think about anything else. It's concerning your mother. And her whereabouts. Take the top newspaper from the pile, Sarah. There's news in there for you.'

News? It was news enough that Laura was in an English prison. Sarah rose and took the top newspaper from the pile. The paper was thin in her hands, and damp. As Beatrice had said, the date was last Sunday, and it had evidently been brought to the Island on last Monday's *Saviour* with Sarah herself. There were mugshots of two men at the top of the article. The headline was *Justice for Saint Gregory's*. Sarah began to read.

These are, finally, the identities of the two men responsible for the church-burning at Saint Gregory's in Berwick on July 4th, 1976, which killed the parish Minister, Rev Ed Williams.

During a raid of a Movement house in Whetstone, North London, Christopher Ware and Thomas Hemming were shot and both killed after they refused to give up their weapons.

For ten years the case has remained unsolved.

The driver of the getaway car, a Mrs Laura Wicks, who was apprehended at the scene, has never revealed the two men's names, even when offered release as part of the terms of the Sunday Agreement.

On hearing about their deaths, Mrs Wicks, now 36, confirmed to the police yesterday that Ware and Hemming were the two men she was with who set fire to the church and murdered Rev Williams. Mrs Wicks, given her cooperation, and time in police custody, will now be released as part of the prisoner roll-out instigated by the Sunday Agreement in 1983.

Sarah stopped reading. There was no photograph of the woman. Just her name.

Laura Wicks.

Beatrice smiled. 'You see. She kept her word. When she told the police their names, it couldn't hurt Tom and Chris. Not any more. She kept her promise right until she had to.'

'Did you know them? These two?'

'No. I never met them. They were very lucky to have Laura as the driver that day. Anyone else would have given them up for a song. And now she's to be released. How lucky she is. Or at least, not lucky. But clever. She was always very clever, your mum.'

Sarah re-read the article. Here it was: the evidence, finally, of Laura's whereabouts. And it had been shipped over in one of the boxes on the boat! All this time, Sarah had been so close to the answer and yet completely unaware of its whereabouts. If only she'd stopped at the newsagent's after the butcher's last Sunday, or watched the television before sneaking off to Newcastle! If only she had opened one of the boxes on the boat that night!

'How old are you now, Sarah?' Beatrice asked.

'Seventeen,' she said, as she re-read the article again.

'Aye, aye,' Beatrice said softly. 'God knows it must have broken her heart to think she might never see you again. And now she's coming home; you might even see her before Christmas.'

'But I'm on the Island.'

'And she's in England. Aye. Well,' Beatrice almost gave a chuckle, 'stranger things have happened. No harm in it now. You'll see her when you're back. Can I ask, Sarah, how it was you managed to come here?'

Now it was time for Sarah to smile. 'I smuggled myself on Monday's boat.'

'A stowaway!'

'It wasn't very hard, you know. Newcastle docks – they're not policed, or anything, I sneaked in when no one was looking. You could do the same, I bet, from the pier, creep in when the Boatman wasn't looking—'

'No,' the woman said, firmly, 'it may not be much, but the Island's home now, aye. I can't go back to England; not after they chucked us out. It wouldn't feel like home, there, not any more. And I have a life here,' she smiled sadly, 'I think.'

Sarah looked at the article again. 'But the whole street thinks she was having an affair with someone from York!'

Beatrice laughed. 'Well. There'll be some issues to iron out, certainly.'

Sarah was tempted to ask Beatrice about her crimes, ask why she was here on the Island, but she stopped herself. She didn't look like she wanted to go over these things. Sarah said thank you, and asked her if she might convey a message to anyone in England.

'No,' Beatrice said. 'But recommend me to Laura. You have her likeness, now that I can see it.'

'And so do you,' Sarah said, almost laughing. 'May I keep this?' she asked, pointing to the paper.

Beatrice nodded, held her hand, and said, 'Goodbye, Sarah Wicks.'

'Thank you, again, for talking to me. I know it was hard.'

From the hallway, putting the newspapers back into her bag, Sarah heard the woman shout after her. 'And you tell those boys to stay away from this house!'

Sarah didn't know whether to laugh or cry. The answer all along had been in one of the boxes in the boat – she might have even been sitting on it. For ten hours, at least, Laura's whereabouts had been under her nose. Under her bottom, in fact. And soon she would meet her. Really meet her. Laura Wicks was coming home. Sarah raced out of the house to tell Nathaniel the news.

26. The Aeroplane

At midday on Sunday, Margaret had fixed herself a decent lunch of baked potato with piccalilli; and had even managed a crossword, going only twice to the dictionary. As the day went on, she sat there happily, ready to cook more fish tomorrow, ready to bring her baby boy back home. Her monkey. He was a naughty boy to be sharking the Island like this, but that's all it was. Mischief – Eliza had said. Tomorrow night, at supper, she might even try a mouthful or two of her meal. Jack would think she was being silly, not eating fish for this long.

After the crossword, Margaret laid the newspaper on her lap and took a small sip of the buttercup syrup. She wouldn't re-order the pills. They were bad for her anyway; she shouldn't be taking them. She would insist on no further cigarettes in the house. And Jake too: he would be banned from supper, or, for that matter, from coming around at all; aye, he had the devil in his eyes.

Margaret closed her eyes. She thought of Jack's letters. *In the summer I close the window, to shut out the sound of the sea, for I know you are jealous of it.* She opened her eyes but it was all right that he was not there because she could not change it and she had to go on for her son. The pen rolled away from her lap. Such a sense of peace in the house today. For most of her life, a Sunday had been a time for burning churches – but how happy she was that all of that was over now. What else was it that he had written? *I'm in love with you, Margaret Malraux – I tell the fishes it every day.* Her eyelids dropped again.

A metallic hum woke her minutes or hours later. She squinted toward the window; there was still some daylight outside. Margaret raised herself from the chair. She did not feel scared about what she was about to do. From behind the chair she brought out her big shawl for warmth. Doubtless, it would be cold outside. Outside.

Margaret opened the first outhouse door and manoeuvred herself down the step. Holding on to the ledge with the plant pots, she made it to the back door. She managed the next step with a little hop, and then the pavement, which led on to a rhubarb bush, the garage, and a tree of unknown name. When Jack had brought her mackerel home from the catch, she would peg the fish up on the clothesline with the socks, to let them dry out in the sun.

The noise was behind her, now, and growing. Evening was coming and with it a great rolling mist that might obstruct her view. The last time she had done this – she knew, quite specifically – was autumn, nine years ago, because Margaret and Jack had not seen another plane together again. They had always come out on the last Sunday of the month, when some plane, on its way to Norway or some other destination, crossed the Island. Perhaps it went somewhere special, or maybe it had come, specifically, to watch them. They didn't know and they didn't care. All Islanders, without exception, loved the plane: suggestive, as it was, of Elsewhere.

In the garden, before it arrived, Jack and Margaret would talk about what they missed from England.

'Spare ribs,' he would say.

And she: 'Steak!'

'Red wine.'

'Nail polish. Nice lipstick.'

'Constant electricity.'

'Cigarettes.'

'More women.' An elbow in the ribs. 'Less men.'

'Fewer. Fewer men.'

'Women who don't correct my grammar.'

And then the plane would come, from nowhere, the sound drilling into the clouds, low and near. They would watch in awe, as if it imparted some vision of the world that was now impossible to imagine.

'How small are we to him?' she asked.

'Can he even see us?'

Margaret and Jack would jump up and down flapping their arms like children. 'Hallo!'

'Can you see us?'

'Yell if you can see us!'

They both wanted to see some passenger's hand flash in the window, or for the pilot to give a debonair salute. Anything to acknowledge they weren't in this alone.

Margaret had not seen the plane since Jack's death, bound, as she was, in the yellowing walls of her house.

She craned her head upward and waited. It emerged,

moments later: its body slipping in and out of the low-banked cloud. It's so beautiful, she thought, this machine, its shape stitching the cloud. How could it be held up like that? Margaret imagined herself in it, racing through air, with a great aerial view of the world, peering down at their tiny Island. She wondered if under the crests of waves the pilot could see shipwrecks and caves and hidden mountains. She wondered if he could see Jack's lost boat or the palace of his bones. She wondered if the plane travelled not just through air and space but time as well, so that the pilot knew what she had just done, as well as what she would do next.

The grey spike tipped out of sight. The sound faded. The shape flashed once or twice in the gaps between the clouds. Margaret stood in the garden until she was sure it had gone. Evening came.

Inside, in the kitchen, Margaret tossed away the last of the cigarettes. She had a moment of doubt, then redoubled her efforts and broke the cigarettes in two, tipping them into the kitchen bin where Thursday's head of bream still eyed her miserably. She would not smoke; no, she would not. She could do this as well, for her son.

They would have a fish supper tonight, just like they did when Jack was here, when he would emerge in his yellow fisherman's trousers, cold and big and starving, and they would eat together and he would jump Nathaniel on his knee. Margaret went to the purple room off the hallway and opened the wardrobe. Her fingers moved gently down the arm's lengths of her coats and dresses, vaguely embarrassed, as if someone might catch her. The fabrics were heavy and well-made, not like what was to be had any more. A box on top of the wardrobe held silk scarves, her old favourites. She tied an orange one at her throat. In the mirror she looked better for it; it gave her some colour in the cheeks, and hid some of the chin.

At the shelves, full of old boy's adventure stories and some philosophy books – they were all Jack's – her recipe book sat on the lowest rung. She hadn't looked at this book since she had given up cooking. In their early married years they had eaten enormously well: Margaret had made a feast every night, and she had been a good cook; still was. The smells of the food came to her, the weight of the dishes she would cook them in, the feeling of sweat escaping squashed breasts under her pinny. She had run a hot kitchen.

There were even, she found, some recipes from before the deportation, which she remembered jotting down – lamb shank roast, pork belly stew – in Newcastle. There was a picture of suet pudding. A small triangle had been cut from the pie, and tallow and kidney spilled onto the plate, steaming in perfection. Margaret tied the knot of the orange scarf tighter.

As she decided on the dish – Arctic char with parsnips – she snapped the book closed and a piece of paper fell from its flush pages. In her hands, the folds were sharp, they had been firmly pressed over the years. Margaret could not believe it. Here, in this book, all this time. So here it was; Jack's last letter, stored here safely and then, in the final negligence of grief, forgotten about.

Margaret read it quickly in the fading evening light.

The Godless Boys

Dear Maggie,

Hello my dear. A short note that should reach you tomorrow. I will be back the day after that, so I really shouldn't write, and save us the expense, but I like to think of your face when you have received a letter, and I imagine you will go and sit out in the garden (if it is fine), on the stripy deck-chair, and sit there for ten minutes or so, reading my words.

How is Nathaniel? Is he behaving himself for his mother? I hope he is not giving you too much trouble. He is as naughty as I was at that age.

It is night-time now, and I am sitting in my cabin, using candle-light to see by. The generator is down again but I do not mind – it makes much less of a noise.

By day I wonder what it is you do when I am on the boat. I think about what you might think about; I wonder what you do – even when you have told me, repeatedly, all that it is you do on a normal day. I think about you taking Nathaniel to the square, to the launderette, to the beach – I think about you putting him to bed and singing that wee song for him.

But somehow I cannot quite grasp together every little moment of your day. I want to know what it is you are doing when I am casting the nets, or pulling in the trawl. Whether you are gardening, or perhaps doing the washing, looking up at the aeroplane without me, or whether you are buying your bream at Stansky's.

But then, even knowing the monuments of your day, I still desire more. It is the long stretches in between buying the fish and cooking it that I most desire to know

about. *These bits, shall we call them your lost time,
when you are walking home or simply sitting in your
armchair, these moments fall out of my scope, and they
fall out of memory, out of remembrance. They are
precious. I wish I could somehow keep them, because
I know that these moments are lost, irretrievably, in
and amongst more important things.*

*My favourite way to imagine you is to think of you at
your armchair. Suddenly, your gaze has fallen into
nothingness, and you stare at nothing. Whatever has
alighted on the bonny shores of your mind has
captivated you, and I know, during these instances, I do
not exist for you. It does not make me anxious. We all
of us have these moments of deep meditation. I wonder
where you are. Are you thinking of Newcastle? The
Grand? Your Pa? Wherever your memory has taken you,
it has bound you fast to the longest minute.*

*If I could make a narrative out of every one of these
lost moments I would be a happy man. I would read
such a book from morning to night, so that I might ken
you better. All the dross: that's what I'd like to know of
you. And in the margins, because isn't that how far we
get in, when we try to map out our lover's mind, only to
the margins – never the heart, no, not really – I will pen
my notes on you. And all of these lost chapters I will
weave into a narrative, and I shan't let a soul read it.
And I will call it, In Search of the Lost Time of Margaret
Malraux. Who would not fall to their knees to hear the
majestic and muddied thoughts of my wife? You're an
irresistible woman – impossible at times.*

Maggie. The candle is sputtering and I am nearly out

of wax. I will put down my pen, and then I will think of
you. Who would have guessed you'd married such a sap?
But there you are. I'm in love with you – I tell the fishes
it every day.

    All my love, all my life,
                Jack

Margaret folded it back to. She carried the recipe book
to her armchair then laid out the letter on the bottom stair
in the hall. Nathaniel should read his father's words. How
beautiful; how sonorous. It might teach him something of
kindness.

She gathered her coat and her purse, checking there
was enough money for the char. And then she did it:
walked out of the front door, and made her way over to
Mr Stansky's.

27. The Fog

Fog filled the garden. Rich with the smell of fish and the sea, fog rolled down the streets and hung about doorways. At first, the air was tissuey, easily broken by the hand, no more than a mist, and then, as the early afternoon tipped quickly into darkness, it thickened into a fog, near the bay at first, as if the salt on the cliffs better attracted it, then it had gone cottony in the streets, and in the square, and up above to Warkworth Town and down into the crowded streets of Lynemouth, so that by evening the fog had come so low it skirted the hill, leaving Marley Hill exposed, the mount poking itself out of the cloud like a leg from a fussy girdle.

Down in the garden of Swanscott House, Sarah and Nathaniel had watched the aeroplane as it flew through the low-banked cloud. It was always sad for Nathaniel to see it: he remembered the times when his mam and dad would watch it together, and he remembered the odd feeling too, of being excluded from the ceremony. He remembered once going out into the garden to join them, and his da saying to him, quite kindly, but firmly, 'No. This is for your mam and dad, just now,' and his parents had cuddled up to each other only when they were sure he was gone. From what English ceremony did they keep him? And is this what they did in England, in Hartlepool and Newcastle, in the places of his parents' birth, stand and whisper to each other and watch aeroplanes? He'd been embarrassed, watching them get syrupy in the garden below, at the way they were acting like kids – despite this evidently being an adult ceremony, from which he was excluded.

Nathaniel had watched it with Sarah, today, although the sense of occasion had been somewhat lost on her, which he didn't mind. It was an Island thing to do, and, more specifically, a thing for old English people to do, like his ma, and his pa; he understood that now, was old enough to understand the significance of what they had lost. When the plane appeared in sight, Sarah had been about to say something, and Nathaniel had wondered if she was about to tell him she had actually been on a real plane. He was glad, if this were true, that she hadn't said anything. He didn't like to think of her gallivanting so far away from him.

As the plane had sounded over the Island, Sarah had, instead, talked of an Englishwoman who was nowhere near the Island, who had remained on English soil all this time. Sarah had looked thrilled, when she'd come back to Swanscott House, after talking with Mrs Spenser, purely talking a mile a minute about her ma being discovered in England, something about the deaths of two men and the confession of their names, the Sunday Agreement, and her mother's release from an English jail. Nathaniel didn't listen so much as watch her: the warmth of her cheeks, the sudden sharpness of her eyes. She was excited. The news of her ma's return had made her buoyant.

*

But Sarah saw how her private happiness seemed to dull him. Nathaniel had watched the plane fly its course overhead with a longing look, and she was aware that his father was not missing, was not waiting to be discovered. Distantly, as she was talking of Laura, and her mother's confession, Nathaniel was toeing the grass with his boot, so that it was almost bald in that patch, and fiddling with one of the studs on the jacket.

Tomorrow, she would go back to England on the boat. And maybe even tomorrow night her mother would be at home with them.

And if she could stay, would she? He was unlike any English boy she had ever met. When they slept in the bed, together, on Friday night, she wondered how it was she had ended up here. Not just on this Island, but with him. And yet it felt right, as if by knowing him she might better know the Island, as if Nathaniel were a kind of map.

Beatrice had seemed frightened by him, which had shocked her, since Sarah had suspected his gang were really only nuisances, not the menaces Nathaniel had tried to impress on her in the beginning. And Beatrice had mentioned something or other, a – what was the word – *crabbing* – that was it – of a Mrs Richards on Wednesday, and only yesterday night he descended to the sleeping bag with the stink of fire on him.

And yet, here he stood, with the aeroplane banking slowly, tipping, at an angle, greyly flying from them, his blue eyes looking sightlessly toward the sky, an emblem of all the good she had found on the Island.

No, she thought, though Beatrice was right about her

mother, she wasn't right about Nathaniel. She couldn't be. He was a good boy; a kind boy.

Sarah stopped talking, all of a sudden, and ran up into the house, past the kitchen with the pushed-back chairs, past the long staircase and up into the bedroom looking out onto the garden. Her fingers knocked the window. Nathaniel looked up at her. All week, she had viewed him as some boy of rebellion and grace, but now she knew him for what he was. Lonely and sad, a boy made from the cold wash of the Sound. She waved down to him. His eyes rounded in delight. A strip of teeth grinned up at her. 'Hello,' she said and Sarah heard her own little voice in the room. He took steps toward the house but she gestured for him to stop. Sarah unlatched the window and removed her jumper, brought the white T-shirt off so that she sat crouched in the pale bra. At her spine she unclipped it. The bones of her ribs curved white; the pink tips of her breasts were hard in the cold. A gamey scent came off her skin, her skin which was the same coolness as the air. She laughed, naked in the fog.

Downstairs, she heard his boot-steps, the sound was now familiar to her. He began on the stairs. Soon he would be at the landing, then at the door. She would stay by the window. She would let him find her.

The boots were behind her now. He must be inches away from her. There was silence for moments but she did not move. Then there were his lips on her neck, a tongue kissing toward her ear. She felt a surge of calm, and pleasure, that she had come here – wrongly, perhaps, but still she had managed to find the truth – and the thought of

Laura returning was perfect, and the thought of the boy, here with her now, was perfect too.

A hand moved her jaw toward him though she didn't turn her hips. She felt the hard plates of his teeth and pressed him closer to her, the buckles of the braces hard against her hips. His fingers came up her thighs and then to her breasts, thumb thumbing a nipple, the other hand bringing her around to face him, so that she saw his whole face in the moonlight. A hand grasped down to her, waiting, she moved against the sill, his finger quick, rounding her. Her legs sided his hips; his skin under his shirt was so white it was almost a glare. She held on to his shoulders.

He looked suddenly bashful and shy, biting his lip. A blush had come up his cheeks. 'Nathaniel?' she said, as he sat down next to her, his knees against her knees. He smelled of apples, and she remembered how, last night, he smelled of soot. 'I want to ask you something.'

'Aye. Go on.'

'When I talked to Mrs Spenser, she said something bad had happened with Mrs Richards, on Wednesday, and that she didn't want it happening to her. What happened, Nath? I think you should tell me.'

He didn't say anything for a few moments. 'Something bad happened with Jake. He did something which I didn't give him permission to do. We were just playing about, and then he took it too far. He always takes it too far.'

'She was scared, Nath. I don't think you should go around the Island frightening people.'

Nathaniel unwrapped her arms from around him. 'Look. I didn't tell you before because you were excited about the news of your mam. But Jake, the one who crabbed Mrs

Richards – he knows about you. He's seen you. He knows you're not from here. And I'm worried about it, about him – he can be such a menace, as I said. He knows you're English, and he'll think you're a threat, and he hates to be left out of things.'

'What does it matter, now, Nathaniel? I'm away tomorrow.'

'Aye. It's just worrying me a bit, that's all. Though it shouldn't do; I know that.'

'It's over now, Nath. I'll stay in all day. Today and tomorrow. And then I'm off. And I'll be far away from him.'

'And from me.'

Sarah brought him back, kissing him. The boy unlaced his boots, took off his socks, and pulled out some handkerchiefs. 'Why've you got hankies in your boots, Nathaniel?'

'They were my da's. Still waiting to fill them.'

Sarah laughed.

When they made love they did it gently as if they were swimmers plumbing the depths of a bay.

28. After the Fire

After the fire last night, Nathaniel had stomped away, unwilling to talk to Jake or give him any further information about the English girl. Oh aye, Jake was in Nathaniel's bad books, but he didn't much care. It had been a triumph, last night, and though Nathaniel still had the English girl under his wing, Jake had won with Verger.

That afternoon, when Sammy questioned him about the English girl, Jake was forced into some amount of lies about where he had spent the day. He told Sammy he'd been down to Swanscott House earlier to talk to Sarah. *Sarah*, he said, as if he were on familiar terms with her. He told Sammy that he'd touched her long copper hair and how she had blushed when she saw him. 'Oh, she is a dolly,' he said, 'despite her Gottery!'

He told Sammy how Old Baldie Boots had stood by mute as Jake laid down the law to her about how they did things on this Island. He told him how she'd bossed Nathaniel about, as if she was his own mam. How he had interrogated Sarah and how he thought this mother story was a cover-up for a much more menacing plan; he told him how frightened she'd become.

The two boys laughed gleefully in Sammy's bedroom as

Mr Carter shouted at them to keep it down – he was waiting for the aeroplane and didn't want to miss it.

None of this was true – Jake had not laid eyes on her since Friday night with Sammy himself – but Sammy seemed to believe him, and they hatched plans for what they would do with Sarah next. Stick her up on a cross or leave her cold in the church or parade her about town pinned in English newspapers. Somehow she would be punished for her English provenance.

No, Jake had not seen Sarah, but, last night, he had dreamed of her.

He dreamed he had been at the mortuary with her. There was no casket in the room; he had thought Mrs Page would still be here, but that was the bad logic of dreams, since he knew in real life that she was already under the waves. The enamel walls gleamed like a bathtub with room enough for two. Seated, Sarah held his hand while he looked down at his lap and tried hard not to laugh. He noticed the tenting of his trousers as the girl's chest heaved up and down and then she looked at him, and smiled, and kissed him softly on the lips. Sarah held him tightly against her bosom, which flattened against him and was as lovely as pudding. He put a finger down the passage between each bosom and then gave each one of them a squeeze. The bulge gave to his clambering hand. His finger strayed to a cold hard nipple. He felt a burst of delight. The girl held him closer. He peered down the black vest and glimpsed there the bra-less epiphany of one of her nipples. The freckles ringed the cool brown tip. He felt a surge of shame and delight, and he wondered, consciously, if he had wet the bed.

Then suddenly, Jake and Sarah were down on a beach and there was nothing but the sea; the North Sea Sound just as it always was. Jake looked down and in his arms he was carrying the girl and her white limp arms were as floppy as a fish. Her ginger hair fanned about her like a crown. She was so lovely and cool and clean and tasted of salt. He was taking her somewhere but he did not know where; he just knew she was an enormous weight, far heavier than she should have been. And then he woke.

Aye, last night's dream was bothering him. He wanted to see Sarah for himself again, to cleanse himself of the image, despite Nathaniel's warnings not to. He left Sammy's house, saying a polite goodbye to Mr Carter, and skirted around Marley Hill toward the Malraux house to see if Nathaniel was in. Mrs Malraux was in the parlour, reading, which was unusual for her; he'd never known her not to be encushioned in her armchair by the fire. She came to the door and looked at him narrowly with a handwritten paper still clutched, and told him Nathaniel was not here. Jake had begun to walk away when she took a step outside and said, 'You be careful, boy, sharking about these parts. You're not as welcome as you might think.' Jake thought back to the summer, when everything had been hot and scratched, the beach like a warm cracked bone, when Mammy Malraux had fed them up on biscuits and tea, and purely he thought she had cared for him, and him for her. He'd even called her Mammy. Well, this was how the Malrauxs turned on you; theirs was a fluid treachery.

But Jake said nothing and set off from the house. He walked quickly, shamefaced by Mammy Malraux's comment, and aware that, despite the dark, he should not be found here along Island paths. People would be looking for them, to hold them to account for Verger's fire. But he thought the silence would stick days longer, and Verger, old and unliked, wasn't likely to grass on them. Perhaps the Malades would never be caught for it; another blameless deed in the anonymity of night! But he walked to Swanscott House, urgently now, wanting to see Sarah just so that he might erase the dreamed image from his mind.

The light was on in the upper room but no one could be seen. He hoped he could crab her alone. At the back, in the garden, the air smelled of pond water. Into the house, the smell continued. Jake checked the rooms but no one was there. Very quietly, he took the stairs. The house was freezing. He heard nothing.

He checked the bathroom and the master bedroom, then pushed at the door of the room he had seen her in on Friday. It gave easily, without a noise. Into the small slot of air he let his eyes fall.

It was them. Together. They were kissing. They were making little sopping noises. They were lying on the bed, naked, the fog, outside, playing on their skin. A shapeless anger spread in Jake. Here it was indeed, for anyone to see, the toppling of a Malade! The English girl's hair was as shiny as a metal. In the light her limbs were almost lavender. Nathaniel moved his hands over her haunches to her breasts, repeatedly, as if he were reminding himself, again and again, that he could. Jake felt a hot, overflowing grief.

He idled by the door. To look away was pure loneliness; but to gaze upon them was agony.

In the last few minutes they'd stopped their wet squelching and fallen into what looked a deep and peaceful sleep. For some reason their stillness panicked Jake more than their smooching. They would be cold like this; naked.

Jake took Margaret's gun from out of his bag and held it out into the quivering air. He put the nozzle to the keyhole, liking the fact it might tunnel through the hole and into the air without splitting the frame. The gun knocked against the wood: the girl stirred but did not wake. Why wouldn't they move, why wouldn't they wake up, so that Jake could be outraged on behalf of the gang? Fog danced on them. He heard her gentle breathing and wondered, *Would it have the same sound on my chest?* From nowhere, a tear came into his eye and his heart felt fit to bursting. Though he knew, as a Malade, he shouldn't, his shoulders started the shake-and-heave, and his nose ran, and he felt the hot tears start to fall unstoppably. Jake thought of their smells together, mingling; he too would like to be inside her stinky crevices; inside, where she'd be as soft as the seabed.

Jake wiped his tears and took a good lungful. He couldn't stand this; not any more. He put the gun back in his bag and rapped on the door. 'Nathaniel?' he whispered. He shook his head to let some cold in. 'Nathaniel?' His voice sounded reedy from the blubbing. No answer, so he hit harder and harder, until Nathaniel shouted, 'Coming!' in an exasperated voice, and Jake stepped away to the banister, where he waited, uselessly, for minutes.

The boy emerged in nothing more than black jeans, doing up the fly with a cig in the crook of his mouth. Boyish skin crested over bones. The light of the match caught all the angles of his face. 'All right, Jakey. To what do I owe this pleasure?' He shut the door behind him, obscuring all view of her.

Jake couldn't quite look at him. 'I came to see the girl.'

'Oh, aye?'

'You promised me you'd show me her. Before the meeting last night, you said that.'

'I said we could all meet, some time. I didn't promise you anything. And I think you've had a good enough grozzly, for tonight, as it were.'

'I haven't even talked to her. This English girl. Found out what she's about.'

'You've had more than a good look. In flagrante, as we were.'

'In flagrante?'

'Aye. Good you didn't catch us actually at it. That might have raised a blush or two.' Nathaniel looked philosophical and smiled, wagging a finger at him. 'It does go to show, though, this theory on Gots and marriage, as we asked Mrs Richards Wednesday. See if she were a Got, Jake, it'd be no bonanza before marriage, get my ken? It's a good test. We're going to have to fuck all the girls on the Island! For the sake of our cause! Ha, ha!'

Jake found his throat very dry. 'Is she a goer, then?'

'Oh, aye,' Nathaniel said. He curled his hands over the banister and leaned back. 'A real cracker-jack.'

'Look.' Jake wouldn't lose this; not yet. 'I haven't told the other boys yet but I will if we don't see more progress. We need to interrogate her, find out what she's really about! Find out what secrets she may be gathering about the Island!'

'In a while. She's here for a while. The whole winter now, if I can get my way. It'll happen in the next few days. Then all the boys will meet her. But on my say so. We need to break them in, slowly, slowly.'

'Aye, aye,' said Jake, 'and we can talk about what sort of thing we should get up to with her. What sort of talking we should do. We might find the stinkiest things in her.'

Nathaniel gave him a curious look. 'That's the right thing. That's the right thing. You're a good boy, lad.'

'I'd do anything for the Malades. Anything you ask. And with the fire we really showed who—'

Nathaniel's face darkened. 'I told you before. It wasn't your place. Listen, Jake. It wasn't your place to suggest Verger. As I said, *immunity*, it was for me to suggest or not to suggest Verger. Do you understand that yet? Thick as two planks, sometimes!'

The girl, and Verger again? Who else might the boy defend? Christ himself could walk the Sound and he would be just as much Malade as they! 'I hate this. I hate what's happened to us! You've changed so much this week it's like you're barely a Malade now!'

Nathaniel looked as if he was about to fly at him, really sock a punch, but instead the boy sighed and asked him to sit on the stairs. He even passed the cigarette over so Jake could have the last draw. 'I know it's hard, Jake, but we've got to remember where we've come from on this. We're brothers, aye, we want the same thing.' There was a sense of weariness to Nathaniel and his voice softened even further. 'Remember, aye, when we had long hair, like a girl's, before we scalped ourselves this summer? Remember how much came off onto the garage floor, and how my ma yelped when she saw us? She said, "Och, look at you, you look like two big babies!" And what your ma said, as well, remember what a bollocking she gave us? Remember, Jake. We're brothers in this.' Nathaniel put his arm around him. The weight was good. 'But I've got to sort out this girl's business, aye, before we give her a galling. And you, out of everyone, should know what these boys are like, they've got no gentleness, they'll be after her like a pack of dogs. No, no; the policy, toward her, stands. The other boys can't ken yet, or else they'll want a looky and then they'll want some scrap and it will end in hardship for everyone. You know this, don't you lad? It'll be our secret, aye, just for this while, between you and me – like old times.' Nathaniel smiled. When the boy was kind and gentle like this, it was like Jake's own da had come back for a month of Sundays. 'I promise to show and share, Jake, once everything's ready. But not before. You need to trust me on this one.'

'Aye, aye, I do.'

Jake squashed the end of the cigarette out, and Nathaniel stood. 'I'll see you tomorrow night after the boat. Gather the boys in the square for nine o'clock or so. But no sooner, aye. I'll have an announcement to make. Of some money we'll see ourselves earning.'

'Money?'

'Aye. A whole lot of it.'

'From what?'

'A shipment. We're shipping out a new product. Forty pounds at least! Can you imagine?'

'What product?'

'Now, now Jake; that's not for your ken. Not right now. But I'll tell you tomorrow. In the square. At nine or so.'

Jake felt a flicker of irritation – *to be left out of the plans again!* – but he told himself to forget about it, while things were going so well. Now he had the boy back in his camp. He was about to suggest a trip to Maiden's Square, with rocks and stones which could be flung at any house, just for the two of them – like old times – but Nathaniel was walking back to the room. Or he thought they might set an agenda for the meeting tomorrow night; anything so that Nathaniel wouldn't descend to the mattress and to the girl, but the boy walked away, and shut the door firmly behind him. That feeling of calm, as if everything had been settled back to the normal way, suddenly broke. Jake stayed for a while, alone on the last stair-board, listening to the soft words of Nathaniel waking her, then the slopped sounds of kissing. And his blood gave that urgent ache again, and Jake ambled outside, into the freezing fog.

The Sound was purely hectic in his ears as he walked back up Marley Hill. Jake thought of the room where they lay rolling atop each other, Nath's black scalp where once it had been beautiful and bald. Cavorting like this with an English girl! Jake should tell Mammy Malraux and watch her blush rise. She would pronounce her son a traitor for this!

There was no one in Maiden's Square: the gang were all in hiding after the fire and cosying up to their mams and watching telly, no doubt. All they wanted was for school to start again tomorrow and for everything to go back to the way it was. But the way it was did not exist, not any more.

Jake was freezing but he went down to Warkworth Beach, his hands balled against the cold, watching the waves draw toward him, wishing for Sammy, or Nicholas; the loneliness in him a barbarous ache. He thought of Nath and Sarah in bed. Jake had wanted nothing more than to join them, that was all; to close himself into the narrow nest of those two exquisite bodies, to put either hand in their hands, and fall asleep with them, as the fog banked silently about the house.

Over the way, the dark roofs in Warkworth Town were beginning to float in the fog. He felt that he must have release or else he too would be lost. Goading himself with the thought of them, he refused to go home until he had shed this feeling.

Men in taverns were drinking and laughing while he stood alone on the cobbled streets. Above the town would be Verger's house, blackening, still hot. He'd like to visit it, to see what the Malades had done, but it was too dangerous, not while the smell of soot was still in his clothes.

Jake walked deeper into Lynemouth Town. He heard a scraping sign and followed the noise. He found the source down a narrow alley and onto the terraced street. The Grand. Promises of kissery and prickery. The expectation of pleasure suddenly lengthened and loosened his spine, flicking his head upright, as the tail of a snake flicks its head. He walked taller as he went in. And the girl and Nathaniel slipped from his thoughts.

*

Supine on the mattress, long-legged, older than the girl; the woman looked toward the window. Her hair was a strip of blonde falling down her back. When she turned, it looked to Jake like she had been crying: all red-rimmed around the eyes, a little wet under the nose. But she was enough to make the heart aloft; enough to give his mind the sense of sailing right out across the Sound.

'Hello,' Jake said, in all quiet tones, remembering how they had crabbed her on Monday night. He'd have to go soft with her, in order not to frighten her.

Her eyes slid up and down the length of him. She didn't say anything, nor did she stand, and Jake stood looming, not quite knowing what to do, or where to place his boots. The silence hung between them until she said: 'What do you want?'

'Eliza,' he said. 'Eliza.'

'Aye,' she said, and still didn't look back: 'That's my name.'

'Eliza—'

'Please go away.'

Jake didn't move.

'I said, go away.'

'Eliza, I've come here . . . ' He didn't know what to say. He thought of Nathaniel in his bedroom, boasting how he, the leader of the Malades, would be the first boy to have her. He remembered the look of complete self-assurance. Tonight, there was something limp about her, but still as lovely. 'I've come here to—'

'I'm sick of the sight of you boys.'

'I'm here alone.'

'I don't care. You're too young. Please go away.'

'I've got the money, I could pay—'

'I said no.'

Nathaniel would expect him to be skittish, like this, frightening at the first task. Jake was scared enough, all right. 'I have five pounds.' Eliza did not say anything but turned to him, stony-eyed. 'Here. Look.' He thought the money would get her. Jake took out the notes, soft as cotton, holding them in his palm. He was pleased to see he did not shake much. Eliza looked at him, something blank about her gaze, like Nathaniel's eyes too when he was lost in the scrap, voided of something important.

She looked at the money as if he were very far away. 'Is it your habit to carry about this amount of money?'

' 'Tis a fortnight's food allowance. Guess my mam will have to be content with tatties for a while.' He smiled at her and expected some warmth but she didn't give any.

She said: 'Ten pounds or nothing.' Her gaze did not leave the money as she picked it up, between forefinger and thumb, as if it was somehow filthy. 'Tomorrow. Come at six. No earlier, and no later. And bring the extra five pounds.'

'I—'

'I don't care. It's ten pounds or nothing.'

'Why? Why do I' – he corrected the whine of his voice to something more gentlemanly – 'have to pay more?'

'Because,' she put the money in the side table by the bed, 'you're a hooligan, Jakob Lawrence. Because you burned down Mr Verger's house. Because you're a child. Because I'd do anything not to do this. But I can't. So bring the ten pounds. Or you get nothing.'

'How'm I meant to find an extra fiver?'

Eliza shrugged. 'Ask your mam for more fish money. I don't particularly care.'

He said, 'Well.' He tried to think of some way of salvaging his triumph. 'It's ten pounds for the whole night. Or there isn't a deal.'

Eliza shrugged her consent. 'How old are you, boy?'

'Fifteen,' he said.

Eliza closed her eyes for just a moment, and then led him to the door. For the second time that night, it was shut right in his face. But this time, Jake was too elated to care. Aye, somehow, tonight, he had won.

29. The Deal

Verger's house was not, of course, the first case of arson on the Island. It was Jack Malraux and John Verger who set their matches on the church's pews in March of '51, and the small blaze rapidly grew, as the Islanders came to observe the last church-burning they would ever see. They watched, the sum of England's Secular Movement, most knowing it was not the church going up in flames, but each person's former life, and it was with a mixture of sorrow and triumph that they observed the fire. It was a last act of defiance, but to whom? No one of clerical consequence saw it. But it still felt deeply necessary. And then soon the bells rang from the cop shop, sirens ringing, telling them to scatter, but not before the church's loot had been divvied up, ready for mantelpieces, tablecloths, and a special place above the telly. And Jack Malraux and John Verger had never – officially – been named as the arsonists.

The culprits of the second fire on the Island, the ones who had set fire to Verger's house, had not yet been found. Verger was ensconced at Caro Kilman's, who was fussing over him as she did Morris. The police, a volunteer group based nominally in Lynemouth Town, were slow in their investigation. People spoke to them of these boys, this gang – they called themselves the Malades – but when Verger had been quizzed about Nathaniel Malraux or Jakob Lawrence, he hadn't said a thing, merely turning a gold ring round and round his index finger. Caro tried to push him into implicating the boys but Verger would say nothing. The policeman asked whether a politic visit to Mrs Malraux would be in order but Caro sighed bullishly and said 'no chance'. The policeman had gathered neighbours' suspicions but, as yet, there were neither witnesses nor evidence.

'Come now,' Caro cajoled Verger, 'try and remember.'

'I do remember, Mrs Kilman. I remember that I saw no one.'

'No one at all?'

'No one.'

Mrs Kilman looked at the chinless policeman with some sense of despair. Verger was wrapped in a tartan blanket, having caught a chill on Saturday night. 'Well,' she said, raising her eyebrows, 'looks like no one saw anything at all. Isn't *that* surprising.'

'In fact, come to think of it, I do recall one thing now,' said Verger. Mrs Kilman's eyes lit up. 'That I might have left the stove on. And what if the kitchen had caught fire, and then the rest of the house? Perhaps it was my fault?'

'Your fault, sir?' the policeman said.

'Aye.'

'But your bedroom was the first room to go up. Not the kitchen. And there was a broken window, as if someone had thrown a missile,' said the policeman. 'A burning missile, sir.'

'Oh. Well. Yes, yes, of course.'

'Can I ask, Mr Verger, where you were last night, when the house first caught fire?'

The old man looked at him frankly, as if he thought this was the first good question the policeman had managed. 'I was down at the church. The ruined one at Lynemouth Town. I was,' he wetted his lips as if they had been scorched from the blaze, 'praying. I was praying.'

Mrs Kilman blushed and looked away, and suggested, in a tactful manner, that the old man was suffering from shock. She suggested the policeman pay a visit to Eliza Michalka, who had picked Mr Verger up outside his home and given him a place to stay for the night. The policeman looked rather pleased at this. 'And I am sure,' Mrs Kilman continued, 'she did it purely out of good thoughts and not out of a general sense of lucre.'

'She profited not a shilling from my being there,' Verger said.

'Aye, well. I doubt she'll implicate anyone,' Caro said, 'now that we have all assumed this rather thick veil of silence.' And she walked off with a cross look and went to see after Morris.

The policeman went round to the Grand, as bidden, to question Musa and Eliza. Neither of them gave up much more than Verger or Mrs Kilman. Eliza admitted picking up Verger outside his house, but she said it was already half-burned by the time she got there, and that she saw no one run off, or acting suspiciously. Musa said he merely provided Verger a safe place to sleep for the night. The policeman asked if the old man paid him for the pleasure, and Musa looked offended: 'Oh no, sir; I don't think we've lost all of our sense of charity.' Eliza raised her eyebrows.

Both were instructed, were they to see either Nathaniel Malraux or Jakob Lawrence, to get in touch with him.

The policeman left with rather a longing look at Eliza.

'Well, well, well,' said Musa, 'looks like the boys are in trouble.' Eliza said nothing. How might she broach the small matter of Jake? Verger's tattoo throbbed. 'And did you really not see anything? Down at his house?'

'I said no. I was telling the truth.'

Musa shrugged. 'Poor Verger. 'Twill be hard with winter coming. And the fog has come so early this year. Well, the Grand is a good place to lick your wounds, so to speak. Still, he was very particular about having no lady visitor *whatsoever*. "Whatsoever!" he said.'

'Come on,' she said. 'He was hardly in a fit state.'

'Aye, well. I would never refuse a lady like you, Miss Eliza. I was always surprised you never did do better here.' Musa looked down at the paper on the desk. 'Ah, well. He will survive. There are provisions enough, I suppose. The pier will be full tonight of English charity and we will see how much can be siphoned off for the old man. 'Twill be a long winter.' Musa sat and studied a paper. 'But then they always are. Well, well, the *Saviour* will be back in February.'

'Aye.'

'And do you feel ready for the winter, Eliza? Have you stored up provisions? Ready for the long hard months?'

'As well as can be expected.'

'You eat like a bird, anyway.' He was still looking down at the paper. 'I'm surprised you haven't come down with the anaemia, you eat so little fish.'

'Went off it, aye, after Mam's death.'

Musa looked up, tipping his head, as if looking at her for the first time. 'Aye. I suppose you did.'

'Well. I'm off to my room. I'm expecting someone.'

He looked surprised. 'Are you?'

'Yes. I am.' Eliza stood to go back to her room. 'Send him through. He'll be here at six.'

'Good, good, good. Some business at last!'

Eliza took a good long breath. 'It's Jake. The boy. It's Jakob Lawrence. The one the policeman was asking after.'

Musa shrugged. 'Just leave my commission.' He said slowly: 'I really don't want to know.' And he turned the leaf of the paper.

Yes, it was the last *Saviour* of the winter. And Eliza would be on it. And Musa didn't have a clue she was escaping. How many times had she traversed this passage from the reception to her room, wondering if there was ever to be an escape from this tread of hall?

Her room was closeted away at the back of the house, with a big window halved by the sea and sky. The sea, this evening, was capped by the approaching fog. She sat and watched. It had not been so bad, really, this Grand life. During that summer, in her fury with Arthur, she had schooled herself into almost enjoying this place. But then time had gone on, and only Mr Carter came now, and she'd grown quite dull, just like the other girls, who grazed and mooched with much the same insolence she had seen of cows on the telly, their eyes full of the same bovine vacuity. Eliza could understand why the Island men shunned the great trough of them. No wonder the Grand was quiet, with girls such as Janey ruling the place.

But now England. Eliza was going to England. She was overjoyed; or thought she should be. It was five o'clock. Eliza passed the brush over her teeth and the comb through her hair. The boy would be here in an hour. Jake, with his babyish mouth, and his constant tic of licking his lips. Jake, who had launched the torch – she was sure it had been him, balder as he was than Nathaniel – on Friday night. Jake, who had terrorized Mrs Richards. Aye, she saw the gang's slug-trail from one spot of terror to the next.

But to refuse Jake meant she would not escape. Eliza had spent the past six months hectoring the thin stiff air asking for respite and here it was: a chance to leave. She reasoned that if there were a God, as Verger had seemed to insist, then this act forthcoming would be squeezed into some dark and unheeded chamber of His heart where it would be, instantly, warmly, forgotten.

In her mind, in the early evening light, it was a much pardonable felony.

Eliza began to pack a bag: a few dresses, jumpers, socks, tights, a pair of good shoes; a newspaper article of London her ma had given her with a map on it, as well as three English banknotes. That afternoon she had sneaked some bread rolls from the kitchen and now she stuffed them in the side pockets of the bag, where the Sound couldn't get a lick on them. Zipped and closed, there was something neat and absurd about the case, as if all the folded clothes were taking her, and not being taken, to a place she had no clear idea of. England. It was a joke, really, for her to go there, a prostitute, from this Island, to the holiest place in the world! But to stay here was another joke, and a miserable joke at that.

Eliza kicked the bag under the bed. Perhaps she should do the right thing and refuse the boy. She should give him back his money and stay. He was a child! A child and an arsonist and a hooligan! But Eliza had not reported the fire, nor stopped the gang when she could have, so what use was it to make her stand of goodness now?

In the mirror, the tattoo of *Verger* was scabbed and raw. How might she mark this? Should she tattoo the word *Jake*, too, on her skull, cosy next to *Verger*, so that she might have victim and criminal squashed together on the same brow? Eliza jammed her fingers into the cut to make it bleed. For moments she nursed her outrage but then gave up and tearfully mopped her forehead with a tissue. Not much point in feeling sorry for herself, since it was not going to stop the crime itself.

There was now half an hour left. The lamp gave off the sallow light of the sick ward. Eliza moved her fingers across her brow, feeling the warm throb of the cut, and then across the walls, trailing them to the contours of the room. She had loved and hated this place; that sea out there; this silence, in here. She remembered Arthur's face that summer, the colour of leather, how the arc of wrinkles fell from his eyes. Leaving, of course, meant leaving him. *Oh, Arthur*, she thought; *the loss of you is the worse part of leaving.*

Eliza had decided she would not say goodbye to him: she would leave silently. She had not been shrewd enough in her life; it was shrewd now, to leave quietly.

At the door, she noticed an envelope. Eliza checked the corridor but there was no one. Might it be from Arthur? A parting note, somehow? Or from Jake? Saying he had changed his mind? Was her passage on the boat less secure than she had hoped? At her bed, she split the top of the envelope and began to read.

Monday 1 December, 1986

Dear Miss Eliza,

I must thank you for the kindness you showed me last night. Without you, as I said, I may have frozen to death outside my house, with such rain as we had early Friday morning. If I could I would offer you some token of my appreciation, but as you know, I have nothing left. Now I am staying at the Kilmans' while I get my things together, which is very kind of them, especially given Morris's ill health.

So instead I would like to give you this prayer, which you may not have ever heard, which is famous across the waters, and which is, to all of us, happily free. It is most of all about forgiveness. I hope in all of this you might forgive yourself. Know that I have. And know that you are loved regardless of anything you might do, or not do. This is what we call Grace, and it is God's dearest gift to us.

What I didn't mention to you yesterday, out of shame (see, we all have it), is my reason for forgiving the boys so quickly after their setting fire to my house. You may not know it, but once I – and another conspirator, namely Nathaniel's father, Jack – set fire to the church down at Lynemouth Bay, back in 1951. It was foolish and childish. We did it to impress the other Islanders, and it did impress some of them. But now we are left with no place for our community to gather, and we are

poorer for it. And I will have to carry this guilt with me
forever.

A few months ago, I found myself at the church
during a particularly hard time, and it was there that
I knew things had come full circle. I found God, there,
Eliza, or should I say; He found me . . . or perhaps, just
that I had never truly been Lost. I heard bells again, as
if they were the bells of the police come to get me, like in
'51, but I knew they weren't: they were soft church bells,
ringing soundlessly, ringing for me.

Just as God forgave me for setting fire to His house,
I must forgive the boys for setting fire to mine. We must,
as it says, 'Forgive those who trespass against us.'

As I get my feet on the ground, and as you formulate
your plan to leave the Grand – I admire your bravery
in this, very much – perhaps we could meet some time
soon, to discuss things. And don't worry about Arthur,
dear: I'm sure it will all work out for the best.

With all best wishes, to you,
And my thanks,
J.V.

I trust you will not show anyone this letter.

She read the prayer at the end. *Forgive us our trespasses,*
she read. *As we forgive those who trespass against us.* It must
have been exactly six. Verger's letter slipped neatly into her
suitcase as she told the boy to come in.

Jake's eyes swung from corner to corner. Here he
was, with his sleek skull and hooligan's clothes. His jacket
was boxy and gave him the look of someone hung from a

scaffold. He smiled. Eliza said his name. All gone was the
nervy regard of last night. Had he taken something, one of
Mrs Malraux's pills, perhaps?

'I brought you the money,' he said. The money, aye. The
money, that tarted up this deed from crime to necessity.
'The last of it,' he said, putting a five-pound note in her
hand. She was terrified of what was happening, and what
was happening so rapidly, but wordlessly she stuffed it into
the cabinet drawer. £50 was there: complete. Before she
had even turned, he put his arms around her.

The boy was kissing her neck. So it had started already,
with so little as a flicker of consent . . . though who was
she fooling, she'd invited him in, had taken his money;
she'd barely simpered, though she had planned a doggish
digging-in of heels! Something about the air had shifted.
Was it a sense of triumph? Aye. All £50 lay crumpled in
the drawer. She was going. She almost smiled. England.
England!

So quickly they were on the mattress and she could
smell the must of one hundred men who'd been on this bed
in years past. She felt his teeth and tongue and gums and
the rise and fall of his breath. Almost erotic; the smell of
his hair, this pomadey smell, and the pressure of his ribs on
her, and the stiff jeans against her thighs. What a girlish
mouth he had, kissing her, squashing her lips with his.
Sheened in sweat, his palms were slick too. The boy was
nearly naked now (how had he managed that so quickly,
in all his trappings?), and he was beautiful and thuggish,
like some god or devil, come down to shame and gratify
her both.

Eliza heard a bang as the jeans hit the floorboards. She

tried to work out what the noise was, a metallic, heavy sound, but he was clambering on top of her now and a bead of sweat had fallen into her eye and was making it smart.

As he started what he had come for, she watched the window. She couldn't bear to look at him. She thought instead of John Verger and his hopeful prayer. She thought of Margaret in her armchair and her chin jogging along with her words. She thought of Linda in her brogues in the coffin. She thought of the Sound, and how surely she had contemplated jumping into it.

A hand, silhouetted in the dark, delved to her breast; he pinned it down with his mouth, a roguish nuzzle.

With doleful grunts, Jake began. It was neither better nor worse than any other customer. He had strangely plump hands, keying them into her mouth. She couldn't do this; but she must! And didn't Verger say the trespass would be forgiven! Jake made boyish mews of pleasure, then with a brute, joyful grunt, the job was over, the deed done, the awful money made.

The boy collapsed. She scooped him off her so that he lay flat next to her. The smell coming off him was as pungent as onion.

Fog banked. Under the flank of her hair she traced the tattoo: *Verger*, it said, and here she was bedding the culprit. How expertly the mind dodged the law when offered a way out of a dilemma! How quickly she had known she would bed him for this sum!

The boy started to snore. Eliza rose and dressed. She put the £50 in her purse, put on the big coat with the fur collar, and her ma's gloves. It was a silliness to write her words in a grave situation such as this, but she couldn't resist. The word Verger was there, now mangled and red. In blue ink, underneath that word, she wrote:

Now I go across the waters.

She screwed in the full stop with some degree of purpose: the little dot was the Island, and she was going far beyond it. Soon the world was about to crack open.

Eliza coaxed out the bag from under the bed and winched open the window. She threw her case and herself over the side onto the flat roof below. A moment of hesitation as she looked back to the room: what if the boy caught a cold, sprawled naked and unguarded on top of the bedspread, with the window open like that? But she had to rush. There was very little time.

30. Foreign Tastes

They'd made love all day in the back bedroom upstairs. The fog was as thick as cotton, and they felt a sense of weightlessness and suspension, as if they were alone on the Island. Exquisite and together, there seemed to be nothing beyond the room but the Sound. And every hour or so a sense of joy burst in them, more intense still for the little time that was left to them. Occasionally, Nathaniel went down to the front garden, to smoke, and watch for Jake. An air of anxiety followed him when he returned up the stairs. Sarah teased him about being scared but he'd looked at her quite seriously and said that he was.

Now, in the early evening, they sat in the kitchen in Swanscott House. It was full of the same metallic light as the bedroom. The tablecloth, which they had found in one of the chests of drawers, was worn and threadbare, with rings of coffee stains and pan marks. The flowers at the bottom of the cloth were fraying at the hem. Sarah had spread it out across the table so that they could eat their last dinner together, and Nathaniel had found a candle, and put it in a glass bottle and lit it for her, so they could eat by the light of the flame. 'I wonder who it was who lived here,' she said. 'Before us.'

'Some Island family.'

'Now English.'

'Aye. Now English, like you.'

'And now we can both remember it as our home. You can visit it and I can think of it. Swanscott House; where I met you. Where we had this.'

Sometimes, panicked, he looked at the kitchen glass, convinced Jake had edged through the overgrown garden and crept up on them without a noise. He had told her Jake had come last night, while she was sleeping, wanting a look at her. He did not want the boy here. Or any of the boys.

She said, 'I'm sure he won't come back. He's feeling abandoned. That's all.'

'Him and everyone else.'

Sarah looked down on the plate. 'I told you. I have to leave. My mum's coming home. Maybe before Christmas.' Her eyes were excited and keen. 'She may even have been released by now. She may be waiting in England. And I couldn't stay anyway. My dad. He's at home, alone. Imagine if I asked you to come back with me. Would you leave?'

'But, Sarah,' he knew his voice sounded syrupy, but perhaps that might help his cause, 'I need you here with me.'

'We can't do it,' she said, with some firmness.

Sarah's skin was soft and lovely in the light. She wore his shirt and braces and her big anorak over the clothes with the red scarf he had given her. It was as if, in here, in the kitchen, the windy kingdom of the Sound had all but disappeared. 'You do have some strange garb,' he said to her, tugging at the end of the scarf. He sighed. 'How can I convince you to stay?'

'You can't. The boat's tonight. I've got to be on it,' she said. She traced one of the tablecloth's flowers. 'You know, I always imagined finding Laura in a grand house. With an open fire and books everywhere. Or on the beach, walking along the bay. I always imagined that when I saw her she would recognize me completely.' She bit at her lip. 'I've no idea who she is. No idea whatsoever. Even if she is back home, I can't think about what I'll say to her, or what she'll say to me. She's a stranger to me, just as you were. And I feel ashamed, at what she did.'

'They didn't do it out of enjoyment. It's not right us being here, stuck on this rock. It's the right cause, Sarah.'

'I know; I know,' she said. 'But a man died for it.'

'Many died for it. On both sides.'

The fog was thickening, so that the landscape looked as if covered with virgin snow. His mam would be alone now, in the living room, waiting for him, but he couldn't bear the thought of Mammy suffering on account of him, and he turned to Sarah and kissed her across the table. Being with Sarah, it was like . . . It was like after hours of the scrap, coming into a warm hot bath where he might stretch out his limbs and enjoy relaxing, because though there was nothing he wanted more than to feel the dark breath of the Island's night air and watch the smash of a window, above all this he wanted to come back home to Sarah, to the neat basin of her lap and the softness of her cheek. Aye, above all, when he was with Sarah, he forgot even what the scrap meant to him.

And the satisfaction of her staying with him far out-weighed the guilt of what he was about to do. Obedient to his love as Arthur was to his, he would not let her go. He could not. And Arthur had advised him on this; and Arthur always kept good counsel.

Nathaniel stood. 'What's this you've got for me?' He read the tin. 'Corned beef? Beef, that's cow, isn't it? It's beef with corn in it?' Nearly three-quarters had already been eaten. 'You didn't leave much for me,' he said. It was moist inside the can, with a strong smell.

'Aye, well, it was my only food, before you arrived.'

'Before I arrived and everything changed.'

'That's right.'

'It smells of old shoe.'

Sarah stood and cut the square loaf he'd brought from home. The meat went lumpishly onto the bread, and she spread it thinly. She hadn't ruled out that he might have some sort of reaction to it. What if it were a kind of poison to his system? The flakes were pink and moist. The smell of it made her salivate; though the sight of it wasn't appe-tizing. Nathaniel sniffed it warily. 'Or foot, aye, it smells of foot,' he said.

'Just try it.'

Nathaniel took a bite. There was something leathery about the taste, and very brown, as if he chewed a piece of particularly expensive furniture. 'It's OK,' he said, 'but not up to much. Still,' he grinned, 'the first Island lad to have the flesh of a cow in me! I was always one for firsts!'

Nathaniel kissed her and he could taste the salt in his own mouth. He felt purely joyous. 'Here, let me make yours.' Sarah sat down at the long kitchen table, the light from the candle playing on her hair. 'You do look lovely, there, Sarah. A real treasure,' he said. She combed the hair back from her face and smiled at him.

Nathaniel spread the last of the beef thickly on the slice. He talked to her, asking her about her dad, and what she'd do when she got back to England, and what she'd tell him about where she had been. He laughed as she imagined all of the stories she could tell them. While she was talking, Nathaniel crushed the sedative in his fingers and spread it thinly onto the chopped tinned beef. With a fork he mashed it in until it couldn't be seen, and then he folded the bread over, just as she'd done. He'd been lucky; there'd only been one left in the small amber bottle in his Mam's bathroom cabinets. It would last the few hours or so that he needed. Sarah would be happy with him, once she saw reason. Once she'd spent the winter here she would realize what a good idea this was, and she could see her ma in good time in the spring. Maybe even let her mam and dad have some quiet time on their own this winter. Tonight, he would persuade the Boatman to take Eliza and he'd come back to the house, as Sarah woke from the love-coma, and he'd be able to show her the money he'd spend on her this winter.

'Here,' he said, passing the plate over to her.

When she ate, she ate heartily. 'Last meal,' she said, but her laugh was quiet, as if the fog had come indoors and muffled her voice.

31. Eliza and Arthur

It was seven o'clock by the time Eliza reached Maiden's Square. Propped in the museum's alcove, that hour bound with every other hour she had spent there, she stood and waited, though she knew it was too late for Arthur to appear. Too late, as well, to say goodbye.

She thought of the English girl. It filled her with regret that she hadn't managed to find her again, that she had slipped out of sight after Mrs Page's funeral. A certain note of anxiety struck her. Eliza wished, dearly, that the girl was well, and being looked after by someone. Perhaps Mrs Malraux had taken her in – or, goodness forbid, Caro Kilman. Or maybe the girl was planning to sneak herself back on the boat tonight, just as she had done last Monday, and they could talk at length while they both hid in the cabin for England.

Eliza could barely see the shop's frontage for all the fog. No shadows to be seen; nothing but this milky swell. Between the folds of her bag Eliza felt for her purse. The money was still there: £35 from her mother's inheritance; £5 from Mrs Page, and a further £10 from Jake. £50 in total. Just as Nathaniel had asked. Her mind emptied. Everything would be fine. The boat would come and take her away to England. And she would be rid, forever, of this Island. But she couldn't leave quite yet. Not without saying a goodbye to Arthur, even if it were just, in effect, a gesture.

Eliza crossed the square and cupped the sides of her temples, peering into the dark room. This window had kept her at the longest distance for so many nights. The gutting knives flashed. Could a message be scrawled on the glass, in the condensation, and might it last till morning? What might it say, but *I love you*, and *goodbye* and *I'll miss you* and *I'm sorry*.

A fluorescent light blinded her for moments. She squinted into it. A lumbering shadow grew larger on the tiled wall, going toward the knives. It had to be Arthur. *He is going to kill me!* was her first thought, but she told herself not to be so melodramatic. Presently, his face was no more than an inch from the other side of the glass, as hers was; straining into the dark and light both. Arthur withdrew; the lock snapped twice. He was locking it against her, she was sure, keeping the slattern on the cold side of the square, but then the door opened and he was standing there: warm, real, breathing, his hands tucked under his arms. Arthur said, 'Hello.'

Her breath left her mouth before she too said hello and then looked down at her shoes.

'Eliza.' It was the first time she had seen him here without the bloodied pinny. He said, 'Come in. Please. There's something rank in that mist tonight.'

She followed him into the shop. The clock at the wall read a quarter past seven. Arthur lifted up the counter and put it back to, so that he was on one side, and she on the other. With a lurch of horror, she wondered if he had assumed she was a late customer and was about to sell her a bream. 'Arthur, I—'

'Eliza.' He turned his back on her, regarding the knives, and she truly did wonder if he was contemplating which one to pluck from the magnet and sink into her heart. But when he turned back to her it was as if his face had aged ten years in the moments just passed. 'Eliza. I've never known how to say sorry. About that night. That night in the Grand this summer. It was unforgivable. Just after your ma's death. It wasn't right, aye.'

'You don't need my forgiveness,' though her voice was surprisingly stern, 'I forgave you a long time ago.'

'Aye, but I've been angry with myself ever since. When your ma died, things moved so fast, and I got scared. And then I got so, so incredibly jealous of you working in the Grand, and I was so angry that you were there . . . I didn't think for a second of your financial situation. And then I came to you, and we . . . I couldn't be sorrier. I'm still so ashamed.'

Eliza didn't say anything.

'And after that, I resolved that I would keep myself to myself and not interfere in your business.' His eyes climbed the walls. 'But I couldn't – I can't – stop thinking about you. Every day when I make up the display, I wonder if it's you who will come and admire the colours. And it's always Mrs Kilman or Mrs Bingley, come to tell me of their husband's bloods, or they fret that the fish were caught where a loved one was lost. I don't say much, I never do, apart from now, it seems, I can't stop talking . . . ' He laughed. Arthur had sounded almost jolly, but now his voice went sort of toneless and flat. 'Every day my heart is as cold as these dead fish. Every day, as I go about my butchering, I seem to get further and further from you, until it's my heart under the knife that I gut and quarter. I can't stand this life without you. I love you.'

'What?'

'I love you.'

'What? Why do you say this now?' Her voice wasn't really much more than a whisper.

He coughed, as if he were embarrassed. 'Mr Verger was in here this morning.'

'Mr Verger?'

'Aye. Talking of you. Saying you had a fair place in your heart for me.'

'No,' she said. 'I'm afraid you're mistaken. He must have been disturbed, perhaps, upset, from the fire. Did you hear, the old man lost his—'

'What do you mean?' Arthur lifted the swing so that he was on her side. The skin by his eyes was dark and she noticed he had not shaved in a while. 'I love you, Eliza. I'll do whatever it takes to make amends. Eliza; dear Eliza.'

She looked at him blankly, as if she had too perfectly managed the art of feeling nothing. Arthur moved to take hold of her arm but she shrugged him off. She would not let him undo her. She had to leave. 'No,' she said again, 'I don't love you.'

'Mr Verger said—'

'Mr Verger got it wrong. Mr Verger was mistaken.'

'He said that you had always wanted to say something, that both of us, we were stuck in shame and I was so—'

'*I'm leaving*, can't you hear me?'

'What?'

'I'm leaving the Island.'

'You can't. I mean. How?'

'I've paid Nathaniel. He'll pay off the Boatman. I've passage on the *Saviour* tonight.'

'How much?'

'Fifty pounds.'

'Fifty pounds! Why? Where are you going?'

'Where else? To England. There's nothing left for me here.'

'But I love you. We could be happy together here, dear Eliza—'

'Why do you have to say this now? Why do you say this tonight, of all nights? I have to go, Arthur.' She hit her palm against the glass case. 'Why could you not have told me before? It's not fair you are saying this to me now!'

Arthur's voice, too, turned flinted. 'Because Mr Verger only said it this morning. *I* had no idea you had plans to get on the English boat. How was I to know?' He stopped. He was quieter now. 'Is your mind made up?'

Eliza saw him, pinny-less, in the glass-and-enamel shop. Here he was in his palace of fish. It would not be a difficult life here. No longer would she be the rag-picker come, in the late nights at the museum, to scavenge off him what she could. She wanted to look after him; wanted to be looked after by him. But she thought of the Island and the Sound and the gossiping women and marauding boys and the thought of Arthur, maybe, failing her again. It would take twenty steps to get off that pier. Twenty steps to England.

The lamp sputtered. It turned dark, and light, and dark again, and all the counters, glass tops and knives were lost completely in the black. 'Arthur?'

'The bulb's gone.' He sounded sad, and faraway. 'A sign, perhaps.'

The light gave a last flicker and they saw each other again, their faces as close as they had been moments ago, though there was no glass between them now, just an inch of air. Then, finally, darkness came: thick, luxurious, depthless. She touched his neck. He gave a sigh. They held each other, willing the other to let go, and he said sorry again. She hushed him and they stood like that for some moments, no more than a statue of an embrace, amongst the sheer tops and polished glass.

He said to her, tell me you will stay with me, tell me you will stay with me here.

And then he kissed her.

She whispered, 'Goodbye,' and fled.

Now, so thick as to be a bog, fog filled the square. Despite herself, despite her twenty-four years here, Eliza could not quite remember which way was which. In an objectless stride she set out. She felt quite dizzy, and freezing cold, and half-blind, and half-witless for losing him. *Arthur!* Aye, here was the sting: here was her punishment enough for Jake, for that merry felony, and it was murder enough.

The air was like a clod of earth. The scrape of the museum sign was somewhere, but she could not tell if it was close or far. Surfacing in her mind came the picture of the deportees, gathered at Newcastle pier, waving their dark documents. And was that where she was going now? To England? What madness did England hold!

She was close enough, now, to see the stonework of the Museum. If she walked away, from this point, she would pass Buttons and the grocer's and Mrs Kilman's, past the surgery and the hardware shop, and if she walked on she would come to the cliffs and the steps down to the pier. Eliza moved herself toward the sound of the sea. This fog held a ratty stink.

'Eliza!' Arthur's voice: where was it coming from? 'Eliza!' There was a lag now, and his voice was thin, as if he was heading down to the cliffs. 'Eliza!'

'Wait,' she said, 'I'm here!'

'Eliza!' he said: he was further off, heading toward Warkworth Bay.

'I'm here!' but she could not throw her voice; not like him, and she knew he was getting further away. She took the narrow path from Maiden's Square out toward the headland, thinking that if she could get to the top of the cliff, the fog might be thinner near the water's edge. She had no idea about the time, or whether she had missed the boat: it seemed like it had been hours between the boy and Arthur.

At the cliff, she saw him: walking toward the pier. How solitary he looked! She scrambled down the cliff steps. 'Arthur!'

He turned and saw her.

'Eliza!' He held something up in his pale hands. 'I'm coming with YOU!' he shouted, as she ran down the last few steps and onto the beach, past the rocks where she had hidden last Monday night. As she came closer she saw more distinctly what it was. Money. 'Arthur!'

He stood there. Smiling. The money outstretched.

'Why on earth have you all this money?' she said, getting the breath back up her.

'Saving up,' he said, 'for a rainy day.'

'Oh, Arthur.'

He brought her closer toward him.

'You know what Mrs Malraux said to me today?'

'What's that?'

'I haven't seen her for years, and you know the first thing she said to me? It was – why are you and Eliza Michalka not hitched already? And I honestly couldn't think of a reason why. Marry me, Eliza, in a big church, in big old England, with a vicar, and music, and plenty of space outside. Will you?'

'Of course, Arthur,' she laughed, and almost couldn't stop, 'of course I will.'

And when he held her for the second time that night, there was no more sadness to speak of. 'England,' he said, 'we're going to England.'

32. The Fugitives

Jake had lost her, briefly, at the square. She had disappeared as surely as if the fog had swallowed her. Then she
had emerged at the headland, squawking, *Arthur, Arthur*,
into the night. And now here they were, man and woman,
Arthur and Eliza, clasped together, all tender embraces at
the pier, even while her smell – like sardines on toast – was
rich on his fingers.

The fog, with the moon on it, was purely white. It was
knuckling cold. Jake squatted down amongst the rocks at
Warkworth Bay, hearing the rattle of crabs by his boots.
He thought of last night: Nathaniel and the English girl
in that room, and the long blue lines of their bodies em-
bracing. Pent in the fog, Eliza and Arthur continued at their
love-making, all kisses, cuddles, caresses. How was it that
everyone so easily betrayed their promises? Barely a day
had passed before Nathaniel had given up on every
Maladey principle to bed this English girl! Not an hour had
passed between Jake's going to Eliza's bed and her leaving
it for this fishmonger!

Jake had skipped school today to get the extra £5,
which he had smuggled out from his mam's savings. A
policeman had called round to the Lawrences' late that
afternoon but Jake had merely watched him from the bed-

room and his mam had lied, saying she didn't know where the boy was. There'd been hell to pay after, but he knew he could rely on his mam, what with his da gone fishing, and her pure dependence on him for the next two weeks, if only for company. No, his mam had not given him up for Verger's fire, and he was ever so proud of her for it. But it did mean he had to spend the day hiding in his bedroom upstairs, with the thoughts of Eliza circling over the anticipated shapes of her hips and breasts.

Oh, this evening, Eliza had made him ache! And now she was here, in the time he had paid for, with this man!

Without a thought, he had followed her here, down to the flat roof and through the winding cobbled streets of Lynemouth Town, over the cliff-tops to the square. All the time, jogging along, yards from her, he could taste her taste, peculiar as a mollusc. Then he had come down to the rocks, witnessing some reconciliation he had no care for, his knees bent and sore against the sand.

And now the fishmonger and Eliza stood at the pier, canoodling and smooching, and Jake was nowhere in her thoughts. He'd paid for the whole night! £10! Eliza had tricked him. She had stolen from him. Last night's ache returned, the one he thought he had quashed. Careless and coquettish, Eliza laughed close to the fishmonger's neck.

The gun was a cold lump at the small of his back.

Jake contemplated breaking them up and demanding Eliza should come back with him to the Grand, just as he had paid for, but the monger was a big man and Jake didn't fancy his chances arguing him down. He didn't know what to do, aside from wait, and watch.

*

There was a sound of footsteps coming down the cliff. A long whistle arced into the cold. The fog was too thick to see anything until Nathaniel emerged at the beach, his skull like a black ball. He waved over to Arthur and Eliza and they waved back to him. Not surprising that Nathaniel should have something to do with her presence here. It would be just Nathaniel's kind of joke to embarrass Jake like this. Perhaps they had planned it together; Nathaniel and Eliza colluding to spoil the night and make him look like the fool.

What was it that the boy had said last night? *We're due to make some money, on a shipment.* What were they shipping? Fish? Seafood? Was this why Arthur was here? But why was Eliza here too? Perhaps she had a cut of the profits, or – and this made Jake gag – perhaps she was a present for the Boatman.

Jake ducked lower behind the rocks as Nathaniel strode toward the pier. The boy looked intolerably cheerful. The scarf was a new addition; he hadn't known Nathaniel to feel the cold and now it flapped redly in the fog and wind. Perhaps Jake could steal back to Swanscott House and finish the night off with the English girl, if Nathaniel was to spend his night here doing business at the pier.

From the rocks, Jake watched the company – the fishmonger, the whore, the leader of the Malades – unable to imagine what on earth they were talking about, or what product they were shipping, until he gave up, and walked, slowed by the sand, toward the waiting pier.

No one turned or heard him coming; they carried on talking in whispers. When would they look? Hadn't they heard him yet? The fog was filling the bay. The *Saviour* would be here soon, and after whatever product had been swapped, he might drag Eliza back to the Grand to have his money's worth. Promises were promises. At the very least, Jake wanted half of his money back. Blondly standing on the pier, her hands clasped about a case as if she were off on holiday, Eliza was nodding her head at Nathaniel, her smile oily and distant.

Yards from the pier, Jake shouted up at them: 'What's going on?'

Nathaniel turned. His eyes slid down Jake's costume, appraising him. It was always on the tip of his tongue for Nathaniel to suggest a corrective, to pull at an escaped shirt-tail, or to point to a scuff on one of his boots. It seemed, though, that the boy couldn't think of a reprimand tonight, because Nathaniel opened his mouth and then closed it again with a snapping sound. Still no one had said a thing. Jake looked at Eliza: she flushed and looked away, narrowing her eyes against the fog. He closed the yards between them and took the steps up to the jetty. 'What's going on here? Why this meeting?'

'Here, Jakey, hallo. Have a cigarette.'

'No. What's going on, Nathaniel?'

'No cigarette? You've changed your stripes, Jakey-boy.'

Eliza's face was ashen now, and she was concentrating on the sea.

'I don't want a cigarette. What's this, then?'

'That shipment. The shipment I was telling you about.' Nathaniel leaned toward him, as if business made them chums again. In a low whisper he said, 'We're due to make a cracking lot of money just now.'

A broad low hum began, though the boat itself could not be seen. 'Ah, the *Saviour* indeed,' said Arthur and everyone looked toward him, then out to the bay. The sound of the engine grew louder. The tide started to rush in toward the water's edge, the scud white in the night. Gulls squawked overhead but neither wing nor beak could be seen. Eliza put herself further into Arthur's shadow.

Nathaniel pulled Jake toward him. 'Look here, Jake: Miss Michalka and Mr Stansky have given us a hundred pounds for their safe passage on the boat.'

Miss Michalka? Mr Stansky? A hundred pounds? This was the shipment? People? Jake could countenance fish or medicine as trades for cigarettes or whatnot, but not people, not when people were the most precious cargo on the Island. 'No. But they can't. No one gets off this Island. Where are they going?'

'Africa, Jake, where do you think? To *England*, of course. Where else would you expect?'

Jake did not know what to say. To England? Surely they hated the English; surely the point was to preserve the Island, not get people over to join them! The leader of the Malades, helping people on their safe passage to England!

'A hundred pounds, Jake, a hundred pounds!' The boy unfurled his fingers, stuffed with banknotes. 'We're rich. Now we can do what we please.' And Jake had effectively put the money directly into Nathaniel's pocket; oh, he had been a foolish lad to bed Eliza for that sum!

'Nathaniel: we can't do this. It's wrong. What'll we tell the lads? We're meant to be stopping the English, not getting people to join them. Nath, it's against everything we believe in, and you know it.'

'Look, even if we give fifty of these to the boatman, we'll be princes of this isle for the whole winter. Don't be crabbing me now with morals, when we've got all this money!' Jake opened his mouth to speak but Nathaniel gave a snap of the notes. Money from the fishery and brothel both. 'Stop your mouth now. This is business. Nothing more. *Enough*, Jake. Your morals tire me out, aye. In fact, they always have.'

'Morals! Morals that *you* gave me. Morals that *we* work for! And what will you spend it on? Your English girlfriend! What a mess, aye, what a fucking hash.'

A horn boomed sadly in the white air. A bow wave carried the waves faster to the beach, spilling over each other in foamy slop. The boat was a smudged shape, in the fog, then more definite, and bigger, then it loomed toward them as it came to the pier. The engine churned the water as the *Saviour* docked at the pier.

When it stopped, the Island felt strangely quiet, though the waves knocked against the boat's hull. The Boatman appeared, large and bald.

'You can't do this, Nath, it's wrong,' he said, but Nathaniel was already halfway down the pier.

Nathaniel shook hands with the Boatman as if they were old friends. They talked for some minutes, then Jake saw money exchanged, and then the boy was waving over to the waiting couple.

The lags between the waves had begun to slow.

Eliza did not look at Jake as she and Arthur began the long walk. He remembered how she had held him, hours ago, and he felt as if his heart were breaking. Maybe he could shout over the fog and tell Arthur what had happened. That would have broken up the little romance. That would have stopped it short. But he had the feeling, indistinctly, that he would not be believed, and they were too far away now, at the end of the pier, chatting aimlessly to the Boatman. Eliza stood laughing, as if she hadn't wronged him, as if she hadn't reneged completely on her promise.

And here it was: the English benefaction; boxed provisions for the hard winter to come when the freezing fog would envelop the Island. The Boatman had each one in hand as Nathaniel followed him counting his money. How the Islanders would grovel and snap at their heels and coo their thank-you's for English charity. England; aye, what had England ever done for them but expel them then throw them the scraps? And now they were putting two on the boat to join them. This was a nasty business.

There was a vague buzzing in his ears. The money went *snap*, *snap*, *snap* in Nathaniel's hands.

With the boxes now at the end of the pier, the Boatman beckoned toward Eliza and Arthur and they were installed up at the driver's section, closeted within. That whore and her man were probably squashed up tight against each other; and Nathaniel, here, was probably only just let loose from his English girl's bed. Long-limbed in the blue light, she'd be at Swanscott House peacefully sleeping and waiting for him, until they could spend the money over the winter and be the Lord and Lady of this isle, dining on bream and scallops and who knew what, with more cigarettes to boot.

'He says he'll use the money in the brothels, Jake! Says

there are none to be found in Godly England, so I don't know how Eliza shall ply her profession. But imagine that, an Englishman in the Grand! They'll have him for breakfast before hell might have a chance. And he didn't even ask for the pills! Just gave me the cigs with a very wide grin. Here, Jake, have one. Have one, our Jake, and get smoothed out. You're all agitated, now.'

'I said I don't want one.' The cargo door was now flush with the rest of the boat. The boatman took the rope from the bollard, grinning insanely, piling the length of rope in his wide fat hands, his bald head greenish in the fog. And then, just as suddenly, the Boatman was inside, and starting the engine, and readying to leave.

Waves lapped gently against the yellow letters of the *Saviour*.

'Are we letting every man and child have his passage to England, then? I thought a Malade such as yourself might feel differently.' Nathaniel only sighed and looked away to an indefinite point. Jake abandoned any fear he had and went at him as if he were not Nathaniel, as if he were just another boy: 'We are the Malades! We're meant to be doing what's right for the Island! Not move people off it! Not so they can abscond to *their* way!'

Nathaniel shoved him in the chest, the force knocking Jake to the pier. The nose of Margaret's gun struck his pelvic bone. The boy stood over him, with that absurd shock of hair. 'Enough,' Nathaniel shouted, the word punctuating the night. 'If only I could tell you how much I've had enough of you! Out of my way, Jake! You're no leader here. You're no man. You're just a boy. A stupid boy who doesn't understand anything!'

Jake looked at him, unable to say anything. The engine gunned.

The sound of steps came from off the cliff. Sarah was quick. She jumped from the steps and ran the length of the bay in very little time at all. The colour of her hair was deeply copper. She gained the pier with a wild look; the freckles flush and dense around her nose, her hands clasped tight to the bag's straps. Nathaniel's face had fallen; lost slack like an old boot.

About the boat there was an upswell so that the waves came quicker to the shoreline. The sound of the engine was convulsive at first, then flattened to a hum. The *Saviour* was readying to leave.

Nathaniel said, 'Sarah.' He held her by the hands and pulled her up to the pier. A gull wailed above the sound of the engine.

She looked around, her skin soft with sleep. She laughed mirthlessly. 'What did you give me, Nathaniel? It sent me to sleep. It knocked me out; I could barely stand.' She squinted over to the end of the pier. 'Is that the boat there?'

'Aye,' he said, but quietly.

Jake gave a whoop, his eyes raking Nathaniel's. 'Another bird to fly the Island, then! Well, miss, I can tell you, you can't, because the boat is all full up, all full up with the others. Did your boyfriend not tell you? He's filled it with a whore and a fishmonger.'

The girl looked from one boy to another. To no one in particular, she said, 'I have to go home. I have to go home.

My dad's waiting for me, and my ma too, when she gets there.'

'*My dad, Nath, my dad!*' Jake mimicked. 'It's to be winter on this isle for you, doll.'

The sound of the engine rose.

'Go on, then,' said Nathaniel. He brought Sarah toward him – just as Jake had brought Eliza toward himself and felt the long sagging in his chest which was love – and kissed her. 'There's still time. He didn't lock the cargo hold. You can still get in. I'm sorry,' the boy said, 'I couldn't bear you going.' Nathaniel looked toward the sea, the hand with the banknotes now loose by his side.

The girl lurched toward the boat, the sound of her shoes smacking the pier. Jake took off behind her. Not paces down the road, he caught up with her and twisted her wrist into the small of her back. He could no longer see Nathaniel behind him. 'No, no, no. Now, Sarah, an Island life isn't so bad!' His feet widened so that he was a scaffold around her, so that he could talk directly into the pleasantly dusted ear. He felt the button of his jeans at her hip, could he be as close to her as Nathaniel had been? His voice coaxed at her: 'We want you here, we want to talk to you. Give up the struggle and it won't hurt so much. That's the truth of it. That'll ease you through. Come now, give up the fight, doll!' Sarah thrashed against him. 'I'll show you how, it's a lovely thing, this Island, when you know it.' He felt his blood, rum and warm, rush about him. The girl wheeled, her body tense in struggle; her face stricken. Jake held both wrists now fixed. Oily smoke joined the mist.

'For God's sake, let me go!'

'No, no, no; no God to help you now.'

The girl turned around and her face was a red blur, all freckles and a blush of fear. Jake felt a wet spray against his face – he thought he had been caught by a wave – but it was her spit, a thick scud. He looked at Nathaniel. The boy stood there, immobile. Why was he not doing anything? Why did he not defend his boy, his Malade? Nathaniel stood there, absolutely still. Jake let go of the girl's wrist.

As soon as he let the gun off, the air about him was hot and sprayed with a smell of pepper. The gun kicked and his hand shook with it. Jake walked toward her fallen shape: twisted, like a downed bird. Distantly he heard the trailing sound of the engine so the boat must have gone now. The girl was flat to the pier, with her thick red hair roping the platform. There was a bone bit visible in her shoulder which made him pure want to gromick. The boy crouched and turned her over so that her face was a white disc; her eyes skipped around the place.

Behind him he heard Nathaniel running up the pier.

She was a thing of beauty amongst the waves, breaking against the pier in the wake of the *Saviour*. The eyes were wild and flashy blue, the black rounds getting bigger and bulging; silky, almost. Jake gave another squeeze of the trigger and her lips opened in an 'o' and about the wound blood pooled. Her breath caught. 'Aye,' he said. He kicked her to the Sound.

As if she were crowned in copper, her hair spread in the water.

Nathaniel, wet-eyed, limp, scrabbled down to the beach and sat nursing her. There were strange sounds coming from his mouth. Yowling softly as if he were a bleeding baby. With the freezing sea up to his chest, he combed back and forth her crown of red hair.

Jake threw the gun to the Sound. Then he ran from them, from the pier, and from the cliffs, back into the impossible light of the Island.

England

Wherever there had been moisture was now frozen. It was early, and the sun had not yet come up far enough to melt the frost. Above her, ragged cloud was breaking away to light.

The fog had lifted, leaving behind a world spun in frost. She heard the stiff iced leaves crack underfoot. She saw the new shops and the old fruit-stalls, selling their mounds of winter fruit. Occasionally people passed her, none whom she recognized, but she did not look for long.

Everywhere in the windows there was an abundance Laura was not accustomed to. Perhaps Trimdon had come into some new source of wealth, though from what, she couldn't imagine. She passed a delicatessen where there were bags of pistachios and berries; a shop, next door, of showers, neat sinks, polished taps and Plexiglas. Light pulled over rooftops. A plane flew under the last of the moon.

Laura passed the butcher's: shoulders of lamb next to the dark mess of liver. She'd probably had meat once a year, at Christmas, since she'd been gone: even then it was only a dry slice of turkey. She was hungry, moved on, passed the grocer's and the pub on the corner.

At the cafe, newly named, a woman in a paper hat

prepared for the day; a man sat in the window, a bald man eating breakfast, the jaw working all the muscles in the gleaming cheeks. He was reading a newspaper: the headline read *A Good Sunday Agreement?* and it showed a picture of Laura, next to the reverend who had died, as well as the mugshots of Thomas and Christopher, the two dead men who she had – finally – been able to name as her accomplices. When she had heard of their deaths, on a quiet news bulletin broadcast in the women's cafeteria, Laura had pushed back her chair and walked straight to the inspector's office. Uttering their names had been like saying obscenities, so skilfully had she schooled herself in the art of silence. In days to come, she had been read her rights from the Sunday Agreement, and, after preliminaries – facts checked, names corroborated, the general closing of the case – preparations for her release had been made.

The date of the newspaper was December 3rd, 1986. More than ten years had passed since the bombing of Saint Gregory's. Her daughter would be a woman, now, she supposed.

Ice cracked under her shoes. Laura followed the stone wall on the sunny side of the street, leading out of the valley, where her boots could find the tarmac and no longer any frost. She thought: if I put my boots down harder the whole world will smash like a glass and I will find that this is a dream.

Laura opened the gate and checked her watch. Her house looked no different. Sarah's curtains were open upstairs;

perhaps her girl was an early riser. At the house, she put her arms up to the doorframe to steady herself. Just a moment to collect, feeling the sun on the back of her neck. The shadow behind her was cruciform in winter light. She remembered the last time she had been here, stepping out into the cool July morning in 1976, though she did not regret Saint Gregory's.

The lock turned the key easily, and why wouldn't it? Did she expect them to have shut up shop without her? The room, then, was just as she had left it, messier perhaps, the dresser still cluttered with things, an old bag of onions, the telephone on its cradle. Green glass bottles near the bin, ready for the bank, a half-litre of whiskey at the table. She was ready to climb the stairs but turned.

There was a bowl of oranges on the side. At the table she put a finger into the seam of the flesh, pulled, felt the skin give.

Into the morning air, the scent spilled. Laura turned to the stairs.

With deep and affectionate thanks to my agent at WME,

Cathryn Summerhayes,

who found this book in a very different form four years ago,

and to my editor at Picador,

Sam Humphreys,

who turned it into what it is today.

picador.com

blog
videos
interviews
extracts